THE JUGGLER

THE JUGGLER

CHARLES EGBERT CRADDOCK

Originally published in 1897.
Published by Wildside Press, LLC.
Visit us online at wildsidepress.com

I.

Mystery was not far to seek, surely. The great gneissoid crags were moulded by the heat from subterranean fires in remote, unimagined æons. From the deep coves, now so heavily wooded, the once submerging waters had long ago ebbed, following undreamed-of lures, drawn seaward or skyward, or engulfed in still lower depths,—who can say?—leaving the ripple-marks on their rocky confines to tell of their being. In the middle of the bridle-path, touched by every careless passing foot, lay a splintered sandstone slab, the fracture revealing a cluster of delicate, cylindrical, stem-like petrifactions, thus preserving, with the comprehensive significance of nature, so slight a thing as the record of the life of a worm long ages agone, in these fossil traces of primordial vermicular burrowings, here in the midst of a scene that was itself as a register of those stupendous revolutions the incidents of which were the subsidence of vast oceans, and the emergence of continents, and the development of the mighty agencies that made and lifted the mountains. All the visible world gave token of the inexplicable past of creation, of the unrevealed future,—those thoughts of God which are very deep thoughts. And yet, in the blunting of daily use, the limitations of dull observation, the unquestioning acceptance of the accustomed routine of nature, there might seem naught before the eye which was not plainly manifest,—mountain, rock, forest,—the mere furniture of existence. One hardly analyzes the breath of life as it is breathed; even when considered as nearly twenty-one per cent. of oxygen to seventy-nine per cent. of nitrogen, are we aught the wiser, for whence comes it, and alas, why does it go? To those creatures of a day, busy with the day, it seemed that mystery and doubt and troublous questioning had first entered Etowah Cove in the guise of a vagrant juggler, their earliest experience of a modern exponent of his most ancient craft.

The light that timidly flickered out of the schoolhouse windows into the bosky depths of the encompassing wilderness, one night, marked a new era in the history of the Cove. It was the first "show" that had ever been given nearer than Colbury, some forty miles distant, unless one might make so bold as to include in the term camp-meetings and revivals, weddings and funerals. The walls of the little log house had hitherto echoed naught more joyous than sermons and "experience meetings,"

5

or sounds of scholastic discipline, or the drone of the juvenile martyr reluctantly undergoing education. The place had long been closed to secular uses, for only at infrequent intervals was the school opened, and a drought of instruction still held sway. To the audience who had been roused from the dull routine of the fireside by the startling and unprecedented announcement that a stranger-man, staying at old Tubal Cain Sims's cabin, was going to give a "show" in the schoolhouse, the flutter of excitement, the unwonted nocturnal jaunt hither, the joyous anticipation, were almost tantamount to the delighted realization. The benches were arranged as for worship or learning, and were crowded with old and young, male and female, the reckless and barefoot, the neuralgic and shod. The men, unkempt and unshaven, steadily chewed their quids of tobacco, and now and then spat upon the floor and grinned at one another. The women conserved a certain graver go-to-meeting air, doubtless the influence of the locality, but were visibly fluttered. Occasionally a big sunbonnet turned toward another, and whispered gossip ensued, as before the first hymn is given out. The lighted tallow candles in small tin sconces against the walls, and a kerosene lamp on the table on the platform, cast a subdued and mellow light over the assemblage. It flickered up to the brown rafters, where the cobwebs were many; it converted the tiny dirt-incrusted panes of the windows to mirror-like use, and was reflected from the dense darkness outside with duplications of sections of the audience; it shone full and bright on the tall, athletic figure of the juggler, appearing suddenly and swiftly from a side door, and bowing low in the centre of the platform with an air of great deference and courtesy to his silent and spellbound audience.

He might have astonished more sophisticated spectators. Instead of wearing the ordinary evening dress or the costume of the Japanese or Hindoo, according to the usual wont of conjurers, he was clad in a blue flannel shirt and a black-and-red blazer, and his blue knickerbockers and long blue hose on his muscular legs impressed the mountaineers as a ballet costume might have done, could they have conceived of such attenuations of attire. A russet leather belt was drawn tightly around his slender waist, and they gazed at him from the tip of his dark sleek red-brown hair, carefully parted in the middle, to the toes of his pointed russet shoes with an amazement which his best feat might fail to elicit. His air of deep respect reassured them in a measure, for they could not gauge the covert banter in his tone and the mockery in his eyes as his sonorous "Ladies and gentlemen" rang forth in the little building. And there was something more in his eyes—of reddish-brown tint like his hair—that the mockery and banter could not hide; for these were transient, and the other—a thought with a fang. It might have been anxiety, remorse, turmoil of mind, fear,—one might hardly say,—plainly to be seen, yet not discerned. Below his eyes, above his cheekbones, that showed their contour, for his face was thin, were deep blue circles, and that unmistakable look of one who has received some serious sudden shock. But the spirit of the occasion was paramount now, and he was as unconscious of the lack in his accoutrements in the estimation of the mountaineers as they were of how the bare feet of sundry of his spectators offended his prejudices in favor of *chaussure*.

"Ladies and gentlemen, we are gathered here to witness some of those feats which are variously ascribed to charlatanry, to skill or sleight of hand, or to certain traffic with supernatural agencies. Those which I shall have the honor to exhibit to this select audience I shall not explain; in fact," with a twinkle of the eye, "some of them are inexplicable, and so may they long continue! I have not thought best to avail myself of the services of an assistant, who is generally, I grieve to say, among most of those of my profession, a mere trickster and accomplice, and therefore you will have the evidence of your eyes to the fact that every feat which I perform this evening is absolutely genuine."

His spirit of rodomontade had reached its limit. Perhaps some of the more finely strung sensibilities in the audience appraised the ridicule in his intention, despite the masquerade of his manner, for a glance of resentment kindled here and there; but before the awed and open-mouthed majority had drawn a breath or relaxed a muscle he changed his tone.

"I have selected a young man from amongst you," he said, quite naturally and pleasantly, "to aid me in finding properties, as it were, for my entertainment; for in apology be it spoken, I am not prepared in any respect for an exhibition of this sort. He has, at my request, borrowed for me this bayonet." He took from the table drawer the weapon, newly cleaned and glistening, and looked at it narrowly as he stood before them on the platform. "I should say it has seen service. Can this gentleman tell me whether it is from a Federal or a Confederate gun?"

He stepped down suddenly from the platform and handed the bayonet to a strong-featured, stern-looking old mountaineer who had earlier regarded him with dawning disfavor.

"It's from a Rebel weepon," the veteran said succinctly.

"It's off a Yankee Springfiel'," a voice came from the other side of the room.

"Enfiel'," said the first speaker doggedly.

"Springfiel'," contradicted his invisible antagonist tersely.

Once more, "Enfiel'."

And again out of the shadow, "Springfiel'."

And the juggler became aware that he had waked up the political dog of the region.

"They are equally digestible," he declared, resuming his place on the platform. "I believe I'll swallow it." And so he did.

For one moment there was an intense silence, while the petrified audience gazed in motionless astonishment at the juggler. Then arose a great tumult of voices; there was a violent movement at the rear of the room; a bench broke down, and in the midst of the commotion, with a gay cry of "Hey! Presto!" the juggler apparently drew the bayonet from out his throat and triumphantly held it up before the people.

An increasing confusion of sounds greeted him. Screams of delighted mirth came from the younger portion of the audience, and exclamations hardly less flattering from the laughing elders. But ever above the babel terrified shrieks, shrill and clamorous, rose higher and higher, and the juggler frowned with sudden sharp annoyance when he distinguished the fact that an elderly woman was crying out that these were the works of the devil,—that here was Satan, and that she would not bide easy till he was bound, neck and heels together, and cast forth into the river. He was not usually devoid of humane sentiments, but he felt vastly relieved when she fell into strong hysterics, and was carried, still shrieking, out to the ox-cart, whence, despite the closed doors and windows, over and over again those weird, unearthly cries were borne in to the audience, as the yoking of the steers for the homeward journey was in progress.

The juggler was out of countenance. "Ladies and gentlemen," he said, with indignation coloring his face to the roots of his hair, "these things are done for amusement. If they fail to amuse, they fail altogether. I will go on, or, if you desire, your money will be refunded at the door."

"Lawd, naw, bub!" exclaimed a toothless old fellow, bent nearly double as he sat on a front bench, his clasped hands between his knees. "We-uns want ter view all ye know how ter do,—all ye know how ter do, son."

Here and there reassuring voices confirmed the spokesman, and as the discomfited juggler turned to the table drawer, resolving on something less bloody-minded, he heard a vague titter from that portion of the building in which, being young, he had already observed that the greater number of personable maidens were seated.

None so dread ridicule as the satirist. He whirled around, his heart swelling indignantly, his eyes flashing fire, to perceive, advancing down the aisle, a fat woman in a gigantic sunbonnet, which, however, hardly obscured her broad, creased, dimpled face, a brown calico dress wherein the waist-line must ever be a matter of conjecture, and a little shoulder-shawl of bright red-and-yellow plaid. She slowly approached him with something of steel glittering in her hands, and at his amazed and dumfounded expression of countenance the girlish cachinnation which he so resented broke forth afresh.

"Beg pardon?" he said more than once, as from his elevation he sought to catch her request. A single tooth of the upper register, so to speak, however ornamental, did not serve to render more distinct the fat woman's wheeze, in which she sought to articulate her desire that he should forthwith swallow her big shears, so fascinated was she by the evidence he had given of his proficiency in the arts of the impossible.

"Certainly, with pleasure,—always anxious to oblige the ladies," he protested, with a return of his covert mockery, as he bowed after a dancing-class fashion, and received from her fat creased hands the great domestic implement with its dangling steel chain. "Ladies and gentlemen," he declared, with his hand upon his heart, as she subsided, shaking with laughter, on the front bench, "I cannot refrain from expressing my flattered sense of this mark of the confidence reposed in me by this distinguished audience, as well as by the estimable lady who is so willing to offer her shears on the altar of science. She is not satisfied with the warlike bayonet. She desires to see the same experiment, *mutatis mutandis*, on a pair of shears, which are devoted to the tender-hearted and affable uses of the work-basket, filled with the love of home and gentle fireside associations, and—and—and other domestic scraps. The rivet is a trifle loose, and I hope I may not be forced to disgorge the blades separately."

He was holding up the scissors as he spoke these words, so that all could see them; the next moment they had disappeared down his throat, as it were, and the astounded audience sat as if resolved into eyes, staring spellbound.

When, a few minutes later, with his cabalistic phrase, "Hey! Presto!" he drew from his open red mouth the shears dangling at the end of the rattling steel chain, which the audience had just seen him swallow, the clamor of exclamations again arose, for the accepted methods of applause had not yet penetrated to the seclusions of Etowah Cove; but there was in this manifestation of surprise so definite a quaver of fear that certain lines of irritation and anxiety corrugated the smooth brow of the young prestidigitator. The tumultuous amazement of the spectators seemed as if it were too great to be realized all at once, and with the sight of the performance anew of the impossible feat, which should have served as reassurance, it degenerated into downright terror which held the possibilities of panic. The idea of panic suggested other possibilities. Albeit their unsophisticated state was highly favorable to the development of emotions of boundless astonishment and absolute credulity, he realized that it was not unattended by some personal danger. After the suggestion of being bound hand and foot and thrown into the river, the juggler was more than once unpleasantly reminded—for he was a man of some reading—of certain fellow craftsmen in the mists of centuries agone, whose wondrous skill in the powers of air, earth, and fire, though great enough to be deemed unlawful traffic with the devil, could not avail to prevent their own earthly elements from going up in smoke and flame, and thus contributing ethereally to the great reserves of material nature. He was here alone, far from help, among the most ignorant and lawless people he had ever seen; and if their dislocated ideas of necromancy and unlawful dealing with the devil should take a definite hold upon them, he might be summarily dealt with as an act of religion, and the world none the wiser. Such disaster had befallen better jugglers, sooth to say, in more civilized communities than Etowah Cove. He sought to put this thought from him, for his heart was sufficiently stout of fibre, but determined that he would not again be diverted from his intention of substituting less blood-curdling feats for the usual experiments with knives and swords. He preserved a calm face and debonair manner, as he carefully wiped the shears free from supposititious moisture on a folded white table-cloth that lay on the platform, and stepped down, and with an elaborate bow presented them to their chuckling and gratified owner.

"Jane Ann Sims wouldn't keer if the Old Nick hisself war ter set up his staff in the Cove, ef he hed some news ter tell or a joke ter crack, or some sorter gamesome new goin's-on that she hed never hearn tell on afore," whispered a lean, towering, limp sunbonnet to its starch and squatty neighbor.

"An' *she* hard on ter fifty odd years old!" said the squatty sunbonnet, malignantly accurate.

As the juggler stepped back to the platform he took up the table-cloth and shook it out, that they might all be assured that there was nothing concealed in its folds.

"Now, ladies and gentlemen," he said, taking heart of grace and his former manner of covert half-banter and mock politeness together, "we all know that it is by the action of the sun on the soil, and the dew and the rain, that the seeds of plants germinate and the green herb grows for the service of men. I propose to show you now a small agricultural experiment which I venture to hope will be of special interest to this assembly, as most of you are engaged in the noble pursuit of tilling the soil, when other diversions cannot by any means be had."

As he clattered off his sentences, garnished now and then with trite bits of Latin, the solemn, stolid, uncomprehending faces ministered to a certain mocking humor which he had, and which was now becoming a trifle bitter with the reluctant realization of a lurking danger.

"Will some gentleman come forward and tell me what kind of a seed this is?"

He held the small object up between his finger and thumb for a moment, but no one approached. He perceived in a sort of helpless dismay that the dread of him was growing. He was fain to step down from the platform and hand the seed to the old man on the front bench, whose bleared eyes were glittering with delight in the greatest sensation that had ever fallen to his lot; for the juggler judged that of all the audience he was nearest the masculine counterpart of the progressive Jane Ann Sims. The old man, in his circle, was not a person of consideration nor accustomed to deference. He was all the more easily flattered to be thus singled out by the juggler, the conspicuous cynosure of all eyes, to give his judgment and pronounce upon the identity of the seed. The love of notoriety is a blasting passion, deadening all considerations of the conformable. Even in these secluded wilds, even in the presence of but a handful of his familiars, even in the lowly estate of a cumberer of the ground, lagging superfluous, it smote Josiah Cobbs. He rose to his feet, whirled briskly around, and, with a manner founded on the sprightly style of the juggler, yet compounded with the diction of the circuit rider, exclaimed, "Yea, my brethren, this hyar be a seed,—yea, it be actually a persimmon seed, though so dry I ain't so sure whether or not it'll ever sot off ter grow like a fraish one might. Yea, my brethren, I ain't sure how long—ah—this hyar persimmon seed hev—ah—been kem out o' the persimmon. Yea"—

He progressed not beyond this point, for the audience had no mind to be entertained with the rhetoric of old Josiah Cobbs, resenting his usurpation of so prominent a position, and his presumption in undertaking to address the meeting. Certain people in this world are given to understand that although their estate in life be not inferior to that of their neighbors, humility becomes them, and a low seat is their appropriate station. More than one sunbonnet had rustlingly communed with another as to the fact that Josiah Cobbs would hardly be heard at an experience meeting, the state of his humble soul not interesting the community. So simultaneous a storm of giggles swept the cluster of girls as to demonstrate that their gravity was of the same tenuous quality as that of their age and sex elsewhere. It was wonderful that they did not sustain some collapse, and this furnishes a pleasing commentary upon the strength of the youthful diaphragm. The men exchanged glances of grim derision, and finally one, with the air of a person not to be trifled with, rose up and stretched out his hand for the bewitched seed, forgetting for the moment all his quondam qualms of distrust.

Josiah Cobbs rendered it up without an instant's hesitation. Precious as was the opportunity in his eyes, preëmpted by his own courage, his was not the type which makes resistance. The hand to despoil him had hardly need to be strong. The will to have what he possessed was sufficient for his pillage. He hardly claimed the merits appertaining to the pioneer. He stood meekly by as the seed was passed from one set of horny finger-tips to another, and the dictum, "It's a persimmon seed, stranger," was repeated with a decision which implied no previous examination.

"A persimmon seed, is it?" said the juggler airily, receiving it back. "Now, gentlemen, you see that there is nothing in this pail of earth but good pulverized soil." He passed his fingers through the surface, shaking them daintily free from the particles afterward, while the hands of the practical farmers went boldly grappling down to the bottom with no thought of dirt. "You see me plant this persimmon seed. There! Now I throw over the pail this empty cloth,—let it stand up in a peak so as to give the seed air; now I place the whole on the table, where you can all see it and assure yourselves that no one goes near it. While awaiting developments I shall try to entertain you by singing a song. It may be unknown to you—yet why this suggestion in the presence of so much culture?—that in the days of eld certain wandering troubadours came to be in some sort men of my profession. In the intervals of minstrelsy they entertained and astonished their audiences with feats of the miraculous,—strange exploits of legerdemain and such light pastimes,—and were therefore termed *jongleurs*. I shall seek to follow my distinguished Provençal predecessors in the gay science *haud passibus æquis*, and pipe up as best I may."

There was a pause while the juggler, standing at one end of the platform, seemed to run over in his mind the treasures of his *répertoire*. The mellow lamplight shone in his reflective brown eyes, cast down as he twisted one end of the long red-brown mustache, and again thrown up as if he sought some recollection among the old rafters. These had the rich reserves of color characteristic of old wood, and the heavy beams of oak showed all their veinous possibilities in yellow and brown fibrous comminglements against the deep umber shadows of the high peak of the roof. The cobwebs adhering here and there had almost the consistency of a fabric, so densely woven they were. One pendulous gauze fragment moved suddenly without a breath of air, for a light living creature had run along the beam beneath it, and now stood looking down at the audience with a glittering eye and a half-spread bat-like wing,—a flying squirrel, whose nest was secreted in the king-post and entered from the outside. So still was the audience,—the grizzled, unkempt men, the sunbonneted women, even the giggling girls in the corner,—he might have been meditating a downward plunge into the room.

Then slightly frowning, but smiling too, the juggler began to sing.

It was a cultivated voice that rang out in the measures of "My Pretty Jane,"—a tenor of good range, true, clear, sweet, with a certain romantic quality that was in some sort compelling and effective. He sang well. Not that the performance would have been acceptable considered as that of a high-grade professional, yet it was far too good for a mere parlor amateur. The rich, vibrant voice, without accompaniment,—grotesque inadequacy to his mind,—filled the little building with a pathetic, penetrating sweetness, and the whole method of rendering the ballad was characterized by that elaborate simplicity and restrained precision so marked in professional circles, so different from the enthusiastic *abandon* of the reckless home talent.

It fell flat in Etowah Cove. There were people in the audience who, if they could not sing, were intimately persuaded that they could; and after all, that is the essential element of satisfaction. The modulation, the delicate shades of expression, the refinement of style, were all lost on the majority; only here and there a discerning ear was pricked up, appreciating in the concord of sweet sounds something out of the common. But there was no sign of approval, and in the dead silence which succeeded the final roulade, coming so trippingly off, the juggler showed certain symptoms of embarrassment and discomfiture. One might easily perceive from the deft assurance of his exploits of sleight of hand that the value he placed upon them was far cheaper than his estimate of his singing. It was a susceptible sort of vanity that could be hurt by the withheld plaudits of Etowah Cove; but vanity is a sensitive plant, and requires tender nurture. He stood silent and flushing for a moment, while still a gentle fibrous resonance seemed to pervade the room,—the memory of the song rather than its echo; then, with a sudden flouting airy whirl, he turned on his heel, and caught off the cloth that had enveloped the pail of earth containing the persimmon seed which he had just planted. And lo! glossy and green and lustrous in the light, there stood a fair young shoot, some two feet in height, and with all its leaves a-rustle. It was a good trick and very cleverly done.

The little building once more was a babel of sounds. The flying squirrel scrambled back to the king-post, pausing once to look down in half-frightened amazement. The window-panes reflected a kaleidoscope of bright bits of color swiftly swaying, for the audience was in a turmoil. It was not, however, the artistic excellence of the feat which swayed the spectators, but its agricultural significance. This, the old farmers realized, was indeed necromancy. Their struggles with the tough and reluctant earth, which so grudgingly responds to toil, oft with such hard-exacted usury, taking so much more than it gives, and which only the poet or the weed-loving botanist calls generous and fruitful, had served to teach them that this kind of growth must needs come only through the wiles of the deluding devil. Not even an agricultural paper—had they known of such a sophistication—could countenance such deceits. A grim, ashen-tinted face with gray hair appeared near the back of the building; a light gray homespun coat accentuated its pallor. A long finger was warningly shaken at the juggler, as he stood, triumphant, flushed, beside the flourishing shoot he had evoked from the persimmon seed, but only half smiling, for something sinister in the commingled voices had again smitten his attention. Then he was arraigned by Parson Greenought with the solemn adjuration in a loud tone, "Pause, Mr. Showman, pause!"

The juggler was already petrified. The spectators obeyed the earnest command, albeit not intended for them. They fell once more into their places; the heads of many turned now toward the juggler, and again back to the preacher, who, in his simplicity, had no idea that he had transgressed the canons of sanctification in visiting a place of worldly amusement, since indeed this was his first opportunity, and greatly had he profited by it, until this last enormity had aroused his clerical conscience. "Mr. Showman," he demanded, "do you-uns call this religion?"

"Religion!" said Mr. Showman, with a burst of unregenerate laughter, for the limits of his patience had been nearly reached. "I call it fun."

"I call it the devices of the devil!" thundered the preacher. "An' hyar ye be,"—he turned on the audience,—"ye perfessin' members, a-aggin' this man on in his conjurin' an' witchments an' Satan tricks, till fust thing ye know the Enemy will appear, horns, hoofs, an' tail, a-spittin' fire an'"—the juggler had a passing recollection that he too could spit fire, and had intended to make his *congé* amongst pyrotechnics of this sort, and he welcomed the thought of caution that was not, like most of its kind, *ex post facto*,—"a-spittin' fire, an' a-takin' yer souls down ter hell with him. Hyar ye be"—

"If you will allow me to interrupt you, sir," the juggler said persuasively, "you are altogether mistaken, and I should like to make a full explanation to a man of your age and experience." His eyes were grave; his face had grown a trifle pale. The danger had come very near. Rough handling might well be encountered amongst these primitive wights, inflamed by pulpit oratory and religious excitement, and abetted by their pastoral guide. "In two minutes," he went on, "I can teach you to perform this simple feat which seems to you impossible to human agency. It is nothing but sleight of hand, a sort of knack."

For one moment Parson Greenought hesitated, beguiled. His eye kindled with curiosity and eagerness; he made as though he would leave the bench whereon he was ensconced, to approach the alluring juggler. Unfortunately, it was at the moment that the young man's hands, grasping the persimmon shoot near the base, drew it forth from the earth with a wrench, so firmly was it planted, and showed to the discerning bucolic gaze the fully developed root with the earth adhering to its fibres; thus proving by the eyesight of the audience, beyond all power of gainsaying, that it had sprouted from the seed and grown two feet high while this juggler—this limb of Satan—had sung his little song about his Pretty Jane.

A man rarely has to contend with an excess of faith in him and his deeds. The juggler was fiercely advised by a dark-browed man leaning forward across one of the benches, with a menacing duplication of his figure and the gesture of his clenched fist reflected in the window, not to try to slip out of it.

And Parson Greenought, with a swelling redundancy of voice and a great access of virtue, gave forth expression of his desire to abide by the will that had ordained the growth of every herb whose seed is in itself upon the earth; he would not meddle and he would not mar, nor would he learn with unhallowed and wicked curiosity thus to pervert the laws that had been laid down while the earth was yet void and without form.

"Well, it never yet was ordained that this persimmon seed was to grow," said the juggler, still game, though with a fluctuating color. He fished the stone out from the earth, and, dusting it off with his fine white handkerchief, put it between his strong molar teeth and cracked it. He would not again invite attention to the reluctance of the audience to approach him, so he laid it down on the edge of the front bench with the remark, "You can see for yourselves the kernel is withered; that thing has no capacities for growth."

One or two looked cautiously at the withered kernel within the riven pit, and then glanced significantly at each other. It was shrunken, old, worthless, as he had said, but then his black art was doubtless sufficient to have withered it with the mere wish.

"I don't know a persimmon sprout from a dogwood, or a sumach, or anything else," declared the juggler. His face was hard and dogged; he was compelled in his own behoof to unmask himself and show how very superficial were his cleverest efforts. He did it as ungraciously as he might. "This young man"—he indicated a bold bluff young mountaineer who was availing himself of the "standing-room only," to which a number of the youths were relegated—"dug up this sprout at my request this afternoon, and hunted out a last year's seed among the dead leaves on the ground."

As his eyes met those of this young fellow the twinkle of mischievous delight in the mountaineer's big blue orbs gave him a faint zest of returning relish for the situation, albeit the primitive denizens of the Cove had been all too well humbugged even for his own comfort.

"This pocket is torn,"—he thrust his hand into it,—"and has no bottom. I therefore slipped this wand into this pocket of these knickerbockers," suiting the action to the word. "You see the leaves all fold together, so that its presence does not even mar the pronounced symmetry of my garments. Then I placed the seed, thus, and threw the cloth over the pail, thus; with my left hand I slipped out the persimmon shoot, and planted it, thus; and it was beneath the cloth that I left in a peak to give it air and to conceal it while I had the honor to entertain you by singing."

He supposed that he would have satisfied even the most timorous and doubtful by this revelation of his methods and of the innocuous nature of his craft, but he could not fail to note the significantly shaken heads, the disaffected whispers, the colloguing of the young mountaineers occupying "standing-room only."

"Ef he hed done it that-a-way at fust, I'd hev viewed it sure. I viewed it plain this time," said one of these.

"He can't fool me," protested a sour-visaged woman who kept up a keen espionage on all the world within the range of her pink sunbonnet.

"One lie never mended another," said the old preacher aside in a low voice to a presiding elder. "Potsherds, lies are, my brother; they hold no water."

The juggler could deceive them easily enough, but alack, he could not undeceive them! He debated within himself the possibility which each of his feats possessed of exciting their ire, as he hurriedly rummaged in the drawer of the table. He closed it abruptly.

"Ladies and gentlemen," he said, "behold this paper of needles; and here also I desire to introduce to your notice this small spool of thread—Has any lady here," he continued, with the air of breaking off with a sudden thought, "any breadths of calico or other fabric which she might desire to have run up or galloped up? I am a great seamster."

Of course, although some had brought their babies, and one or two their lunch to stop the mouths of the older children, many their snuff or their tobacco, no one had brought work on this memorable outing to the show in the Cove.

"What a pity!" he cried. "Well, I can only show you how I thread needles. I swallow them all, thus," and down they went. "Then I swallow the thread," and forthwith the spool disappeared down his throat.

The audience, educated by this time to expect marvels, sat staring, stony and still. There was a longer interval than usual as he stood with one hand on the table, half smiling, half expectant, as if he too were doubtful of the result. Suddenly he lifted his hand, and began to draw one end of the thread from his lips. On it came, longer and longer; and here and there, threaded and swaying on the fine filament, were the needles, of assorted sizes, beginning with the delicate and small implement, increasing grade by grade, till the descending scale commenced, and the needles dwindled as they appeared.

Parson Greenought had risen when the thread was swallowed, but he lingered till the last cambric needle was laid on the table, and the prestidigitator had made his low bow of self-flattery and triumph in conclusion. Then having witnessed it all, his forefinger shaking in the air, he cried out: "I leave this place! I pernounce these acts ter be traffickin' with the devil an' sech. Ef I be wrong, the Lord will jedge me 'cordin'; ez he hev gin me gifts I see with my eyes, an' my eyes air true, an' they war in wisdom made, an' war made ter see with. Oh, young man, pause in time! Sin hev marked ye! Temptation beguiles ye! I dunno what ye hev in mind, but beware of it! Beware of the sin that changes its face, an' shifts its name, an' juggles with the thing ez is not what it seems ter be. Beware! beware!"

As he stalked out, the juggler sought to laugh, but he winced visibly. The spectators were on their feet now, having risen with the excitement of the moment of the old man's exit. There was, however, a manifest disposition to linger; for having become somewhat acclimated to miracles, their appetite for the wonder-working was whetted. But the juggler, frowning heavily, had turned around, and was shaking the cloth out, and banging about in the drawer of the table, as if making his preparations for departure. The people began to move slowly to the door. It was not his intention to dismiss the audience thus summarily and unceremoniously, and as the situation struck his attention he advanced toward the front of the platform.

"Ladies and gentlemen," he began; but his voice was lost in the clatter of heavy boots on the floor, the scraping of benches moved from their proper places to liberate groups in order to precede their turn in the procession, the sudden sleepy protest of a half-awakened infant, rising in a sharp crescendo and climaxing in a hearty bawl of unbridled rage.

"Ladies and gentlemen!" he cried vainly to the dusty atmosphere, and the haggard, disheveled aspect of the half-deserted room. "Oh, go along, then," he added, dropping his voice, "and the devil take you!"

His mountain acquaintance had come to the side of the platform, and stood waiting, one hand on the table, while he idly eyed the juggler, who had returned to rummaging the drawer. He was a tall strong young fellow, with straight black hair that grew on his forehead in the manner denominated a "cowlick," and large contemplative blue eyes; his face showed some humor, for the lines broke readily into laughter. His long boots were drawn high over his brown jeans trousers, and his blue-checked homespun shirt was open at the neck, and showed his strong throat that held his head very sturdily and straight.

He was compassionate at the moment. "Plumb beat out, ain't ye?" he said sympathetically.

"I'm half dead!" cried the juggler furiously, throwing off his blazer, and wiping his hot face with his handkerchief.

The open door admitted the currents of the chill night air and the pungent odors of the dense dark woods without. Calls to the oxen in the process of gearing up sounded now and again droningly. Occasionally quick hoofbeats told of a horseman's departure at full gallop. The talk of waiting groups outside now came mingled to the ear, then ceased and rose anew. More than once a loud yawn told of the physical stress of the late hour and the unwonted excitement. The young mountaineer was going the rounds of the room extinguishing the tallow dips laboriously; taking each down, blowing gustily at it, and replacing it in the sconce. The juggler, as he passed, with his blazer over his arm, quenched the lights far more expeditiously, but mechanically, as it seemed, by fanning the timorous flames out *seriatim* with his hat in quick, decisive gestures. When he stood in the door, the room dark behind him, there was no life, no motion, in the umbrageous obscurity at hand; naught gave token of the audience so lately assembled save the creak of an unoiled axle far away, and once the raucous cry of a man to his team. Then all was still. In the hush, a vague drowsy note came suddenly from a bird high amongst the budding leaves of a tulip-tree hard by. An interval, and a like dreamy response sounded from far down the slope where pendulous boughs overhung the river. Some sweet chord of sympathy had brought the thought of the one to the other in the deep dark night,—these beings so insignificant in the plan of creation,—and one must needs rouse itself with that veiled reedy query, and the other, downily dreaming, must pipe out a reassuring "All's well."

The suggestiveness of this lyric of two tones was not lost on the juggler. He was pierced by the poignancy of exile. He could hardly realize that he was of the same species as the beings who had formed the "cultivated and intellectual audience" he had had the honor to entertain. Not one process of his mind could be divined by them; not one throb of their superstitious terrors could he share.

"The cursed fatality," he growled between his teeth, "that brought me to this God-forsaken country!"

"Waal," drawled the young mountaineer, whom he had forgotten for the moment, "they won't be so tur'ble easy skeered nex' time."

"They won't have another chance in a hurry," retorted the juggler angrily, as they walked away together in single file.

The night was very dark, although the great whorls of constellations were splendidly abloom in the clear sky. If a raylet fell to earth in the forest, it was not appreciable in the sombre depths, and the juggler, with all his craft, might hardly have made shift to follow his companion but for the spark and the light luminous smoke of the mountaineer's pipe. Suddenly, as they turned a sharp edge of a series of great rocks, that like flying buttresses projected out from the steep perpendicular wall of a crag above them, all at once growing visible, a white flare shone before their eyes, illumining all the surrounding woods. There in an open space near the edge of a bluff was a great fire of logs burning like a funeral pyre. The juggler had paused as if spellbound. From the opposite side of the glowing mass a face, distorted, tremulous, impossibly hideous, elongated almost out of the proportion of humanity, peered at him.

"For God's sake, what's that?" he cried out, clutching at his guide's arm.

The slow mountaineer, surprised out of his composure, paused, and took his pipe from his mouth to stare uncomprehendingly at his companion.

"Jes' burnin' lime," he said.

Their shadows, suddenly evolved, stretched over the ground in the white flare. The Cove, not far beneath, for this was on a low spur of the great range, now flickered into full view, now receded into the darkness. Above the vague mountain the stars seemed all gone, and the sky was elusive and cloaked. For all the art of the juggler, he could show naught of magic more unnatural, more ghastly, than the face of the lime-burner as it appeared through the medium of the heated air arising from the primitive kiln,—protean, distorted by every current of the night's breath,—although it was of much significance to him, and later he came to know it well to his cost. As the man caught the sound of their approach, he walked around to the side of the kiln, and his face and figure, no longer seen through the unequally refracting medium of the heated air, dwindled to normal proportions. It was not a prepossessing face in its best estate,—long, thin-lipped, grim, with small eyes set close together, and surmounted by a wide wool hat, which, being large for his head, was so crushed together that its crown rose up in a peak. His clothes were plentifully dusted with powdery flakes, and the scalding breath of the unslaked lime was perceptible to the throats of the newcomers.

"Ye 'pear ter be powerful late," the young mountaineer hazarded.

"Weather-signs air p'intin' fur rain," replied the lime-burner. "I ain't wantin' all this lime ter git slacked by accident." He glanced down with a workman's satisfaction at the primitive process. Between the logs of the great pile layers of the broken limestone were interposed, and were gradually calcined as the fire blazed. Although some of it was imperfectly consumed, and here and there lay in half-crude lumps, the quantity well burned was sufficient to warrant the laborer's anxiety to get it under shelter before it should sustain the deteriorating effects of moisture.

"Gideon Beck war a-promisin' ter kem back straight arter supper," said Peter Knowles, "an' holp me git it inter the rock-house thar." He indicated a grotto in the face of the cliff, where, by the light of the fire, one might perceive that lime had already been stored. The beetling rocks above it afforded adequate protection from falling weather, and the small quantity of the commodity was evidently disproportionate to the ample spaces for its accommodation within. "I felt plumb beset an' oneasy 'bout Gid," added Knowles. "He mought hev hed a fit, or suthin' may have happened down ter his house, ter some o' the chil'n o' suthin'. He married my sister Judy, ye know. They don't take haffen keer o' them chil'n; some o' them mought hev got sot afire o' suthin', or"—

"They *mought*, but they ain't," exclaimed Jack Ormsby, the young mountaineer, with a laugh. "Gid's been down yander ter the show, an' all the chil'n, an' yer sister Judy too."

"What show?" demanded Knowles shortly, his grim face half angry, half amazed.

"The show in the schoolhouse in the Cove. This hyar stranger-man, he gin a show," Ormsby explained. "I viewed 'em all thar, all the fambly."

There was a momentary pause, and one might hear the wind astir in the darkness of the woods below, and feel the dank breath of the clouds that invisibly were gathering on the brink of the range above. One of the sudden mountain rains was at hand.

"An' I wish I hed every one of 'em hyar now!" exclaimed Peter Knowles in fury. "I'd kiver 'em all up in that thar quicklime,—that's what I'd do! An' thar wouldn't be hide, hawns, or taller lef' of none of 'em in the mornin'. Leave *me* hyar,—leave *me* hyar with all this medjure o' lime, an' I never see none so stubborn in burnin', the timber bein' so durned green an' sappy, the dad-burned critter promisin' an' promisin' ter kem back arter he got his supper,—an' go ter a show, a damned show! What sort'n show war it?"

The juggler burst out laughing. "Come ahead!" he cried to Ormsby. "Lend a hand here!"

He had a strong sense of commercial values. To let a marketable commodity lie out and be ruined by the rain was repellent to all his convictions of economics. It might have been as much for the sake of the lime itself as from a sort of half-pity for the deserted lime-burner—for

Peter Knowles had not the cast of countenance or of soul that preëmpted a fellow feeling—that he caught up a great shovel that lay at hand.

"I'll undertake to learn the ropes in a trice," he declared, throwing his coat on the ground.

Knowles only stared at him in surly amazement, but Ormsby, who had often seen the process, threw aside the half-burnt-out logs and followed the lead of the juggler, who, tense, light, active, the white flare, terrible so close at hand, on his face and figure, began to shovel the lumps into the barrow or cart made to receive the lime. Then, as the wind swept by with a warning note, Knowles too fell to work, and added the capacities of his experience to the sheer uninstructed force of the willing volunteers. They made it short work. The two neophytes found it a scorching experiment, and more than once they fell back, flinching from the inherent heat of the flying powder as they shoveled it into the mouth of the grotto.

"I had no idea," the juggler said, as he stood by the embers when it was all over, looking from one smarting hand to the other, "that quicklime is so very powerful, so caustic an agent. I can believe you when you say that if you should put a body in that bed there it would be consumed by morning,—bones and all?" He became suddenly interrogative.

"Nare toe nor toe-nail lef'," returned Peter Knowles succinctly, as if he had often performed this feat as a scientific experiment.

The juggler lifted his eyes to the face of the man opposite. They dilated and lingered fascinated with a sort of horror; for that strange anamorphosis had once more possessed it. All at variance it was with its natural contours, as the heated air streamed up from the bed of half-calcined stone,—trembling through this shimmering medium, yet preserving the semblance of humanity, like the face of some mythical being, demon or ghoul. A dawning significance was on his own face, of which he was unconscious, but which the other noted. How might he utilize this property of air and heat and quicklime in some of those wonders of jugglery at which he was so expert? More than once, as he walked away, he turned back to gaze anew at the phenomenon, his trim figure lightly poised, his hand in his belt, his blazer thrown over his arm, that gleam of discovery on his face.

As the encompassing rocks and foliage at last hid him from view, Peter Knowles looked down into the fire.

"That air a true word. The quicklime would eat every bone," he said slowly. "But what air *he* aimin' ter know fur?" And once more he looked curiously at the spot where the juggler had vanished, remembering the guise of discovery and elation his face had worn.

II.

LATE that night old Tubal Sims lingered on his hearthstone, brooding over the embers of the failing fire. As he reviewed the incidents of the evening, he chuckled with a sort of half-suppressed glee. His capacities for enjoyment were not blunted by the event itself; the very reminiscence afforded him a keen and acute pleasure. In all his sixty years he had never known such a vigil as this. He could not sleep for the crowding images with which his brain teemed. Each detail as it was enacted returned to him now with a freshened delight. The objections urged by the audience on the score of necromancy gave him peculiar joy; for he and his wife were of a progressive tendency of mind, and had that sly sense of mental superiority which is one of the pleasantest secrets to share with one's own consciousness. As he sat on a broken-backed chair, his shoulders bent forward and his hands hanging loosely over his knees, the hard palms rubbing themselves together from time to time, for the air was growing chilly, the light of the embers on his shock of grizzled hair, and wrinkled face with its long blunt nose and projecting chin, and small deep-set eyes twinkling under their overhanging brows, he now and again lifted his head to note any sudden stir about the house. So foreign to his habit was this long-lingering wakefulness that it told on his nerves in an added acuteness of all his senses. He marked the gnawing of a mouse in the roof-room, the sound of the rising wind far away, and the first stir of the elm-tree above the clapboards. A cock crew from his roost hard by, and then with a yawn Tubal Sims pulled off one of his shoes and sat with it in his hand, looking at it absently, and laughing at the thought of old Parson Greenought and his interference to discourage Satan. "I wisht I could hev knowed what the boy would hev done nex', if so be he hed been lef' alone." He made up his mind that he would ask the juggler the next day, and if possible induce a private repetition of some of the wonders for the appreciation of which, evidently, the public sentiment of Etowah Cove was not yet ripe. For the juggler was his guest, having reached his house a few evenings previous in the midst of a storm; and asking for shelter for the night, the wayfarer had found a hearty welcome, and was profiting by it. Sims could hear even now the bed-cords creak as he tossed in uneasy slumber up in the roof-room, so still the house had grown.

So still that when a deep groan and then an agonized gasping sigh came from the sleeper, the sounds were so incongruous with the trend of old Tubal Sims's happy reflections that he experienced a sudden revulsion of feeling that was like a shock. The rain began to fall on the roof; it seemed to come in fine lines on a fluctuating gust, for it was as if borne away on the wings of the wind, and the eaves vaguely dripped.

"But oh," cried the sleeper, "the one who lives! what can I do!—for whose life! his life! his life!" and spoke no more.

Yet the cabalistic words seemed to ring through the house in trumpet tones; they sounded again and again in every blast of the wind. The place had grown cold; the fire was dead on the hearth; it was the unfamiliar midnight. Old Tubal Sims sat as motionless as if petrified. He had never heard of the process of mind-reading, but he would fain decipher these sleeping thoughts of his guest. He found himself involved in tortuous and futile speculations. Who was "the one who lives," whose life this stranger grudged? And following the antithesis,—not that Tubal Sims would have thus phrased it,—was there then one who died? And why should the recollection return in the deep slumbers of the night and speak out in this weird dreaming voice.

It occurred to Tubal Sims, for the first time, that there was something inexplicable about this man. Apparently, he had no mission here save for the exhibition of jugglery,—how suddenly it had lost its zest! He knew naught of the people or the surrounding region; he had no baggage, no sort of preparation for continued existence, not even a change of clothes. Mrs. Sims, being subsidized to supply this deficiency, had already constructed for him one blue homespun shirt, which evidently astounded him when he first beheld it, so different it was from the one he wore, but which he accepted meekly enough. Tubal Sims told himself that he had been precipitate in housing this stranger beyond a shelter during the storm.

To this it had come,—the happy dreaming over the fire, renewing a pleasure so rare,—to these vague fears and self-reproaches and suspicions and anxious speculations. He stumbled to bed at last in the dark, yet still the words and the tone haunted him. It was long ere he slept, and more than once he was roused from slumber to the dark silence by the fancy that he heard anew the poignant iteration.

If the juggler had dreams, they may have weighed heavily upon him the next day, for he came down the rickety stairs, pale and silent, with heavy-lidded eyes and dark blue circles beneath them. Under Mrs. Sims's kindly ministrations he sought in vain to eat the heavy thick biscuit, the underdone fried mush, and the fat greasy bacon; for Mrs. Sims was not one of those culinary geniuses sometimes encountered at humble boards; in good sooth, but for her cows and chickens, in these early days of his stay in Etowah Cove, he would have fared ill indeed.

"Ye make a better out at swallerin' needles 'n ye do swallerin' fried 'taters," she declared, with a reproachful glance, supplemented by her good-humored chuckle.

He could make no sort of compact with the beverage she called coffee, and after the merest feint of breakfast he took his host's angling-tackle and wended his way down to the river, observing that the fish would bite well to-day, since it was so cloudy. Cloudy it was, undoubtedly, sombre and drear. Now and then drizzling showers fell, and when they ceased the mists that rose in the ravines and skulked in every depression were hardly less dank and chill. The river, in its deep channel between jagged rocky gray bluffs and shelving red clay banks of the most brilliant terra-cotta tones, was of the color of copper instead of the clear steel-gray or the silvered blue it was wont to show, so much of the mud of its borders did it hold now in solution, brought down by the rains of the night. Here and there slender willows hung over it in lissome and graceful wont, with such vivid vernal suggestions in the tender budding foliage as to cause the faint green tint to shine with definite lustre, like the high lights in some artificial landscape of a canvas, amidst the dark dripping bronze-green pines of the Cove, which from this point the young man could see stretching away in sad-hued verdure some three or four miles to the opposite mountain's base,—the breadth of the restricted little basin. This was the only large outlook at his command; for behind the house he had quitted, the slopes of the wooded mountain rose abruptly, steep, rugged, soon lost among the clouds. He gazed absently at the little cabin, the usual structure of two rooms with an open passage, as he lay on the shelving rock high above the river, the fishing-pole held by a heavy boulder fixed on it to secure it in its place, his hands clasped under his head, his hat tilted somewhat over his eyes; for despite the paucity of light in the atmosphere the mists had a certain white glaring quality.

Meanwhile, he was the subject of a degree of disaffected scrutiny from indoors.

"Jane Ann," said Tubal Sims, suddenly interrupting the loud throaty wheeze by which his help-meet beguiled the tedium of washing the dishes, and which she construed as that act of devotion commonly known as singing a hymn, "that thar man ain't got no bait on his hook."

Jane Ann set the plate in her hand down on the table, and turned her broad creased face toward her husband as he sat smoking in the passage, just outside the door.

"Then he ain't goin' ter ketch no feesh," she replied logically, and lifting both the plate and her droning wheeze she resumed her occupation.

Tubal Sims, like other men, fluctuated in his estimation of his wife's abilities according as they seemed to him convertible to his aid. Ordinarily, he was wont to commend Jane Ann Sims's logical common sense as "powerful smartness," and had been known to lean on her judgment even in the matter of "craps," in which, if anywhere, man is safe from the interference and even the ambition of woman. He rejoiced in her freedom from the various notions which appertain to her sex, and felt a certain pride that she too had withstood the panic which had so preyed upon the pleasures of the "show." But now, when her lack of the subtler receptivities balked him of a possible approach to the key of the mystery which he sought to solve, he was irritated because of her density of perception, and disposed to underrate her capacities to deduce aught from that cabalistic phrase which he alone had heard uttered in the deep midnight and from such slender premises to frame a just conclusion. And furthermore, with the rebuff he realized anew that Jane Ann Sims was a woman, incompetent of reason save in its most superficial processes, or she would have perceived that the significance of the unbaited hook lay in the strange mental perturbation which could involve the neglect of so essential a particular, not in the obvious fruitlessness of the labor. Jane Ann Sims was a woman. Let her wash the dishes.

"Naw," he said aloud, half scornfully, "he'll ketch no feesh."

Mrs. Sims ceased to wheeze, and her fat face relapsed from the pious distortions of her psalmody into its normal creases and dimples. "I be plumb fit ter fly inter the face o' Providence," she said, as she moved heavily about the table and slapped down a blue platter but half dried.

"What fur?" demanded the lord of the house, whose sense of humor was too blunted by his speculations, and a haunting anxiety, and a troublous eagerness to discuss the question of his discovery, to perceive aught of the ludicrous in the lightsome metaphor with which his weighty spouse had characterized her disaffection with the ordering of events.

"Kase Euphemy ain't hyar, o' course. Ye 'pear ter be sorter dunder-headed this mornin'!" Thus the weaker vessel!

She wheezed one more line of her matutinal hymn in a dolorous cadence and with breathy interstices between the spondees; then suddenly and finally discarding the exercise, she began to speak with animation: "I hev always claimed an' sot out ter be suthin' of a prophet,—ye yerse'f know ez I be more weatherwise 'n common. I be toler'ble skilled in cow diseases, too; an' I kin say 'forehand who be goin' ter git 'lected ter office,—ginerally, though, by knowin' who hev got money an' holds his hand slack; an' I kin tell what color hair a baby be goin' ter hev whenst he ain't got so much ez a furze on the top o' his bald pate; an' whenst ye 'low ye air strict sober of a Christmastime or sech, I kin tell ter a—a quart how much applejack hev gone down yer gullet; an'"—

He sacrificed his curiosity as to her other accomplishments as a seer, and hastily inquired, "What on the yearth hev sot ye off ter braggin' this-a-way, Jane Ann? I never hearn the beat!"

"I ain't braggin'," expounded Mrs. Sims. "I be just meditatin' on how forehanded I be in viewin' facts in gineral; an' yit,"—her voice rose in pathetic exasperation,—"the very day o' the evenin' this hyar stranger-man got hyar I let Euphemy go over ter Piomingo Cove ter visit her granny's folks; an' the chile didn't want ter go much,—war afeard o' rain, bein' dressed out powerful starched; an' I, so forehanded in sight, told her 'twarn't goin' ter rain till evenin'."

"Waal, no more did it. Phemie war under shelter six hours 'fore it rained."

"Lawd-a-massy!" cried Mrs. Sims, at the end of her patience. "What war the use o' creatin' man with sech a slow onderstandin'? I reckon the reason woman war made arterward war ter gin the critter somebody ter explain things ter him! Can't you-uns sense"—she directly addressed her husband—"ez what I be a-tryin' ter compass is why—why—I could tell ter a minit when the storm war a-comin', an' yit couldn't tell the juggler war comin' with it?"

Tubal Sims, staring up from under his shaggy eyebrows, his arms folded on his knees, his cob pipe cocked between his teeth, could only ejaculate, "I dunno."

"Naw, you-uns dunno," flouted Mrs. Sims, "an' you-uns dunno a heap besides that."

He received this fling in humble silence. Then, after the manner of the henpecked, unable to keep out of trouble, albeit before his eyes, and flinching at the very moment from discipline, he must needs inquire, "Why, Jane Ann, what you-uns want the pore child hyar fur? Ye git on toler'ble well with the cookin' 'thout her help. Let Phemie git her visit out ter her granny in Piomingo Cove," he concluded expostulatingly.

There was not a dimple in Mrs. Sims's face. It was all solid, set, stern, fat. She sunk down into a chair and folded her arms as she gazed at him. "Tubal Cain Sims," she admonished him solemnly, "ef I hed no mo' head-stuffin' 'n you-uns, I'd git folks ter chain me up like that thar tame b'ar at Sayre's Mill, so ez 'twould be knowed I warn't 'sponsible. Ye hev yer motions like him, an' ye kin scratch yer head like him, too; but he can't talk sense, an' ye can't nuther." She paused for a moment; then she condescended to explain: "I want that child Euphemy hyar kase she oughter hed a chance ter view that show las' night."

His countenance changed. He too valued the "show" as a special privilege. He was woe for Euphemia's sake, away down yonder in the backwoods of Piomingo Cove.

"Mebbe he mought gin another show over yander ter the Settlemint," he hazarded. "The folks over thar will be plumb sharp-set fur sech doin's whenst they hear 'bout'n it."

The sophistications of polite society are not recognized by the medical faculty as amongst the epidemics which spread among mankind, but no contagious principle has so dispersive a quality in every feature of the malady. Given one show in Etowah Cove, and Tubal Cain Sims developed the acumen of a keen *impresario*. He saw the opportunity, counted the chances, evolved as an original idea—for the existence of such a scheme had never reached his ears—a successful starring tour around the coves and mountain settlements of the Great Smoky range.

The melancholy expressed in the slow shaking of Mrs. Sims's head aroused him from this project.

"Naw," she said; "the fool way that the folks tuk on 'bout Satan—they'd better hev the high-strikes 'count o' thar sins—an' thar theatenings an' sech will purvent him. He won't show agin. An' I be plumb afeard," she cried out in renewed vexation, "the man will get away from hyar 'thout viewin' Euphemy. I'll be bound he hev never seen the like of her!" with a joyous note of maternal pride.

The pipe turned around in Tubal Sims's mouth, and the charge of fire and ashes and tobacco fell unheeded on the floor. Like a voice in his ears the echo of that strange cry of the sleeper came to him out of the deep darkness of the stormy midnight, with the problem of its occult significance, with the terror of its possible meaning, and every other consideration slipped from his consciousness. The perception of the mental trouble expressed in the man's face, its confirmation even in the trifle of the unbaited hook, returned to Sims, with the determination that he must know more of him or get him out of the Cove before Euphemia's return. "The man's dad-burned good-lookin'," he said to himself, perceiving the fact for the first time, since it had a personal application. "An' Phemie be powerful book-l'arned, an' be always scornin' the generality o' the young cusses round about, kase she knows more 'n they do. Mebbe he knows more 'n she do." He pondered for a moment on the improbability that daughter Euphemia's knowledge, acquired at the little schoolhouse where the "show" had been held, was exceeded by the fund of information stored in the brain-pan of any single individual since the world began. At all events, anxiety, complications, familiar association in the sanctions of the fireside, impended. This was a man with a secret, and, innocent or guilty, a stranger to his host. He must be quick, for Mrs. Sims—transparent Mrs. Sims!—was even now evolving methods by which Euphemia might be summoned peremptorily from Piomingo Cove, and canvassing means of transportation. She chuckled even amidst her anxieties. The juggler, in all his experience,—and his conversation now and again gave intimations that he was a man of cities and had seen much folk in his time,—had never viewed aught like Euphemia, and if scheming might avail, he should not leave Etowah Cove till this crowning mercy was vouchsafed him.

Whether Tubal Sims vaunted his wife's mental qualities or derided them,—and his estimate swung like a pendulum from one side to the other, as her views coincided with his or differed from them,—he knew that on this topic she was immovable. To pierce the juggler's heart by a dart still more mystic and subtle than aught his skill could wield was her motive. Help must come, if at all, from without the domestic circle. He waited, doubtful, until after dinner, and as he looked about for his hat, his resolution taken after much brooding thought, he noted a change in the weather-signs. The wind was blowing crisply through the open passage. The mists had lifted. The river, dully gurgling in the dreary early morning, had begun anew its lapsing sibilant song that seemed a concomitant of the sunshine; for the slanting afternoon glitter was on the water here and there, and high on the mountain side all the various green possible to spring foliage was elicited by the broad expanse of the golden sheen that came down from the west. He noted, as he took his way along the road, that the recumbent figure once again on the ledge below was not asleep, for the juggler lifted his hand as the rocks above began to reflect the beams on the water in a tremulous shimmer, and drew his hat further over his eyes. "Ye mought hev better comp'ny 'n yer thoughts, Mr. Showman, I'm a-thinkin'," Tubal Sims muttered, and he mended his pace.

His path, much trodden, wended along about the base of the range, and finally, by a series of zigzag curves, began to ascend the slope. The clouds, white, tenuous, were flying high now. The sun had grown hot. Already the moisture was dried from the wayside foliage of laurel as he came upon the projecting spur of the range where the lime-burners worked. The logs, protected from the rain by a ledge of the cliff, had been piled anew with layers of limestone, and the primitive process of calcination had begun once more. Here and there were great heaps of fragments of rock placed close at hand, and numerous trees had been felled for fuel and lay at length on the ground, yet so dense was the forest that the loss was not appreciable to the eye. The stumps and boles of these trees furnished seats for a number of lounging mountaineers, in every attitude that might express a listless sloth. Those who had come to work felt that they had earned a respite from labor, and those who had come to talk hastened to utilize the opportunity. Their conversation was something more brisk than usual, accelerated by interest in a new and uncommon topic. As Sims had foreseen, the events of the previous evening occupied every thought, and several of the group experienced a freshened joy in detailing them anew to Peter Knowles, who alone of all the neighborhood for a circuit of twenty miles had been absent. He had heard every incident repeatedly rehearsed without showing a sign of flagging interest. Now and then he bent his brows and looked down at the quicklime scattered on the ground, and silently meditated on its capacity to destroy flesh and bone and on the juggler's unhallowed curiosity.

"A body dunno how ter git his own cornsent ter b'lieve his own eyesight," one of the men reflectively averred. The interval since witnessing the astounding feats of the prestidigitator had afforded space for rumination, and but served to deepen the impression of possibilities set at naught and miracles enacted.

"That thar man air in league with Satan," declared another, "Surely, surely he air." He accentuated his words with his long lean forefinger shaken impressively at the group.

"Ye mark my words," said Peter Knowles suddenly, still eying the refuse of quicklime on the ground, "no good hev kem inter the Cove with that thar man."

"Whar'd he kem from, ennyhows?" demanded the first speaker.

"Whar'd he kem from?" repeated Knowles, peering over the great kiln. "From hell, my frien',—straight from hell."

He had the combined drone and whine which he esteemed appropriate to the clerical office; for although he had never experienced a "call," he deemed himself singularly fitted for that vocation by virtue of a disposition to hold forth at great length to any one who would listen to his views on religious themes,—and in this region, where time is plenty and industry scanty, he seldom lacked listeners,—a conscience ever sensitive to the sins of other people, and great freedom in the use of such Scriptural terms as are debarred to persons not naturally profane or suffering under the stress of extreme rage.

"Waal, sir!" exclaimed old man Cobbs, sitting on a stump and gently nursing his knee. He spoke with a voice of deep reprehension, and as simple an acceptance of the possibility of hailing from the place in question as if it were geographically extant.

Ormsby, who had been standing leaning on an axe, silently listening, laughed slightly at this,—an incredulous laugh. "Folks ez git ter that kentry don't git back in a hurry," he drawled negligently, but with a manifest satisfaction in the circumstance, as if he knew of sundry departed wights whom he esteemed well placed.

"How d'ye know they don't?" demanded Peter Knowles. "Ain't ye never read the Scriptures enough ter sense them lines, 'Satan was a-walkin' up and down through the yearth,' ye blunderin' buzzard, an' *he* fell from heaven?"

The young fellow's robust figure was clearly defined against the western sky. He swung his axe nonchalantly now, for to be an adept in reading and remembering the Scriptures was not the height of his ambition. Nevertheless, the idea of the possibility of being in the orbit, as it were, of an earthly stroll of the Prince of Darkness roused him to argument and insistence on a less terrifying solution of the mystery.

"He telled it ter me ez he kem from Happy Valley," he volunteered.

The elders of the party stared at one another. The fire roared suddenly as a log broke, burned in twain; the limestone fragments, still crude, went rattling down into the crevices its fall had made. Peter Knowles's arm, with the free ministerial gesticulation which he was wont to copy, fixed the absurdity upon Ormsby even before he spoke.

"Don't ye know that thar Philistine ain't got sech speech ez them ez lives in Happy Valley, nor thar clothes, nor thar raisin', nor thar manners, nor thar ways, nor thar—nuthin'? Don't you-uns sense that?"

"I 'lowed ez much ter him," replied Ormsby, a trifle browbeaten by the seniority of his interlocutor and the difficulty of the subject. "I up-ed an' said, 'Ye ain't nowise like folks ez live in Happy Valley. Ter look at ye, I'd set it down fur true ez ye hed never been in the shadder o' Chilhowee all yer days.'"

"An' what did he say, bub?" demanded old man Cobbs gently, after a moment of waiting.

"Great Gosh, yes!" exclaimed Peter Knowles explosively. "We-uns ain't a-waitin' hyar ter hear you-uns tell yer talk; ennybody could hev said that an' mo'. What did the man say?"

Ormsby turned doubtfully toward the descending sun and the reddening sky. "We-uns war a-huntin', me an' that juggler. I seen him yestiddy mornin'. I went down thar ter Mis' Sims' an' happened ter view him. An' I loant him my brother's gun. An' whenst I said that 'bout his looks an' sech, we war a-huntin', an' he 'peared not ter know thar war enny Happy Valley 'way over yander by Chilhowee. An' I tuk him up high on the mounting whar he could look over fur off an' see the Rich Woods an' Happy Valley, an'—an'"—He paused.

"An' what did he say?" inquired Knowles eagerly.

Ormsby looked embarrassed. "He jes' say," he went on suddenly, as if with an effort, "he jes' say, 'Oh, Dr. Johnson!' an' bust out a-laffin'. I dunno what the critter meant."

Once more Ormsby turned, swinging his axe in his strong right hand, and glanced absently over the landscape.

The sun was gone. The mountains, darkly glooming, rose high above the Cove on every side, seeming to touch the translucent amber sky that, despite the sunken sun, conserved an effect of illumination heightened by contrast with the fringes of hemlock and pine, that had assumed a sombre purple hue, waving against its crystalline concave. In this suffusion of reflected color, rather than in the medium of daylight, he beheld the scanty fields below in the funnel-like basin; for this projecting spur near the base of the range gave an outlook over the lower levels at hand. Some cows, he could discern, were still wending homeward along an undulating red clay road, which rose and fell till the woods intervened. The woods were black. Night was afoot there amongst the shadowy boughs, for all the golden glow of the feigning sky. The evening mists were adrift along the ravines. Ever and anon the flames flickered out, red and yellow, from the heap of logs. Not a sound stirred the group as they pondered on this strange reply, till Ormsby said reflectively, "The juggler be toler'ble good comp'ny, though,—nuthin' like the devil an' sech; leastwise, so much ez I know 'bout Satan,"—he seemed to defer to the superior acquaintanceship of Knowles. "This hyar valley-man talks powerful pleasant; an' he kin sing,—jes' set up an' sing like a plumb red-headed mock-in'bird, that's what! You-uns hearn him sing at the show,"—he turned from Knowles to appeal to the rest of the group.

"Did he 'pear ter you-uns, whilst huntin', ter try enny charms an' spells on the wild critters?" asked Knowles.

"They didn't work ef he did!" exclaimed Jack Ormsby, with a great gush of laughter that startled the echoes into weird unmirthful response. "He shot one yallerhammer arter travelin' nigh ten mile ter git him." After a pause, "I gin him the best chance at a deer I ever hed. I never see a feller hev the 'buck ager' so bad. He never witched that deer. He shot plumb two feet too high. She jes' went a-bouncin' by him down the mounting,—bouncin' yit, I reckon! But he kin shoot toler'ble fair at a mark." The ready laughter again lighted his face. "He 'lows he likes a mark ter shoot at kase it stands still. He's plumb pleasant comp'ny sure."

"Waal, he ain't been sech powerful pleasant comp'ny down ter my house," protested Tubal Sims. "Ain't got a word ter say, an' 'pears like he ain't got the heart ter eat a mouthful o' vittles. Yander he hev been a-lyin' flat on them wet rocks all ter-day, with no mo' keer o' the rheumatics 'n ef he war a bullfrog,—a-feeshin' in the ruver with a hook 'thout no bait on it."

"What'd he ketch?" demanded one of the men, with a quick glance of alarm. Miracles for the purpose of exhibition and cutting a dash they esteemed far less repellent to the moral sense than the use of uncommon powers to serve the ordinary purposes of daily life.

"Pleurisy, ef he got his deserts," observed the disaffected host. "He caught nuthin' with ez much sense ez a stickle-back. 'Pears ter me he ain't well, nohow. He groaned a power in his sleep las' night, arter the show. An'"—he felt he ventured on dangerous ground—"he talked, too."

There was a significant silence. "That thar man hev got suthin' on his mind," muttered Peter Knowles.

"I be powerful troubled myself," returned the level-headed Sims weakly. "I oughtn't ter hev tuk him in,—him a stranger, though"—he remembered the hospitable text in time for a flimsy self-justification. "But 'twar a-stormin' powerful, and he 'peared plumb beat out. I 'lowed that night he war goin' inter some sort'n fever or dee-lerium. I put him inter the roof-room, an' he went ter bed ez soon ez he could git thar. But the nex' day he war ez fraish an' gay ez a jaybird."

"What's he talk 'bout whenst sleepin'?" asked Peter Knowles, his covert glance once more reverting to the refuse of quicklime at his feet.

"Suthin' he never lays his tongue ter whenst wakin', I'll be bound," replied Tubal Sims precipitately. Then he hesitated. This disclosure was, he felt, a flagrant breach of hospitality. What right had he to listen to the disjointed exclamations of his guest in his helplessness as he slept, place his own interpretation upon them, and retail them to others for their still more inimical speculation? Jane Ann Sims,—how he would have respected her judgment had she been a man!—he was sure, would not have given the words a second thought. But then her habit of mind was incredulous. Parson Greenought often told her that he feared her faith was not sufficient to take her to heaven. "I be dependin' on suthin' better'n that, pa'son," she would smilingly rejoin. "I ain't lookin' ter my own pore mind an' my own wicked heart fur holp. An' ye mark my words, I'll be the fust nangel ye shake han's with when ye git inside the golden door." And the parson, impaled on his own weapons, could only suggest that they should sing a hymn together, which they did,—Jane Ann Sims much the louder of the two.

Admirable woman! she had but a single weakness, and this Tubal Cain Sims was aware that he shared. With the returning thought of their household idol, Euphemia, every consideration imposing reticence vanished.

"Last night," he began suddenly, "I war so conflusticated with the goin's-on ez I couldn't sleep fur a while. An' ez I sot downsteers afore the fire, I could but take notice o' how oneasy this man 'peared in his sleep up in the roof-room. He sighed an' groaned like suthin' in agony. An' then he says, so painful, 'But the one who lives—oh, what can I do—the one who lives! fur his life!—his life!—his life!'" He paused abruptly to mark the petrified astonishment on the group of faces growing white in the closing dusk.

An owl began to hoot in the bosky recesses far up the slope. At the sound, carrying far in the twilight stillness, a hound bayed from the door of the little cabin in the Cove, by the river. A light, stellular in the gloom that hung about the lower levels, suddenly sprung up in the window. A tremulous elongated reflection shimmered in the shallows close under the bank where the juggler had been lying. Was he there yet? Sims wondered, quivering with the excitement of the moment.

His anxiety was not quelled, but a great relief came upon him when Peter Knowles echoed his own thought, which seemed thus the natural sequence of the event, and not some far-fetched fantasy.

"That thar man hev killed somebody, ez sure ez ye live!" exclaimed Peter Knowles. "'But the one who lives!' An' who is the one who died?"

"Jes' so, jes' so," interpolated Sims, reassured to see his own mental process so definitely duplicated in the thoughts of a man held to be of experienced and just judgment, and much regarded in the community.

"He be a-runnin' from jestice," resumed Knowles. "He ain't no juggler, ez he calls hisself."

There was a general protest.

"Shucks, Pete, ye oughter seen him swaller a bay'net."

"An' Mis' Sims tole him she'd resk her shears on it, she jes' felt so reckless an' plumb kerried away. An' he swallered them, too, an' then tuk 'em out'n his throat, sharp ez ever."

"An' he swallered a paper o' needles an' a spool o' thread, an' brung 'em out'n his mouth all threaded."

There was a delighted laugh rippling round the circle.

"Look-a-hyar, my frien's," remonstrated Peter Knowles in a solemn, sepulchral voice, "I never viewed none o' these doin's, but ye air all 'bleeged ter know ez they air on-possible, the devices o' the devil. An' hyar ye be, perfessin' Christians, a-laffin' at them wiles ez air laid ter delude the onwary."

There was a general effort to recover a sobriety of demeanor, and one of the men then observed gravely that on the occasion when these wonders were exhibited Parson Benias Greenought taxed the performer with this supposition.

"Waal," remarked Ormsby, "ye air 'bleeged ter hev tuk notice, ef ye war thar las' night, ez old Benias never moved toe or toe-nail till arter all the jinks war most over. He seen nigh all thar war ter see 'fore he 'lowed how the sinners war enj'yin' tharse'fs, an' called up the devil ter len' a han'."

"What the man say?" demanded Peter Knowles.

"He 'peared cornsider'ble set back a-fust, an' then he tried ter laff it off," replied Gideon Beck. "He 'lowed he could l'arn sech things ter folks ez he had l'arnt 'em, too."

"Now tell me one thing," argued Peter Knowles; "how's a man goin' ter l'arn a pusson ter put a persimmon seed in a pail o' yearth, an' lay a cloth over it, an' sing some foolishness, an' take off'n the cloth, an' thar's a persimmon shoot with a root ez long ez my han' a-growin' in that yearth?"

There were sundry gravely shaken heads.

"Mis' Jernigan jes' went plumb inter the high-strikes, she got so skeered, an' they hed ter take her home in the wagon," said Beck.

"Old man Jernigan hed none; the las' time I viewed him he war a-tryin' ter swaller old Mis' Jernigan's big shears hisse'f," retorted Ormbsy.

"Mis' Jernigan ain't never got the rights o' herself yit, an' her cow hev done gone dry, too," observed Beck.

"Tell me, my brethren, what's them words mean,—'the one who lives'?" insisted Peter Knowles significantly. "Sure's ye air born, thar's another verse an' chapter ter that sayin'. Who war the one who died?"

Once more awe settled down upon the little group. The wind had sprung up. Now and again pennons of flame flaunted out from the great heap of logs and stones, and threw livid bars of light athwart the landscape, which pulsated visibly as the blaze rose and fell,—now seeming strangely distinct and near at hand, now receding into the darkness and distance. Mystery affiliated with the time and place, and there was scant responsiveness to Ormsby's protest as he once more sought to befriend the absent juggler.

"I can't git my cornsent ter b'lieve ez thar be enny dead one. I reckon the feller war talkin' 'bout his kemin' powerful nigh dyin' hisself. He 'lowed ter me ez he hed a mighty great shock jes' afore he kem hyar,—what made him so diff'ent a-fust."

"Shocked by lightning?" demanded Peter Knowles dubiously.

"I reckon so; never hearn on no other kind."

"Waal, now," said Tubal Sims, who had sought during this discussion to urge his views on the coterie, "I 'low that the Cove ought not ter take up with sech jubious doin's ez these."

"Lawsy massy!" exclaimed Beck, with the uplifted eyebrows of derision, "las' night you-uns an' Mis' Sims too 'peared plumb kerried away, jes' bodaciously dee-lighted, with the juggler an' all his pay-formances!"

There is naught in all our moral economy which can suffer a change without discredit and disparagement, barring what is known as a change of heart. It is a clumsy and awkward mental evolution at best, as the turncoat in politics, the apologist for discarded friendships, the fickle-minded in religious doctrines, know to their cost. The process of veering is attended invariably with a poignant mortification, as if one had warranted one's opinions infallible, and to endure till time shall be no more. Tubal Cain Sims experienced all the ignominious sensations known as "eatin' crow," as he sought to qualify his satisfaction of the previous evening, and reconcile it to his complete change of sentiment now, without giving his true reason. It would involve scant courtesy to the absent Euphemia to intimate his fears lest she admire too much the juggler, and it might excite ridicule to suggest his certainty that the juggler would admire her far too much. Sometimes, indeed, he doubted if other people—that is, above the age of twenty-five—entertained the rapturous estimate of Euphemia, which was a subject on which he and Jane Ann Sims never differed.

"I did,—I did," he sputtered. "Me an' Jane Ann nare one never seen no harm in the pay-formance. An' Jane Ann don't know nuthin' contrarious yit, kase I ain't tole her,—she bein' a 'oman, an' liable ter talk free an' let her tongue git a-goin'; she dunno whar ter stop. A man oughtn't ter tell his wife sech ez he aims ter go no furder," he added discursively.

"'Thout he wants all the Cove ter be a-gabblin' over it nex' day," assented a husband of three experiments. "I know wimmin. Lawsy massy! I know 'em now." He shook his head lugubriously, as if his education in feminine quirks and wiles had gone hard with him, and he could willingly have dispensed with a surplusage of learning.

"But arter I hearn them strange words," resumed Tubal Cain Sims,—"them strange words, so painful an' pitiful-spoken,—I drawed the same idee ez Peter Knowles thar. I 'lowed the juggler war some sort'n evil-doer agin the law,—though he didn't look like it ter me."

"He did ter me; he featured it from the fust," Knowles protested, with a stern drawing down of his forbidding face.

There was a momentary pause while they all seemed to meditate on the evidence afforded by the personal appearance of the juggler.

"I be afeard," continued Sims, glancing at Knowles, "like Pete say, he hev c'mmitted murder an' be fleein' from the law. An' I be a law-abidin' citizen—an'—an'—he can't stay at my house."

There was silence. No one was interested in the impeccability of Tubal Cain Sims's house. It was his castle. He was free to say who should come and who should go. His own responsibility was its guarantee.

It is a pathetic circumstance in human affairs that the fact of how little one's personal difficulties and anxieties and turmoils of mind count to one's friends can only be definitely ascertained by the experiment made in the thick of these troubles.

With a sudden return of his wonted perspicacity, Sims said, "That thar man oughter be gin notice ter leave. I call on ye all—ye all live round 'bout the Cove—ter git him out'n it."

There was a half-articulate grumble of protest and surprise.

"It's yer business ter make him go, ef yer don't want him in yer house," said Peter Knowles, looking loweringly at Sims.

"I ain't got nuthin' agin him," declared Sims excitedly, holding both empty palms upward. "I can't say, 'Git out; ye talk in yer sleep, an' ye don't talk ter suit me!' *But*," fixing the logic upon them with weighty emphasis and a significant pause, "you-uns all b'lieve ez he air in league with Satan, an' his jinks air deviltries an' sech. An' so be, ye *ought* ter make him take hisself an' his conjurin's off from hyar 'fore he witches the craps, or spirits away the lime, or tricks the mill, or—He ought ter be gin hours ter cl'ar out."

Peter Knowles roused himself to argument. He had developed a vivid curiosity concerning the juggler. The suggestion of the devil's agency was a far cry to his fears,—be it remembered he had not seen the bayonet swallowed!—and he had phenomenal talents for contrariety, and graced the opposition with great persistence and powers of contradiction.

"Bein' ez ye hev reason ter suspect that man o' murder or sech, we-uns ain't got the *right* ter give him hours ter leave. Ye ain't got the *right* ter turn him out'n yer house ter escape from the off'cers o' the law."

The crowd, always on the alert for a sensation, pricked up their willing ears. "Naw, ye ain't," more than one asseverated.

"'Twould jes' be holpin' him on his run from jestice," declared Beck. "Further he gits, further the sher'ff'll hev ter foller, an' mo' chance o' losin' him."

"They be on his track now, I reckon," said old Josiah Cobbs dolorously.

"It's the jewty o' we-uns in the Cove," resumed Peter Knowles, "ter keep a stric' watch on him an' see ter it he don't git away 'fore the sher'ff tracks him hyar."

Tubal Sims's blood ran cold. A man sitting daily at his table under the espionage of all the Cove as a murderer! A man sleeping in his best feather-bed—and the way he floundered in its unaccustomed depths nothing but a porpoise could emulate—till the sheriff of the county should come to hale him out to the ignominious quarters of the common jail! Jane Ann Sims—how his heart sank as he thought that had he first taken counsel of her he would not now be in a position to receive his orders from Peter Knowles!—to be in daily friendly association with this strange guest, to be sitting at home now calmly stitching cuffs for a man who might be wearing handcuffs before daylight! Euphemia—when he thought of Euphemia he rose precipitately from the rock on which he was seated. In twenty-four hours Euphemia should be in Buncombe County, North Carolina, where his sister lived. The juggler should never see her; for who knew what lengths Jane Ann Sims's vicarious love of admiration would carry her? If the man were but on his knees, what cared she what the Cove thought of him? And Euphemia should never see the juggler! Tubal Sims hurried down the darkening way, hearing without heeding the voices of his late comrades, all dispersing homeward by devious paths,—now loud in the still twilight, now veiled and indistinct in the distance. The chirring of the myriad nocturnal insects was rising from every bush, louder, more confident, refreshed by the recent rain, and the frogs chanted by the riverside.

He had reached the lower levels at last. He glanced up and saw the first timid palpitant star spring forth with a glitter into the midst of the neutral-tinted ether, and then, as if affrighted at the vast voids of the untenanted skies, disappear so elusively that the eye might not mark the spot where that white crystalline flake had trembled. It was early yet. He strode up to his own house, whence the yellow light glowed from the window. He stopped suddenly, his heart sinking like lead. There on the step of the passage sat Euphemia, her elbow on her knee, her chin in her hand, her eyes pensively fixed on the uncertain kindling of that pioneer star once more blazing out the road in the evening sky.

III.

EUPHEMIA could hardly have said what it was that had brought her home,—some vague yet potent impulse, some occult, unimagined power of divination, some subjection to her mother's will constraining her, or simply the intuition that there was some opportunity for mischief unimproved. Tubal Cain Sims shook his head dubiously as he canvassed each theory. He ventured to ask the views of Mrs. Sims, after he had partaken of the supper set aside for him—for the meal was concluded before his return—and had lighted his pipe.

"What brung her home? Them stout leetle brogans,—that's what," said Mrs. Sims, chuckling between the whiffs of her own pipe.

"Course I know the chile walked. I reckon she'll hev stone-bruises a plenty arter this,—full twelve mile. But what put it inter her head ter kem? She 'lowed ter me she ain't dreamed o' nuthin', 'ceptin' Spot hed a new calf, which she ain't got. Reckon 'twar a leadin' or a warnin' or"—

"I reckon 'twar homesickness. Young gals always pine fur home, special ef thar ain't nuthin' spry goin' on in a new place." And once more Jane Ann Sims, in the plenitude of her triumph, chuckled.

It chanced, that afternoon, that when the red sunset was aflare over the bronze-green slopes that encircled the Cove, and the great pine near at hand began to sway and to sing and to cast forth the rich benison of its aroma to the fresh rain-swept air, the juggler roused himself, pushed back his hat from his eyes, and gazed with listless melancholy about him. Somehow the sweet peace of the secluded place appealed to his world-weary senses. The sounds,—the distant, mellow lowing of the kine, homeward wending; the tinkle of a sheep-bell; the rhythmic dash of the river; the ecstatic cadenzas of a mocking-bird, so intricate, delivered with such dashing *élan*, so marvelously clear and sweet and high as to give an effect as of glitter,—all were so harmoniously bucolic. He was soothed in a measure, or dulled, as he drew a long sigh of relief and surcease of pain, and began to experience that facile renewal of interest common to youth with all its recuperative faculties. It fights a valiant fight with sorrow or trouble, and only the years conquer it at last. For the first time he noted among the budding willows far down the stream a roof all aslant, which he divined at once was the mill. He rose to his feet with a quickening curiosity. As he released the futile fishing-rod and wound up the line he remarked the unbaited hook. His face changed abruptly with the thought of his absorption and trouble. He pitied himself.

The road down which he took his way described many a curve seeking to obviate the precipitousness of the descent. The rocks rose high on either side for a time, and when the scene beyond broke upon him in its entirety it was as if a curtain were suddenly lifted. How shadowy, how fragrant the budding woods above the calm and lustrous water! The mill, its walls canted askew, dark and soaked with the rain, and its mossy roof awry, was sombre and silent. Over the dam the water fell in an unbroken crystal sheet so smooth and languorous that it seemed motionless, as if under a spell. Ferns were thick on a marshy slope opposite, where scattered boulders lay, and one quivering blossomy bough of a dogwood-tree leaned over its white reflection in the water, fairer than itself, like some fond memory embellishing the thing it images.

With that sudden sense of companionship in loneliness by which a presence is felt before it is perceived, he turned sharply back as he was about to move away, and glanced again toward the mill. A young girl was standing in the doorway in an attitude of arrested poise, as if in surprise.

Timidity was not the juggler's besetting sin. He lifted his hat with a courteous bow, the like of which had never been seen in Etowah Cove, and thus commending himself to her attention, he took his way toward her along the slant of the corduroy road; for this fleeting glimpse afforded to him a more vivid suggestion of interest than the Cove had as yet been able to present. For the first time since reaching its confines it occurred to him that it might be possible to live along awhile yet. Nevertheless, he contrived to keep his eyes decorously void of expression, and occupied them for the most part in aiding his feet to find their way among the crevices and obstacles with which the road abounded. When he paused, he asked, suffering his eyes to rest inquiringly on the girl, "Beg pardon, but will you kindly inform me where is the miller?"

The glimpse that had so attracted him was, he felt, all inadequate, as he stood and gazed, privileged by virtue of his simulated interest in the absent miller. He could not have seen from the distance how fair, how dainty, was her complexion, nor the crinkles and sparkles of gold in her fine brown hair. It waved upward from her low brow in a heavy undulation which he would have discriminated as "à la Pompadour," but its contour was compassed by wearing far backward a round comb, the chief treasure of her possessions, the heavy masses of hair rising smoothly toward the front, and falling behind in long, loose ringlets about her shoulders. She had a delicate chin with a deep dimple,—which last reminded him unpleasantly of Mrs. Sims, for dimples were henceforth at a discount; a fine, thin, straight nose; two dark silken eyebrows, each describing a perfect arc; and surely there were never created for the beguilement of man two such large, lustrous gray-blue eyes, long-lashed, deep-set, as those which served Euphemia Sims for the comparatively unimportant function of vision. He had hardly been certain whether her attire was more or less grotesque than the costume of the other mountain women until she lifted these eyes and completed the charm of the unique apparition. She wore a calico bought by the yard at the store, and accounted but a flimsy fabric by the homespun-weaving mountain women. It was of a pale green tint, and had once been sprinkled over with large dark green leaves. Lye soap and water had done their merciful work. The strong crude color of the leaves had been subdued to a tint but little deeper than the ground of the material, and while the contour of the foliage was retained, it was mottled into a semblance of light and shade here and there where the dye strove to hold fast. The figure which it draped was pliant and slender; the feet which the full skirt permitted to be half visible were small, and arrayed in brown hose and the stout little brogans which had brought her so nimbly from Piomingo Cove. Partly amused, partly contemptuous, partly admiring, the juggler remarked her hesitation and embarrassment, and relished it as of his own inspiring.

"Waal," she drawled at last, "I don't rightly know." She gazed at him doubtfully. "Air ye wantin' ter see him special?"

He had a momentary terror lest she should ask him for his grist and unmask his subterfuge. He sought refuge in candor. "Well, I was admiring the mill. This is a pretty spot, and I wished to ask the miller's name."

There was a flash of laughter in her eyes, although her lips were grave. "His name be Tubal Sims; an' ef he don't prop up his old mill somehows, it'll career down on him some day." She added, with asperity, "I dunno what ye be admirin' it fur, 'thout it air ter view what a s'prisin' pitch laziness kin kem ter."

"That's what I admire. I'm a proficient, a professor of the science of laziness."

She lifted her long black lashes only a little as she gazed at him with half-lowered lids. "Ye won't find no pu*pils* in that science hyar about. The Cove's done graduated." She smiled slightly, as if to herself. The imagery of her response, drawn from her slender experience at the schoolhouse, pleased her for the moment, but she had no disposition toward further conversational triumphs. There ensued a short silence, and then she looked at him in obvious surprise that he did not take himself off. It would seem that he had got what he had come for,—the miller's name and the opportunity to admire the mill. He experienced in his turn a momentary embarrassment. He was so conscious of the superiority of his social status, knowledge of the world, and general attainments that her apparent lack of comprehension of his condescension in lingering to admire also the miller's daughter was subversive in some sort of his wonted aplomb. It rallied promptly, however, and he went on with a certain half-veiled mocking courtesy, of which the satire of the sentiment was only vaguely felt through the impervious words.

"I presume you are the miller's daughter?"

She looked at him in silent acquiescence.

"Then I am happy to make an acquaintance which kind fortune has been holding in store for me, for my stay in the Cove is at the miller's hospitable home." He concluded with a smiling flourish. But her bewitching eyes gazed seriously at him.

"What be yer name?" she demanded succinctly.

"Leonard,—John Leonard,—very much at your service," he replied, with an air half banter, half propitiation.

"Ye be the juggler that mam's been talkin' 'bout," she said as if to herself, completing his identification. "I drawed the idee from what mam said ez ye war a old pusson—at least cornsider'ble on in years."

"And so I am!" he cried, with a sudden change of tone. "If life is measured by what we feel and what we suffer, I am old,"—he paused with a sense of self-betrayal,—"some four or five hundred at least," he added, relapsing into his wonted light tone.

She shook her head sagely. "'Pears like ter me ez it mought be medjured by the sense folks gather ez they go. I hev knowed some mighty young fools at sixty."

The color showed in his face; her unconscious intimation of his youth according to this method of estimate touched his vanity, even evoked a slight resentment.

"You are an ancient dame, on that theory! I bow to your wisdom, madam,—quite the soberest party I have seen since I entered the paradisaical seclusion of Etowah Cove."

She appreciated the belligerent note in his voice, although she scarcely apprehended the *casus belli*. There was, however, a responsive flash in her eye, which showed she was game in any quarrel. No tender solicitude animated her lest unintentionally she had wounded the feelings of this pilgrim and stranger. He had taken the liberty to be offended when no offense was intended, and perhaps with the laudable desire to give him, as it were, something to cry for, she struck back as best she might.

"Not so sober ez some o' them folks ye gin yer show afore, over yander at the Notch. I hearn they war fit ter weep an' pray arterward. Mam 'lowed ye made 'em sober fur sure."

He was genuinely nettled at this thrust. His feats of jugglery had resulted so contrary to his expectations, had roused so serious a danger, that he did not even in his own thoughts willingly revert to them. He turned away on one heel of the pointed russet shoes that had impressed the denizens of Etowah Cove hardly less unpleasantly than a cloven hoof, and looked casually down the long darkly lustrous vista of the river; for the mill so projected over the water that the point of view was as if it were anchored in midstream. The green boughs leaned far over the smooth shadowy current; here and there, where a half-submerged rock lifted its jagged summit above the surface, the water foamed preternaturally white in the sylvan glooms. He had a cursory impression of many features calculated to give pleasure to the eye, were his mind at ease to enjoy such trifles, and his sense alert to mark them: the moss on the logs, and the lichen; the tangle of the trumpet-vines, all the budding tendrils blowing with the breeze, that clambered over the rickety structure, and hung down from the apex of the high roof, and swayed above the portal; even the swift motion of a black snake swimming sinuously in the clear water, and visible through the braiding of the currents as through corrugated glass.

"No," he said, his teeth set together, his eyes still far down the stream, "I did my little best, but my entertainment was not a success; and if that fact makes you merry, I wish you joy of your mirth."

His eyes returned to her expectantly; he was not altogether unused to sounding the cultivated feminine heart, trained to sensibility and susceptible to many a specious sophistry. Naught he had found more efficacious than an appeal for sympathy to those who have sympathy in bulk and on call. The attribution, also, of a motive trenching on cruelty, and unauthorized by fact, was usually wont to occasion a flutter of protest and contrition.

Euphemia Sims met his gaze in calm silence. She had intended no mirth at his expense, and if he were minded to evolve it gratuitously he was welcome to his illusion. Aught that she had said had been to return or parry a blow. She spoke advisedly. There was no feigning of gentleness in her, no faltering nor turning back. She stood stanchly ready to abide by her words. She had known no assumption of that pretty superficial feminine *tendresse*, so graceful a garb of identity, and she could not conceive of him as an object of pity because her sarcasm had cut deeper than his own. He had an impression that he had indeed reached primitive conditions. The encounter with an absolute candor shocked his mental prepossessions as a sudden dash of cold water might startle the nerves.

He was all at once very tired of the mill, extremely tired of his companion. The very weight of the fishing-rod and its unbaited hook was a burden. He was making haste to take himself off—he hardly knew where—from one weariness of spirit to another. Despite the lesson he had had, that he would receive of her exactly the measure of consideration that he meted out, he could not refrain from a half-mocking intimation as he said, "And do you propose to take up your abode down here, that you linger so long in this watery place,—a nymph, a naiad, or a grace?" He glanced slightingly down the dusky bosky vista.

She was not even discomfited by his manner. "I kem down hyar," she remarked, the interest of her errand paramount for the moment, "I kem down ter the mill ter see ef I couldn't find some seconds. They make a sort o' change arter eatin' white flour awhile."

He was not culinary in his tastes, and he had no idea what "seconds" might be, unless indeed he encountered them in their transmogrified estate as rolls on the table.

"And having found them, may I crave the pleasure of escorting you up the hill to the paternal domicile? I observe the shadows are growing very long."

"You-uns may kerry the bag," she replied, with composure, "an' I'll kerry the fishin'-pole."

Thus it was he unexpectedly found himself plodding along the romantic road he had so lately traversed, with a bag of "seconds" on his shoulder,—"a veritable beast of burden," he said sarcastically to himself,—while Euphemia Sims's light, airy figure loitered along the perfumed ways in advance of him, her cloudy curls waving slightly with the motion and the breeze; the fishing-rod was over her shoulder, and on the end of it where the unbaited hook was wound with the line her green sunbonnet was perched, flouncing like some great struggling thing that the angler had caught.

It did not occur to him, so impressed was he with the grotesque office to which he had descended and the absurd result of the interview, that her errand to the mill must have anticipated some burlier strength than her own to carry the "seconds" home, until as they turned an abrupt curve where the high rocks rose on either side they met a man with an axe in his hand walking rapidly toward them. He paused abruptly at the sight of them, and the juggler laughed aloud in scornful derision of his burden.

Then recognizing Ormsby he cried out cheerily, "Hello, friend, whither bound?" So acute had his sensibilities become that he had a sense of recoil from the surly mutinous stare with which his friendly young acquaintance of the previous evening received his greeting. Ormsby mumbled something about a fish-trap and passed on swiftly toward the river. Swift as he was it was obviously impossible that he could even have gained the margin and returned without a pause when he passed again, walking with a long rapid stride, swinging his axe doggedly, his hat pulled down over his brow, his eyes downcast, and with not even a flimsy affectation of an exchange of civilities.

"Now, the powers forbid," thought the juggler, "that I shall run into any such hornet's nest as interfering with this Corydon and Phyllis. Surely sufficient vials of wrath have been poured out on my head without uncorking this peculiar and deadly essence of jealousy which all three of us cannot hope to survive."

He looked anxiously up from his bent posture, carrying the bag well up on his shoulders, at the quickly disappearing figure of the young mountaineer. He did not doubt that Ormsby knew that Euphemia's domestic errands would probably bring her to the mill at this hour, and the bearing home of the bag of "seconds" was his precious dévoir most ruthlessly usurped. "I only wish, my friend," thought the juggler, "that you had the heavy thing now with all its tender associations." He glanced with some solicitude at the delicate lovely face of the girl. It was placidity itself. He had begun to be able to read it. There was an implication of exactions in its soft firmness. She would make no concessions. She would assume no blame not justly and fairly to be laid at her door. She would not rend her heart with those tender lies of false self-accusation common to loving women who find it less bitter to censure themselves than those they love, and sometimes indeed more politic. She would not bewail herself that she had not lingered, that Ormsby, who came daily to examine his fish-traps, might have had the opportunity of a long talk with her which he coveted, and the precious privilege of going home like a mule with a flour-bag on his back. It was his own fault that he was too late. She could not heft the bag. If he were angry he was a fool. On every principle it is a bad thing to be a fool. If God Almighty has not seen fit to make a man a fool, it is an ill turn for a man to make one of himself.

As the juggler divined her mental processes and the possible indifference of her sentiments toward the disappointed Ormsby, he realized that naught was to be hoped from her, but that probably Ormsby himself might be less obdurate. Doubtless he had had experience of the stern and unyielding quality of her convictions, and had learned that it was the part of wisdom to accommodate himself to them. Surely he would not indulge so futile an anger, for it would not move her. After an interval of solitary sulking in the dank cool woods his resentment would wane, his jealousy would prompt a more zealous rivalry, and he would come to her father's house as the evening wore on with an incidental expression of countenance and a lamblike manner. The juggler made haste because of this sanguine expectation to leave the field clear for the reconciliation of the parties in interest. He deprecated the loss of one of the very few friends, among the many enemies, he had made since his advent into Etowah Cove. The frank, bold, kindly young mountaineer had, in the absence of all other prepossessions, somewhat won the good opinion of the juggler. With that attraction which mere youth has for youth, he valued Ormsby above the other denizens of the Cove. Jane Ann Sims was possessed of more sterling worth as a friend than a battalion of such as Ormsby. But the juggler was a man of prejudices. Mrs. Sims's unwieldy bulk offended his artistic views of proportion. The slow shuffle of her big feet on the floor as she went about irritated his nerves. The creases and dimples of her broad countenance obscured for him its expression of native astuteness and genuine good will. Therefore, despite her appreciation of the true intent of the feats of a prestidigitator he was impatient of her presence and undervalued her hearty prepossessions in his favor. He heard with secret annoyance her voice vaguely wheezing a hymn, much off the key, as after supper she sat knitting a shapeless elephantine stocking beside the dying embers, for the night was chilly. Her husband now and again yawned loudly over his pipe, as much from perplexity as fatigue. Outside Euphemia was sitting alone on the step of the passage. The juggler had no inclination to linger by her side. Except for a lively appreciation of the difference in personal appearance she was not more attractive to him than was her mother. He passed stiffly by, with a sense of getting out of harm's way, and ascended to his room in the roof, where for a long time he lay in the floundering instabilities of the feather-bed, which gave him now and again a sensation as of drowning in soft impalpable depths,—a sensation especially revolting to his nerves. Nevertheless, it was but vaguely that he realized that Ormsby did not come, that he heard the movements downstairs as the doors were closed, and when he opened his eyes again it was morning, and the new day marked a change.

If anything were needed to further his alienation from the beautiful daughter of the house, it might have been furnished by her own voice, the first sounds of which that reached his ears were loud and somewhat unfilial.

"It's a plumb sin not ter milk a cow reg'lar ter the minit every day," she averred dictatorially.

"Show me the chapter an' verse fur that, ef it's a sin; ye air book-l'arned," wheezed her mother, on the defensive.

"I ain't lookin' in the Bible fur cow-l'arnin'," retorted Euphemia. "There's nuthin' in the Bible ter make a fool of saint or sinner."

"Thar's mo' cows spoke of in the Bible 'n ever you see," persisted Mrs. Sims, glad of the diversion. "Jacob hed thousands o' cattle, an' Aberham thousands, an' Laban thousands, not ter count Joseph's ten lean kine an' ten fat kine, what I reckon war never viewed out'n a dream, an' mought be accounted visions."

"Waal, I ain't ez well pervided with cattle ez them folks, neither sleepin' nor wakin'," said Euphemia. "I 'lowed ye'd milk pore Spot reg'lar like I does, else I wouldn't hev gone away."

"I slep' till nigh supper-time," apologized Mrs. Sims unctuously, pricked in conscience at last, "else I'd hev done it. Want me ter go walkin' in my sleep, an' milk the cow?"

Euphemia said no more, but there rose an energetic clashing of pans and kettles, intimating that the explanation had not mitigated the enormity of the offense. It was with a distinct sentiment of apprehension that the juggler made himself ready and descended the stairs. The place was evidently under martial law. The slipshod, easy-going liberty which had characterized it was a thing of the past. He might hardly have recognized it, so different was the atmosphere, but for the fixtures. The perfumed air swept through and through the rooms that he had found so close, from open window to open door. The floors had been scrubbed white, and were still but half dry. The breakfast-table was set in the passage, and the graceful vines which grew over the aperture at the rear showed the morning sunshine only in tiny interstices, as they waved back and forth with a fluctuating glimmer and an undertone of rustlings and murmurs; through the drooping boughs of the elm at the opposite entrance might be caught glimpses of the silver river and the gray rocks and the purple mountains afar off.

Here he found Euphemia and her parents. The irate flush was still red on the young girl's cheeks, and her eyes were bright with the stern elation of victory. But if submission entailed on Mrs. Sims no effort, she was not averse to subjugation. The juggler was pleased for once to perceive no diminution in the number and depth of her dimples as she welcomed him.

"Ye'll hev ter put up with Phemie's cookin', now. I don't b'lieve in no old 'oman cookin' whenst she hev got a spry young darter ter do it fur her. I reckon ye'll manage ter make out. She does toler'ble well fur her, bein' inexperienced an' sech; but I can't sense it into the gal how ter git some sure enough strong rich taste on ter the vittles."

Old Sims's grizzled, stubbly, unshaven countenance expressed a rigid neutrality, as if he intended to abide by this impartiality or perish in the attempt. His art had sufficed to keep him out of the engagement this morning, and his success had confirmed his resolution.

It seemed afterward to the juggler that this meal saved his life. He ate as if he had not tasted food for a week. He partook of mountain trout broiled on the coals, and of "that most delicate cate" constructed of Indian meal and called the corn dodger. The potatoes were roasted in the ashes with their jackets on, and crumbled to powder at the touch of a fork. He drank cream instead of buttermilk,—it had been too much trouble for Mrs. Sims to skim the big pans when she could tilt the churn instead; and there was a kind of dry, crisp, crusty roll compounded of the seconds that he had brought to the house on his shoulder yesterday, and which was eaten with honey and the honeycomb. He watched the river shimmer between the green willows of the banks. He noted the white mists rise on the purple mountain sides, glitter prismatically in the sun, tenuously dissolve in fleecy fragments, and vanish in mid-air. The faint tinkle of a sheep-bell sounded,—pastoral, peaceful; he heard a thrush singing with so fresh, so matutinal a delight in its tones.

"If this is the line of march," he said to himself, as he maintained a decorous silence, for the state of the temper of the family was too precarious to admit of conversation, "I don't care how soon I fall into ranks."

It is supposed by those who affect to know that the seat of the intellectual faculties is the cerebrum situated in the brain-pan. Still, science cannot deny that the stomach is a singularly intelligent organ. Through its processes alone the juggler perceived how well subjection becomes parents, especially a female parent addicted to the use of the frying-pan; realized Euphemia's strength of character, unusual in so young a person, and conceived a deep respect for her mental and industrial capacities. He appreciated an incongruity in his bantering style and his mocking high-sounding phrases. His manner toward her became characterized by a studious although apparently incidental courtesy, which was, however, compatible with a certain cautious avoidance.

These days passed eventlessly to him. Much of the time he strolled listlessly about, so evidently immersed in some absorbing mental perturbation that Tubal Sims marveled that its indicia should not attract the attention of the womenfolk, who esteemed themselves so keen of discernment in such matters. He still affected to angle at times, but his hook was hardly less efficient when it dangled bare and farcical in the deep dark pool than when the forlorn minnow it pierced stirred an eddy in the shadowy depths. He did not seem annoyed by his non-success. Mrs. Sims's banter scarcely grated on his nerves or touched his pride. But indeed Mrs. Sims herself did not think ill of the unachieving; somehow the aggressive capability of Euphemia made her lenient. If there were more people like Euphemia, Mrs. Sims might have felt in conscience bound to move on herself. As to the daughter, her little world hastily conformed itself to its dictator, and she ruled it with an absolute sway. Triumphs of baking or butter-making ministered amply to her pride. Even the dumb creatures seemed ambitious to meet her expectations and avoid her censure. The dogs, who had sat so thick around the hearthstone in her absence as to edge away the human household, and had so independently tracked mud over the floors, now never ventured nearer than the threshold; yet there was much complimentary wagging of tails when she appeared on the porch. Sometimes the clatter of the treadle and the thumping of the batten told that the great loom in the shed-room was astir. Sometimes the spinning-wheel whirred. Occasionally she was busily carding cotton, and again she was hackling flax.

One afternoon he found her differently employed. She sat near the window and caught the waning light upon the newspaper which she held with both arms half outstretched as she read aloud. Mrs. Sims glanced up at the young man with a radiance of maternal pride that duplicated every crease and every dimple. Even Tubal Sims, who, as the juggler had fancied of late, was wont to look at his guest askance, lifted his eyes now with a smile distending his gruff, lined countenance, as he sat with his arms folded in his shirt-sleeves across his breast, his chair tilted back on its hind legs against the frame of the opposite window, his gaze reverting immediately to the young elocutionist. With a good-natured impulse to minister to the satisfaction of the old couple, the juggler silently took a chair hard by, and suppressed his rising sense of ridicule.

For, alack, Euphemia's accomplishments were indeed of manual achievement. He listened with surprise that this should be the extent of her vaunted book-learning, knowing naught of how scanty were her opportunities, and what labor this poor proficiency had cost. Subjugation is possible only to superior force. In the instant his former attitude of mind toward her had returned, on this pitiful exhibition of incapacity which she herself and her prideful parents were totally incompetent to realize. She droned on in a painful sing-song, now floundering heavily among unaccustomed words, now spelling aloud one more difficult than the others, while he had much ado to keep the contemptuous laugh from his face, aware that now and again his countenance was anxiously yet triumphantly perused by the delighted old people, to lose no token of his appreciation and wonder.

To bear this scrutiny more successfully he sought to occupy his thoughts in other matters. His practiced eye noted even at the distance that the newspaper must be some county sheet,—published perhaps in the town of Colbury. He congratulated himself that the girl had evidently exhausted the columns of local news, and was now deep in the contents of what is known as the "patent outside." Otherwise his polite martyrdom might have been of greater duration. He felt that neither her interest nor that of her audience would long sustain her in the wider range of subjects and the more varied and unaccustomed vocabulary of the articles, copied from many sources, which made up this portion of the journal.

The next moment he could have torn it from her hands. His heart gave a great bound and seemed to stand still. His eyes were fixed and shining. He half rose from his chair; then by an absolute effort resumed his seat and resolutely held himself still. In the throe of an inexpressible suspense every fibre of his being was stretched to its extremest tension as, slowly, laboriously, pausing often, the drawling voice read on anent "Young Lucien Royce. Details of his Terrible Death." For so the headlines ran.

IV.

THE account which the newspaper made shift to give was but a bald, disjointed recital of the superficial aspect of events to one whose memory could so nearly reproduce the vivid fact; and where memory and experience failed him, his imagination, conversant with the status depicted, could paint the scene with all the tints of actuality. A recent steamboat accident on the great Mississippi River had resulted in much loss of life. The words, as Euphemia droned them, still holding the newspaper with both arms outstretched, brought back to one of her listeners the sensation of forging tremulously along in midstream at nightfall, the shimmer of the shaking chandeliers of the great flimsy floating palace, the white interior of the ladies' cabin, with the "china finish" of the painted and paneled walls, its velvet carpet and furniture, its grand piano. He heard anew the throb of the engines, and the rush of water from the great revolving wheels; he had the sense, too, of the immensity of the vast river, gleaming with twinkling points of light close at hand, where the waves caught the glitter from the illuminated craft, and tossed it from one to another as the surges of the displaced water broke about the hull; further away could be seen the swift current hurrying on, a different dusky tint from the darkness; and still further, where the limits of vision were reached, one had even yet some subtle realization of that unceasing irresistible flow, although unseen and unheard. He remembered leaning over the guards and idly watching a number of mules on the deck below, crowded so thickly that they seemed only a dark restlessly stirring mass, until at some landing, when they were excited by the clamors of the roustabouts loading on more cotton, the pallid glare of the electric light rendered distinguishable the tossing snorting heads and wild dilated eyes. An ill-starred cargo! The frantic struggles of this animated mass caused much loss of human life; many a bold swimmer might have gained the land but for the uncontrolled plunging of those heavy hoofs. And there was no lack of light to reveal the full horrors of the fate: those huge piles of bales of blazing cotton illumined the river for twenty miles. How unprescient, how strangely stolid, the human organism, the phlegmatic mind, the insensate soul, that no nerve, no faint tremor of fear or forecast, no vague presentiment, heralded the moment when every condition of life was reversed!

Up in the pilot-house he was now, with the captain and the pilot and the great shadowy wheel. The ladies had all vanished, leaving the cabin below deserted and a trifle forlorn. Once he had taken his way through those sacred precincts, affecting to be searching for some one; and so he was,—to discover if any one there was worth looking at twice: and this he esteemed a justifiable if not a laudable enterprise, for were the ladies not welcome to look at him? His trim business suit he felt was quite the correct thing. He had entire confidence in his tailor, and he swore by his barber! His proper thankfulness to his Creator, too, was not impaired by any morbid self-depreciation. With his strong, alert, handsome figure, his dark red-brown hair, his eyes of the same tint, only kindled into fire, his long dark lashes, his drooping mustache, and the features with which nature had taken some very particular pains,—the ladies were quite welcome not to turn their heads away, if they chose.

However, his vanity was not insatiable. He had made his triumphal progress through the circle earlier in the evening, and now he was relishing the captain's surprised laughter at sundry feats that he was exhibiting with a silver dollar and a goblet which did not always hold water. One moment the silver dollar was under it, glimmering affably through the thin glass; then, with no human approach to it, the goblet was empty. It seemed the problem of life to the jolly captain to discover how this was done, and being an ambitious wight, he assured his passenger, with a wild wager of ten dollars to nothing, that, after the boat should leave the bank again, he would be able to do the trick himself before they could make another landing. Before they made another landing he was initiated into deeper mysteries.

The boat was heading slowly for the shore. For the whistle, in loud husky amplitudes of sound, overpowering when heard so close at hand, had broken abruptly on the air, and the echoes of all the wild moss-draped cypress woods on either hand were answering the accustomed sound through the dark aisles of the swamp. To many a far cabin up lonely bayous they carried the note of the progress of "de big boat up de ribber." The great tremulous craft was swinging majestically round in midstream. Now and again sounded the sharp jangling of the pilot's bell. Then the boat paused with a quivering shock, backed, veered to one side, approached the shore, paused again, and then smoothly glided forward, trembled anew, and was still.

He had gone out on the hurricane deck. The wind blew fresh from the opposite shore; he was sensible of a certain attraction in the aspect of the gloom which was as above a darkling sea, for the further bank was hardly visible by day, and utterly effaced by night. The stars were in the water as well as in the sky. He looked up at them above the two dusky columns of the boat's chimneys, which were bejeweled now with swinging lights. The sudden stillness of the machinery gave one to hear the sounds from the land. A crane clanged out a wild woodsy cry from somewhere in the darkness. An owl, hooting from the bank, sent its voice of ill omen far along the currents of the great deep silent river. The clamor from the landing caught his attention, and he turned back to look down at the cluster of twinkling lights,—for the place was a mere hamlet. And but for the shifting of his attitude,—oh, could he but have contented his gaze with the sad spring night by the riverside, the lonely woods, the waste of waters, the reflection of the stars in the depths and the stars themselves in the infinite heights of the dark sky,—could this have sufficed, he said to himself as the girl read aloud the story of his fate, he might be living now.

For alive as the man looked, he was dead!

And the end of Lucien Royce—for this was his real name—came to pass in this way.

That night, as he shifted his position on the hurricane deck, a young fellow coming up the broad landing-stage amongst the neighborhood loafers bound to take a drink at the bar of every passing steamboat, caught sight of him in the steady pervasive radiance of the electric search-light now aflare on the boat, and lifted his voice in a friendly hail. This young fellow was very visible in the warm spring afternoon in the far-away mountains, where he had never been. The juggler inadvertently glanced down at the russet shoes on his feet, for this man had then stood in them. It was he who wore, that night, the long blue hose, the blue flannel shirt, the black-and-red blazer, the knickerbockers, and the tan-colored belt, which was drawn an eyelet or so tighter now, for the juggler was slighter of build. Notified by the whistle of the boat of its approach, he had come down to the landing on his bicycle, merely for the break in the monotony of a long visit at a relative's plantation. Royce remembered how this other fellow had looked in this toggery, grown so familiar, as they stood together at the bar, and he asked of the newcomer more than once what he would take. Very jolly they were together at the bar. It was hard to part. Lucien Royce could scarcely resist the pressing insistence to return at an early day and visit this friend at his sister's place, a few miles back from the river, where he himself was a guest. But John Grayson was the prodigal son in an otherwise irreproachable family, and Royce preferred more responsible introduction to make his welcome good. With this hampering thought in mind he was not apt at excuses. John Grayson, noting that he was ill at ease, instantly attributed it to commercial anxiety, and asked, with rude curiosity, how his firm was weathering the flurry. For this was a time of extreme financial stress. A general panic was in progress. Assignments were announced by the dozen daily. The banks were going down one upon another, like a row of falling bricks. With business much extended, with heavy margins to cover and notes for large amounts about to fall due, the cotton commission firm, Greenhalge, Gould & Fife, of St. Louis, of which his late father had been a partner, and of which he was an employee, had made great efforts to collect all the money due them in the lower country, and Lucien Royce had been sent south on this mission. He had succeeded beyond their expectations. Owing to the prevalent total lack of confidence in the banks, he had been instructed to transmit a considerable sum by express. This, however, was promptly attached in the express office at St. Louis to satisfy a claim against the firm; and although they were advised it could not be sustained in court, the proceeding greatly embarrassed them, being, in fact, designed at this crisis to force a compromise in order to release the surplus funds. To furnish security proved impossible under the circumstances; and the firm being thus balked, Royce telegraphed in cipher to them for authority to bring the remainder home on his person, that it might be in readiness to take up their paper. Although he was rarely troubled by the weight of the money-belt which he thus wore, containing a large sum in bills and specie, he was very conscious of it now when Grayson, who with all the rest of St. Louis had heard of the attachment suit, abruptly demanded, with a knitting of his brow, "How in the world do you get your collections to them, if you can't send the money by express or draft?"

Royce controlled his face, and replied evasively, "Oh, the financial situation is on the mend now. As to the firm, it will pull through all right, without a doubt."

John Grayson listened, his auburn head cocked to one side. He winked a roguish dark eye. Then, with a sudden jocose lunge at his friend, he slipped his arm around his waist, feeling there the heavy roll of the belt, and burst into rollicking laughter. The scuffling demonstration—for Royce had violently resisted—was eyed with stately disapproval by an elderly planter of the old régime, who possessed now more manners than means; evidently contrasting the public "horse-play," as he doubtless considered it, of these representatives of the present day with the superior deportment of the youth of the punctilious past.

Lucien Royce remembered that he had been secretly perturbed after this, for he knew that Grayson drank to excess and talked wildly in his cups; and although, in view of his own safety, he would hardly have cared to make public the character of his charge, he realized with positive dismay that it might be fatal to the interests of the firm should he encounter some legal process at the wharf in St. Louis, the result of this discovery.

But he was simple-hearted, after all. He did not suspect John Grayson of aught dishonorable. To the world at large he seemed a fine young fellow, of excellent forbears, merely sowing his wild oats,—a crop which many men have harvested in early years with scant profit, it is true, but without derogation to common honesty and repute.

Royce subsequently sought to urge in compassion for his friend that the turpitude of the crime was insomuch the less that it was not deliberate and premeditated. Certain it was that Grayson's cry of amazement and his plunge toward the guards were very like the precipitancy of dismay when he found that the huge boat was sheering off; she was turning as he dashed down the stair, and was headed once more on her course when he realized that in their conviviality he and his friend had failed to hear the sonorous panting of the engines again astir, the jangling of the bell, the heavy plashing of the buckets striking the water as the wheels revolved anew, and that the landing was now a mile down the river.

The captain showed much polite concern when the two young men resorted hastily to the "texas" and found him seated at a table, eying, with an air of great cunning and a robust intention to solve the mystery forthwith, a silver dollar which was securely invested under an inverted glass goblet, and which, so far as his powers were capable of extricating it thence, save by the rule of thumb, as it were, was the safest silver dollar ever known.

He desisted from this occupation for the moment to master the new perplexity that confronted him, and to express his most affable and ceremonious regret; for his boat carried all the cotton shipped from the rich sister's plantation, and the dictates of policy aided his constitutionally kindly disposition.

"Why, I wouldn't have kidnapped you this way for"—his eye fell on the bit of silver shining through the goblet—"for a dollar," he concluded modestly. "I'll put you ashore in the yawl, if you like. I would turn downstream and land again, but"—he faced half round from the table, with the lightness characteristic of some portly men, and sat with one hand on the back of the chair, and the other on the goblet—"but the truth is I'm running pretty much on one wheel; there was an accident to the other before we were a hundred miles from New Orleans, and with this wind blowing straight across the river it's mighty difficult getting out from the left bank; she can hardly climb against the current."

John Grayson appeared for a moment to contemplate the suggestion of going ashore in the yawl. The wind came in a great gust through the towering chimneys, the lights flickered, the texas seemed to rock upon the superstructure of the hurricane deck. "I don't believe I care to be on the river in a yawl in this wind, this dark night," he said, evidently debating the matter within himself.

"Then go to St. Louis and back with us!" exclaimed the hospitable captain. "Shan't cost you a cent, of course. We'll make our next landing a little after midnight, I reckon, and I'll telegraph Mrs. Halliday from there."

The jovial evening seemed to the juggler, as he listened to the girl reading aloud, and stared at her with eyes blank of expression and that introverted look which follows mental processes rather than material objects, like an experience in another planet, so far away it was, as if so long ago. He remembered that he scarcely dared to touch a glass, with the consciousness of the treasure he carried in the belt he wore and all its interdependent interests, but John Grayson drank blithely enough, and the generous liquor relaxed beyond all precedent his loosely hinged tongue. Lucien Royce kept close by his side as he wandered about the boat, having developed a fear that he would tell the secret that had come so unwarrantably into his possession; and when the captain asked as a favor that, on account of the crowded condition of the boat, Royce would share his stateroom with the guest, he acceded at once, preferring to have Grayson able to talk only to him until such time as he should be once more duly sober.

He consigned the guest to the upper berth, thinking that thus Grayson could not leave the stateroom without his knowledge. He lay awake by a great effort until he was sure from the snores of his jovial friend that Grayson was asleep; and when he dropped into slumber himself, as he was young and tired, having been much in the open air that day, to which he was unaccustomed in his clerical vocation, he slept like a log.

His consciousness was renewed, after a blank interval, with the sense of being awakened in his berth by a violent jar, and of striving to rouse himself, and of falling asleep again. Another interval of blankness, and he remembered definitely the grasp of John Grayson's hand on his shoulder, roughly shaking him, with the terrified announcement that there was something the matter. He experienced a sort of surprise that John Grayson was in the stateroom; then—it was strange that his mind should have thus taken cognizance of trifles—he recalled the crowded condition of the boat, and realized that his friend was leaping down from the upper berth. He stated, with drowsy dignity, that he did not care a damn what was the matter; that he had paid for his stateroom, which was more than *some* people could say, and that if he were not allowed to sleep in it, he would give bond that he would know the reason why.

The next thing of which he was aware was a flash of light in the room. The door had opened from the saloon, and a clerk had put in his head to say that there was no danger. The boat had struck a snag, it was true, but the damage was slight. Somehow Royce slept but lightly after this. The unreasoning sense of impending misfortune had come to him at last. Presently he was awake and conscious that he was alone. He lifted himself on his elbow and listened. What was that low roar? The wind? That sound of banging timbers must be the flapping of shutters or doors as the gust rushed across the river. He heard a clamor on the boiler deck. Voices?—or was it the wind, screaming wildly as it went? And why did they run the engines at that furious rate? He could feel the strain of the machinery in the very floor under his feet.

As he slipped out of the lower berth he perceived that the gray dawn was in the contracted little room; he could see through the glass of the door opening on the guards the tawny-tinted stretches of water, the sad-hued cypress woods on a distant bank, draped with fog as well as with hanging moss, and down the stream the whiter tints of an island of sand covered with sparse vegetation, locally known as a "tow-head," for which the disabled boat was running with every pound of pressure which the engines could carry. There was, in truth, something the matter, for the tow-head would have been given a wide berth in a normal state of affairs; getting aground, when the lesser of two evils, showed a crisis indeed.

He looked about hastily for his clothes. They were gone, and in their place John Grayson's toggery lay in a heap. In his panic and the darkness Grayson had probably caught the garments nearest to his hand. His deserted friend hastily invested himself in the suit of clothes that John Grayson had left. As he was drawing on the blazer, suddenly a hoarse cry smote his ear. "No bottom!" sang out the leadsman. They were taking soundings. "No-o bottom!" And he felt the vibrations of the tone in the very fibres of his quaking heart.

He plunged out at the door on the guards, and as he stood there gasping for a moment he realized the situation. The boat was sinking fast; evidently in striking a snag the craft had sprung a leak. He saw on the deck the frightened passengers huddled together in groups, here and there a man anxiously fastening life-preservers on the women and children of his kindred. Again the leadsman's cry, "No-o bottom!" floated mournfully over the water, and the frantic panting of the engines seemed redoubled. He saw the captain, cool and collected, at his post; the other officers appeared now and again among the groups of passengers, soothing, reassuring, and doubtless their lies were condoned for the mercy of the intention. As he passed on amongst them all, nowhere did he catch a glimpse of John Grayson. "If I didn't know the fellow wouldn't play such a fool trick at such a time, I'd think he was dodging me," he muttered. The next moment he had forgotten him utterly.

"Deep four!" called the leadsman.

As Royce listened he stood still, holding his breath in suspense.

"Mark three!" called the leadsman, sounding again.

Royce heard the plunging of his heart as distinctly as the echoes of the cry clanging from the shore. But suddenly they were blended with a new refrain,—"A quarter twain!"

He gave a great sigh of relief, and checked it midway to listen anew.

"Mark twain!" called the leadsman, with a new intonation.

There was no longer doubt,—they were in shallow water. A great exclamation of delight rose from the crowd. The very hope was like a rescue,—the relief from the blank despair! Here and there the hysterical sobbings of the women told of the slackening of the tension of suspense.

"Quarter less twain!" cried the leadsman, sounding anew.

The juggler remembered how free he had felt, how safe. The boat, even if her engines could not run her aground, would soon settle in shallow water, and rescue would come with some passing steamer.

A blinding glare, a thunderous detonation that seemed to shatter his every nerve, and he was weltering in the river; now sinking down with a sense of the weight of infinite fathoms of water upon him, and now mechanically trying to strike out with an unreasoning instinct like an animal's. When he could understand what had happened he was swimming fairly well, although greatly hampered by the clinging blazer that John Grayson had left on the floor, and which he now wore. The long reaches of the river, the shore, the dim dawn, were all lighted with a lurid glare; for the boat had taken fire with the explosion of the overstrained boiler. The roar of the flames mingled with the heart-rending screams of those whom hope had so cruelly deluded. But the sounds were all faint at the distance, and he never could understand how he had been thrown, unhurt, so far away. He saw none of the human victims of the disaster. Now and again charred timbers, shooting by on the current, threatened him, and to avoid them necessitated some skillful management. A far greater danger was the proximity of two horses, also gallantly swimming, who followed him with loud whinnies of inquiry and distress, appealing in their way for aid and guidance, leaning on the humankind as if recognizing his superior capacity. More than once, one of them, a spirited mare, intended for new triumphs at the Louisville races, swam close in front of him, pausing, as if to say, "Mount, and let us gallop off on dry ground;" deflecting his course, which was already beset with abnormal difficulties. For when almost exhausted, he saw that the land he was approaching, half veiled with the gray fog, was a bluff bank, thirty feet high at least, and as far as eye could reach up and down the river there was no lower ground. To scale it was impossible. His heart sank within him. He felt that his stroke was the feebler when hope no longer nerved it. In his despair he could hardly make another effort. And although he had feared the horses, with their lashing hoofs and their unearthly cries, when the mare—the more importunate in dumb insistence that he would succor them—threw up her head, and with a wild inarticulate scream went struggling down into the depths to rise no more, he felt a choking sob in his throat, his eyes were blurred, he could scarcely keep his head above the surface. If he were further conscious, the faculty was not coupled with that of memory, for he never knew how he came to be in a flatboat floating swiftly down the stream from the scene of the disaster, and he never saw his other comrade again. Once more there came an interval void of perception; then he was vaguely aware that the flatboat was tied up in the bight of a bend; the shadowy cypresses towered above it,—he heard their waving boughs,—the water lapped gently about it; then blankness again, and he never knew how long this continued.

One morning he awoke, restored to his senses, in a bunk against the wall; he felt the motion of the river, and he knew that the flimsy craft with the rickety little cabin in its centre was again afloat upon the stream. Every pulse of the current set his own pulses a-quiver. The very proximity of the fearful river induced a physical terror that his mind could not control. It was only by a mighty wrench that his thoughts could be forced from the subject, and fixed as an alternative on his surroundings. The interior of the cabin consisted of two apartments: one for bunks and cooking purposes; the other, apparently, from the glimpse through a door, fitted up as a store, with small wares, such as threads and perfumery, soaps and canned goods, and showy imitation jewelry calculated to take the eye and the earnings of the negroes at the various landings where the craft, locally called the "trading-boat," tied up. Through a further door he had an outlook upon the deck. An elderly woman with rough red arms was sitting there on a stool, peeling potatoes; a half-grown boy, cross-legged on the floor, tailor-wise, was sawing away on an old fiddle. Beyond still was the vast spread of the tawny-tinted rippling floods and the sad hues of the nearer shore. Lucien Royce recoiled at the very sight and turned away his eyes. Within, much of the wearing apparel of the proprietors dangled from the rafters. There were bunks on the opposite wall, imperfectly visible through the smoke from the tiny stove, which, despite a great crackling of driftwood, seemed to labor with an imperfect draft. Two men were seated close to it, and were talking with that security which presumes no alien ear to listen. A certain crime of robbery absorbed their interest, and Royce gathered that, fearing they might be implicated in it, they had silently fled from the locality before their presence was well recognized. They had evidently had naught to do with it. They only wished they had!

A great swag it was, to be sure. The man had worn a money-belt,—a rare thing in these times. Heavy it must have been and drawn tight, for both hands had stiffened on its fastenings as if striving to tear it off. Its weight had doubtless drowned him. It was no joke to swim the Mississippi at high water, completely dressed and with a tight belt stuffed with money—gold or silver? And how much could the sum have been?

Whenever this point was broached, a glitter of greed was in the eyes of each which made the grizzled-bearded faces alike despite the variations of contour and feature. Always a long pause of silent speculation ensued, and whenever the supposititious sum total was mentioned, it had augmented in the interval. No one knew where the man went down; the body—the face beaten and bruised by floating timbers out of all semblance to humanity—had been swept upon a sand-bar. There some pirates of the river-bank had found it, had cut the belt open, had taken the money and fled, leaving the empty belt to tell its own futile story. At this point the flatboatmen would pause, and once more gloomily shake their heads and spit tobacco juice on the tiny stove, till it was as vocal as a frying-pan, and obviously wish that the chance had been theirs.

Thus it was that Lucien Royce had been apprised of John Grayson's death and of the loss of the funds with which he himself had been entrusted. Until this moment he had never missed the belt. Doubtless Grayson took it from him at the first alarm of striking the snag before the dawn, when he vainly sought to rouse his friend to a sense of danger. Was it possible, he marveled, that Grayson, leaving him to drown, as he supposed, had thought that the good money need not be wasted? Had its custodian been rescued, however, probably Grayson would have restored it; otherwise suspicion would have fallen upon him, since they had occupied the same stateroom. But if not, if Lucien Royce's body had gone to the bottom of the river, and no one the wiser that the money-belt did not go with it,—was it upon this chance, in that supreme moment of terror, that Grayson had had the forethought to act? He was not a man who made much account of the rights of others when his own comfort or his own pleasure was at stake. But his life—did he risk the precious moment that might mean existence to save a sum of money for a St. Louis cotton commission firm of which he did not know a single member? Would he have jeopardized his chances in the water with this weight, with this fatally close-gripping python of a belt, for a mere commercial matter? It was needless to argue the question. Royce knew right well, both then and now, that in no event, had he not survived, did Grayson intend to restore the money. Evidently the idea had flashed upon him when, in seeking to rouse his companion, his hands came in contact with the belt and the opportunity was his own. And so Grayson had gone to his death, drowned by the weight and the pressure of the stolen money. It seemed a grim sort of justice that with the last movements of his hands in life, the last effort of his will, he sought to tear it off, to cast it from him, as he went down into the hopeless depths.

Royce experienced hardly a regret for his false friend,—not more than a physical pang of sympathy, an involuntary shudder, his very nerves instinct with the terror of the water. Had Grayson not tampered with a secret that was not his own, the belt would now be safe. Royce himself had had the strength to sustain its weight in the water. He was used to it, and its size had been carefully adjusted to his slender figure. Now the money was gone,—the belt was found on another man. They would seem to have been confederates in the robbery of the fund. He was responsible for it. He could not reasonably account for its being out of his own possession without incriminating himself. Should he seek to inculpate the dead man alone, he was aware that the fact that Grayson could not speak for himself would speak for him. Nothing could palliate the circumstance that the belt was found on another man than its proper custodian, and that the leather had been slit and the money extracted. He would have to account for this, and improbable excuses would not go far with men smarting under a ruinous loss from the carelessness or the drunkenness or the cupidity of their employee. He could not go back. He could never face the firm!

So light of heart he had always been, so light of heel, so light, so very light of head, that the anguish which pierced him at the idea of the loss of public esteem, of his commercial honor, of the confidence of the firm, involved in his seeming failure of probity, subacutely amazed him at its keen poignancy. He had hardly known how he valued these spiritual, immaterial assets. More than life,—far, far more than life! He began to contemn the struggle he had made in the water; he had been wondering and calculating, with an early gleam of consciousness and an athlete's stalwart vanity, how far he had swum, how long he had sustained himself in the great flood; for what purpose, he thought now, what melancholy purpose, to save his life for the ignominy of an episode behind the bars for breach of trust, embezzlement, robbery—he hardly cared what might be the technical rank of the crime of which he would so certainly be accused. Every reflection brought confirmations of the popular suspicion which would be so false, and which could not, alas, be disproved. With a mechanical review, as of a life when it is closed, sundry gambling escapades of John Grayson's recurred to his mind, in which he had been nearly concerned and which had attained a certain degree of notoriety. On one occasion, indeed, when he was younger and more easily led by his friend, a gambling establishment had been raided by the police, the two had been among the captured players, and being arraigned, although under false names, were nevertheless recognized. The exploit was so well bruited abroad that the senior member of the firm, who had been a friend as well as a partner of his father's, had given him what the old gentleman was pleased to term a "remonstrance," and what he himself denominated a "blistering." "Mark my words," had been its conclusion, "that fellow

Grayson will ruin you." Was it possible that this prophet of evil would fail to note the fulfillment of the prognostication? Would this event give no color to the supposition that he had been gambling with the money, that Grayson had won it, and then was drowned and robbed?

Oh, why, why had he so struggled to save his wretched life? The terrors of the water no longer shook his nerves. As he noted the trembling of the little craft,—the flimsiest thing, he thought, that he had ever seen afloat,—he said to himself that it would be the luckiest chance that had ever befallen him should the flatboat suddenly disintegrate, timber from timber, on the swelling centre of the tide, engulfing him never to rise again. "I would not move a hand to save my life. I wish I were dead," he said, his white face turned to the wall. "I wish I were dead." And then he realized that he had his wish. He was dead.

For the flatboatmen were talking again, with a morbid revolving around the subject. From their disjointed dialogue it appeared that the "stiff" was not on the sand-bar now; it had been removed in obedience to a telegram from a firm in St. Louis,—Greenhalge, Gould & Fife, cotton commission merchants. One of their clerks had come down by train on the other side of the river, "nigh tore up" about the belt and the loss of the money. He recognized the dead man by his clothes, and the color of his hair and eyes,—"there was no other way to know him, he was such a s'prisin' bruised-up sight." This clerk had once given the man a meerschaum pipe that was in the breast-pocket yet, and some papers were dried off, and read and identified. He was shipped by train. They would bury him where he came from. The firm and its employees would turn out, probably, and do the handsome thing. "Good for trade, I reckon," remarked the proprietor of the flatboat store, with an appreciation of sentiment as an agent of profit.

"What's the man's name?" demanded the other.

"He never left no name as I heard. He loafed round Kyarter's sto' over thar in the bend awhile, an' a nigger rowed him over in a dug-out to see the stiff, an' he give his orders an' put out fur the up-country quick."

"I ain't talkin' 'bout *him*. I mean the stiff. What was the stiff's name?"

"Oh, Royce. Lucien Royce,—that's the stiff's name. Lucien Leonard Royce."

And thus it was that the juggler realized that he was dead.

He made haste to leave the trading-boat as soon as he could stand, however unsteadily, on his feet. And the boatmen were not ill pleased to see him go. The humane search for all survivors of the wreck and the rescue of the bodies had been in progress for some days, but with a vague terror of implication in crime which must indeed be appalling to the poor, who believe that justice is meted out according to the price the victim can pay for it, the flatboatmen were drifting night and day further and further away from the dreaded locality. When they had chanced to meet the skiffs sent out by the search-parties for victims of the disaster, they had said naught of the man whom they had rescued, who lay between life and death in the bunk. They had even relinquished the opportunity of "scrapping" about the waters for floating articles, of scant value in themselves, hardly worth the gathering of them together by the owners, but precious indeed to those of so restricted opportunities,—tins of edibles, cutlery, bedding, cooking utensils, bits of furniture, table-ware, garments, and the like. Once a stranger had boarded the craft, but he came no further than the door of the store, where he was furnished with a flask of whiskey needed for a half-drowned man lying hard by on a sand-bar. So when their guest was at last on his feet again they bade him farewell with a right good will, and the trifle of change that was in the pocket of poor John Grayson's knickerbockers was a superfluity to their satisfaction.

They set Royce ashore one night at a point which they stated was half a mile from the railroad; it seemed a league or more through the dense oak forests, clear of undergrowth, level as a park, before he sighted a red lantern and an empty box car on a siding near a great tank. There was apparently not another soul in the world, so unutterably lonely was the spot. He clambered into the car, knowing that he could not well play the rôle of tramp on any discerning train-man while wearing Grayson's expensive russet shoes, albeit somewhat the worse for water, and his natty knickerbockers and blazer. He would invent some story and beg a ride. He lay down behind a pile of bagging, and when he awoke he saw that the car was moving rapidly, that it was half full of freight, that an afternoon sun was streaming in dusty bars through the chinks in the door, that he must have traversed many a mile of the inland country from the scene of the disaster; so many miles that, the next morning, when the car was opened in the yard of the freight depot of a small town, the whole landscape was as strange to him as if he had entered a new world. Great purple mountains, wooded to their crests, encircled the horizon, itself seeming lifted to a great height, in contrast with the low-lying skies of the swamp country; and now and again, where the summit-lines were broken by gaps, further visions of enchanted heights in ethereal tints of blue and alluring sun-flooded slopes met his gaze. There was a river, too, narrow, smoothly flowing, but cliff-bound, crystal-clear in a rocky channel that curved between the mountains it reflected. The sunshine was so dazzling that he made scant shift to see the men, who, in moving the freight, discovered him. The first demonstration of the yardmaster was wrathful bluster because of the impudent device of the supposed tramp and his success in stealing a ride. But as Lucien Royce rose to his feet, and his costume that of a young gentleman of bucolic proclivities taking his ease and dispensing with ceremony, became visible, he was received with banter and laughter. He was presumed to be engaged in some kind of adolescent escapade,—stealing a ride for a wager, perhaps; and as, with his quick intelligence, he perceived this fact, he answered in the same vein. He leaped out of the car, made his way from the yard and up the main street of the town, and when, reaching its opposite extremity, he was out in the country, he walked as if for his life. All day long he trudged at the top of his speed. Pedestrianism had been one of his many fads, and he wished more than once for his pedometer, that he might have his score to boast of and break the record of the pedestrian club of which he was an active member; and then he would check himself suddenly, remembering that it was decreed that he should never see his old comrades again. He was dead! His safety imperatively required that he should remain dead.

Apparently he left the sunshine behind him; the wind flagged and fell back; only certain clouds maintained an equal pace, congregating about the summits of the mountains, showing tier on tier above them, so darkly purple that sometimes he could hardly tell which was shadowy earth and which over-shadowing sky. Always, as he clambered over the flank of some great ridge and looked upon the deep dells of the valley, these clouds were already crossing it, and rising, peak on peak and towering height over height, above the crest of the mountains still beyond. In one of these sequestered nooks among the vast ranges, when the swift lightnings were unleashed and the thunder reverberated from dome to dome and the weighty rain fell in tumultuous torrents, he dragged his stumbling feet to a lighted window dimly flickering in the gloom, and found the latch-string of Tubal Cain Sims's door on the outside, as the hospitable mistress of the cabin said it always should be, when she welcomed the wayfarer.

And thus it came to pass that within a fortnight after the disaster the juggler sat listening to the miller's daughter as she read the account of the terrible death of young Lucien Royce. He could have given the journalist many points on the details of the accident. But his mind ceased its retrospection, and he hearkened with keen interest, for one so very dead, to the narrative of the supplemental events occurring in the city of his home. As Euphemia droned drearily on, he gathered that the firm had made an assignment, the result of the loss of the funds of which Lucien Royce had been robbed, and their consequent inability to take up their paper. The amount was stated at thrice the reality, and his lips curved with a scornful wonder as to whether this was a commercial device to render the failure more seemly and respectable, or was merely due to the magnifying proclivities natural to the race of reporters. "It lets the house down easier,—that's one good thing," he reflected. And then he checked himself, marveling if other people who were dead could not immediately dissever their interests and affections from those subjects and associations that had once enthralled them. "It must take a long time to get thoroughly acclimated to another world," he thought, realizing that the impulse of satisfaction which he had experienced because the "break" had its justification in the eyes of the commercial world was the loyal sentiment to the firm shared by every man on their pay-roll. "We could have weathered the flurry easily enough but for this," he knew the various employees were all severally saying to their personal friends and such of the general public as came within their opportunity. It seems that cynicism is not a growth exclusively native to this sphere, for he presently found himself attributing to a wish to fix general attention on this subject of the loss of the money the firm's elaborate attention to the details of the obsequies of their unfortunate employee. But they would not overdo it, he realized even before Euphemia, hobbling painfully among words whose existence had hitherto been undreamed-of by her, and whose structure would serve to render them obsolete forever in her vocabulary after this single usage, had reached the description of the funeral arrangements. He had feared she would flag, and would thus balk his palpitating curiosity; but the mournful pageantry of death has its fascination for certain temperaments, and it is fair to say she would not have read so long, nor would Tubal Sims and his wife have waking listened, had the theme been more cheerful.

No, the firm would not overdo it. They were men of good taste and acumen. The public received sundry reminders that Lucien Royce's deceased father had been a member of the firm for many years, and much of the quondam prosperity had been due to his sagacity and sterling qualities. The young man's inherited interest in the business was of course swamped with the rest. And all this made the presence of each of the partners and of all the employees, together with large and showy floral tributes at St. —— Church, the more appropriate and natural. As no simple interment could have done, however, it had also riveted attention on that especial feature, the loss of the money, which was in itself calculated to excite much sympathy and commiseration in the commercial heart, and to be of service in securing a composition with creditors and the possibility of continuance.

"They needn't have been so mighty particular," he said to himself a moment afterward, his eyes bright and shining, the color in his cheeks. "I could have gotten up a big enough blow-out all by myself."

For that meed of popularity which many better men never achieve had been a gratuitous gift to Lucien Royce, who had never done aught to secure it or given it a thought in his life. His gay young friends were bereaved. All experiencing a sense of personal loss, all struck aghast with dismay and pity, those attended in a body who were of his many clubs and societies, and others singly if they happened to be merely friends outside the bonds of fraternities. The church was densely thronged; a wealth of flowers filled the chancel. The words of a popular hymn were sung by a member of the Echo Quartet, a singer of local renown, to an air composed by the late Lucien Royce,—so pathetic, with such sudden minor transitions, such dying falls (it had been a love-song, and he had written the words as well as the music), that the congregation were in tears as they listened.

"Ah ha, my fine first tenor!" the juggler said to himself in prideful triumph at the praise of print. "And how about that final phrase of each refrain that you persisted ought to resolve itself into the major, and not the minor chord? Oh, oh! Mightily pleased to stand up before a big crowd and sing it now, for all its faulty harmony!"

But if he had already been gratified, he was shortly delighted. The account digressed to the personal qualities of the deceased, his exceptional popularity, the high esteem in which he was held by his business associates, the great affection which his personal friends entertained for him, the extraordinary versatility of his talents. He was a wonderful athlete for an amateur. (The juggler listened with a critical jealous ear to the detail of certain feats of lifting, walking, and swimming. "I can break that record now," he muttered.) He was a very acceptable amateur actor. He sang delightfully, and composed charming songs with words of considerable merit; in fact, he had a gift of light, easy versification. He was hospitable and joyous, and fond of entertaining his friends, to whom he was much attached,—the more as he was so alone in the world, having no near kindred since the death of his father. There was no bitterness in his mirth; he laughed with you rather than at you. ("Don't be too sure of that," said the juggler, in his sleeve.) He was wonderfully quick in learning, even quick in acquiring any mechanical art that struck his attention. He had really become a skillful prestidigitator (how the juggler blessed the six-pronged unpronounceable word as Euphemia struggled to take hold of it, and finally left it as incomprehensible!): and this came about partly through his extraordinary quickness, and partly because no one could resist his fascinating *bonhomie*, and many a traveling artist in legerdemain had imparted his professional secrets to him from sheer good will and liking. He was the same to all classes; he had an easy capacity for adapting himself to the company he was in for the time being, as if it were his choice. Many a pleasant haunt of his friends would lack its relish after this, and it would be long before the name or face of Lucien Royce would be forgotten in St. Louis city.

"Well," mused the juggler, with a sigh, as the reading concluded, "it's worth dying once in a while, to get a send-off like that."

"Pore young man!" ejaculated Mrs. Sims, looking up with a sigh too, the relief from the long tension, her big creased solemn face bereft of every dimple.

The juggler caught himself hastily. "The paper doesn't say what Sabbath-school he was a member of," he observed, with mock seriousness.

"That's a fac'," returned Euphemia, unfolding the upper part of the journal to reperuse with a searching eye the portion relating to biographical detail. After an interval of vain scrutiny she remarked, "Nor it don't say nuther whether he war a member o' the Hard-Shell Baptis' or Missionary or Methody."

"He mought be a sinner, an' the paper don't like ter say it, him bein' dead," wheezed Mrs. Sims lugubriously, intuitively seizing upon a salient point of polite modern journalism. The anxious speculation in her fat overclouded countenance was painful to see, for Mrs. Sims believed in a material hell with a plenitude of brimstone and blue blazes.

"I dare say he *was* a sinner!" exclaimed the juggler, with his manner of half-mocking banter. "Poor Lucien Royce!"

Only late that night, when all the house was still, and darkness was among the sombre mountains, and the absolute negation of vision seemed to nullify all the world, did his mood change. He lay staring with unseeing eyes into the void gloom about him, yet beholding with a faculty more potent than sight the decorated chancel, the clergyman in his surplice, the crowds of sympathetic faces, the casket with the funeral wreaths covering it,—the hideous mockery that it all was, the terrible hoax!

V.

THE juggler was hardly disposed to felicitate himself upon this feat of simulation which had served to deceive the whole of his native city, and to bury a stranger, as it were, in his own grave. He began to pity the plight of the dead if they could so yearningly remember the life they had left. Return for him was impossible. Glimpses of the moon might shadow forth spirits revenant, but for him memory only must serve. He wondered that he could not accept conclusions so evidently final, for over and again, in the deep watches of the night, he would argue anew within himself the chances *pro* and *con* of transforming these immutable fictions into fact, of overcoming the appearance of crime by his previous high character, of relying on the good feeling of the firm, and the futility of the proceeding, to save him from prosecution. Then always, when he would reach this point, and his heart would begin to beat fast with the hope of restoration to life, it would stand still with a sudden paralysis and sink like lead; for there were interests other than those of revenge or justice, or preserving the public morals by enforcing penalties for the infringement of the law to be served by his incarceration in a good strong safe prison. There existed a certain corporation, the Gerault Bonley Marble Company, that he knew would give much money to be able to lay hands upon him now, and that had doubtless grieved for his demise like unto Rachel mourning for her children. The Gerault Bonley Marble Company had, in the past few years, been greatly enriched by the discovery of beds of a very fine marble in a large body of Tennessee land, in which, however, they merely held an estate *per autre vie*,—limited to the duration of Lucien Royce's natural existence. In this unique position of a *cestui que vie* he had at first felt a certain glow of pride. It was characteristic of his knack of achieving importance and prominence with so slight effort that he seemed, as it were, born to a certain preëminence. He recollected the prestige it added to his personality at the time when it was discovered that there were great beds of marble in the almost worthless tract, and the sensation of pleased notoriety he had experienced when Mr. Gerault Bonley, the president of the company, a well-known broker, had dropped in at the office to look at him—he had never taken the trouble before—and have a word with him. "Remember your business is to *live*, young man," he had said in leaving, flushed and elated with success. "That's all you have to do. And if you ever find any hitch about doing it pleasantly, come to us, and we will help you eke it out. You are the one who lives, you understand." And he walked out, portly and rubicund, his eye kindling as he went.

Lucien Royce had ridden up town on the cable car one evening, a day or two afterward, and he had noticed with new interest a man, forlorn, shabby, chewing the end of a five-cent cigar so hard between his teeth as he talked that he was unaware that its light had died out, who railed at life and his luck in unmeasured terms that astonished the passengers precariously perched on the platform of the rear car. This was the unsuccessful speculator who, some years earlier, had sought to mortgage the land in question to Mr. Gerault Bonley, the broker, who had bought up his paper and was disposed toward thumbscrews. It was not a good day for mortgages, somehow, but, with the desperation of a man already pressed to the wall, about as badly broken as he was likely to be, the debtor would not consent to an absolute transfer of the title.

"The land will be sold under execution, then," he of the thumbscrews had said.

"The law allows two years for redemption, in Tennessee," the owner had retorted, with the expectation of better times in his face.

Perhaps because of the resistance,—the broker always said he did not know why he had wanted the land, for although he was aware that a little marble quarry had once been worked there, it had been abandoned as not worth the labor,—still protesting that he could not avail himself of the property unless for a term of years, at least, he finally offered the bait of enough ready money to extricate the speculator, and give him another show amongst the bulls and bears, and the conveyance was made for the uncertain term of the life of another. Lucien Royce had chanced to drop in on some business for Greenhalge, Gould & Fife, the cotton commission firm, a lithe, muscular young fellow, the ideal of an athlete, and the thought suggested itself to the broker that the estate should be limited to the duration of his life. The proposition was carelessly acceded to by the young man, attracted for the moment by the novelty of the proceeding, apprehending in the matter the merest formality. This was the conclusion.

"And now you'll live forever!" cried the disappointed speculator, suddenly recognizing, in the uncertain light on the platform of the car, the features of the stalwart *cestui que vie*. Once more he was chewing hard on his cigar, once more inveighing against his accursed luck, as he stretched the newspaper toward the dull lamp of the car, indicating with a trembling hand the big head-lines chronicling the discovery, while the cumbrous vehicle went gliding along through the blue haze of the dusk and the smoke and the dust,—the medium through which the looming blocks of buildings and the long double file of electric lights were visible down the avenue. "You'll live forever, while those men make millions on the tract they euchred me out of at ten dollars an acre! It would be a charity for you to fall off the car and break your backbone. They tell me concussion of the brain is painless. I'll swear I'd feel justified if I should hide in a dark alley, some night, and garrote you as you go by to the club."

"There's another case of garroting in the paper," observed a mutual acquaintance by way of diversion.

"I noticed it. That's what reminded me of it. It's like lassoing. I lived a long time in Texas," he said, as he swung himself off at a side-street, and disappeared in the closing haze that baffled the incandescent lights showing upon its density in yellow blurs without illuminating it.

"You'd better look out for that man, sure enough," the literal-minded mutual acquaintance warned Lucien Royce. "He feels mighty sore. This company is going to make 'big money' on his land."

But Royce laughed it off. "I am the one who lives," he boasted.

He found it not altogether so careless an existence since it was worth so much financially. His acute sensibilities realized a sort of espionage before he was definitely aware of it. He came to know that he was reckoned up. What he did, where he went, how he felt, were matters in which other people were concerning themselves. He resented the irksome experience as an attack on his liberty. He felt no longer a free man. And this impression grew as the yield from the property promised more and more. The Bonley Company had gone to heavy expenses. They had put in costly machinery. They had hired gangs and gangs of men. They had built miles of narrow-gauge railroad, to convey the stone by land as well as by water. It had become a gigantic venture. The jocose "Take care!" "Live for *my* sake!" "Be good to yourself!" which had at first formed the staple of the injunctions to him when he chanced to encounter any member of the company, changed to serious solicitous inquiry which affronted him. More than once Mr. Bonley called upon him to remonstrate about late hours, heavy suppers, and the disastrous effects upon the constitution of drinking wine and strong waters. Thus the rubicund Mr. Gerault Bonley, whose countenance was brilliant with the glow of old Rye! In one instance, when Royce's somewhat cavalier and scornful reception of these kind attentions served to rouse Mr. Bonley to the realization that the *cestui que vie* claimed the right to have other objects in existence than merely to live for the corporation's sake, the president of the company apologized, but urged him to consider, for the justification of this anxiety, what large financial interests and liabilities hung upon the thread of his life. There was a panic among the company whenever he went to the seashore for a short vacation, and once he allowed himself to be persuaded out of a trip to Europe, of which acquiescence he was afterward ashamed,—so much so that when a place in the office of the Bonley Company was offered him, with a large increase of salary, but with the unavowed purpose of keeping him under surveillance, that he might always be at hand and easily reckoned up, he declined it with such peremptoriness as to cause the company to relax this unwise exhibition of solicitude for the time, and greatly to please his own firm, Greenhalge, Gould & Fife, who had not relished the effort to decoy a confidential clerk from their employ. On one occasion when, in training for a boat-race, he was suddenly prostrated by the heat, the anxiety of the Gerault Bonley Marble Company knew no bounds, and its manifestation more than verged upon the ridiculous; it was the joke of the whole town. The claims of his own personal friends—he had no near relatives—were set at naught. The company took possession of him. He came to himself in one of the well-appointed guest-chambers of Mr. Bonley's own house; and when he rallied, which he did almost immediately, with the recuperative powers of youth and his great strength, he was detained there several days longer than was necessary by his host's insistence, until indeed the physician in charge laughed in the face of Mr. Gerault Bonley, the broker.

"Take care you don't do anything eccentric," the doctor said in parting at last from his patient. "That company might shut you up in a lunatic asylum or a sanitarium, where you would be ready for inspection at all hours,—just to make sure you are alive, you see."

It was meant for a joke, but it grated on the nerves of the *cestui que vie*. And now it came back as he lay under the dark roof of Tubal Cain Sims's house, staring into the unresponsive night, with the thought that a good strong state prison would serve the purpose of the Marble Company, looking toward his safekeeping, more effectually still. He could well understand their despair upon the supposed determination of the life estate, for since they had secured the land at slight cost, the vast profits of the industry were to the ordinary business mind all the dearer, being the favor, as it were, of chance, or the uncovenanted mercy of Providence,—"clean make." How could they survive the reversion of the property, with all its present wealth and its future prospects, to the original grantor? His imagination, alert as it was, failed to respond to so heavy a demand upon its resources. Should they find that the death of the *cestui que vie* was spurious, their tenancy not yet expired, should they be restored to their former status, what a warning this untoward alarm would seem, what restraints upon his liberty might not be attempted! The idea bereft him of his last hope. Could he reasonably expect to escape prosecution when his custody in the clutches of the law was so obviously to the interests of a powerful corporation like this? Even if his own firm of Greenhalge, Gould & Fife should be averse to it to avenge their losses, what powerful influence would be brought to bear upon them by the Gerault Bonley Marble Company; what substantial values were to be dangled before the eyes of a broken firm in the friendship and backing of a strong financial association like this! The Marble Company would move heaven and earth to place him behind the bars. There could Mr. Bonley come and look at him any fine day, as he sat making shoes and saddles,—he had heard that at the penitentiary they put their swell guests to such occupations, and his deft fingers might commend their utility in this service to the commonwealth,—or perhaps busied in some clerical capacity to which his long experience in counting-rooms rendered him apt. Mr. Bonley's scarlet countenance and bristly white mustache were of a calmer aspect as they appeared in this vision than they had worn in reality for many a long day! The menu would contain naught to destroy the digestion of the *cestui que vie* or affright the Marble Company in the way of midnight suppers and unlimited champagne. There would be no wild uproarious companions, no gambling escapades, no perilous activities on the horizontal bar,—what war had Mr. Bonley waged against his attachment to the gymnasium!—no swimming-matches, no boat-races, no encounters with gloves or foils. Truly Mr. Bonley's estate would be gracious indeed!

No; Lucien Royce felt that his escape was a crowning mercy vouchsafed. His most imperative care should be to make it good, or he might well spend a decade of the best years of his life behind the bars for a crime he had not committed. His incarceration would easily be compassed, were his defense far more complete than perverse circumstance rendered possible, by the craft and persistence of men who had such large interests at stake on the life and well-being of a wild, adventurous, hairbrained boy. His supposititious death had saved his name, his commercial honor, which he held dear. John Grayson, with the theft of the belt and its treasure, had also taken his life—for he had no life left! He was dead! He was very dead! And let the Gerault Bonley Marble Company mourn him. With a laughing sneer on his face, he cursed again, as he had cursed a thousand times, the plastic folly, or the vagary of chance, or whatever fate it was that induced him to lend himself to the broker's scheme; for although he had thought it a mere formality, it had in effect sold him into a species of slavery for the rest of his natural life. "But is not my advice good advice?" Mr. Bonley had more than once urged upon his recalcitrant mood. "Is it not in your *own* interests as well as in ours? Is it not exactly the advice I would give to my own son?"

"He needs it. Give it to *him*," the *cestui que vie* would reply in flippant despair. But Mr. Bonley's son was not worth so much money to the company, and he went his own ways with some celerity, all unchecked.

The continually administered cautions, the sense of sustaining anxiety, espionage, criticism, of thus sharing his life, had made it in some sort a burden to the merry *cestui que vie*; and therefore, in the first days of his escape, the realization of the petty persecutions, the irksome advice of the ill-advised Mr. Bonley, shaken off and forever thwarted, seemed to the young man only matter for self-gratulation. In the accumulation of these trifles in his thoughts, he had lost sight of the far-reaching significance of the event until he had reached the haven of Etowah Cove, and his bodily fatigue and distress of mind were somewhat allayed. Then he began to perceive that in this fictitious death a great property had changed hands, a definite right was subverted; a terrible fraud had been practiced on the tenants *per autre vie*, in that the life estate was not yet terminated. Mr. Gerault Bonley was mulcted of his prominence as a ludicrous, pertinacious, troublous bore, and the personality of the company was asserted as possessors of certain rights and large interests of which they were to be bereft through his agency. He was offered his choice,—to stay dead, or to go back and serve a term in the penitentiary for a crime he had never committed, to benefit the financial interests of Mr. Gerault Bonley and his associates. He sought now and again some solace in reflecting upon the hard bargain that Mr. Bonley had driven with the original owner, the poetic justice that his lands should revert to him in his lifetime, their value enhanced a thousandfold by their own inherent natural wealth, which had been merely developed, not bestowed, by the Marble Company. "I have made one poor soul happy, anyhow! It's just as well that he should get the land before they have sold and shipped all the rock in it. He would have nothing left except a hole in the ground but for this," he muttered to his pillow. For the Marble Company had been exempted by the terms of the grant from "any impeachment of waste," and had successfully defended a suit brought by the reversioner, who sought to restrain their operations by showing that not even the surface of his tract would be left to him upon the determination of the estate *per autre vie*. "He never seemed to have any grudge against me, and I can't say I blame him for being glad I am dead," said Royce, seeking to gauge the sentiments of the joyful reversioner.

Nevertheless, all his commercial instincts revolted. They would not support this arbitrary dispensing of justice. The Gerault Bonley Marble Company's right was definite and indefeasible, and unlawfully he had divested them of it. The idea was abhorrent to his commercial conscience. All the depth of character which he possessed lay in this endowment. He had no religious convictions, no spiritual estimate of the abstractions of right and wrong. To him the thought of religion was like a capitulation. It had never occurred to him as a thing to live by. It seemed of the nature of mortuaries, akin to last wills and testaments, of the very essence of finality. His moral structure was the creation of correct commercial principles,—sound enough, but limited. It was an impenetrable external shell, at once an asset, a protection, and a virtue, but it had no intimate inner tissues. His soul languished inert within it. As far as his financial integrity was concerned, there had been no leanings to the wrong, no struggles against temptation, not even temptation; he was proof against it. His integrity diminished even his capacity for repentance. He had never felt himself a sinner. On the contrary, he thought he had done mighty well. He had been for years in touch with the markets at home and abroad, but he could quote no spiritual values. For the first time in his life, he groped for a knowledge of the right, he strove with the definite sense of wrong-doing. His supposed death had all the taint of dishonor; it affected him as a false entry might have done. The indirect good that it wrought, the natural justice that it meted out, appealed to him no more than the success of speculating with the funds of the firm that employed him might serve to commend this peculation to his incorruptible commercial honor.

He fared better when he sought to protest an irresponsibility. It was the Marble Company's affair to disprove his death if they could, to maintain themselves in continual assurance of his life. "I've seen old Bonley perform so long like a hen with one chicken that I imitate him instinctively. I assume a sort of guardianship of the Gerault Bonley Marble Company as they assumed it of me, and one is as absurd as the other. The company's counsel ought to be equal to the situation. I have nothing to do with them. Their property is held for a term of years, which happens to be the duration of my life. I take on as if a *cestui que vie* was a salaried officer of the Bonley Company,—as if I were paid for drawing the breath of life. It is no part of my duty to report continually for observation. I forfeit no pledge. I violate no trust. And self-preservation is the first law of nature."

With these vacillations he had struggled in throes of mental agony as he lay on the ledges of the rocks above the river and affected to angle; or as he wandered alone through the woods; or when he sat, unheeding the drawling talk of his host, in the open passage where they lighted their pipes together, his evident preoccupation shrewdly noted by the suspicious mountaineer; or, more than all, in the silent watches of the night, before physical fatigue could coerce sleep to his aid,—always arguing the wrong that his silence and absence wrought to others, yet the false suspicion on the part of Greenhalge, Gould & Fife, and the consequent terrible fate that his return would bring upon himself; the intrinsic justice in the restoration to the reversioner of his plundered lands, and yet the positive legal rights which the Gerault Bonley Marble Company held in their unexpired tenancy *per autre vie*; the lies that thus conspired in their masquerade as truth, yet the fact that the truth unmasked would prove the falsest of them all. He had never in all the exercitations of his various problems seemed so near a definite and final decision as now. Never had he reverted so often to one basis of action. He determined that he would not return to the certainty of an ignominious imprisonment on a false suspicion for the sole benefit of a strong corporation of financial sharks, who, on the pretext of a tenancy *per autre vie*, were tearing the estate of their grantor from off the face of the earth; the reversioner would have nothing left but literally a hole in the ground! This awful sacrificial surrender would serve no moral right, but one of those legalized robberies which arise from a fault of the law through its constitutional deficiencies, being at last only of human device. And if, he argued, it was not his function to remodel the laws, and administer them according to the moral basis of evident right, it was in this instance his privilege to dispense even-handed justice.

But when he fell asleep, and his will lay dormant, and his reasoning faculties were blunted, and only his conscience vaguely throbbed with an unassuaged wound, the sense of the commercial wrong that he did, the realization of the definite legal right that he extinguished, the weight of responsibility with which his mere breathing the breath of life had burdened him, all were reasserted without the connivance of volition, and over and over again that poignant cry, "But the one who lives—the one for whose life—his life—his life—his life!" rang through the house with all the pent-up agony of his days of doubt and strivings and distress in its tone.

It was a silent house. No wind stirred. Not a leaf rustled. One might hear the ash crumble covering the embers on the hearth. A vague monotone came from the river. Outside, the still radiance of a late-risen moon lay pallid and lonely on the newly ploughed fields. Here and there crevices in the chinking between the logs of the walls made shift to admit a ray, sending its slight shaft through the brown gloom of the interior, visible itself and luminous in its filar tenuity, yet dispensing no light. One of these rays glimmered through the clapboards of the roof on the face of the sleeper, which showed in the dusk, with all its wan trouble on it, with the distinctness of some sharply cut cameo, to Tubal Cain Sims, who, half dressed and with shock head and bare feet, had climbed the stair, and lurked there listening, that perchance he might hear more to convey to the sharp-set curiosity of the magisterial lime-burner.

This involuntary lapse of his resolution left no trace on the juggler's consciousness when he awoke the next morning. He was not aware that he had dreamed, that in sleeping he had swerved from his intention, far less that he had cried out in his unrealized mental anguish. He took comfort from his stanch mental poise. The fact that he held fast to his conclusion seemed to confirm the validity of his judgment. Here he was to begin life anew, and it behooved him to make the most and the best of it. For one moment the recollection of the world he had left almost overcame him,—the contrast it bore to his sorry future! Even its workaday aspect,—the office, his high desk by the window, the thunder of the cotton-laden wagons in the streets and the clamor of voices impinging so slightly on his absorption in his work as to be ignored,—even this wrung a pang from him now. How much more the thought of the club, with its brilliant lights, and its luxury of furnishing, and its delectable cuisine, and the pretensions of its elder members, and the countenance they were pleased to show him; of the fraternity halls where he was so prime a favorite; of the gymnasium he affected, and the boating and swimming clubs; of his choice social circle, with its germans and musicales, its little dinners and tally-ho drives, its private theatricals, its decorous parlors of refined and elegant suggestions, of which he valued the *entrée* in proportion as he had once felt it jeopardized by the bruiting abroad of that wild gambling escapade, which he feared, in the estimation of the severe and straight-laced matrons and delicate-minded young girls, ill became a member of so elevated a coterie. They seemed, in his recollection, of an embellished beauty and aloof majesty infinitely removed from his sordid plight and maimed estate. He faltered as he thought of his hopeless alienation from it all, his dreary exile.

And then, with a sudden bracing of the nerves, he reflected on the view which this refined society would entertain of the alternative that fate presented; the disgrace which he would sustain in his return was hardly to be mentioned to ears so polite! Was he farther from his friends here than he would be there? Was he more definitely banished from his wonted sphere? He was dead to them,—forever dead,—and the sooner forgotten the better!

In pursuance of his determination, he went downstairs arrayed in the blue-checked homespun shirt and gray jeans trousers which Mrs. Sims with so great and dilatory labor had contrived. He thought he looked the typical mountaineer in this attire, with a pair of long cowhide boots, purchased at the cross-roads store, drawn up to his knees over the legs of the trousers, and a white wool hat of broad brim set far back on his dark red-brown hair. He could hardly have deceived even an unpracticed eye. The texture of his skin, shielded by his vocation from wind and weather; the careful grooming which was the habit of years; the trained step and pose and manner, unconscious though they were; the hand, delicate, however muscular, and white, and with well-tended nails; the silken quality of his smooth hair and mustache; the expression of the eye;—he looked like a young "society swell" dressed for a rural rôle in private theatricals.

Mrs. Sims, who was languidly setting the table in the passage, while Euphemia, clashing the pots and pans and kettles in the room to the left, was "dishin' up" breakfast, paused in her wheezing hymn, catching sight of him, to survey her handiwork.

"Waal!" she exclaimed in delighted pride, appropriating to her own skill the credit of the effect of his symmetry. "Now don't them clothes jes' set! I'll be boun' nobody kin say ez I ain't a plumb special hand fur the needle an' shears! I jes' want Tubal Cain Sims ter view them 'vain trappin's,' ez the hyme calls 'em,—though ez we ain't endowed by Providence with feathers, thar ain't no use in makin' a sin out'n hevin' the bes' clothes what we kin git."

The juggler was as vain as a young man can well be. But he had seldom encountered such outspoken admiration, and was a trifle out of countenance; for what Mrs. Sims conceived to be the excellence of her own proficiency as a tailor he apprehended was due to the graces of his personal endowment. He made her a flourishing bow of mock courtesy, and then stood leaning against the jamb of the door, one hand in the pocket of the gray trousers, the other readjusting the wide low shirt-collar about his throat.

"I'd like ter know what Tubal Cain Sims *will* say now!" exclaimed Mrs. Sims, pursuing corollaries of the main proposition of triumph. "He 'lows, whenst I make him ennythin' ter wear, ez he kin sca'cely find his way inter sech shapen gear. An' whenst in 'em, he 'lows he'll never git out no mo', an' air clad in his grave-clothes—goin' 'bout workin' an' sech—in his grave-clothes! It's a plumb sin, the way he talks!"

Her face clouded for an instant, remembering the ungrateful flouts; then as her gaze returned to her guest, she dimpled anew.

"But laws-a-massy!" she cried, "how peart ye do 'pear in them clothes, to be sure! A heap more like sure enough folks than in them comical little pantees ye hev been a-wearin'."

He could not forbear a laugh at her criticism of the spruce knickerbockers; but with the thought of the varying standards of a different status of life the realization of his exile came to him anew, and imbittered the decoction called coffee which Mrs. Sims handed to him, and although his eyes were dry, as he gulped it down, he tasted tears.

It was difficult for him to resent any admiration of himself as too redundant, but she could not quit the subject, and pointed out to Tubal Cain Sims, when he entered, the excellence of the fit of the shirt about the shoulders and its flatness in the back; apparently arguing that if this shirt fitted the juggler, it was only Tubal Cain Sims's rugged temper and finical fancy that *his* shirt did not fit. The old man's prominent shoulder-blades were not long destined to be concealed by the worn cloth drawn taut across their recurved arches as he leaned slouchingly forward, and the loose amplitudes over his narrow bent chest might well have been economized for a supplement across the shoulders. It never seemed to occur to either of them that the cloth should be cut to suit the figure, or at all events the bearing, of the wearer. She only tortured her helpless partner with her adherence to a pattern at least fifty years old, and which had fitted him well enough twenty-five years ago; but as seam, gusset, and band burst under the stress of his crookedness and increasing slouch, he considered that the hand of Jane Ann Sims had utterly forgotten its cunning, and talked as if his clothes were a trap requiring a certain diligence of investigation to get into, and from which there was no escape.

The juggler grew restive lest Euphemia should enter while he was a bone of contention between the two, for Mrs. Sims was still disposed to call on all who might behold to note the beauty of the fit of his shirt, and Tubal Cain Sims as resolutely refused to admire. Royce was ready to laugh at himself that he should thus desire to shirk these personalities in Euphemia's presence, and that he should assume for her a delicacy in the discussion which he was very sure Mrs. Sims would not appreciate. Yet he was not so coxcombical as to preëmpt for her Mrs. Sims's standpoint; he realized that she might be as stolidly unadmiring as Tubal Cain himself. He finished his breakfast with a hasty swallow or two, and was about to take himself off with his fishing-rod down to the river, hearing Mrs. Sims remarking after him, "Ye oughter thank the Lord on your bended knees, young man, fur the fit o' them clothes," and Tubal Cain Sims's growl of objurgation that "folks oughter have better manners an' sense 'n ter be thankin' the Lord for the set o' thar clothes on the blessed Sabbath day."

"Is this Sunday?" asked the juggler, and stood stock-still.

"It air the blessed Sabbath," said Tubal Cain, his eyes still full of the misfit rancor and his mouth full of corn dodger.

Ah, how Lucien Royce heard across the silent Cove the bells ringing from the church towers of St. Louis, hundreds of miles away! He distinguished even the melody that the chimes were rippling out,—he would have sworn to it amongst a thousand,—and the booming of heavier metal sounding from neighboring steeples. He knew just how a certain dissonance impinged upon the melodious tumult,—the bell of an old church below Seventeenth Street that had a crack in it and rang false. The raucous voices of newsboys were calling the Sunday papers, much further up town than on week-days. The clanging of the cable cars sounded here, there, everywhere; the sunlit streets were full of people. And then, as his heart was throbbing near to breaking for this his world, his home, of which he was bereft, he realized how his imagination had cheated him. Across the Cove the slanting sun-rays had not yet reached the levels of the basin;

the red hue of the dawning still tinged them. The mists of the night clung yet in purple shadowy ravines. The dew was in the air. Away—away—the far city of the mirage lay sluggard and asleep. No bell rang there save the Angelus. Now and again a figure slipped along to early mass. The rumbling wheels of a baker's wagon or the tinkle of a milkman's bell might sound,—a phase of the town, an hour of the day he did not know and for which he did not care. And so he was admonished to beware of fancies. This—*this* was his home, and here he was to spend his life.

He hardly knew how he might contrive to spend the day, he said, as he flung himself down on a ledge of the rock overlooking the river. He appreciated how he would value the rest, had a week of hard work preceded it. He was no Sabbatarian on religious principles, but adhered to the theory as physically economical. As he lay smoking, he argued that much of his tendency to revert to the troubles that had whelmed him, to pine for even the minutiæ of his old life,—aught that suggested it was dear!—to forget that it had gone forever and could never be conjured back, and that a far different fate awaited him in his familiar world, was only an indication of the morbid influence of idleness and mental solitude. The persistence of the activities of the human mind is but scantily realized. Given adequate subjects to work upon, to engross it,—a stent, so to speak,—and its powers seem rarely greater than its task; but remove the objective point of occupation, and the complications of the engine, its normal strength yet its perilous fragility, its inherent tendencies to dislocation, its perpetual uncontrollable subjection to any idea, evolved at haphazard, clutched with a tenacity as of the muscles of a galvanized grasp, result in a chaos of disaster, the mere contemplation of which is wonderfully conducive to energy and the embellishment of toil.

Blessed are the hard workers, for their minds and their hearts shall be sound. This truth was most deeply felt by the young exile from the business world as well as the world of pleasure.

"I must get at something," he said to himself. "I must realize that I am here to stay. This juggling money"—he rattled in his pocket the silver that he had earned the evening of his ill-starred entertainment—"won't last forever, even at the rates of board and lodging in Etowah Cove. It would be the part of wisdom to ingratiate myself with the miller,—cross-grained old donkey,—help him with the mill, marry the miller's daughter, and succeed to the throne."

He laughed, with a mocking relish of the incongruity of the idea. Then, as he thought of the miller's daughter, a vague perception came to him that he had never before encountered a woman apparently so indifferent to him; for indifference was not the sentiment which he was wont to excite. He remembered, too, his hasty retreat from the table, lest her delicacy be offended if his garments were descanted upon in her presence. "Am I going to persuade myself that I am in love with this rural Napoleon in petticoats?" he asked himself scornfully. Then he argued that it was merely because he was not used to such critical scrutiny of his vestments except by his tailor. "All the same, I got out of there before the lady Euphemia appeared." He thus took as dispassionate note of the fact as if he were discussing the state of mind of another person. "I might meet a worse fate. She could be trusted to keep me extremely straight from now till the Judgment Day. She is so pretty—that—if she were a trifle softer—a trifle different, it wouldn't be such hard lines to make love to her."

Perhaps it did not seem such "hard lines" when she suddenly came out of the house, later in the day; for as he glanced up the slope and beheld her, he rose promptly and went to meet her.

It was a tortuous way up the slope; the outcropping ledges here and there projected so heavily that it was easier to skirt around than to climb over them. Brambles grew in shaggy patches; trees intervened; more than once, gnarled roots, struck but half in the ground, the bole rising at a sharp angle with the incline, threw him out of the line of a direct approach. He saw, in drawing near, that he was as yet unperceived, as she made her way slowly along the road. Her wonderful eyes were fixed meditatively, softly, upon the blue mountains beyond the Cove, showing through the gap of the nearer purple ranges. Her lips had a drooping curve. The golden glimmers of her brown hair, rising in dense fairness above her white brow, had never seemed to him so distinct. She carried her pink sunbonnet in her hand; the large loose curls floated on the shoulders of her calico dress. It was of a sleazy texture, and the skirt fell in starchless folds from a short waist to the tops of her low-cut shoes. The color was a rose pink, and on it was scattered a pattern of great roses of the darkest red hue, and she looked as fantastic as if she were attired for a fancy-dress ball. Somehow, this accorded better with his humor than the sombre homespun attire which the mountain women as a rule affected. Her costume, regarded as a fad, did not so diminish her beauty. He could judge better of it, as he paused, still unperceived because of the intervening brambles, hardly ten feet from her. She looked like some old picture, as, swinging the bonnet by one string, she stood still for a moment, with an intent expression in her lovely eyes.

"Ef he speaks so agin," she said slowly, "ef he speaks so agin afore them all, I dunno *how* I kin abide it."

There was a look of pain on her face which, however, did not promise tears. He realized that tears were scarce with her and came hard. It was the look of one whose heart is pierced, and whose pride is bent, and whose endurance flags. Then, with an access of resolution visible in her soft face, she suddenly moved onward, and the swaying sprays of the brambles painted the picture out.

He had hardly time to take stock of his impressions, or note his own surprise, or marvel of what or of whom she spoke, when Mrs. Sims issued, waddling, from the house. She perceived him readily enough, having him in mind, perhaps, and called to him to hurry up, "for we-uns air all goin' ter meetin' over yander at the church-house, whar ye gin that show o' yourn," displaying a fat dimply smile too jolly for the occasion, and all un-meet to companion the Sabbath-day expression on the sour visage of old Tubal Cain Sims, who was shuffling out with high shoulders and hollow chest and bent knees to join the family procession.

Lucien Royce welcomed the summons with the half-bewildered delight of one unexpectedly rescued from the extremest griefs of ennui. His first instinct was to run and dress. Then remembering that he wore the best clothes he had, he composed himself with the reflection that he was in the fashion as it prevailed here. He was consoled, too, as he strolled along beside Mrs. Sims, for the lack of a younger companion, by reflecting that he wanted to make no mischief among any possible lovers of Euphemia, which his public appearance walking with her to church was well calculated to do.

"I think I am safe with Mrs. Sims," he said to himself. "I suppose nobody is in love with her,—not even old Tubal Cain, whatever he may once have been."

He cast a glance at the lean and active partner of Mrs. Sims's joys and sorrows, forging along at a brisk pace which was certain to land him in church before the rest of the household had achieved half the distance.

VI.

THE Cove was no longer silent. Akin to the cadence of the echo, one with the ethereal essence of the sighing and lapsing of the mountain stream, the distant choiring of the congregation in the unseen "church-house" seemed some indigenous voice of the wilderness, so sylvan, so plaintive, so replete with subtle solemn intimations, was the sound. The juggler did not at once distinguish it. Then it came anew with more definite meaning, and it smote upon his quivering, lacerated sensibilities. Not that in the sophisticated life which he had quitted he had valued the Sunday sermons, or cared for the house of the Lord, save architecturally; but he had loved the Sunday singing; the great swelling reverberations of the organ were wont to stir his very heart-strings; and while he appreciated the scope and the worth of the standard compositions of sacred music, he was always keen and critically alert to hear any new thing, with due allowance for the lower level. And should the consecrated hour prove heavy to his spirits, did not his seat near the door, his hat at hand, his quick, noiseless, deft step, provide amply for his retreat? With the realization of the loss of his life, his home, poignantly renewed by the vibrations of the long, sustained, psalmodic tones, he would fain have turned back now; but the idea of the tedious solitude on the ledge of the river-bank, his heavy thoughts, the dread of the remonstrances and urgency of Mrs. Sims, constrained him. So he listened to the solemn rise and fall of the hymning in the Cove, rising and falling with the wind, with a new sense of aghast trouble fixed upon him, as if some spectral thing had revealed itself in the wilderness as he walked unwary.

Now and then, as they wended along amongst the great boles of the trees, with a narrow brook splashing and foaming in the deep rocky gully at one side of the red clay road, or losing itself in the densities of the laurel pressing so close on either hand, he caught in sudden turns through gaps in the foliage glimpses of the winding way further on and of Euphemia's rose-hued dress. She was making but indifferent speed, despite the nimbleness of those "stout little brogans" that could cover the ground so fast when the will nerved them. Once he saw her standing in an open space and looking over the levels of the Cove below. Her pink bonnet was on her head now, its flaring brim pushed far back, and revealing that Pompadour-like effect of her fair hair which he so much admired, and here and there the large loose curls straying on her shoulders. With the short waist of her dress, and the long, straight, limp skirt, the picture-like suggestion was so complete that he had not one throb of that repulsion which ignorance and coarse surroundings occasioned his dilettante exactingness. He looked at her with a kindling eye, a new and alert interest. He began to seek to divine her mental processes. Why was she so reluctant? why did she hesitate? It could not be that the prospect of the dull droning of the preacher affrighted her; she was not wont to seek her ease, and he knew instinctively that her Spartan endurance would enable her to listen as long as the longest-winded of the saints could hold forth. Were her lips moving? He could not be sure at the distance. Was she saying once more, "Ef he speaks so agin afore 'em all, I dunno *how* I kin abide it"?

He wondered who "he" could be—not Jack Ormsby, he was very sure. He wondered how Euphemia should have mustered the feeling to care. She seemed to him not complex, like other women. Her character was built of two elements, kindred and of the nature of complement one to the other,—pride and the love of power, the desire to rule. He had thought her possessed of as much coquetry at eighteen as her grandmother might have at eighty-five. And who was this "he" who brought that look of sweet solicitude, almost a quiver, to her lips?

"I should like to knock 'him' down," he said to himself, humoring the theory of his pretended infatuation.

She turned suddenly, holding up her head with a look of determination, and went on as before.

Far afield might Pride seem, to be sure, in the humble ways of these few settlers in the wilderness, yet here he was in full panoply, to walk, almost visibly, alongside the simple mountain maiden, to enter even the church with her, and to take his seat beside her on one of the rude benches, already crowded.

Her mother and the juggler were later still. The diurnal aspect of the little gray unpainted building in the midst of the green shadows of the great forests, with the wide-spreading boughs of the trees interlacing above its roof, was not familiar to Royce, who had been here only after dark on the evening of his memorable entertainment. The array of yokes of oxen, of wagons, of saddle-horses hitched to the trees, had been noisily invisible in the blackness, on that occasion. The group of youths hanging about the sacred edifice outside had a prototype in the Sunday curbstone gatherings everywhere, and he at once identified the species. A vague haze of dust pervaded the interior; it gave a certain aspect of unreality to the ranks of intent figures on the benches, as if they were of the immaterial populace of dreams. A slant of the rich-hued sunlight fell athwart the room in a broad bar of a dully glamourous effect, showing a thousand shifting motes floating in the ethereal medium. A kindred tint glowed in the folds of a yellow bandanna handkerchief swinging from one of the dark brown beams, and served to advertise its loss by some worshiper at the last meeting. Not so cheerful was another waif from past congregations,—a baby's white knitted woolen hood; it looked like the scalp of this shorn lamb of the flock, and was vaguely suggestive of prowling wolves. On the platform were four preachers who were participating in the exercises of the day. Two of muscular and massive form had an agricultural aspect rather than that of laborers in a spiritual vineyard, and were clad in brown jeans with rough, muddy cowhide boots; they were dogmatic of countenance, and evidently well fed and pampered to the verge of arrogance; they sat tilted back in their splint-bottomed chairs, chewing hard on their quids of tobacco, and wearing a certain easy, capable, confident mien as of an assurance of heavenly matters and a burly enjoyment of worldly prominence. They listened to a hymn which the third—whom Royce recognized as old Parson Greenought—was "lining out," as he stood at the table, with a kind of corroborative air as became past masters in all spiritual craft. They had traveled the road their colleague sought to point out in metre, and were not to be surprised at any of its long-ago-surmounted obstacles. At the end of every couplet, each of them, while still seated, burst into song with such patent disregard of the pitch of the other, the whole congregation blaring after, that the juggler quaked and winced as he sat among the men,—the women being carefully segregated on the other side of the church,—and had much ado to set his teeth and avoid wry faces. The fourth minister was not singing. He sat with his head bowed in his hand, his elbow supported by the arm of his chair, as if lost in silent prayer. The juggler watched his every motion as for deliverance from the surging waves of sound, permeated with that rancorous independence of unison, which floated around him, for he divined that this was the orator of the day. This young man lifted his face expectantly after a time,—a keen, thin, pale face, with black hair and dark gray eyes, and an absorbed ascetic expression. But Parson Greenought still "lined out" the sacred poetry, which was hobbling as to metre, and often without connection and bereft of meaning; and with a wide opening of the mouth and a toss of the head, the two musically disposed pastors resolutely led the singing, and the congregation chorused tumultuously. It was in some sort discipline for Brother Absalom Tynes to be obliged to sit in silence and wait while stanza followed stanza and theme was added to theme in the multifarious petition psalmodically preferred. The words were on his lips; his heart burned for utterance; he quivered with the very thought of his pent-up message. He was of that class of young preachers who have gone into the vineyard early, and with a determination to convert the world single-handed. Nothing but time and Satan can moderate their enthusiasms; but time and Satan may be trusted. Too much zeal,—misdirected, young, unseemly, foolish,—Brother Tynes had been given to understand, was his great fault, his besetting sin; it would do more harm than good, and he had been admonished to pray against it. Perhaps the exhibition of it grated on his elder *confrères* as an unintentional rebuke, beneath which they secretly smarted, remembering a time long ago—but of short duration, it may be—when they too had been fired with wild enthusiasm and were full of mad projects, and went about turning every stone and wearying even the godly with the name of the Lord. So, to use the phrase of the politicians, they "paired off" with Satan, as it were; forgetting that zeal is like gunpowder, once damped, forever damaged, and that their own had caught no spark from any chance contiguous fire this many a long day.

That singing praises to the Lord should be a means of "putting down" Brother Tynes savors of the incongruous; but few human motives are less complex than those which animated Parson Greenought as he combined the edification of the congregation, the melody of worship, and the reduction of the pride of the pulpit orator, whose fame already extended beyond Etowah, and even to Tanglefoot Cove. The science of "putting down" any available subject is capable of utilizing and amalgamating unpromising elements, and as Parson Greenought cast up his eyes while he sang, and preserved a certain sanctimonious swaying of the body to and fro with the rhythm of the hymn he "lined out," the triumph of "simulating" these several discordant mental processes cost him no conscious effort and scarcely a realized impulse.

The juggler looked about him with a sort of averse curiosity; the traits of ignorant people appealed in no respect to his somewhat finical prepossessions. Among his various knacks and talents was no pictorial facility, nor the perception of the picturesque as a mental attitude. He resented the assumption of special piety in the postures and facial expression here and there noticeable in the congregation; he could have singled out those religionists whom he fancied thus vying with one another. One broad-shouldered and stalwart young man was given to particularly conspicuous demonstrations of godliness, exemplified chiefly in sudden startling "A-a-a-mens" sonorously interpolated into the reading, a breathy, raucous blare of song as he lifted up his voice,—inexpressibly off the key,—and a sanctimonious awkward pose of the head with half-shut eyes. The juggler could have trounced this saint with hearty good will, for no other reason than that the man took pleasure in showing how religious he was! Only Mrs. Sims exhibited no outward token of her happy estate as a "perfesser," but her salvation was considered a very doubtful matter, and even that she had "found peace" problematical, since she did not believe in special judgments alighting on the mistaken or the unconverted, and had surmised that the Lord would find out a way to excuse "them that had set on the mourners' bench" in vain. "Ef you hev jes' started out," she would say to those unfortunate wights whom the members were allowed to persecute with advice and exhortation as they cowered before the throne of grace, "don't *you* be 'feard. The Lord will meet ye more 'n halfway. Ef ye don't see him, 'tain't because he ain't thar. Jes' start out. That's all!"

But Parson Greenought had warned her to forbear these promissory pledges of so easy a salvation. For he wanted sinners all to gaze on that lake of brimstone and fire which none but him could so successfully navigate; and now and again he had his triumph when some wretch in agonies of terror would screech out that he or she was "so happy! so happy!" since to be "happy" by main force, so to speak, was the alternative he offered to the prospect of weltering there forever. So Jane Ann Sims held her peace, and preserved a fat and placid solemnity of countenance, and sang aloud in such wheezy audacity that the juggler could hear her breathe across the church.

Only one countenance was doubtful, wistful, its muscles not adjusted to the discerning gaze of the congregation. Euphemia Sims sat near a window, the tempered light on the soft contours of her face. The flaring pink sunbonnet framed the rising mass of fair hair; she gazed absently down at the floor; her delicate young shoulders were outlined upon the masses of green leaves fluttering above the sill hard by. Her look so riveted Royce's attention that he sought to decipher it. What did she fear? There was a suggestion of wounded pride, most appealing in its incongruity with her normal calm, or hardness, or unresponsiveness, or whatever he might choose to call the nullity of that habitual untranslated expression. Why was she so grave, so sad? The sudden lifting of her long lashes and the intent fixing of her eyes directed his attention to the pulpit, and there he perceived that Brother Tynes was standing at last, beginning to elucidate his text. The juggler, relieved of the torture of the singing, braced his nerves for the torture of the sermon. Here he might have had a recourse in his facility of abstracting his mind. He had sat through many a sermon in this unreceptive state. He had cast up accounts, preserving a duality of identity in the secular activity of his mental faculties and the sabbatical decorum of his face and listening attitude. Between firstly and secondly he had once chased down three vagrant cents,—an error which had cost him fifteen hours of labor out of regular working time,—without which he could not balance his accounts. Once—it was during the Christmas holidays—he had utilized the peroration of a long and searching discourse by the bishop of the diocese to evolve certain new and effective figures for the german which he was to lead the next evening, and he had always esteemed that hour a most fruitful occasion. And again, during a special sermon, on foreign missions, he evolved a little melody, hardly more than a repetitious phrase, forever turning and coiling and doubling on itself, to which he adapted the artfully repetitious words of a dainty chansonnette of a celebrated French poet with such skill and delicate inspiration of fitness that he often sang it afterward in choice musical circles to unbounded applause. He had sat under the sound of the gospel all his life, and he was as thorough a pagan as any savage. But alack! his was not the only deaf ear in those congregations—more's the pity! and while we send missionaries to China and the slums of our own great cities, our civilized heathen of the upper classes are out of reach.

It was perhaps because he now had no thought that would let him be friends with it—no sedulously conserved accounts, no *bizarreries* of the german to devise, no inspiration of melody in mind (the psalmody of Etowah Cove was enough to strike the music in him dumb for evermore)—that he followed the direction of Euphemia's gaze and composed himself to listen.

He encountered a sudden and absolute surprise. The sermon was one of those examples of a fiery natural eloquence which sometimes serve to show to the postulant of culture how endowment may begin at the point where training leaves off. The rapt silence of Brother Tynes's audience and their kindling faces attested the reciprocal fervors of his enthusiasms. He was awkward and unlettered, with uncouth gestures and an uncultivated voice, but there burned like a white fire in his pale, thin face a faith, an adoration, an exultation, which transfigured it. He had a fine and lofty ideal in the midst of the contortions of his ignorance, which he called doctrines, and presently he spoke only and in proteanwise of the mystery and the mercy of Redeeming Love. The idea of reward, of punishment, of the hope of heaven and the fear of hell, did not seem to enter into his scheme of salvation. He sought to grasp the realization of an infinite sacrificial love, and he adjured his people to fall on their faces, with their faces in the dust, before the sacred marvel of the Atonement. The text "He first loved us" rang out again and again like a clarion call. Its simple cogency seemed to need no argument. How could the politic and mercenary motives of securing exemption from pain or the purchase of pleasure enter herein? That phase of striking a fair bargain, so controlling to sordid human nature, was for the moment preposterous. Many a one of his simple hearers knew the joy of unrequited labor for love's sweet sake, of self-denial, of being hungry or tired or cold, in sacrificial content. More than one mother could hardly have given a practical reason why the crippled child or the ailing one should be the dearest, when its nurture could rouse no expectation that it might live to work for her sake. More than one gray-haired son loved and honored the paralytic troublous old dotard in the warmest corner of the fireside all the more for his helplessness and the toil for his sake. Love makes duty dear. Love makes service light. In some one phase or other they all knew that love is for love's own sake.

And this was all that he demanded in the great prophetic name of Christ even from the dread heights of Calvary, "My son, give me thine heart."

Now and again sobs punctuated the discourse. Before there was any call for mourners to approach the bench, an old white-headed man, who had resisted many an appeal to his fears on behalf of his soul, rose and shambled forward; others silently joined him where he sat looking at them over his shoulder, very conscious, a trifle crest-fallen, if not ashamed, thus to be forced from the stanch defenses which he had defiantly held through many a siege. The assisting ministers occasionally cleared their throats and shifted their crossed legs, with an expression of countenance which might be interpreted as deprecation of the factitious excitements of a sensational sermon.

Euphemia Sims hearkened with a face of perfect decorum and superficial receptiveness. In her heart, rather than in her mind, she missed the true interpretation of the discourse. It did not seem to her so wonderful that she should be of a degree of importance to merit salvation. To be sure, in the sense of sharing original sin she supposed she was a sinner,—born so. But her life was ordered on a line of rectitude. Who kept so clean a house, who wove and milked and cooked and sewed so diligently, as she? Who led for years the spelling-class in this very house, whose brown walls might tell of her orthographic triumphs? And she had got her religion, too, and had even shouted one day, albeit a quavering, half-hearted hosanna. So she looked on with a calm post-graduate manner at the gathering penitents at the mourners' bench. She too had passed through the preliminary stages of spiritual culture, and had taken her degree.

The juggler, as he listened, repeatedly felt that cold thrill which he was wont to associate with a certain effect on his critical faculties. Only a high degree of excellence in whatever line appealing to them was capable of eliciting it. He had experienced it in this measure hitherto only in the pleasurable suspense and excitement, so intense as to be almost pain, in the dress circle of some crowded play-house, at the triumphant moment of a masterpiece in the science of histrionism.

The orator was approaching his climax. To so great a height had he risen that it seemed as if his utmost power could not reach beyond; every moment tingled with the expectation that the next word must herald a collapse, when, suddenly throwing himself on his knees, he cried, "Lead us in prayer, Brother Haines,—lead us in prayer to the foot of the cross!"

There was a startled movement among his colleagues of the pulpit, charged with the prosaic suggestion that if they could they would deny Brother Haines—apparently a layman and seated among the congregation—the opportunity of thus publicly approaching the throne of grace; but the people already had crowded upon their knees, and a suppliant voice, pitched on a different key, rose into the stillness.

Euphemia Sims sat for a moment as if she were turned to stone. A light both of pain and of anger was in her eyes. Her lips were stern and compressed. She felt her blood beating hard in her temples. Then she remembered the exacting decorums of the exercise, gathered her trim pink skirts about her, softly knelt down, and Pride knelt down beside her.

She hardly heard the voice of Brother Owen Haines at first, as she put her dimpled elbows on the hard bench and held her head between her hands, so tumultuous were the surging pulses of humiliation and fear, and of love, too, in a way. And then it asserted itself upon her senses, although she was conscious first merely of tones, rich, mellow, of delicate modulations and lingering vibrations,—differing infinitely from the clear, incisive, somewhat harsh utterances of the preacher; but at last words came gradually to her comprehension.

Commonplace words enough, to be sure, to excite so poignant a torture of agonized expectation in that heart, beating as one with Pride's, but presently too oft repeated. Now and again a raucously cleared throat amongst the row of kneeling ministers told of a nervous stress of anxiety as to these verbal stumblings and inadequacies. Sometimes a sentence was definitely broken, subject and predicate hopelessly disjointed. Sometimes a clause barely suggested the thought in the brain, an irremediable solution of continuity in its expression. More than once occurred a painful pause, in which the heads of certain newly regenerate sinners, easily falling again under mundane influences or the control of Satan, turned alertly from the prayerful attitudes still conserved by their bodies to covertly survey the spellbound suppliant. Like unto these was the juggler. He had, on the first summons to prayer, decorously assumed that half-crouching posture common to devotionally disposed men, which intimates to the surrounding spectators the fact of a certain polite subduement of mind and body to divine worship. Then, remembering suddenly the character of mountaineer which he designed to assimilate, he plumped down on his knees—for the first time in many a long day—like the rest. And if in the ensuing excitements his mind did not match his lowly attitude, the juggler is not the only man who has ever been upon his knees with no prayer in his heart. Taking license from the stir near at hand, he too shifted his posture that his furtive glance might command a view of the man thus deputed to pray.

The suppliant was among the congregation, but his face, as he knelt in an open space near the pulpit, was irradiated by the slant of the sunset glow. Beheld above the benches and the kneeling congregation, it had a singularly detached effect,—it was like the painting of a head; all else was canceled. For a moment, the juggler, his eyes growing intent and grave as he gazed, could not account for a sense of familiarity with it, of having seen it often before. Then, with a reminiscence of dim religious surroundings, of tempered radiance streaming through translucent mediums, of flecks of deep rich tints,—red and blue and purple and amber, always with emitted undertones of light,—he realized its association with church windows, with the heights of clerestory twilight, with catherine-wheels luminous in dark transepts, with trifoliated symbols in chancel arches. It might have seemed, the idealizing glamour of the sunset in the rapt devotional expression, a study for a seraph's face; in truth, one could hardly desire a more fitting presentment of the angelic type. The fair hair, not gold even under the heightening sunlight, lay in gentle infantile curves along the broad forehead; as it fell to the shoulder it showed tendencies to heavy undulations that were scarcely curls or ringlets, and that grew diaphanous and cloudy toward their fibrous verges. The large languid blue eyes had long dark lashes, and the pathetic fervors, the adoration, the entreaty of their expression, moved sundry covert glances to a twinkle of laughter; for this surpassed in some humorous sort the liberal limits assigned to the outward show of devotion in Etowah Cove. None of its other denizens ever looked like that, saint or sinner! It was a subtle and complex expression, and, being incomprehensible, it struck most of the observers as simply funny. The high cheekbones and the pale unrounded cheek might have impressed an artist as somewhat too attenuated of contour to suggest the enjoyment of the eternal bliss of heaven, but they added to the extreme spirituality of the effect of the eyes, and with the congruous but delicate irregular nose and full lips made the face unusual and individual.

An odd face for the butt of a coarse joke. The congregation, still kneeling, stirred with a ripple of silent laughter. Here and there, as the glances of curious worshipers, looking furtively over the shoulder, encountered one another, a gleam of caustic comment or deprecating amusement was exchanged; and once a newly caught saint, not yet having wholly dropped the manners and quirks of the Old Man, from force of habit winked, wrinkled his nose, and grinned. For the halting supplication, still offered in that melting melody of intonation, had passed from its disconnected plea for mercy, for the conversion of sinners, for the guidance of the congregation, for the spiritual profit of the meeting, and had boldly entered on a personal and unique petition, a prayer for the power to preach the gospel. The day of miracles, the learned say, is past. Even the illiterate congregation in Etowah Cove expected none to be wrought in its midst. And surely only the hand of God could touch that faltering tongue to the full expression of the thought that trembled impotently upon it. What subtle unimagined rift was it between the mind and the word, what breach in their mysterious telegraphy! Elsewhere the phenomenon exists: the silent poet, whose metre beats in certain dumb fervors of the pulse; the painter, whose picture glows only upon the retina of the mind's eye; or those, unhappily not quiescent, who blurt and blunder as did Owen Haines in his incoherent monologue to Almighty God. But he was the single example in the experience of Etowah Cove, and to the literal-minded saints the spectacle of a man bent upon preaching the gospel, and yet so ill fitted for the task that he could scarce put half a dozen words into a faltering sentence, moved them now to mirth and now to wrath, according to the preponderance of merry or ascetic religionists in the assembly. Again and again, whenever an opportunity was vouchsafed, Owen Haines, with his illumined face and passionate appealing voice, publicly besought of God in the congregations of worshipers, where he felt prayer must most surely prevail, with the pulse and the heart and the word of all his world to bear him company to the throne of grace, the power to preach the gospel:—in such phrase, such few repetitious disjointed words, *disjecta membra* of supplication, with so flagrant a display of hopeless incapacity, that it became almost the scandal of the meetings, and there had been a tacit agreement among the ministers who were to conduct the revival that he should not be called upon to pray. The exhibition of his eloquent burning face and his halting words, his faith and its open reiterated denial, was not deemed edifying; and indeed it had latterly begun to affect the gravity of certain members of the congregation of whose conversion the leaders had had great hopes.

"He hev got ter fight that thar question out alone," said old man Greenought in indignation. "I won't gin him nare 'nother 'Amen.' He an' his tomfool wantin' ter preach the gorspel whenst he can't pray a 'spectable prayer is a puffick blemish on the divine service; it's fairly makin' game o' serious things,—his prayin' fur the power,—an' I dunno what the Lord is a-goin' ter do about it, but *I* ain't a-goin' ter lend *my* ear nare 'nother time."

It was this choleric gentleman who at last half rose from his knees, and with a peremptory jerk of his thumb toward the failing sunlight brought Haines's aspiring spirit back to earth. He had gone far on the wings of those poor words, he had flown high. His thought had so possessed him that he did not realize what slight tincture of it his speech distilled for those who heard him. The ministerial thumb jerking a warning of the flight of time, a certain covert jeer in the bent half-covered faces of those about him, brought the fact to him that this prayer was like so many others, voiced only in the throbs of his heart. The light was dying out of his eyes, the sunset glow had quitted him; no fine illumined countenance now he bore, as of one who looks on some transcendent vision; only a conscious disciplined face, quiet and humbled and so patient! He broke off suddenly to say "Amen," for he sacrificed no connection,—he hardly knew whither he was rambling,—and the people scrambled noisily to their feet, eager for dispersing.

"What did you-uns call on him fur, ennyhow?" said old Greenought bluffly to Absalom Tynes. He had somewhat of a swaggering manner as he came up close to the thin, pallid young man. He took great joy in all the militant tropes descriptive of the Christian estate, and with the more liberty suited his secular manner to his ministerial rhetoric. Since he waged so brisk a warfare against Sin and Satan, he often seemed about to turn his weapons, as if to keep his hand in, against his unoffending fellow man.

Absalom Tynes did not flinch. "I called on him," he said a trifle drearily, for the fire of his exaltation, too, was quenched in that pathetic and ineffectual "prayin' fur the power," "kase ez I war a-preachin' the word I knowed he war a-followin' me, an' I 'lowed I hed got him ter the p'int whar surely he mought lift up his heart. I 'lowed the Lord mought take pity on him ez longs ter serve him, an' so touch his lips an' gin him the gift o' a tongue o' fire. I can't sense it, somehow,—I don't onderstand it."

"I do," Parson Greenought capably averred. "The Lord's put him in the place whar he wants him, an' he'll be made ter stay thar,—jes' a-persistin' in prayin' fur the power!"

"Thar ain't no lock an' key on prayer ez I knows on," responded the other a trifle testily. "A man kin pray fur what he wills."

"Yes, an' he kin do without it, too, unless the Lord wills. Fight the devices o' Satan, an' don't git ter be a beggar at the throne fur gratifyin' yer own yearthly quirks. Prayin' an' a-prayin' fur the power! The power's a gift, my brother, a free gift, an' no man will git it by baigin' an' baigin' an' teasin' fur it."

He strode off, feeling that he had had the best of the discussion. He was discerning enough to be conscious that, despite his belligerencies, he was often inferior to his youthful *confrère* in the rhetoric of the pulpit, and he relished the more worsting him in argument, thus proving the superiority of his judgment and solid reasoning capacities.

Outside the door a group of loiterers still lingered. The juggler's prudential motives had collapsed utterly in the prospect of Mrs. Sims's society in the long walk home. He looked about him with a desperate hope of diversion, in which Euphemia and the curiosity she had newly excited were factors. But he was fain to be content with his elderly companion, for as Euphemia's rose-hued dress blossomed in the portal against the dark brown background of the interior he noticed that Owen Haines was standing at the foot of the steps evidently awaiting her. The mountaineer gave her no greeting, but walked beside her as if his companionship were a matter of course.

"Warn't that a plumb special sermon?" he said enthusiastically, turning his candid eyes upon her. "'Pears like ter me 'twar the best, the meltin'est, the searchin'est discourse I ever hear."

There was a measure of contempt in her face. She would not have admitted that she thought herself too good for the need of salvation, but the theme with all its cognate elements was palling. She replied with a definite note of sarcasm in her voice. "The bes'? Waal, I hev hearn ye say that time an' time agin. The sermons air *all* the bes', 'cordin' ter you-uns."

"Yes," he admitted a trifle drearily, "ef I lose my soul, 'twon't be bekase I ain't hed the bes' chance fur salvation. I hev sot under a power o' good an' discernin' sermons in my time."

The seraphic suggestions of his face, now that he was recalled to earth, were little marked, and presently totally merged when he clapped his big broad-brimmed hat upon that mass of cloudy, fine-fibred fair hair. The irreverent juggler could have laughed at the swiftness and completeness of the transition. Haines still wore that dreamy, far-away look which, however, with mundane associations and modern garb, is apt to indicate an unpurposeful nature and a lack of energy rather than any lofty ideals and high resolves. The perfect chiseling and contour of his countenance and its refined intimations were still patent to the discerning observer; but without the preconceived idea drawn in the church from the aspect of his head, with the soul revealed for one rapt moment through its facial expression,—picture-like, dissevered from the suggestion of body—Royce would hardly have perceived any spiritual trait of a higher type in the young mountaineer. Thus it is that only the outer man is known of men, and that ethereal essence of thought and emotion, the real being, is a stranger upon earth and foreign from the beginning.

Royce, greedily snatching at the very straws of abstraction, watched the young couple as they strolled slowly along the red clay road. The slouching, thin, languid figure of the tall youth, the ill-fitting suit of brown jeans with the coat hanging so loosely from the narrow shoulders, the big white hat, the rough crumpled boots all appealed to him with a pleasant sense of incongruity as the accoutrement of this object of mistaken identity, when a golden harp and a white robe and a sweep of wings would better have become the first glimpse caught in the church. Now and again, mechanically, involuntarily, Euphemia looked furtively back over her shoulder at Royce. With all that surging pulse of pride in her heart she was strangely bereft of her wonted assurance. It would never have occurred to her, in her normal sphere of thought and action, to refer aught that concerned her to the judgment, the problematic opinion of another. But although she gave him so slight thought, although she could not definitely gauge its objects and interests, she had not been unnoting of that subtle pervasive mockery which characterized the juggler's habit of mind. Until now, however, she had not cared at what or at whom the "game-maker" laughed, how loud, how long. The laughter of folly cannot serve to mock good substantial common sense which affords no purchase for ridicule; it rebounds only upon the mocker. She apprehended naught in herself, her home, her parents, the Cove, deserving of scorn or sneers. Her pride was proof against this. It was because she herself deemed her lover ridiculous that she winced from Royce's imagined laugh now, as she had shrunk from the criticism of the rest of the congregation. But this mockery was of the intimate fireside circle. For Royce would go home with them, and bring it in his laugh, his glance; nay, she would be conscious of it even in his silent recollections. She felt she had no refuge from it. She told herself that because she loved Haines she deprecated mockery as unworthy of him, she would fain shield him from the sneers of those not half so good as he. She would rather he should eat out his heart in silence than besiege the throne of grace in any manner not calculated to inspire respect and admiration in those who heard his words addressed to the Almighty. As to the Deity, the goal of all these petitions, she never once thought of their spiritual effect, the possibility of an answer. She esteemed the prayer as in the nature of a public speech, a public exhibition, which, glorious in success, is contemptible in its failure in proportion to the number of witnesses and the scope of the effort. How could Owen Haines pray for the power to preach, when there was Absalom Tynes looking on so vainglorious and grand, doubtless esteeming himself a most "servigrous" exhorter, and obviously vaunting his own godliness by implication in the fervor with which he called sinners to repentance? How could Owen Haines seek so openly, so painfully, so terribly insistently, as a privilege, a boon, as an answer to all his prayers, as a sign from the heavens, as a token of salvation, as the price of his life, that capacity which was possessed so conspicuously, without a word of prayer, without a moment of spiritual wrestling, without a conscious effort, by Absalom Tynes?

"I'd content myself with the power ter plough," she said to herself.

Then, as he fell into retrospective thought, she said aloud,—her voice not ringing true as was its wont, but with a tremulous uncertain vibration,—"'Pears like ter me, ez ye hain't been gin the power arter sech a sight o' prayer, 'twould be better ter stop baigin' an' pesterin' the Lord 'bout'n it."

There was a moment's silence, during which the little roadside rill flung out on the air the rudiments of a song,—a high crystalline tremor, a whispering undertone, a comprehensive surging splash as of all its miniature currents resolved into one chord *con tutta forza*, and so to whispering and tentative tinklings again. He had turned his clear long-lashed blue eyes upon her, and she saw the reproach in them. That courage in the feminine heart which dares wreak cruelty on its own tender fibres urged her.

"I hev tole ye that afore," she added sternly.

He was still silent. So sacred was that disregarded petition of his that, despite the publicity of its preferment, its free unrestrained fervors, he could hardly discuss it, even with her.

"Ye hain't hed no advices from the Lord," she argued. "Ye hev been prayin' fur the power constant, ever since ye got religion, an' the Lord don't take no notice o' ye."

A shadow was on his face, pain in his eyes. Any one more merciful than the proud woman who loved him, and who would fain conserve his pride, might have pitied the sudden revulsion from the enthusiastic pleasure in the sacred themes of the sermon so late upon his lip and firing his eye—which she accounted merely the triumphs of Absalom Tynes—to this abasement and sorrow and prescient despair.

"I kin wait on his will," he said humbly.

"Waal, ye better wait in silence," Euphemia declared, near to the brink of tears,—angry and wounded and scornful tears.

"'Ask an' ye shall receive, seek an' ye shall find,'" he quoted pertinently, with that upbraiding look in his eyes which hurt her for his sake, and which she resented for her own.

"How long! how long!" she cried impetuously. "Will ye spen' yer life askin' fur what's denied ye, seekin' fur what's hidden from ye? The Lord's got nuthin' fur ye, Owen, an' by this time ye oughter hev sensed that."

"Then I kin pray fur the grace ter take denial from his hands like a rich gift," he declared, his face kindling with an illumined, uplifted look.

"Oh, yer prayin' an' prayin'! I'm plumb wore out with it!" she cried, stopping still in the road; then realizing the advance of the others she walked on hastily, and with the affectation of a careless gesture she took off her bonnet and swung it debonairly by the string, lest any emotional crisis be inferred from her abrupt halt. "Owen Haines," she said, with sudden inspiration, "ye air deceived by Satan. Ye ain't wantin' the power ter preach the gospel ter advance the kingdom. Ye want the power ter prance ez prideful ez a peacock in the pul-*pit*, like Absalom Tynes an' them other men what air cuttin' sech a dash afore the yearth ez keeps 'em from keerin' much *how* the nangels in heaven air weepin' over 'em."

He recoiled from this thrust, for, however his charity might seek to ignore the fact, however his simplicity might fail to discern it, his involuntary intuition made him well aware that "prancing ez prideful ez a peacock" was not altogether foreign to the pulpit here or elsewhere, and that undue vainglory must needs wait on special proficiency. She felt that she struck hard in imputing to him a motive of which he knew himself to be incapable. Perhaps he would have pleased her better had he combined his religious fervors with any intention so practical, so remunerative, so satisfying to the earthly sentiment of one not too good to live in this world.

It was eminently in keeping with that phase of his character which she most contemned that he should, with his cheek still flushed, with his eyes wincing and narrowing as from a blow, begin a vehement defense, not of himself and his motives, but of Absalom Tynes.

She would hardly listen. "I hev hearn ye talk about Absalom Tynes, an' I don't want ter hear no mo'. I know what I know. Tell me thar ain't no pride in the pul-*pit*,—a-readin' an' a-talkin' an' a-preachin' so glib an' precise, an' showin' off so gran' afore the wimminfolks, an' a-singin' so full-mouthed an' loud, an' bein' the biggest man thar; fur Satan, though he often gits his club-foot on the pul-*pit* stairs, ain't never been knowed ter step up! Ye tell me that ain't true 'bout some, ef not that precious friend o' yourn, Absalom Tynes?"

"Euphemia," he said sternly in his turn, and her heart was full at the tone of his voice, "I dunno what idee you-uns hev got; ye 'pear so—so—diff'unt—so"—He hesitated; his words were not wont to be ready.

"So diff'unt from what? From you-uns? I reckon so! Ef I war ter drap dead this minit, nuthin', nuthin' could hev made me act like you-uns, prayin' an' prayin' fur the power ter preach—whenst—whenst—Owen Haines, ye ain't even got the power ter pray! The Lord denies ye that—even the power ter ax so ez—ter be fitten fur *folks* ter hear!"

"The Lord kin hear, Euphemy; he reads the secret thoughts."

"Let yourn be secret, then!" cried Euphemia. "Fur the folks air listenin' too ter the thoughts which the Lord kin hear 'thout the need o' words—listenin' an'—an', Owen Haines, laffin'!" She choked back a sob, as her eyes filled and the tears ran out on her scarlet cheek. With a stealthy gesture she wiped them away with the curtain of her pink sunbonnet, carrying herself very stiffly lest some unconsidered turn of the head betray her rush of emotion to the other church-goers loitering behind. When she lifted her eyes, the flow of tears all stanched, her sobs curbed, she beheld his eyes fixed sorrowfully upon her.

"D'ye 'low I dunno that, Euphemy?" he said, his voice trembling. "D'ye 'low I don't see 'em an' hear 'em too when I'm nigh the Amen?"

Her tears burst out anew when she remembered that the "Amen" was often said for him by the presiding minister, with such final significance of intonation, ostentatiously rising the while from the kneeling posture, as to fix perforce a period to this prolix incoherency of "prayin' fur the power."

"Ye don't *feel* it," she protested, very cautiously sobbing, for since her grief would not be denied, she indulged it under strict guard,—"ye don't *feel* it! But me,—it cuts me like a knife!"

"Why, Phemie," he said softly, walking closer to her side,—noticing which she moved nearer the verge of the stream, that she might keep the distance between them exactly the same as before, not that she wished to repel him, but that the demonstration might escape the notice of those who followed,—"'pears ter me like ye oughtn't ter keer fur the laffin' an' mockin', fur mebbe I'll be visited with a outpourin' o' the sperit, an' be 'lowed ter work fur my Lord like I wanter do."

She turned and looked at him; they had reached the top of a sort of promontory that jutted out over a leafy sea of the budding forests on the levels of the Cove below. The whole world of the spring was a-blooming. Even the tulip-trees, with their splendid dignity of height and imposing girth, seeming well able to spare garlands, wore to their topmost sprays myriads of red and yellow bells swaying in the breeze. The azaleas were all a-blow, and a flowering vine, the merest groundling, but decked with delicate white corymbs, lay across the path. The view of the sinking sun was intercepted by a great purple range, heavy and lowering of shadow and sombre of hue, but through the gap toward the west, as if glimpsed through some massive gate, was visible a splendid irradiation overspreading the yellow-green valley and the blue mountains beyond; so vividly azure was this tint that the color seemed to share the vernal impulse and glowed with unparalleled radiance, like some embellishment of the spring which the grosser seasons of the year might not compass. From below, where the beetling rock overhung a wilderness of rhododendron, voices came up on the soft air. The others of the party had taken the short cut. She heard her mother's wheeze, the juggler's low mellow voice, her father's irritable raucous response, and she realized that she might speak without interruption.

"The Lord's got nuthin' fur ye," she averred vehemently; "he don't need yer preachin' an' he don't listen ter yer prayers. Ye hev come ter be the laffin'-stock o' the meetin' an' the jye o' the game-makers o' the Cove. An' ef—ef ye don't gin it up—I—I—ye'll hev ter gin me up—one or t'other—me or that."

Haines was not slow now. He understood her in a flash. The covert grin, the scornful titter, the zestful wink,—she cared more for these small demonstrations of the unthinkingly merry or the censorious scoffer than for him or the problematic work that his Master might send him the grace to do. Nevertheless, he steadied himself to put this into words that he might make sure beyond peradventure. He had taken off his hat. The wind was blowing back the masses of his fine curling fair hair from his broad low brow. His cheeks were flushed, his eyes alight and intense. He held his head slightly forward. "I must gin you up, or gin up prayin' fur the power ter preach?"

"Prayin' in public—'fore the folks—I mean; in the church-house or at camp-meetin'. Oh, I can't marry a man gin over ter sech prayin' afore the congregations! but ye kin go off yander alone in the woods or on the mountings, an' pray, ef so minded, till the skies fall, for all I'm keerin'."

"Ye mind kase people laff," he said slowly.

"Ef people laff at me kase I be foolish, I mind it. Ef people laff at me kase *they* air fools, they air welcome ter thar laffin' an' thar folly too." This discrimination was plain. But as he still looked dreamy and dazed, she made the application for him. "Ye can't preach; ye can't pray; ye make a idjit o' yerself tryin'. I can't marry no sech man 'thout ye gin up prayin' 'fore folks."

"Ye think mo' o' folks 'n the Lord?" Haines demanded, with a touch of that ministerial asperity expert in imputing sin.

But so widely diffused are the principles of Christianity that the well-grounded layman can rarely be silenced even by a minister with a call, much less poor uncommissioned tongue-tied Owen Haines.

"The Lord makes allowances which people can't an' won't," she retorted. "He hears the thought an' the sigh, an' even the voice of a tear."

"He does! He does!" cried Owen Haines, fired by the very suggestion, his face, his eyes, his lips aflame. "An' may my tongue cleave to the roof of my mouth an' my right hand be withered an' forget its cunning, may agues an' anguish rack my body an' may my mind dwindle ter the sense of a brute beastis, ef ever I promise ter put bonds on prayer or eschew the hope of my heart in the house of God. I'll pray fur the power—I'll pray fur the power ter preach till I lose the gift o' speech—till I kin say no word but 'the power!—the power!—the power'!"

Euphemia cowered before the enthusiasm her chance phrase had conjured up. She had not, in a certain sense, doubted the sincerity of her lover's religious fervor. She secretly and unconsciously doubted the validity of any spiritual life. She could not postulate the sacrificial temperament. She could not realize how he would have embraced any votive opportunity. He was of the type akin to the anchorite, the monastic recluse,—who in default of aught else offers the kernel of life, if not its empty shell,—even the martyr. For he had within him that fiery exaltation which might have held him stanch at the stake, and lifted his voice in triumphant psalmody above the roar of the flames. But although he had had his spiritual sufferings of denial, and floutings, and painful patience, and hope that played the juggler with despair, he had anticipated no ordeal like this. He looked in her eyes for some token of relenting, his own full of tears above the hardly quenched brightness of his fervor of faith, a quiver on his lips.

Her face was set and stern. With a realization how deeply the fantasy had struck roots in his nature, she perceived that she must needs share it or flee it. She was hardly aware of what she did mechanically, but as she painstakingly tied the pink strings of her bonnet under her dimpled chin it was with an air of finality, of taking leave. She was not unconscious of a certain pathetic appeal in his life, seemingly unnoted by God, yet for God's service, and rejected by love. But she thought that if he pitied himself without avail she need not reproach herself that she did not pity him more. And truly she had scant pity to spare. And so he stood there and said "Farewell" as in a dream, and as in a dream she left him.

VII.

It created something of a sensation, one morning, when the juggler—for the mountaineers as solemnly distinguished him by the name he had given them of his queer vocation as if it were the serious profession of law—appeared among the lime-burners on the slope of the mountain. With his sensitive perceptions, he could not fail to notice their paucity of courtesy, the look askance, the interchanged glances. Singularly obtuse, however, he must have seemed, for he presently ensconced himself, with a great show of consideration for his own comfort, as if for a stay of length, in the sheltered recess where the lime-burners were seated at some distance from the fire, for the heat was searching and oppressive. The heavy shadow of the cliff protected them from the sun. Below, the valley was spread out like a map. If one would have dreams, a sylvan ditty that an unseen stream, in a deep ravine hard by, was rippling out like a chime of silver bells swaying in the wayward wind came now to the ear, and now was silent, and somehow invited the fantasies of drowsing. Everything that grew betokened the spring. Even the great pines which knew no devastation of winter bore testimony to the vernal impulse, and stood bedecked with fair young shoots as with a thousand waxen tapers.

The juggler, lying at full length on the moss, his hands clasped under his head, watched their serried ranks all adown the slope, broken here and there by the high-tinted verdure of the deciduous trees. He conserved a silence that seemed unintentional and accidental, perhaps because of his unconstrained attitude and of his casual expression of countenance, since he apparently took no note of the cessation of conversation among the lime-burners which had supervened on his arrival.

Talk was soon resumed, however, curiosity becoming a factor.

"Who's 'tendin' the pertracted meetin' down yander, from Sims's?" demanded Peter Knowles, looking at Royce to intimate whom he addressed.

"Only the head of the house," responded the juggler: "Tubal Cain, the man of might, himself."

Peter Knowles still gazed at him with frowning fixity. "That thar Jane Ann Sims ain't got no mo' religion 'n a Dominicky hen," he observed.

"Well," the juggler was fain to contend in a sentiment of loyalty to the roof that sheltered him, "she is busy; she has her household duties to look after."

"Shucks, ye young buzzard! ye can't fool me!" exclaimed Tip Wrothers, in half-jocular triumph. "Don't all the Cove know ez Jane Ann Sims don't turn a hand ef Phemie's thar ter do it fur her?"

"Yaas," drawled Gideon Beck, "an' Phemie ain't got much mo' religion 'n her mammy. Jes' wunst hev she been 'tendin' on the meetin',—an' this air Thursday, an' the mourners constant, an' a great awakenin'. Phemie Sims would set the nangel Gabriel down ter wait in the passage whilst she war a-polishin' of her milk-crocks, ef he hed been sent ter fetch her ter heaven, an' she warn't through her dairy worship."

"If Mrs. Sims doesn't turn her hand, there's obliged to be somebody there to turn one. We don't have any rations of manna served out these days," argued the juggler. "It's well that somebody stays at home. Tubal Cain and I are enough church-goers for one house."

"Air you-uns a mourner?" demanded Beck, with a sudden accession of interest.

"No," answered the juggler, "though I've lots and cords to mourn over." He shifted his position with a sigh.

Wrothers and Knowles exchanged a significant glance which Beck did not observe. With a distinct bridling he said, "*I* be a perfesser. *I* hev been a perfesser fur the past ten year."

"It must be a great satisfaction," responded the juggler.

It was something, however, which he did not envy, and this fact was so patent that it roused the rancor of Beck. One of the dearest delights of possession is often the impotent grudging of him who hath not.

The juggler, despite his assured demeanor, had reverted to that sense of discomfort which had earlier beset him when he went abroad in the Cove. In the church he had marked a certain agitated curiosity as members of the congregation who had been at the "show" recognized the man who was deemed so indisputably in league with Satan. But this was merged in the fast accumulating interest of the meetings, and upon a second attendance, barring that he was here and there covertly pointed out to wide-eyed newcomers, denizens of further heights and more retired dells, his entrance scarcely made a ripple of excitement. This he accounted eminently satisfactory. It had been his intention to accustom the mountaineers to the sight of him, to have his accomplishments as a prestidigitator grow stale as a story that is told, to be looked upon as a familiar and a member of the Sims household; all this favored his disguise and his escape from notoriety and question. He had been prepared for the surprise and curiosity which the presence of a stranger in so secluded a region naturally excites. Since learning somewhat of the superstitions and distorted religious ideas which prevailed among so ignorant and sequestered a people, he could even understand their fear of his simple feats of legerdemain, and the referring of the capacity to work these seeming miracles to collusion with the devil. But altogether different, mysterious, threatening, unnerving, was the keen inimical vigilance which he discerned in Peter Knowles's eye; the sense of some withheld thought, some unimagined expectation, which might be apprehended yet not divined, roused afresh the terror of detection which had begun to slumber in the security of this haven with its new life and absolute death to the old world. As the juggler lay on his back, with his eyes fixed on that deep blue sky of May, fringed about with the fibrous pines above his head, he tried to elucidate the problem. Something alien, something dangerous, something removed it was from the fantasies of the ignorant mountaineers. But for all his keenness and his long training in the haunts of men, for all his close observation and his habit of just deduction, that thin-lipped, narrow, ascetic visage gave him no inkling what this withheld thought might be,—how it could be elicited, met, thwarted. Only one gleam of significance from the eye he interpreted, a distinct note of interrogation. Whatever the expectation might be, to whatever it might be leading, it was not devoid of uncertainty and of involuntary inquiry.

He attempted to reassure himself. He tried to argue that it was only his consciousness surcharged with its weighty secret which made him flinch when any questioning eye was turned upon him. What could this mountaineer, ignorant and inexperienced as the rest, divine or suspect,—how could he dream of the truth?

And yet, so much was at stake: his liberty, his name, his honor,—nay, the sheerest commercial honesty. And so far all had gone well! He clung now to his fictitious death as if the prospect of this existence in the Cove had not well-nigh made it real, so had his heart sunk within him at the thought of the future. He said to himself sharply that he would not be brought to bay by this clumsy schemer. Surely he could meet craft with craft. The old habit of transacting business had no doubt sufficed to keep his countenance impassive, and he would set himself to add to the little they knew circumstances of which they did not dream, well calculated to baffle preconceived theories.

"No, I'm not a mourner," he replied to Beck's sanctimonious gaze,—"not much! The kind of sinner I am goes to meeting to see the girls."

A momentary silence ensued. Not that this pernicious motive for seeking the house of worship was unheard of in Etowah Cove. There as elsewhere it was a very usual symptom of original sin. Few saints, however indurated by holiness against such perversion of the obvious uses of the sanctuary, but could remember certain soft and callow days when the theme of salvation held forth no greater reward than the occupancy of crowded back benches and the unrestricted gaze of round young eyes. It was, nevertheless, a motive so contrary to the suspicion which Knowles and Sims himself had entertained of the juggler's sojourn here and had grafted on the credulity of their cronies,—a lightsome motive, so incompatible with the grisly suggestions of murder, and flight from justice, and the expectation of capture and condign punishment,—that it could not be at first assimilated with his supposed identity as a fugitive and criminal. His sudden unaccounted-for presence here, the unexplained prolonged stay, the report of the silent preoccupied hours which he spent on the ledges over the river, fishing with an unbaited hook, the troubled silence, the answers at haphazard, the pallid languid apparition after sleepless nights, and, more than all, the agonized cries from out the feigned miseries of dreams, all tallied fairly and justified the theory built upon them. But this new element interjected so abruptly had a disintegrating subversive effect.

"Waal, ain't all the gals in the kentry mighty nigh down yander at the meetin' now?" demanded Beck.

He spoke mechanically, for he had lost sight of his effort to induce the juggler to attend upon the means of grace, if ever he had seriously entertained it, and he would not, on sober reflection, have offered this frivolous inducement as a loadstone to draw the reluctant heavenward,—let perdition seize him first!

"Plenty there, no doubt," said the juggler uncommunicatively, as if having taken counsel within himself.

Old Josiah Cobbs chuckled knowingly, as he sat on the stump of the tree which he most affected and nursed his knee. "The *right one* ain't thar,—that's the hitch! All the gals but one, an' that one wuth all the rest, hey?" He chuckled once more, thinking he was peculiarly keen-witted to spy out the secret of the juggler's indifference to prayer and praise. He perceived naught of the subtler significance of the disclosure, and easily quitting the subject he turned his head as if to listen.

The sound of the hymning rose suddenly on the breeze. From far away it was, if one must mete out the distance by the windings of the red clay road and the miles of fragrant springtide woods that intervened. But the music came straight through the air like the winged thing it is. And now it soared in solemn jubilance, and now it sank with soft fluctuations, and presently he recognized the tune and fell to humming it in unison with that far-away worship and with that air of soft pleasure in the religious cadences which one may often see in the aged, and which suggests the idea that in growing old hymns become as folk-song on the lips of the returning exile, and in every inflection is the rapture of going home.

The others neither heard nor heeded. They reminded Lucien Royce, as they were grouped around him,—some standing, some sitting or reclining on the mossy rocks in the flickering shade, but every eye fixed speculatively on him,—of that fable in many tongues wherein the beasts of the field find a sleeping man and hold a congress to determine the genus of the animal, his capacities and utilities. He looked as inadvertent as he could, and but for the jeopardy of all he held dear he might have discovered in the situation food for mirth.

Jack Ormsby, who had not spoken heretofore, sat with a great clasp-knife in his hand whittling into thin slivers a bit of the bird's-eye maple that lay prone on the ground as if it had no better uses in manufacture than to furnish fuel to burn lime. He suddenly said, regardless of the possible inference and with a certain surly emphasis, "I hev hearn tell ez Euphemia Sims air a-goin' ter marry Owen Haines."

"I don't believe it!" cried the juggler.

Swift significant glances were exchanged among the others as he pulled himself into a sitting posture and looked with challenging controversy at Ormsby. The young mountaineer seemed surprised at this direct demonstration.

"They hev been keepin' comp'ny cornsider'ble, ennyhow," he persisted.

"Let bygones be bygones," the juggler said, with his wonted easy flippancy.

Old Cobbs rejoiced in the idea of love-making in the abstract. He had not realized who was the girl whose absence apparently rendered the crowded church but a barren desert. He only apprehended that one of the disputants advanced the possibility of a future marriage which the other denied. He sided at once with conjugal bliss.

"I reckon it must be true," he urged. "Thar ain't nuthin' ter be said agin it."

"Except he's a fool!" exclaimed the juggler, with rancor.

"Ye mean 'bout prayin' fur the power?" asked Beck.

"A tremendous fool! He can't preach. He hasn't the endowment, the gift of the gab. He has no call from above or below."

Royce felt no antagonism toward the man, and he realized that they all shared his standpoint, but he was not ill pleased that he should seem to be jealously decrying Euphemia's lover.

"Phemie don't 'low he be a fool, I'll be bound," said old Cobbs. "I hev viewed a many a man 'counted a puffick idjit, mighty nigh, at the sto' an' the blacksmith shop, yit at home 'mongst his wimminfolks he be a mo' splendugious pusson 'n the President o' the Nunited States."

"I reckon Jack's right," remarked Beck. "I reckon they'll marry." This stroke, he reflected with satisfaction, cut not only the juggler, but Ormsby also, notwithstanding the fact that it was the theory advanced by the young mountaineer himself.

"I'll bet my hat they don't," declared the juggler eagerly.

This suggestion of superior knowledge, of certainty, on the part of a stranger angered Jack Ormsby, who vibrated between his red-hot jealousy of the juggler on one side and of Owen Haines on the other.

"We-uns know Phemie Sims better'n ye do!" he said, as if this were an argument despite the chameleon-hued changes of the feminine mind. "Ye never seen her till ye kem ter Etowah Cove."

"How do you know I didn't?" retorted the juggler warily. He sat leaning forward, his hat in his hand; his hair, grown longer than its wont, was crumpled on his forehead; he looked at Ormsby with a glitter of triumph in his red-brown eyes.

"Whar'd ye kem from jes' afore ye got hyar?" demanded Ormsby huskily.

"I don't know why you are so inquisitive, my son," returned the juggler, airily flouting, "but since you wish to know—from Piomingo Cove."

This was true in a literal sense. Since he had been here, and had sought, with that instinct natural to civilized people, to grasp the details of the surrounding country,—some specimens of the genus not being able to sleep until the points of the compass are satisfactorily indicated and arranged in their well-regulated minds,—he had learned that the rugged valley which he had traversed, with only another cove intervening before he reached Etowah, was Piomingo Cove. They all remembered Euphemia's recent visit there. The inference was but too plain. He had doubtless seen her at her grandmother's house down in Piomingo Cove, and, fascinated by her beauty and charm, he had followed her here. And here he lingered,—what so natural! A proud, headstrong maiden like Euphemia was not to be won in a day; and should he leave her, with Jack Ormsby and Owen Haines inciting each other to haste and urgency, were matters likely to remain until his return as they were now? Most of the lime-burners' clique never hereafter believed aught but that this was the solution of the mystery of the juggler's sojourn in Etowah Cove.

Royce went down the mountain flushed with victory. He had descried a strong and favorable revolution in popular sentiment toward him, and the duty nearest at hand was to make the illusion true and lay siege to the heart of Euphemia.

He was not concerned as to how his wooing should speed. It was only essential that it should be a demonstration sufficiently marked to justify his lingering presence here and sustain the impression which he had made on the lime-burners. He said this again and again to himself, to appease a certain repugnance which he began to experience when the idea with which he had lightly played became a definite and constraining course of action. He remembered that in reverie he had even gone so far as to canvass the disguise which marriage might afford, settling him here permanently as if he were a native, and, as time should pass, lessening daily the chance of the detection of his identity and of his life heretofore. He realized that for the next twenty years this discovery would be impending at any moment. He had a great respect for the truth as truth, and its inherent capacity for prevailing; and this led him to fear it the more. A lie has so fatal a proclivity to collapse. He had often told himself that it was the part of policy to accept life here as one of the mountaineers, content with their portion of the good things vouchsafed, the brand of undeserved shame evaded, the hardship of ignominious imprisonment eluded, the struggle of poverty reduced to its minimum in this Arcadian existence; for sometimes he realized anew, with a half-dazed sense, that the old life was indeed gone forever,—if for naught else, by reason of his financial losses in the collapse of the firm of Greenhalge, Gould & Fife.

He now stipulated within himself, however, that this was to be only a feint of love-making,—a flirtation, he would have termed it, were it to be illumined by wax candles, or the electric light, or gas, in lieu of the guttering tallow dip. He adduced with a sense of protection—and he could not forbear a laugh at himself and his sudden terrors—the certainty with which he had cause to know that the heart of the fair daughter of the miller was already bestowed on the young "crank," as he called the man "who was fool enough to pray for what he wanted." Yet for all it was to be only a mere semblance of capture, he could but be dubious of these chains with which he was about to invest himself of deliberate intention; heretofore he had fallen headlong in love and headlong out, and would not have shackled himself of his own volition. Thus he rattled Cupid's fetters tentatively, timorously, judging of their weight, and with a wish to be safely out of them as well as swiftly into them.

It was but a feint, he reassured himself. On her part, she would have an additional conquest to boast of; and as to him, all the world—of Etowah Cove—would see with what grace he would "wear the willow-tree."

"Since Phyllis hath forsaken me!" he sang airily, as he made his way down the sharp declivity.

Never in all his mental exercitations did he dream of difficulty in conveying to her intelligence an intimation of the supposed state of his heart. It had been his experience that such intimations are like spontaneous combustion: they take fire from no appreciable provocation. Nay, he had known of many wills-o'-the-wisp in this sort, suggesting flame where there was no fire, for it is a trait of the feminine creature to often overrate the power of her charms, and to predicate desolation therefrom in altogether thriving insensible hearts. But perhaps because of her absorption Euphemia took no notice of a certain change in his manner toward her, which had been heretofore incidental and non-committal and inexpressive. Mrs. Sims, however, with that alertness to which the meddler in other people's love affairs is ever prone, marked it with inward perturbation, lest it should attract the attention of Tubal Cain Sims, whose evident antagonism to the juggler she had ascribed merely to a perverse humor. From the beginning, however, Royce had found especial favor in her eyes,—at first because he was so travel-worn and rain-soaked, and fevered and exhausted. Mrs. Sims had not experienced such solicitude since her only child was an ailing infant. Although he disproved her diagnosis of his illness and her arbitrary plans of treatment by appearing fresh and well the next morning, as if he had been newly created, she forgave him his recovery, and liked him because he was so strong and handsome and pleasant-spoken, and in some vague way, to her groping inexperienced realization of the various strata of human beings, so different, and so superior, and so capable of appreciating the wonderful Euphemia that he was really to be accounted worthy of the relenting of fate which permitted him to see her. After Euphemia's return Mrs. Sims suffered a certain disappointment that the young people took such scant notice of each other in coming and going the household ways, and she was wont to console herself now and then by contemplating them furtively as they sat opposite, one on each side of the table, and fetching the fattest of her sighs to think what a handsome couple they would make! She remembered, however, as in duty bound, Owen Haines, and perhaps she drew from this consciousness deeper sighs than either of the young lovers could have furnished to any occasion. She was not so proud as Euphemia, and she thought that if the Lord visited no judgment on Owen Haines for his pertinacity in praying for the power, his fellow saints or fellow sinners—whichever they might be most appropriately called—ought to be able to endure the ten minutes wasted in the experiment to win the consent of Heaven. But she wished that her prospective son-in-law could be more practical of mind. She realized that Haines was dreamy, and that his spiritual aspirations were destined to be thwarted. They had sent deep roots into his nature, and she fancied that she could foresee the effect on his later years,—years pallid, listless, forever yearning after a spiritual fantasy always denied; forever reaching backward with regret for the past wasted in an unasked and seemingly a spurned service. Her motherly heart went out to Owen Haines, and she would fain have coddled him out of his—religion, was it? She did not know; she could not argue.

But Euphemia was her only child, and it is not necessary that the materials shall be ivory and gold and curious inlay to enable a zealous worshiper to set up an idol. Mrs. Sims looked into the juggler's handsome face with its alert eyes and blithe mundane expression, and as proxy she loved him so heartily that she did not doubt his past, nor carp at his future, nor question his motives. The fact of his lingering here so long—for he had asked only a night's lodging, and afterward had taken board by the week—occurred to her more than once as a symptom of a sentimental interest in Euphemia; for otherwise why did he not betake himself about his affairs? This theory had languished recently, since naught developed to support it.

Now when she began to suspect that this vicarious sentiment of hers on Euphemia's account was about to meet a return, Mrs. Sims's heart was all a-flutter with anxiety and pity and secret exultation. One moment she trembled lest Euphemia should mark the thoughtful silent scrutiny of which she was the subject, but when she chanced to lift her long-lashed eyes, the juggler reddened suddenly, averted his own, and drank his coffee scalding hot. Euphemia evidently was oblivious of him, and Mrs. Sims became wroth within her amiable-seeming mask, and said to herself that she would as soon have a dough child, since one could "take notice ez peart ez Phemie." Perhaps because of Mrs. Sims's superabundant flesh, which rendered her of a quiescent appearance, however active her interest, and perhaps because she did not appeal in any manner to the ungrateful juggler's hypercritical and finical prepossessions, he had no subtle intimations that she was cognizant in a degree of his mental processes, and had noted the fact of the frequent serious dwelling of his eyes, and manifestly his thoughts, upon Euphemia.

The girl had never been so beautiful as now. In these later days, that saddened pride which at once subdued and sustained her added a dignity to her expression of which earlier it would have been incapable. It spiritualized her exquisite eyes; so often downcast they were and so slowly lifted that the length of the thick dark lashes affected the observer as a hitherto unnoted element of beauty. Her eyes always had a certain look of expectation,—now starlike as with the radiance of renewing hope, now pathetic and full of shadows. It seemed to the juggler, unconsciously sympathetic, that those incomparable eyes might have conjured the man bodily into the road where they looked so wistfully to see him, so vainly.

"Confound the fellow!" he said to himself. "Why doesn't he come? I'd like to hale him here by the long hair of that tow-head of his—if she wants to see him." And his heart glowed with resentment against poor Owen Haines, who thought in his folly that a woman's "No" is to be classed among the recognized forms of negation, and was realizing on far Chilhowee all the bitterness of rejected love and denied prayers.

After a while Royce despaired of drawing her attention to himself,—he who had been in his own circle the cynosure of all youthful eyes. "There's nothing in the world so stupid as a girl in love," he moralized, irritated at last.

This state of unwilling obscurity developed in him a degree of perversity. He was prepared to assume an attitude of lowly admiration, of humble subservience, the kiss-the-hem-of-your-robe-save-for-the-foolishness-of-it sort of look which might impress her and the rest of the Sims family and all admiring spectators with the fact of how stuck full of Cupid's arrows he had now become. But no man can play the rôle of lover, however lamely, when the lady of his adoration notices him no more than a piece of furniture.

As he went through the passage one day, she happened to be there alone, tilted back in her chair against the wall, her small feet upon one of the rungs, her curls stirring in the breeze, droning laboriously aloud from the Third Reader, the pride and limit of her achievement.

"Here," he said cavalierly, reaching out and taking the book quickly from her hand, "let me show you how *I* read that."

Now elocution had been one of the versatile juggler's chief accomplishments. He read the simple stanzas in a style of much finish. His voice was of a quality smooth as velvet, and his power of enunciation had been trained to that degree that its cultivation was apparent only in the results, and might have seemed a natural endowment, so scantily was the idea of effort suggested. His special and individual capacity lay in the subtle inflections of tone, which elicited from the verses meanings hitherto undreamed-of by her. It was as if a stone had been flung into still water. Above these suddenly interjected new interpretations the circles of thought widened from one elastic remove to another, and Euphemia sat dazed in the contemplation of these diverse whorls and concentric convolutions of the obvious idea. She said nothing as he handed back the book with an elaborate ballroom bow, but gazed up at him with an absorbed, serious face, all softened and gently appealing like a bewildered child's, and then fixed her eyes intently upon the page, as if seeking to find and hold those transient illusions of fickle fancy that had glimmered so alluringly through the plain, manifest text. He left her thus as he put on his hat and stepped out upon the path leading down the slope. He glanced back once, to see her still sitting there, motionless but for the wind which swayed the fair loosely curled hair of her bent head and the folds of her faint green dress as it did the sprays of the vines on the opposite side of the passage, which grew so thick that they formed a dark background for her figure in the cool shadowy green dusk; otherwise he might not have been able to distinguish it from out the glare and glister of the open sunny space where he stood. He gazed unobserved for a moment; then he turned and went on in much dissatisfaction of spirit. It was no way, he argued within himself, to assume the character of a lovesick swain by demonstrating his superiority to the fair maiden,—to flout her poor and painful efforts by the exhibition of his glib accomplishment. "I must needs always have an audience,—be always exhibiting my various feats and knacks. I was born a juggler," he said ruefully.

But that evening when they sat at supper,—much later than usual, since the favorite Spot had wandered far into the forest, and did not return till she was sought and found and driven reluctantly home, with many pauses by the way,—the furtive glances across the table did not emigrate from his side of it. The meal was served in the main room of the cabin, to avoid the cloud of moths which the light outside in the passage would attract. In the white, languid, dispirited glow of the tallow dip the furnishings of the apartment were but dimly visible. Now and again the flicker of the wind set astir the pendent strings of pepper and bunches of dried herbs and various indiscriminate gear that swung from the beams. The red embers where the supper had been cooked were spread apart on the hearth that the heat might be lessened, and here and there through the white efflorescence of the ash only a tinge of the vermilion hues of the coals could be discerned. Despite its subdued red glare the failing fire had little irradiating effect, and added scantily to the cheer of the apartment. The batten shutter flapped back and forth with a wooden clamor; the wind had brought clouds and rain impended, and Tubal Cain Sims's corn was not yet all planted, and the ground would probably be too wet to plough for a week or more. Grum and indignant because of this possible dispensation of Providence, he sat in his shirt-sleeves, with his shock head bent, only looking up from under his grizzled shaggy eyebrows to discern in the glimmer of the candle the food he wanted, and only speaking to growl for it. The one crumb of comfort he coveted was denied him. A certain johnny-cake had burnt up "bodaciously" on its board as it baked before the fire, and it would seem that Tubal Cain Sims, from his youth up, had subsisted solely on the hope of this most dainty of rural cates, so surlily did he receive the news, and so solemnly did he demand to be told how in the name of Moses a cake that never was put near the fire, but baked by the heat thrown on the hearth, could be reduced to cinders.

"Witched somehows, I reckon," suggested Mrs. Sims easily; and since argument could not move that massive lady, Tubal Cain resorted to silent sulks, not in the vain hope of shaking her equilibrium, but for the sake of their own solace to the affronted spirit.

Although this disaster chanced within Euphemia's own jurisdiction and beneath her presidial care, she took no part in the spirited colloquy on the subject, but seemed absorbed in thought, ever and anon casting a covert look at the young man. As of late he had fallen into the habit, with the opportunity afforded at meal-times, of contemplating her with swift and furtive glances, more than once their eyes met, to the visible embarrassment of both; the juggler, to his astonishment, coloring furiously as might any country boy, and a touch of surprise and almost inquiry becoming visible in the eyes of Euphemia. Strange that so poor and primitive a contrivance as a pallid tallow dip could set such stars of radiant beauty in those long-lashed pensive orbs. They looked bewilderingly lovely to the young man as they were suddenly fixed upon him, intent with the first intimation of personal interest which he had ever discerned in their depths.

"How long hev you-uns hed schoolin'?" she demanded abruptly.

"Schooling? I? Oh yes. From the time I was six years old till I was twenty-two," he replied.

Her face was a study of amazement. "Did school keep reg'lar all them years in the cove whar you-uns lived?" she asked.

"Oh yes, school kept as regular as taxes." He had half a mind to explain that it was not always the same institution which had the honor of training his youthful faculties, and to enumerate the various gradations which had their share in his proficiency, from the kindergarten, and the grammar school, to the academic and collegiate career; but he stopped short, reflecting that this might result in self-betrayal in some sort.

Her mind was at work. Her eyes and face were troubled. "We-uns hev hed school in the Cove two years consider'ble time ago," she remarked. "They 'low the money air short, somehows."

"That ain't no differ ter we-uns," said Mrs. Sims cheerily. "Phemie l'arned all thar is ter know."

Even old Tubal Cain threw off dull care for a moment and vouchsafed a prideful refrain: "I 'lowed the chile would put out her eyes studyin' an' readin' so constant, but she hev got her eyesight and her l'arnin' too."

But Phemie's face was flushed with a sudden painful glow. "I ain't got ez much ez some," she faltered, her head drooping slightly.

In the midst of the clamor of denial of any greater possible proficiency, from the two old people, who had not heard the juggler's reading during the afternoon, she involuntarily cast upon him so appealing, so disarming a glance that for once he was ashamed to even secretly laugh at them.

"If it's erudition that goes," he said afterward, lighting his pipe under the stars and finding the grace to laugh instead at himself, "I am the learned man to suit the occasion."

* * * *

VIII.

EUPHEMIA's interest did not relax. What strange perversity of fate was it that this little clod of humanity, so humbly placed, upon the very ground of existence, as it were, should have been instinct with that high, keen, fine appreciation of learning for its own sake?—for she knew naught of its more sordid rewards, and could not have dreamed that the relative estimation of these values, even by those of happiest opportunities, is often reversed, the reward making the worth of the learning. She did not realize an aspiration. Her wings simply fluttered because she felt the impulse to rise. Royce could not have conceived of aught more densely ignorant. He had known no mind more naturally intelligent. Its acquisitiveness hardly differentiated its objects; it only grasped them. The Third Reader bade fair to become a burden. He could scarcely put his foot on the sill of the passage before he heard the flutter of its leaves, and the much-thumbed, dog-eared old volume was offered to his hand with the restrained enthusiasm of the remark, "Ye'll hev time ter read a piece afore dinner," or supper, or bedtime, as the case might be. There was a certain embarrassment in these symposia. Mrs. Sims, it is true, looked on smilingly, with her vicarious affection shining in her eyes, but a chance question developed the fact that she understood hardly one word out of ten, the vocabulary of ignorance being of most constricting limitations; while Tubal Sims openly and gruffly sneered down the performance, tossing his shock head at every conclusion, and protesting that the young man read so fast, an' with so many ups an' downs, an' with such a clippin' an' bob-tailin' of his words that it was plumb ridic'lous. For him, give him good Scriptur' readin', slow an' percise, like the l'arned men in the pul-*pit*. Did Pa'son Tynes read in that flibberty-gibberty way? He reckoned not. And he wagged his head as if he would fain take his oath on that, the spirit of affirmation so possessed him. Moreover, Royce did not consider this Third Reader a particularly meritorious compilation; he often flung its pages back and forth in vain search of a satisfactory selection, and doubtless would have declined to waste the merits of his rendering on the least vapid had it not been for the submissive, expectant face of Euphemia, as she sat waiting in her chair, bolt upright, school-wise, with her hands clasped in her lap, the subdued radiance of her eyes capable of making a much wiser man do a more foolish thing. For his own sake—he did not dream of the possibility of the development of her taste—he would fain have had a wider choice that his delicate perceptions might suffer no despite, and one day he bethought himself of the resources of memory. The young people were both down at the mill. Some domestic errand had brought Euphemia there, and he chanced to be on a ledge near at hand languidly essaying to fish. He asked her a question touching the further course of the stream and the locality of a notable fishing-ground further down. As she replied, she paused and stood expectantly in the doorway, dangling her green sunbonnet by the string.

The mill was silent, as was its wont; the afternoon sunlight glinted through the dense laurel and the sparse spring foliage of the deciduous trees; the great cliff on a ledge of which Royce was standing beetled above the smooth flow of the stream. Many a fissure broke the massive walls of stone; here herbage grew and vines swung, and the mould was moist and fragrant; the perfume of the wild cherry tree in a niche on the summit filled all the air. Close by, a great sycamore which had fallen in a storm stretched from one bank to the other: its white bark and bare branches were reflected in the clear water with wondrous fidelity; even a redbird with his tufted crest, as he fluttered and strutted up and down the white boughs, now and again uttering sharp cries of alarm; and even a nest in a crotch, and his sober-hued little brown-feathered mate with her head, devoid of any decoration in the way of unnecessary and vainglorious tufts, stretched far out in anxiety and trembling.

Euphemia pointed out these reflections in the water, and after another long pause, "Ef we-uns hed the book now, ye could read," she sighed regretfully.

He played his line negligently; he cast his eyes to the far, far sky, as if his memory dwelt on high. Then he began to recite. The wind stirred in the trees; on the dark lustrous water a shimmer of sunshine fluctuated like some ethereal golden mesh. Once, the joy of spring and the bliss of love and the buoyancy of life overcame the fear in the redbird's heart, and he sang out suddenly, as if he too would have to do with the poetry of thought and the melody of utterance, and the little brown bird in the nest listened in admiring silence. All the time Royce was conscious of Euphemia's amazed eyes on his face; when he had finished he could scarce trust himself to meet the mute rapture of her gaze. He looked down at his futile line dragging on the water, and among the sounds of the sibilantly lapsing currents and the leaves wafted by the wind he heard her long-drawn sigh of the relaxing of the tension of delight, and he turned and met her eyes with a laugh in his own in which there was only a gentle mirth.

After this he had no peace. He was reminded of the importunacy of juvenile consumers of stories, whose interest seems whetted by the incapacity to read and thus purvey romance for their own delectation. He found it conducive to his entertainment to relapse into prose, and he rehearsed many a work of fiction from memory, failing seldom of the details, but in such lapses as must needs come boldly supplying the deficit by invention. It is true that in these recitals Euphemia was debarred the graces of the style of the authors, but then the juggler thought he had a very good style of his own. All this involved long digressions, historical, geographical, astronomical, political, to explain the status of the personnel or the *locus in quo*; and while he talked her eyes never left his face. He had a habit of looking straight at his interlocutor, whoever this might be, and it was thus, perhaps, that he could with such distinctness conjure the image of those eyes of hers upon the retina of his mind at moments of darkness or absence or reverie, as he would. Much that he said she could not at first comprehend, and again he was reminded of the inquisitors of the nursery in the multitude and unsparingness of her questions; only, so searching and keen and apt were these that sometimes there was an experience of surprise and pleasure on his part.

"I tell you, Phemie," he said one day, "you are most awfully clever to have seen that."

The blood rushed to her cheeks in the joy, the triumph, of his commendation. Pride, the love of preëminence, the possession of worthy endowment,—these sentiments were her soul, the ethereal essence of her life. She had no definite ambition; she had no definite mental paths. She had groped in the primeval wildernesses of mind, as if there had been no splendid line of pioneers who had blazed out a road for all the centuries to come.

In the midst of his utter idleness, in the turmoil of his troublous thoughts, this review of the literature that had been dear to him was at first a resource and a distraction, and later it became a luxury. He began to be only less eager than she to resume the discourse where it had left off. Thus it was that he joined her in sundry domestic duties, so that while mechanically busy they might be mentally free, in Scotland, or Norway, or Russia, or on the wild, wild seas. He was wont to go with her to drive up the cows; and surely never in such company did the old fancies tread this New World soil,—knights in armor and ladies fair and all the glittering hordes of chivalry crowding the narrow aisles of the wilderness, and following hard the fairies and demons of many an antique legend. Once on the summit of a crag he looked out upon the world beyond the Cove, for the first time since his arrival here. Fair, oh, very fair it was, in the yellow haze of the declining springtide sunshine, and far it stretched in promissory lengths, like all the vague possibilities of the future. Parallel with the massive green heights near at hand ran others growing amethystine of hue, showing many a gray cliff and many a gleam of silver mountain streams winding amongst the divergent spurs and ravines and coves. Beyond lay the levels of a great valley, and here were brown stretches of ploughed fields, and here gleamed the emerald of winter wheat, and here swept the splendid free curves of the Tennessee River, flowing the color of burnished copper, so did the sunlight idealize the hue of the spring floods, between the keen high tints of the green foliage fringing its banks where the rocks failed. To the north a thousand minor ridges continued the parallelism which marks the great mountain system, and these were azure of an indescribably exquisite and languorous shade, rising into a silver haze that was itself like an illumination. And where it seemed that the limits of vision must surely be reached, the abrupt steeps of the eastern side of Walden's Ridge, stretching diagonally across the whole breadth of the State, shadowy purple, reflecting naught of the sunset, rose against the west, and there the sun, all alive with scarlet fire, was tending downward, with only one vermilion flake of a cloud in all the blue and pearly-green and amber crystal sky. He paused on the verge of the cliff and gazed at it all, while she stood and looked expectantly at him. Perhaps with her woman's intuition she divined that this moment was in some sort a crisis in his mind. She was inexplicably agitated, breathless. But as he gazed his heart did not stir the faster. Here and there he marked a brilliant slant of glitter where a steeple caught the sun, now to the north and again to the southwest, beyond a space a hand might seem to cover, but which he knew measured fifty or a hundred miles. These indicated towns. There beat the full pulses of the life he had left; and still at sight of them his heart did not plunge. He looked down at her with an expression in his eyes all new to them and which she could not interpret. Nevertheless it set her happy heart a-flutter. Nothing was said of the view, and with one accord they sat down on the verge of the cliff. His boots dangled over the sheer spaces a thousand feet below, but he could not repress a shiver at her attitude as she leaned over the brink of the precipice.

"I wish you would move farther back from the edge," he said, with a corrugated brow. "I am afraid you may slip over, you are so little, and"—

"That would put an e-end to the readings mighty quick," she said, as she still leaned over to peer down at the tops of the trees in the valley, and he turned sick and dizzy at her very gesture. He hardly dared to speak lest an unconsidered word might flutter her nerves and cause her to lose her hold. She had no intention of thus teasing his vicarious fright, but drew back presently to a safe distance. "Wouldn't it?" she asked, recurring to her remark as she executed this manœuvre.

"You mean if you should slip over into this dreadful abyss? I should never, never have the heart to read another word as long as I should live!" he protested.

He caught the look of exultant joy in her surprised and widely opened eyes for one moment, and then she turned them discreetly on the splendid vastness of that great landscape in its happiest mood. He realized that she had no difficulty in comprehending the obvious inference. Her experience as a rural beauty and belle heretofore had doubtless served to acquaint her with the hyperbole of a lover's language. There were Haines and Ormsby within his own knowledge, and he could not guess how many suitors hitherto,—confound them all! he muttered as he thought of them. He had not intended to win her heart. In view of her feeling for Owen Haines he had not deemed it possible. With the suspicion, which he would fain call realization, for it had all the importunacy of hope, he experienced a rush of elation, of soft delight, which amazed him, while it almost swept him off his feet. Had not he too fallen in love during his "readings"?—for thus they both called his recitals. He knew that he had only to look into her eyes to make his heart flutter; but then it was a susceptible heart and easily stirred. She had grown dear to him in many ways, and he had learned this even when he did not dream of other result of their companionship than the broadcast impression that he lingered here for her sake. He began to strive to separate his ideal of womanhood from those merely arbitrary values which fashion and artificial life bestow. Is it a French man milliner only who establishes the criterion of beauty? He had but to glance at the face and form beside him. She was beautiful; she was good; she was of a singularly strong and individual character; her natural mind was quick and retentive and discerning, and of a remarkable aptness. She was so endowed with a keen perception of real excellence that knowledge had but to open its doors to her, for she possessed as a gift the capacity of worthy choice. She loved with spontaneous affection those things which other people are trained to love; she seized on the best of her own devout accord, unaware of aught of significance save her own preference. She could easily acquire all he could teach her. With her quick grasp and greed of learning there would soon be little disparity. He began to meditate on the arbitrary methods of appraisement in the world. How sadly do we richly rate, not our own preference, but that which is valued by others: hence the vyings, the heart-burnings, the ignoble strife, the false pride, of many mundane miseries. He knew her real identity. Her nature would befit any station. Her beauty,—even the reference to the immutable standards of his own world could avail no detraction here,—it was preëminent. Having lived his life in one sphere, why should he, being dead to it forever, let its rigid conventionalities follow him into his new world? As to the coming years and the monotony of rounding out a long life in this narrow circuit, let the coming years take thought for themselves. For a moment the words pressed to his lips. Then he realized that this was no ordinary self-committal. To pledge himself to marry a woman of her degree in life—an ignorant mountain girl of an inexpressible rusticity and lack of sophistication, as far removed from a comprehension of the conventions in which he had been reared and the cultivated ideals still dear to him as if she were a denizen of a different planet—was a serious step indeed; he winced, and was silent.

This day marked a change. When they reached home the sky was red, and a white star was alight in the zenith. Spot stood lowing at the bars, and Mrs. Sims's dimples deeply indented her plumpness as she addressed the young people in pretended reproof.

"I sent you-uns arter Spot. From now on I be a-goin' ter sen' Spot arter you-uns."

Summoned by the sound of her chuckle out came briskly Tubal Cain, venomous with fault-finding and repining. "Hyar ye be, Euphemy Sims," he said, more harshly than he had ever before spoken to her, "a-foolin' away yer time huntin' fur a cow what war standin' at the bars sence long 'fore sundown, ez sensible ez grown folks, an' Pa'son Tynes a-settin' an' a-settin' hyar waitin' ter see ye."

Euphemia answered with an affronted coolness: "Pa'son Tynes? An' what do I keer ter see Pa'son Tynes fur?"

"Pa'son Tynes keer ter see you-uns, Phemie: that's what makes yer dad hop roun' like a pea on a hot shovel," said Mrs. Sims.

Royce began to have an illuminating sense that "Daddy Sims" was flattered to have so distinguished a guest as Pa'son Tynes, with his widespread oratorical fame, awaiting by the hour Euphemia's return, and that he could hardly forgive his idol that these precious moments had been wasted in the juggler's society. Royce perceived the farcical antithesis of the theory which he had been arguing all the afternoon, and realized that there are arbitrary gradations in less sophisticated society than that on which he had predicated the proposition. He felt very small indeed, being thus called upon to look up to Pa'son Tynes.

"I dunno what he be wantin' ter see *me* fur," said Euphemia, still with the resentment of being esteemed dilatory, and evidently apprehending a purpose in the call other than the enjoyment of her conversation.

"Me nuther," chuckled Mrs. Sims; "you-uns bein' seen a outdacious ugly gal ez all the menfolks be compelled ter shade thar eyes whenst ye kem about."

Mrs. Sims's vicarious coquetry was unblushingly fickle. She did not wait for Euphemia to be quit of the old love before she was on with the new. Nay, in the very presence of the superseded swain she prospectively and speculatively flirted with his problematic successor.

"A plague on all fat old women!" thought the juggler, ill at ease and out of countenance.

"I hev got my religion," said Euphemia stiffly, her pride revolting at the idea that perchance Pa'son Tynes had presumed her to be still

116

unconverted, and that his call was pastoral. "I *dunno what* he kin be a-comin' pesterin' round about me fur."

"Waal," said her mother, still chuckling, "he be a-comin' agin ter-morrer ter see you-uns. He axed me special ter keep ye home ter view him—no, that wasn't the way; he knows thar's better things ter be viewed in this world 'n a lantern-jawed, tallow-faced preacher-man, though from thar own account thar'll be a power o' nangels featured like that in heaven—he axed me special ter keep ye home till he could *view you-uns!*" And Mrs. Sims's chuckle of enjoyment broke from its habitual bounds and into the jolliest of obese laughter. It might have been termed infectious had any one present been sufficiently in spirits to be susceptible to its influence. The juggler was disconcerted and strangely cast down; Euphemia, doubtful, antagonistic, prophetically affronted; and old Tubal Cain's interest still hinged on the topics of the conversation during the several hours while he had borne the parson somewhat weary company.

"He hev hed great grace in the pertracted meet-in'," her father rattled on, still flustered by the occurrence. "He hev converted fifteen sinners; some hardened cases, too. An' he hev preached wunst a day reg'lar, an' sometimes twict."

"Let him go preach some mo', then," retorted Euphemia, vaguely resentful.

She was silent during the serving of supper, carrying her head high, with her cheeks flushed and her eyes alight. Royce's glance forbore to follow her. He ate little, and with a downcast, thoughtful mien he found his pipe after supper and took it out upon the rocky slope that led to the river. The moon was up; long, glamourous slants of light lay athwart the Cove; the shadows of the pines were dense along the slope, but through their fringed branches the light filtered like a shower of molten silver. The river was here touched with a crystalline glitter, and here a lustrous darkness told of its shaded depths. Looking across the levels of the Cove, one had a sense of the dew in the glister and sparkle of the humid leaves. Above all rose the encompassing mountains, imposing, dark, and stern. The little log cabin with the swaying hopvines and the window flaringly alight, and the glittering reflection so far in the swift current below, had its idyllic suggestions in the moonlight, but he was not alive to the interests of the picturesque in humble environment, and had no fibre that responded to the enthusiasm of the *genre* painter. He looked toward the house not to mark how the silver-gray hue of its weathered logs was heightened by the smooth effect of the moonbeams. He did not even feign to care that one of the clay-and-stick chimneys leaning from the wall was so awry against the sky as to give a positive value of individuality in composing; what it did in regard to the proper emission of smoke was of no consequence, since it so served the airy designs of the possible painter. He approved of the cant of the roof no more than if he had been an architectural precisian. He looked with all his eyes for what he presently saw,—a shadowy figure stole out and sat down on the step of the passage and gazed disconsolately, as he fancied, up at the moon.

"Euphemia, come down here," he called in a low voice.

She started, stared out into the mingled shadow and sheen with dilated eyes; then, as he advanced she rose and went down toward him.

As they stood there together, the girl looked out from the shadow of the tree above them at the blended dew and glimmer, and he looked imperiously down at her.

"See here, Phemie, why is that man coming to see you to-morrow?"

"I dunno," she responded vaguely.

"Ah, but you guess;" he caught both her hands. "Tell me why you think he is coming."

She lifted her eyes to his, which had a constraining quality for her. "He be kemin' ter see me—'bout—'bout Owen Haines—him—him ez prayed fur the power—I reckon. They be mighty close friends."

He gave a short laugh of ridicule.

She could not join in his mirth. Only so short a time ago its cause had been the tragedy of the world to her. She could hardly bring herself to admit even to herself that now, scarcely three weeks later, she cared as little for it as if it had never been. But her world had changed. How it had developed! There were new countries; strange peoples had been discovered; a marvelous scope of emotion had been evolved. Romance had unfolded its wondrous page. She had seen Poetry trim its pinions and wing its flight. She had lived a new life; she was a changeling. Where was her old self? Her fancied love for the young religionist, her wounded pride for his sake, her scorching, fiery compassion for her own—all had fled. She remembered herself in these emotions as if she were another being. She could hardly pity Owen Haines. If he did not care for the fleer of ridicule, why should she? For since—she had lived an enchanted life.

"What will he want of you?" demanded Royce gravely.

She faltered. She feared Tynes and his powers of argument. She dreaded, not being convinced, but the rigors of the contest. And if Owen Haines should, as a sacrifice to love, agree to relinquish his "praying fur the power," she dreaded the renewal of their old status of "keepin' comp'ny."

"He will want me ter take Owen Haines back."

"But you wouldn't, Phemie, you wouldn't?" urged Royce breathlessly.

"He mought gin up prayin' fur the power. I turned him off fur that," she hesitated.

118

Royce's scheme was complete. All the Cove and the mountain regarded him as a dangler after Euphemia Sims. He could feign a hopeless jealousy. He could hold aloof for a time, and the old status would doubtless readjust itself with the ease and security imparted by habit. He had gone as far as he had ever planned. Now he could leave the rest to chance.

But if the life here had afforded so arid a prospect heretofore, how could he contemplate it without Euphemia? His very speech no other creature could understand. He felt that he would be as isolated as if he were on a desert island, and he had a fiery impatience of time,—the years that were coming seemed such long years. He had never been more in earnest in his life, as he looked down into her beautiful illumined face.

"But you will not, Euphemia," he said, slipping his arm around her waist. "You don't love him."

Beyond a start, half surprise and half coyness, she had not moved.

"Tell me—you care nothing for him?"

"Not now," she faltered. And she felt anew a pang for her lack of constancy.

He revolted at the partial admission with all a lover's insistence on preëminence. "Never—never! You *could*n't care for such a fool. And he doesn't love you, or he would have given up that folly at once—or anything you wished."

Even now he hesitated. The breeze swayed the branches above them, and all the draping pendent wild grapevines that clung about the tree were suddenly astir. The circle of dark shadow in which they stood was inlaid with silver glintings as the moonlight struck through the foliage; the soft radiance fell full in her eyes.

"*I* would give up all the world for you," he cried impulsively, "because I love you!"

She drew back a trifle, and looked over her shoulder into the glittering idealization of the familiar scenes of her life in the glamours of the moonlight and of love. She heard the low dryadic song of the leaves; she heard the beating of her own heart.

"Tell me that you love me, Euphemia," he pleaded. "Tell me that."

Amidst all the joy in her face there was a flash of triumph. She was withdrawing her hands from his, and the realization how like she was to women of a higher sphere, despite her limitations, came to him with a certain surprise. No sooner did she feel her power than she had the will to wield it. The humble little rustic was expressed only in her outer guise. No finished coquette could have given him a more bewildering broadside of beautiful eyes as she said, joyously laughing, "What makes you ask such impossible questions?"

The phrase was borrowed of him, in his frequent despair of elucidating the whole scheme of civilization to her ignorance, in their readings. He could not laugh when it was so dexterously turned on himself. "Tell me," he persisted earnestly, "tell me, Phemie—or I'll—I'll"—the assertion had little humility, but he divined its effectiveness—"I'll go away, and never come back again."

She was still laughing, but he marked that she no longer drew back. "Do you have to be told *everything*?" she quoted anew from his remonstrances because of her catechistic insistence. "Can't you see through anything without having it point-blank?" with his own impatient intonation.

He allowed himself to be decoyed into a hasty smile. "And you'll send that fellow to the right-about to-morrow?" he urged gravely.

"Oh, I'll be glad enough ter git rid of him!" she cried, in the extremity of her relief.

He realized with a momentary qualm that the new situation must be avowed openly to justify the position which Euphemia would sustain in case Owen Haines should offer to relinquish, as a sacrifice to love, the pernicious practice of "prayin' fur the power" in public. He recognized this step as a certain riveting of his chains; yet had he not been eager but a moment ago to assume them? And even now, as he looked down into her face, radiant with that joyous sense of supremacy in his heart, and seeming to him the most beautiful he had ever seen, the most tender, as it responsively looked up to his, he wondered that his untoward fate had so relented as to bestow upon him, in his forlorn exile, this creature, so delicately endowed, so choicely gifted, that even his alien estimate of values wrought no discord in the simple happiness that had come to him.

And it was he who revealed to Jane Ann Sims the altered state of things when the two went presently back to the little cabin on the slope. There she sat in bulky oblivion of the things of this world, and especially the dish-pan. Her spectacles were awry on her nodding head. The dish-towel was limp in her nerveless hand. The tallow dip was guttering in the centre of the table, and about it the moths circled in fond delusions, regardless of the winged cinders that lay, now still, and now with a quiver of departing life, on the cloth. She made a spasmodic offer to resign the dish-towel to Euphemia, waving it mechanically at her with a fat, dimpled hand and a gesture of renunciation; but the girl, all unallured, passed without a word into the shed-room beyond, and the juggler sat down on the opposite side of the table with one elbow on it as he looked steadily across at Mrs. Sims's face, which was all lined with the creases of fat that were usually dimples. She had roused into that half-dazed condition characteristic of the sudden and unwelcome termination of the sleep of fatigue, and the tallow dip swayed reduplicated before her eyes like a chandelier. Mentally she seemed no clearer of perception. Royce had realized her maternal fondness for him, ungratefully requited, and he could not altogether reconcile this with the agitated and alarmed mien with which she received his disclosure.

"Marry Phemie!" she exclaimed in a sort of drowsy affright, as if her mental capacities had not yet laid hold on something that had roused her more alert apprehensions.

He was irritated for a moment. He knew in his secret soul that he forswore much, overlooked much, bestowed much, in this mad resolution, and this knowledge, quiescent under the immediate influence of the girl's beauty and charm and his loneliness, became tumultuously assertive in the society of Mrs. Sims.

"Why not? I love her, and I want to marry her. Is there anything so astonishing in that?"

"Laws-a-massy, no, honey!" Mrs. Sims sputtered, her eyelids faltering before the myriad-flamed tallow dip. She apprehended his rising wrath, and, somnambulistically waving her hand, seemed to seek to appease it. "Mighty nigh every young fool ez ever seen her sets up the same chune. 'Tain't astonishin'—but—honey"—she looked at him with sleepy admonition, still waving her hand—"don't talk 'bout sech so brazen an' loud." Then sinking her voice to a husky whisper that could have been heard in South America, "Shet that thar door ahint ye. Tubal Cain be asleep in thar." Her gesture, indicating the door, was accompanied by a premonitory jerk of her body which usually preceded rising.

"Don't disturb yourself, I beg," said Royce, still nettled.

He leaned back in his chair, and catching the door by the latch brought it to with a brisk bang. Mrs. Sims pursed up her mouth with a warning hiss imposing silence to preserve the gentle slumbers of old Tubal Cain, and neither noticed that the latch had failed to catch, and that the door, although apparently closed, stood slightly ajar.

"Phemie says—at least she gives me to understand that my affection is returned," Royce went on, in better humor.

"I hope she ain't tellin' no lies 'bout'n it this time, ennyhow," said Mrs. Sims waggishly; and it seemed to Royce that he was capable of singular temerity when he had risked the perils of seriously falling in love by simulating the tender passion in any instance in which Mrs. Sims was to be considered, however remotely. To be good-natured in ridicule by no means implies good nature in being ridiculed.

"You have a right to say anything you like, I suppose, about your own daughter," he rejoined angrily. "She doesn't look like a liar. For my part, I believe her."

"Shucks! Shucks!" Mrs. Sims shook a mildly admonitory head at him. "I'm jes' funnin'. An' yit I kin 'member tellin' Tubal Cain things cornsider'ble short o' the truth whenst I war a young gal like Euphemy, an' he war a-sparkin' round."

The young man looked uneasily out of the window. Could time really work such metamorphoses as these? Had she ever been young and lissome and soft-eyed and fair, and was Euphemia to grow old thus?

Perhaps it was well for the broken snatch of Love's young dream that there against the darkness he suddenly saw the bending boughs of an elder bush all whitely abloom, and among them, the fairest blossom of all, Euphemia's face, half touched with the moonlight, yet distinct in the radiance that came from the candle within, smiling upon him as she played the eavesdropper, her dimpled elbows on the window-sill and her fair hair blown back in the wind.

"Nothing was said about it till this evening," he went on, his satisfaction restored in an instant, "and I thought it was only the fair thing to let you and Mr. Sims know; you have both been so kind since I have been here."

Mrs. Sims's preliminary apprehension, which she seemed to have forgotten, was once more aghast upon her face. She raised a warning forefinger, and she spoke in her husky penetrating whisper: "Don't you-uns say nare word ter Tubal Cain Sims. Leave him ter *me*. I'll settle him."

"Why not?" asked the young man, alert to any menace, however remote.

Mrs. Sims knitted her brows in embarrassment. "Waal," she said, composing herself to divulge the truth so far as she knew it, since no polite subterfuge was handy, "he air cantankerous, an' quar'lsome, an' hard-headed, an' powerful perverse. An' he 'pears ter be sot agin ye, kase, I reckon, I like ye,—me an' Phemie, though Phemie never tuk no notice o' ye in this worl' till 'bout three weeks ago whenst ye ondertook ter set up ter her so constant. Ye hev witched that gal; ye jes' *made* her fall in love with ye, whether or no."

The juggler laughed at this, casting a bright glance at the dusky aperture of the window where the white blossoms all stirred by the wind seemed to be leaning on the sill and eavesdropping too. They might not have all been so happily at ease had they known that, close by the door, still slightly ajar, and awakened by the bang which the juggler had dealt it, lay old Tubal Cain Sims, grimly listening to this conversation.

"I can't agree to that," said Royce, after a moment's reflection. He was certainly nothing of a prig, but he had his own views of honor, and they controlled him. "This is Mr. Sims's house; and I was received into it first as a guest, and it is as a privilege that I have been allowed to remain. I can't make love to any man's daughter, under these circumstances, on the sly."

"But s'pose he won't agree—an' the critter is ez *contrary* ez—ez"—Comparisons failed Mrs. Sims, and she could only shake her head warningly.

"Oh well, everything having been aboveboard, I'd take the girl and elope!" cried the juggler, his eyes alight at the mere prospective fanning of the breeze of adventure. "Being an educated man, Mrs. Sims, I could make a living for myself and my wife in a dozen different ways, in any of these little towns about here. Why—what"—

Mrs. Sims, bulkily rising, had almost overturned the table and the crockery upon him. Her fat face was pallid and flabby, and it shook as she gazed, speechless and wild-eyed, at him. Her puffy hand besought him in mute entreaty before she could find words to blurt out, "Good Gawd A'mighty, John Leonard, don't lay yer tongue ter sech ez that! Don't s'picion the word ez ye'd steal my darter away from me. It would kill me—an' I hev stood yer frien' from the fust, even whenst they all made out ez ye war in league with Satan an' gin over ter witchments. It would kill me, bodaciously! Don't ye steal my one leetle lamb—thar's plenty o' gals in the worl', ready an' willin'—steal them—steal them! I want my darter ter live hyar with me, married an' single,—ter live hyar with me. We ain't got but the one lone, lorn leetle chile. Don't—don't"—The tears stood in all her dimples and she was speechless.

"Well, upon my word!" exclaimed Royce indignantly, but pausing, with that care which he bestowed upon all manner of possessions representing property, however meagre, to right the table and restore the imperiled crockery. "What sort of a frenzy is this, Mrs. Sims? Am I going to run away with your daughter? Have I shown any symptoms of decamping? Strikes me I have come to stay. I make a point of telling you—because I know that I am not here under your roof for any small profit to you, but as a matter of kindness and courtesy—of telling you all about it within the hour that I know it myself, and this is my reward!"

Poor Mrs. Sims, having sunk back in her chair, and the young man still remaining standing, could only look up at him with piteous contrition and anxious appeal.

"I hope Mr. Sims won't give me any reason to contemplate elopement. Wasn't he willing for his daughter to marry Owen Haines, they having been 'keepin' comp'ny,' as I understand?"

She silently nodded.

"My Lord! what have I come to!" Royce cried, lifting his hands, then letting them fall to his sides, as if calling on heaven and earth to witness the absurdity of the situation. "I think I might be considered at least as desirable a *parti* as that pious monkey praying for the power!" He gave that short laugh of his which so expressed ridicule, turned, secured the end of tallow candle placed for him on the shelf, and, lighting it, ascended the rickety stairs to the roof-room.

The suggestion of an elopement was not altogether unacceptable to him. If there should be any objection urged against him,—and he could hardly restrain his mirth at the idea,—an elopement into some other retired cove in these regions of nowhere would result not infelicitously, affording still further disguise and an adequate reason for both him and his wife to be strangers in a strange land. "A runaway match would account for everything: so bring on your veto and welcome!" he said to himself.

Next morning, however, he found his disclosure to Tubal Cain Sims postponed. His host had left the house before dawn, and although he did not return for any of the three meals Mrs. Sims felt no uneasiness, it being a practice of Tubal Cain Sims's, in order to assert his independence of petticoat government, to deal much in small mysteries about his affairs. All day—her equanimity restored by the half-jocular, half-affectionate raillery of Royce, who had roused himself to the realization that it was well to continue friends with her—she canvassed her husband's errand, and guessed at the time of his probable return, and speculated upon his reasons for secrecy. Night did not bring him, and Royce, who had been now laughing at Mrs. Sims's various theories, and now wearying of their futile inconsistencies, began to share her curiosity.

It was the merest curiosity. He did not dream that he was the chief factor in his host's schemes and absence.

IX.

TUBAL CAIN SIMS still continued to harbor the theory that the juggler's unexplained and lingering stay in Etowah Cove betokened that he sought immunity here from the consequences of crime, and that he was a fugitive from justice. In no other way could he interpret those strange words, "—But the one who lives—for his life!—his life!—his life!" cried out from troubled dreams in the silence of the dark midnight. Although this view had been shared by the lime-burners when first he had sought to enlist their prejudice, for he would fain rid his house of this ill-flavored association, of late their antagonism had flagged. Only Peter Knowles seemed to abide by their earlier impression, but Peter Knowles was now absorbed heart and soul in burning lime, as the time for its use was drawing near. Sims began to understand the luke-warmness of the others when he noted the interest of the young man in his beautiful daughter: they deemed him now merely a lover. This discovery had come but lately to Sims, for he was of a slow and plodding intelligence, and hard upon it followed the revelations he had overheard through the open door the previous evening. It was evidently an occasion for haste. While he loitered, this stranger, encouraged by the vicarious coquetry of Jane Ann Sims, might marry Euphemia; and when the juggler should be haled to the bar of justice for his crimes, the Cove would probably perceive in the dispensation only a judgment upon her parents for having made an idol of their own flesh and blood.

He realized, as many another man has done, that in extreme crises, involving risk, quondam friendships are but as broken reeds, and he was leaning stoutly only upon his own fealty to his own best interests, as he jogged along on his old brown mare, with her frisky colt at her heels, down the red clay roads of the cove, and through rugged mountain passes into still other coves, on his way to Colbury, the county town. His heart burned hot within him against Jane Ann Sims when he recalled her advice to the man to say nothing to him, the head of the house and the father of the girl! She'd settle *him*! Would she, indeed? And he relished with a grim zest, as a sort of reparation, the fright she had suffered at the bare possibility of an elopement. Then this recollection, reacting on his own heart, set it all a-plunging, as he toiled on wearily in the hot sun, lest this disaster might chance during his absence, and he found himself leaning appealingly, forlornly, on the honor of the very man whom his mission was to ruin if he could. It was he who had refused to dispense with the father's consent could it be obtained, and the perfidious Jane Ann Sims had counseled otherwise; he who had taken note of hospitality and courtesy,—much of which, in truth, had been mere seeming. More than once it almost gave Sims pause to reflect to whom he was indebted for any show of consideration. He had, however, but one daughter. This plea, he felt, might serve to excuse unfounded suspicion, and make righteous a breach of hospitality, and even justify cruelty. "One darter!" he often said to himself as he went along, all unaware that if he had had six his cares, his solicitude, his paternal affection, would have been meted out six-fold, so elastic is the heart to the strain upon its resources.

For this cause, despite his softened judgment toward the juggler, he did not flinch when he reached Colbury, and made his way across the "Square," where every eye seemed to his anxious consciousness fixed upon him, as if attributing to him some nefarious designs on the liberty of an innocent man. But in reality the town folks of Colbury were far too sophisticated in their own esteem to accord the slightest note to an old codger from the mountains,—a region as remote to the majority, save now and then for a glimpse of an awe-stricken visitor from the backwoods, as the mythical island of Atlantis. For such explorations into the world at large as the ambitious citizens of Colbury adventured led them not into the scorned rural wilds comprehensively known to them as "'way up in the Cove."

Tubal Cain Sims had been here but twice before: once when there was a political rally early after the war, and later as a witness for the defense in a case of murder. The crowded, confused, jostling political experience still thronged unintelligibly the retina of his mind's eye, but order and quiet distinguished the glimpse vouchsafed him of the workings of justice. He had evolved a great respect for judicial methods, and he felt something like a glow of pride to see the court-house still standing so spacious and stately, as it seemed to him, within its inclosures, the surrounding grass green and new, and the oak boughs clustering above the columns of the porch. He was not aware how long he stood and gazed at it, his eyes alight, his cheek flushed. If the question had been raised, he would have known, of course, that the Juggernaut car of justice had held steadily on its inexorable way through all the years that had since intervened, and that his individual lack of a use for it had not banished it from the earth; but Tubal Cain was not a man of speculation, and it smote him with a sort of gratified surprise to see the court-house on its stanch stone foundations as it was in the days when he and it conserved so intimate a relation. There were two or three lawyers on the steps or passing in at the gate, but he eyed these members of the tribe askance. The value which he placed on counsel was such confidence as he might repose in a shooting-iron with a muzzle at both ends,—as liable to go off in one direction as in the other; and thus it was that, with a hitch of the reins, he reminded himself anew of his errand, and took his way down the declivity of a straggling little street, where presently the houses grew few and small, dwindling first to shabby tumble-down old cottages, then to sundry dilapidated blacksmith shops, beyond which stretched a rocky untenanted space, as if all habitation shrunk from neighboring the little jail which stood alone between the outer confines of the town and the creek.

Here also he came to a halt, looking at the surly building with recognizing eyes. And to it too these years had not been vacant. All the time of his absence, in the far-away liberties of the mountains, with the unshackled wind and the free clouds and the spontaneous growths of the earth out of its own untrammeled impulse, this grim place had been making its record of constraints, and captives, and limits, and locks, and longing bursting hearts, and baffled denied eyes, and yearning covetings of freedom, the bitterness of which perhaps no free creature can know. Surely, surely, these darkening elements of the moral atmosphere had turned the bricks to their dingy hue. The barred windows gave on vague black interiors. A cloud was in the air above, with now and then a mutter of thunder, and the sullen jail lay in a shadow, and the water ran black in the green-fringed creek at the foot of the hill, while behind him at its summit, where the street intersected the open square, the sunlight fell in such golden suffusions that a clay-bank horse with his rider motionless against the blue sky beyond might have seemed an equestrian statue in bronze, commemorating the valiance of some bold cavalry leader. Tubal Cain wondered to see the jail so still and solitary; and where could be the man whom he had pictured sitting in all the luxury of possession on the front doorsteps, smoking his pipe?

This man of his imagination was the sheriff of the county, who did not avail himself of his privilege to appoint a jailer, but turned the keys himself and dwelt in his stronghold. He was of an over-exacting cast of mind. He could never believe a prisoner secure unless with his own hands he had drawn the bolts. On account of the great vogue attained by various crimes at this period, and the consequent overcrowding of the prisons throughout the State, a considerable number of captured moonshiners had been billeted on the Kildeer County jail while awaiting trial in the Federal Court, and by reason of this addition to his charge his vigilance was redoubled. In all the details of his office he carried the traits of a precisian, and was in some sort a thorn in the side of the more easy-going county officers with whom his official duties brought him into contact. Even the judge in his high estate on the bench was now and again nettled by the difficult questions of punctilio with which this servant of the court could contrive to invest some trifling matter, and was known to incline favorably to the salutary theory of rotation in office,—barring, of course, the judicial office. But the sheriff had three minie balls in him which he had collected on various battlefields in the South; and although he had fought on a side not altogether popular in this region, they counted for him at the polls in successive elections, without the formalities of statutory qualifications and with a wondrous power of reduplication in the number of resulting votes. He was reputed of an extraordinary valor on those hard-contested fields where he had found his bullets, but there were advanced occasionally caviling criticisms of his record on the score that, being incapable of originating a course of action, it never occurred to him to run away when his command was ordered to advance, and that his bravery was simply the fixed stolidity of adhering to another man's idea in default of any ideas of his own. In proof of this it was cited that when he was among a guard detailed to hold a gin-house full of cotton, and the enemy surprised the sentinel and captured the building, he alone stood like a stock with his rifle still at a serene "shoulder-arms," where it was ordered to be, while his comrades undertook a deploying evolution of their own invention at a mad double-quick, without a word of command, showing the cleanest of nimble heels across the country. But he was esteemed by these depreciators a lucky fool, for since the war, having an affinity for the office of sheriff, he had more than once been obliged to decline to make the race, and lie off a term or two, because of the law which will not permit the office to be held by the same person eight years without an interval. His fad for being in the direct line of the enemy's fire had not resulted more disastrously than to give him some painful hospital experience; the balls had come to stay, and apparently the hard metal of his constitution served to assimilate them easily enough, for he was hale and hearty, and bade fair to live to a green old age, and they never made themselves heard of save at election times, when in effect they stuffed the ballot-box.

Having voted for him so often, and with that immense estimate of the value of a single ballot common to the backwoodsman little conversant with the power of numbers, Tubal Cain Sims felt a possessory claim on the sheriff as having made him such. He stood in dismay and doubt for a moment, gazing at the stout closed door that opened, when it opened at all, directly on the descending flight of steps, without any ceremonial porch or other introduction to entrance; then, after the manner of Etowah Cove, he lifted up his voice in a stentorian halloo and hailed the grim and silent house.

The sound seemed a spell to waken it into life. The echo of his shouts came back from the brick walls so promptly as to simulate two imperative voices rather than acoustic mimicry. Sudden pale faces showed at the bars, wearing the inquiring startled mien of alarm and surprise. The rattle of a chain heralded the approach of a great guard-dog dragging a block from around the corner. With his big bull-like head lowered and his fangs showing between his elastic lips, he stood fiercely surveying the stranger for a short time; then—and Tubal Cain Sims could have more readily forgiven a frantic assault, for he had his pistol in his hand—the sagacious brute sat down abruptly, and continued to contemplate the visitor, but with a certain air of non-committal curiosity, evidently realizing that his vocation was not to deter people from getting into jail, but to prevent them from getting out. The pallid faces at the windows were laughing, despite the bars; and although nettled by the ridicule they expressed, Tubal Sims made bold to lift up his voice again: "Hello, Enott! Enott Blake! Lemme in! Lemme in, I say! Hello, Enott!"

The faces of the spectators were distended anew. At those windows where there was more than one, they were turned toward each other for the luxury of an exchange of winks and leers. When a face was alone it grinned jocular satisfaction to itself, and one man, with a large red and facetious countenance, now and again showed a lifted hand smiting an unseen leg, in the extremity of solitary joy. The dog, with his big head still lowered and his drooping lips a-quiver, gave a surly growl of displeasure, when the colt, having somewhat recovered from the fatigues of its long journey, began to frisk nimbly, and to curvet and caracole; the mare turned her head anxiously about as she watched these gyrations. Tubal Cain glared at the men at the windows. They had little to laugh at, doubtless, but why should they so gratuitously laugh at him? A tide of abashed mortification carried the blood to his head. His stanch self-respect had heretofore precluded the suspicion that he was ever the object of ridicule, and now his pride revolted at his plight; but since he could not get at his mockers and inflict condign punishment, naught remained but to manfully persist in his course as if they were not. He dismounted, threw the reins over a hitching-post, advanced through the gate of the narrow yard, his pistol in his hand for fear of the formidable dog, and ascended the steps with a resolute tread. He dealt a resounding double-knock with the butt end of his shooting-iron, crying as he did so upon Enott Blake as a "dad-burned buzzard" to unlock the door or he would break it down. Suddenly it opened, and by the force of his expectant blow he fell forward into the hall; then it closed behind him with a bang that shook the house.

"What does this mean?" exclaimed an irate voice. "Jeemes, take his weepon."

And albeit Tubal Sims stoutly held on to it, a scientific crack on the knuckles administered by a dapper light-haired young man caused the stiff old fingers to relax and yield the pistol to the custody of the law.

Tubal Sims confronted a tall, spare, vigorous man about fifty-five years of age, with iron-gray hair worn with a certain straight lank effect and parted far on the side, a florid complexion, and a bright yellowish-gray eye which delivered the kind of glance popularly held to resemble an eagle's. His look was very intent as he gazed in the twilight of the grimy hall at Tubal Cain Sims, who began to feel a quiver at the lack of recognition it expressed. To be sure, Tubal Sims knew that he had no acquaintance with the man, but somehow he had not counted on this total unresponsiveness to his claim upon the officer.

"I hev voted fur you-uns fur sher'ff nine time out'n ten," he said, with the rancor of reproach for benefits conferred unworthily.

He stood with a very large majority of the enlightened citizens of the county. Enott Blake had been but recently reëlected, but if his canvass were to be made anew it is barely possible that he would have fancied he might have weathered it without the support of this ancient adherent. His office was of the sort which is not compatible with any show of personal favor, and he resented the reminder of political services as an imputation.

"Well, ye have got a sheriff that knows what attempted house-breaking is," he said severely. "And unless ye can show a good reason for tryin' to break into that door, ye'll find ye have got a sheriff that will take a power o' pains ye don't break out again soon."

Tubal Cain's face, all wind-blown and red with the sun, and rugged with hard grooved wrinkles, and nervous with the untoward complications of achieving an audience with the man he had ridden so far to see, was shattered from the congruity of his gravity into a sort of fragmentary laughter out of keeping with the light of anxiety in his eyes.

"Did ye ever hear of a man tryin' ter break inter a jail?" he demanded.

"I caught you doin' it to the best of your ability," returned the literal-minded sheriff.

Tubal Cain would have felt as if he were dreaming had it not been for sundry recollections of stories of the matter-of-fact tendencies of the officer which were far from reassuring. He felt that he could hardly have faced the situation had not the dapper round-visaged young deputy, whose blond hair curled like a baby's in tendrils on his red, freckled forehead, glanced up at him with a jocose wink as he proceeded to draw the cartridges from the mountaineer's shooting-iron; the triumph of capture was still in his eye, while he lounged carelessly over the banisters of the staircase to evade the responsibility and labor of standing upright.

"Own up, daddy," he cavalierly admonished the elder. "Tell what you were aimin' to do. To rescue prisoners"—his superior snorted at the very word—"or rob us of our vally'bles?" The sheriff turned upon the deputy with a stare of inquiry as if wondering what these might be; then, vaguely apprehending the banter, said severely:—

"Cuttin' jokes about your bizness, Jeemes, so constant, makes me 'feard it's a leetle bit too confinin' for such a gay bird as you. Bar-keepin' in a saloon would fit your build better'n the sort o' bar-keepin' we do here, I'm thinkin'."

Enott Blake might be laughed at on occasion, but he had a trick of making other men as serious as himself when he sought to play upon their foibles. The blond deputy's countenance showed that it had another and deeper tinge of red in its capacity; he came to the perpendicular suddenly as, without lifting his eyes, he continued to revolve the cylinder of the pistol and to draw the cartridges seriatim. He was but newly appointed, and zealous of the favor of his superior.

"I dunno how I could bear up, though," he said, with apology in the cadence of his voice, "if I didn't crack a joke wunst in a while, considering I'm just broke into harness."

"That's a fact," admitted the martial elder, visibly and solemnly placated. "Do you know what we were doin' while you yelled, an' capered, an' cut up them monkey-shines in front of the jail?" he demanded sternly, turning to Tubal Cain Sims. "We were cuttin' a man down that tried to hang himself."

"Suicidin'," put in the deputy, as if making a nice distinction between this voluntary suspension and the legal execution.

"An' we were bringin' the man to himself agin."

"He's crazy, crazy as a loon," interpolated the deputy in a mutter, pulling the trigger and snapping the hammer of the empty weapon, and sighting it unpleasantly down the hall, aiming alternately at the sheriff and at Tubal Cain Sims, who could scarcely repress an admonition, but for awe's sake desisted.

"Or more likely, simulatin' insanity," said the sheriff; "it's plumb epidemic nowadays 'mongst the crim'nals."

"Well, he come mighty nigh lightin' out for a country where no vain pretenses avail," remarked the loquacious deputy, one eye closed, and drawing a very fine line from the bridge of old Sims's nose with the empty pistol.

"This is a country where they don't avail, either," retorted the sheriff, "not with any reasonable jury. And twelve men, though liable to be fools, ain't fools o' the same pattern. That's the main thing: impanel a variety o' fools, an' the verdic' is generally horse sense. Now, sir," turning on Tubal Cain Sims, who could feel his hat rising up on his hair, "what do you want, anyhow?"

"Ter git out,—that's all; ter git out o' hyar!" exclaimed Tubal Sims, sickened with a ghastly horror of the presentment of the scene they had left, the walls that harbored it, the roof that sheltered it. Oh for the free pure mountain air, the wild untrodden lengths of the mountain wilderness, fresh with the sun and the dew, and the vigor of natural growths, and the sweet scent of woodland ways! As he cast up his eyes to the high window above the staircase he could have cried out aloud to see the bars, and he gazed at the door in a desperation that started the drops on his brow and brought the blood to his face, as if the intensity of his emotion had been some strong physical effort.

"What did you get in here for, then?" demanded the sheriff. "Most folks have to be fetched."

Tubal Cain Sim's heart failed him. Could it be possible that he had ever designed a fate like this for the man who had slept under his roof; who had eaten his bread; who had refused to maintain secrecy against him; who considered him and his claims, when his own, his very own, passed them by? He could not realize it. He refused to credit his cherished scheme; he felt that if once away from the paralyzing sight of the place, invention would rouse itself anew. Some other device would serve to rid the Cove of the man, and to frustrate his elopement with Euphemia. Tubal Sims was sure he could compass a new plan if once more he were free in the clear and open air.

The eagle eye of the sheriff marked the alert turning of Sims's head toward the door. "What did you come here for, then?" he again demanded.

With hot eyes glancing hither and thither like a wild thing's in a trap, Tubal Sims replied, with the inspiration of the moment, "I wanted ter view the man I hev voted fur so often an' so constant."

Now, the sheriff, like many other great men in their several places, had his vanity, and it is not hard to convince one who has been before the public eye that he fills that orb to the exclusion of any less worthy object. That Tubal Cain Sims should have journeyed fully thirty-five miles from the mountains to contemplate the resplendent dignity of the sheriff in his oft-resumed incumbency seemed possibly no disproportionate tribute to Enott Blake's estimate of his own merits. But this view, however flattering, was hardly compatible with the lordly manner in which the old mountaineer had beaten upon the door of the jail, and the imperative tones with which he had summoned forth the servant of the public who owed his high estate to the suffrages of him aided by the likes of him.

A wonderful change is wrought in the moral atmosphere of a man by the event of an election. The candidate's estate is vested by the announcement of the result. He owns his office for the time, and he breathes a free man. It is interesting to see how the muscles of his metaphorical knees straighten out, for the day of genuflection is over. Independence is reasserted in his eye; he bears himself as one who conquers by the prowess of his own bow and spear; and men whom he would fain conciliate last week need to search his eye for an expression they can recognize. They will be treated no more to that mollifying demonstration, the candidate's smile.

The defeated aspirant's once bland countenance, however, has assumed all the contours of the cynic's. A bitter sort of nonchalance with a frequent forced laugh goes better combined with peanuts, if the place is not too high in the official scale and the candidate of no great social pretensions, since the hulls can be cast off with a flouting gesture which aids the general implication that the constituency may appropriately go hang, for all he cares. He is not hurt,—not he! He made the race to oblige his friends and party, and he now and again throws out intimations of a bigger piece of pie saving for him as a reward for filling the breach. Meantime peanuts perforce suffice.

Enott Blake, through much place-holding, had become imbued with the candidate's antagonism to that assumption of all the power residing in the voting masses common to the arrogant but impotent unit. He was never elected by any one man, nor through any definitely exerted political influence. He served the people, and incidentally his own interest, and mighty glad they ought to be to get him, and this was what he felt especially after elections. If ever in the course of a canvass he had a qualm,—and it is said that the least imaginative of men are capable of nightmare,—he had the satisfaction of calling himself a fool thereafter, to think less of himself than people thought of him, and of counting endearingly his minie balls. He was a rare instance of a great personal popularity, and he had no mind to abate his pretensions before the preposterous patronage of this old mountaineer who possibly had not paid poll-tax for twenty years. He could no more be said to possess an enlightened curiosity than the hound trained to trail game could be accredited with an inquisitive interest in the natural history of the subject of his quest. It was only with a similar rudimentary instinct of the pursuit of prey that he felt stirring an intention to wring from the intruder the real reason for this strange entrance.

"No, no, my friend," he said, with a kindling of his keen eye which expressed a degree of ferocity, "you can't come it that-a-way on me. I'm a mighty fine man, I know, but folks ain't got to sech a pass yet as to break into jail for a glimpse of me. You don't get out of that door"—he nodded his head at it—"till you give me a reasonable reason for your extraordinary conduc'."

Tubal Cain Sims was silent. His hard old lips suddenly shut fast. His eyes gleamed with a dogged light. He would not speak had he no will to speak, and the officer should see which could hold out the longest at this game. He remembered how often he had hearkened to the complaints of the preternatural quality of his obstinacy with which Jane Ann Sims had beguiled the conjugal way since, a quarter of a century ago, they had left the doorstep of Parson Greenought's house man and wife. Surely, if it had time and again vanquished Jane Ann Sims, how could the sheriff, a mere man, abide it? He had not, however, reckoned on certain means of compulsion which were not within the power of the doughty contestant for domestic supremacy.

There was no visible communication between the older officer and the deputy when the young man said appealingly, "Ye won't need handcuffs, Mr. Blake? Leastwise not till after we come from the jestice's?"

"Handcuffs!" screeched Tubal Sims, as violently cast out from the stronghold of his obstinate silence as if he had been hurtled thence by a catapult. "Ye hev got no right to handcuff me! I kem hyar of my own free will an' accord. I ain't no prisoner. Open that thar door," he continued, lowering his voice to a tone of command and turning majestically to the sheriff. "Open that door, or I'll hev the law of ye."

"Not till I have had the law of you," replied the imperturbable functionary. "But, Jeemes,"—he turned with a disaffected aside to his young colleague,—"what d'ye go namin' irons for? 'Tain't polite to talk 'bout ironin' a man old enough to be your father."

The deputy looked about in vague despair. He had but sought the effect upon the imagination of the mention of shackles, and indeed his words had potently affected the fancy of the only man in the room who possessed that illusive pictorial faculty. The stanch old mountaineer was all a-tremble. What would Jane Ann Sims think of this? He might have known that this journeying abroad in secret and without her advice would result disastrously! What indeed would Jane Ann Sims think of this?

"Open that door!" he vociferated. "Ye hev got no right ter detain ME!"

"What for not?" demanded the sheriff sternly. "What d'ye call this fix'n'?" He opposed to Tubal Cain Sims's nose, with the trifling intervenient space of an inch, his own pistol.

"Shootin'-iron!" sputtered Tubal, squinting fearfully at it.

"Worn in defiance o' the law and to the terror o' the people," said the sheriff frowningly. "I have got to be indicted myself or to arrest you on that charge. And I reckon you know you ain't got no right to carry concealed weapons."

"Ain't got no right ter w'ar a shootin'-iron!" exclaimed Tubal Sims, his eyes starting out of his head.

"Agin the law," said the deputy airily.

"Agin the law!" echoed Tubal Sims, his back against the wall, and his eyes turning first to one, then to the other of his companions. "Lord! Lord! I never knowed afore how fur the flat-woods war abint the mountings! How air ye goin' ter pertec' yerself agin yer neighbor 'thout no shootin'-iron?" he asked cogently.

"By the law," said both officers in unison.

"Thar ain't no law in the mountings, thank Gawd!" cried Tubal Sims.

"There is law here," declared the sheriff, "and a plenty of it to go round."

"Thank Gawd!" echoed the pious deputy.

"Come, old man!" said the sheriff. "Come in here an' set down, an' sorter straighten out, an' tell me what in hell ailed ye to come bangin' on the jail door with a weepon called a shootin'-iron till you git yourself arrested for crim'nal offense. Surely, surely, you have got *some* reason in you."

He flung open a door close at hand, and Tubal Cain Sims, his knees trembling under him, so great was the nervous reaction in his metamorphosis from the masterful accuser to the despairing accused, was ushered into a room which seemed to him dark despite the glare of sunlight that fell broadside half across the bare floor from two tall windows,—a gaunt and haggard apartment suggestive of the intention of the building of which it was a part. These windows were not grated, but the fleckings of moving clouds barred the sunlight on the floor, and the mutter of thunder came renewed to the ear. The dust lay thick on the table in the centre of the room. A lounge covered with a startlingly gay quilt was in one corner, where Tubal Cain presumed the sheriff, in moments of fatigue which might be supposed to overpower even his stiff military figure in the deep midnight, slept with one eye open. A desk in the jamb by the fireplace held several bulky books, a large inkstand, a bag of fine-cut tobacco, a coarse glass tumbler which had nothing in it but a rank smell of a strong grade of corn whiskey, and a pipe half full of dead ashes, which the sheriff had hastily laid aside when summoned to the scene of the horrors perpetrated by a forlorn human being in the desperation of the fear of still greater horrors to come.

Tubal Cain Sims's mind, unaccustomed to morbid influences, could not detach itself from the idea. Despite his absorptions on his own account, he followed as an independent train of thought futile speculations as to where in the building this man might be,—close at hand, and he felt a nervous thrill at the possible propinquity, or in some remote cell and out of hearing; what had he guiltily done, or was he falsely accused; had he been really resuscitated, or had the potentialities of life merely

135

flickered up like the spurious quickening of a failing candle before the moment of extinction, and was he even now, while the officers lingered here, dead again, and this time beyond recall; or would he not, left to his own devices, once more attempt his life? The old mountaineer could not forbear. He turned to the sheriff with an excited eye.

"Ain't ye 'feard he'll hang hisself again?" he said huskily.

The officer stared. "Who?" he inquired, with knitted brow, as if he had forgotten the occurrence absolutely; then with renewing recollection, "You can bet your life he won't."

"Why not?" asked Sims, the clatter of his boots on the bare floor silent as he stopped short.

The deputy gave a fleering laugh, ending in a "ki-yi" of the extremity of derision. He had flung himself into a chair, and, with his elbows on the table, looked up with a scornful grin at Tubal Cain Sims, who seemed to entertain solicitude as to the capacities for management and discipline of Enott Blake, famous as the veriest martinet of a drill-sergeant years before he ever saw the inside of Kildeer County jail.

This absurd officiousness, however, met with more leniency from the sheriff. Whether it was that, from his steady diet of commendation, his vanity could afford to dispense with such poor crumbs as Tubal Cain Sims might have it in his power to offer, or whether he was desirous of the emollient effects of indulgence to loosen his visitor's tongue, he apparently took no heed of this breach of the proprieties.

"He's all right now. You needn't have no anxiety 'bout him," he said, as if it were a matter of course to be brought to book in this way.

"He can't hurt himself nor any one else now," echoed the deputy, taking his cue.

Sims turned from one to the other inquiringly.

"Got him in a cage," said the sheriff grimly.

For one moment Tubal Cain Sims silently cursed his curiosity that had elicited this fact for his knowledge and provision for future nightmares. It was of the order of things that sets the natural impulses of humanity and sympathy adverse to all the necessities of law and justice. He stared at the two officers, as if they were monsters. Perhaps only his weapon, empty in the deputy's pistol-pocket, persuaded his apparent acquiescence.

"Good Lord!" he gasped, "that's powerful tur'ble,—powerful tur'ble!"

The sheriff was no mind-reader. He deemed that the allusion applied to the unjudicial hanging.

"Not so very," he said, seating himself in a splint-bottomed chair, and elevating his boots to the topmost bar of the rusty, fireless grate. "'Tain't nigh so bad as havin' 'em fire the jail," he added gloomily. "They have played that joke on me five times. All this part o' the buildin' is new. Burnt spang down the last time we had a fire."

"Take a chair, sir, take a chair," said the conformable deputy, perceiving that politeness had come to be the order of the day.

Tubal Sims, almost paralyzed by the number and character of the new impressions crowded upon his unaccustomed old brain, still stood staring from one to the other, his sunburned, grooved, lank-jawed face showing a sharp contrast with his shock of tow hair, which, having been yellow and growing partially gray, seemed to have reverted to the lighter tint that it had affected when he came into the world. His hat was perched on the back of his head, and now and then he reached up to readjust it there; some subtle connection surely exists between the hat of a man and his brain, some obscure ganglion, for never does embarrassment beset his intellect but the solicitous hand travels straight to the outer integument. His creased boots moved slowly forward with the jeans-clothed continuations above them. He doubtfully seized on the back of a chair, and, still gazing from one to the other of his companions, deposited himself with exaggerated caution on the stanch wooden seat as if he half expected it to collapse beneath him.

"Now," said the sheriff smoothly, "you are a sensible man, I know, an' I wish you well."

"How 'bout that thar pistol?" said Tubal Cain Sims, instantly presuming upon this expression of amity.

"I didn't make that law," said Enott Blake testily. "But I'm here to enforce it, and you'll find that I know my duty an' will do it."

Tubal Sims relapsed into his friendless despair. And once more the deputy essayed a new device.

He turned his round, red, freckled, good-natured face full upon the visitor across the table, and, pushing back his black hat from the blond tendrils that overhung his forehead like an overgrown infant's, he said, fixing a grave blue eye upon Tubal Sims, "You came here to tell us about some crime you've s'picioned."

The sheriff plucked up his faculties as if an inspiration had smitten him. "You were going to give us the names an' fac's as far as you knew or they had developed," he followed hard on the heels of the pioneering deputy.

"You caved after you got here, 'cause you wished the man no harm, and the sight o' the jail sorter staggered you," pursued the subordinate.

"But you had some personal motive," interjected the sheriff, suddenly solicitous for the verisimilitude of the sketch of the interior workings of Tubal Cain's astounded intellect. "It has to be a mighty plain, open case, with no s'picion 'bout it, when information ain't got some *personal* motive,—justifiable, maybe, and without direct malice, but *personal* motive."

Tubal Cain Sims's head turned from one to the other with a pivotal action which was less suggestive of muscles than of machinery. His eyes were starting from beneath his shaggy, overhanging eyebrows. His lower jaw had dropped. Thus dangled before him, his own identity was as recognizable to him as to their divination. If he had had time to think, there might have seemed something uncanny in this facile meddling with the secrets of his inner consciousness, hardly so plain to his own prognosis as in their exposition, but moment by moment he was hurried on.

"Your personal motive in giving this information," continued the deputy, "is because you are afraid of the man."

"Not for myse'f," blurted out Tubal Sims. "Before Gawd, I'll swear, not for myse'f." He was all unaware of an impending disclosure of the facts that he had resolved to hide, since the horrors of the jail, the true, visible presentment of the abstract idea of imprisonment, had burst upon his shuddering realization. He had forgotten his caution. His obstinate reticence relaxed. All the manhood within him roused to the alarm of the possibility that these officers should impute to him fear of any man for his own sake. He lifted a trembling, stiffened old hand with a deprecatory gesture. "Jes' one—jes' one darter!" He lowered his voice in expostulation.

"One daughter!" echoed the sheriff in surprise.

"Gittin' interestin'," murmured the flippant deputy.

"An' this hyar man wants ter marry her, an' she is willin' ter marry him, an'—an' he spoke of runnin' away." Tubal Cain Sims brought this enormity out with a sudden dilation of the eyes irresistible to the impudent deputy.

"Powerful painful to the survivors!" he snorted in a choking chuckle, "but not even a misdemeanor agin the law o' the land."

The sheriff's countenance changed. Not that he apprehended any cause for mirth, for it might be safely said that he had not laughed at a joke for the past six years, and it would have been a matter of some interest to know how he appraised the cachinnation habitually going on all around about him, and which he was temperamentally debarred from sharing. His face merely took on a perplexed and keenly inquisitive expression as he bent his brow as to a worthy mystery.

"You know a man can't be arrested for runnin' away with a young woman an' marryin' her," he expostulated. "You ain't such a fool as to think you can take the law to him to prevent that."

There are few people in this world who do not arrogate to themselves special mental supremacy. Folly is like unto the jewel in the forehead of the toad in that the creature thus endowed is unaware of its possession. Tubal Cain Sims had perceived subacutely the acumen of both the officers, and was emulous of demonstrating his own intellectual gifts. The word "fool" is a lash that stings, and, smarting, he protested:—

"The law would purvent it mighty quick by not waitin' fur him, ef he hed commit crimes."

"What'd he ever do?" demanded the sheriff incredulously. And the deputy sat very still and silent.

Now, the peculiarity of being literal-minded has special reference to exoteric phenomena introduced for mental contemplation, but is easily coexistent with the evolution of an esoteric train of ideas, the complication of which is nullified by familiarity incident to their production. The sheriff was a plain man, a serious-minded man, who could not see a joke when it was before his nose; so literal-minded a man that because he never perceived the latent scheme of another, he himself was never suspected of scheming.

"What'd he ever do?" he repeated, and it did not occur to Tubal Cain Sims that he had not yet mentioned the juggler's name, nor so much as suggested his own or the locality whence he came.

"I ain't keerin' ter know *whut* he done!" he asseverated, led on by the non-compliant look of the other. "I *know* he done *somewhut*; an' Phemie ain't goin' ter be 'lowed ter marry no evil-doer an' crim'nal agin the law."

The pause that ensued was unbroken, while the thunder rolled anew, and the dashing of the water of the surly black creek at the foot of the hill came to their ears. The sunshine on the floor faded out suddenly and all at once, and the murky gray light was devoid of any lingering shimmer. If the deputy breathed, he did not hear the heaving of his own chest, so still he was.

The sheriff, having allowed in vain a goodly margin for continuance, went on abruptly: "That's the way you fellows, with no sense of the obligations of the law, carry on. You have got no information to give. You have got some personal motive, an' that's the way to get an officer into trouble,—false arrests an' charges of stirrin' up of strife an' such like,—an' it's personal motive always. I'll bet this man o' yourn ain't committed no crime," and he turned his calm gray eyes on Tubal Cain Sims, seated in the midst of his consciousness of a fool errand to the great county town. Mortified pride surged to his face in a scarlet flood, and vehement argument rose to his lips.

"Why can't he sleep quiet nights in his bed, then?" he retorted. "Why do he holler out so pitiful, fit ter split yer heart, in his sleep. 'What can I do? For his life!—his life!—his life! Oh, what can I do—for his life!—his life!—his life'?"

The wind came surging against the windows with a sudden burst of fury, and the sashes rattled. As the gust passed to the different angles of the house, the sound of other shaking casements came from the rooms above and across the hall, dulled with the distance, till a single remote vibration of glass and wood told that even in the furthest cells the inmates of this drear place might share the gloomy influences of the storm, though fair weather meant little to them, and naught the sweet o' the year. A yellow flash, swift and sinister, illumined the dull, gray room, that reverted instantly into gloom, and, as if the lightning were resolved into rain, the windows received a fusillade of hurtling drops, and then their dusty, cobwebbed panes were streaked with coursing rivulets mingling together here and there as they ran.

The sheriff sat silently awaiting further disclosures, his eyes on the window, his guarded thoughts elsewhere. "The same words every night?" he asked at last.

"The same words every night," repeated Tubal Cain reluctantly, as if making an admission.

"Oh, you can't arrest a man for talking in his sleep," put in the deputy, with the air of flouting the whole revelation as a triviality; and he yawned with much verisimilitude, showing a very red mouth inside and two rows of stanch white teeth. "I ain't sech a fool ez that, Mr. Dep'ty," snarled Tubal Sims raucously; "but puttin' sech ez that tergether with a pale face an' blue circles round the eyes, in the mornin', o' the stronges', finest-built, heartiest young rooster I ever seen in my life,—he could fling you or the sher'ff from hyar clean acrost that creek,—an' layin' on the ruver-bank day arter day fishin' with no bait on his hook"—

"What'd he catch?" queried the deputy, affecting anxious eagerness.

"All he expected, I reckon," retorted Sims. "A-layin' thar, with his hat over his eyes, day arter day; an' his eyes looked ez tormented ez—ez a deer I shot wunst ez couldn't git up ter run an' couldn't hurry up an' die in time, an' jes' laid thar an' watched me an' the dogs come up. An' this man's eyes looked jes' like that deer's,—an' I never let the dogs worry him, but jes' whipped out my knife an' cut his throat."

The deputy's eyes widened with pretended horror. He snatched a pair of handcuffs from the drawer at the side of the table, and, rising, exclaimed dramatically, "You say, in cold blood, you whipped out your knife and cut the man's throat!"

"Ye think ye air powerful smart, Mr. Dep'ty," sneered Sims, out of countenance, nevertheless. "But thar ain't much credit in baitin' an' tormentin' a man old enough ter be yer father," remembering the sheriff's rebuke on this score, and imputing to him a veneration for the aged.

"Yes, stop that monkeyin', Jeemes," Blake solemnly admonished his junior. Then, after silently eying the rain still turbulently dashing against the windows, he said reflectively, "Don't ye think, Mr.—Mr.—I disremember your name?"

"Sims,—Tubal Cain Sims," replied the owner of that appellation.

"Oh yes; Mr. Sims. Don't you think the feller's jest a leetle lazy? There's no law against laziness, though it needs legislation, being a deal more like the tap-root of evil than what money is,—though I don't set up my views against the Good Book."

"'Pears like 'twarn't laziness, which may be a sin, but makes men fat, an' ez long ez the pot holds out ter bile, happy. This man warn't happy nor fat, an' he looked like the devils hed thar home with him."

"Where did he come from, and what's his name?"

"He 'lowed, one day, from Happy Valley, but he didn't know whar Happy Valley war. An' he talks like a town man, an' reads a power, an' tells tales ez Phemie say air out o' books; an' he gin a show"—

"A show?" the sheriff interrupted.

"A juggling show," pursued Tubal Sims, in higher feather since they no longer dissimulated their absorption in these details. "He calls hisse'f a juggler, though his name is John Leonard."

"What's he live on?" demanded the sheriff.

"The money he made at his show. He 'lowed ter gin more shows, but the church folks gin it out ez he war in league with Satan, an' threatened ter dump him in the ruver, so he quit jugglin'."

The deputy with difficulty repressed a guffaw, but asked, with a keen curiosity, "Was it a pretty good show?"

"Ye never seen nuthin' like it in yer life. He jes'"—

"What sort of lookin' man is he?" interrupted the sheriff. He cast a glance at the deputy, who unobtrusively began to busy himself with pen, ink, and paper, and was presently scribbling briskly as Tubal Cain Sims sought to describe the stranger.

"He looks some like a mountain feller now," he said. "He paid my wife ter make him some clothes; but shucks!" his eye kindling with the glow of discursive reminiscence, "the clothes he kem thar in war a sight fur the jay-birds,—leetle pants ez kem down no furder'n that, an' long stockin's like a gal's, an' no mo' 'shamed of 'em 'n I am o' my coat-collar; a striped black-an'-red coat he hed on, an' long, p'inted reddish shoes." He paused to laugh, while a glance of fiery excitement and significance shot from the eyes of one officer into those of the other.

Far better than Tubal Sims they knew how to place the wearer of this sophisticated costume. For although their bailiwick was the compass of the county, their official duties carried them occasionally to neighboring cities and their suburbs; and while rolling so rapidly was not conducive to gathering moss for personal embellishment, it afforded opportunity for observation not altogether thrown away. This man was out of place,—a wanderer, evidently; but whether a fugitive from justice remained to be proved.

And while Tubal Cain Sims talked convulsively on, hardly realizing whither his reminiscences led, the expert penman was quietly noting down all the personal traits of poor Lucien Royce,—his height, his weight, his size, the color of his hair and eyes, the quality of his complexion, the method of his enunciation, and the polish of his manner,—all in the due and accepted form of advertisement for criminals, minus the alluring sum offered for their apprehension by the governor of the State.

Tubal Cain Sims did not note the cessation of the scraping of the pen, but the sheriff did, and it was within a few moments that he said, "Well, Mr. Sims, this offers no ground for arrestin' the man. But I'll give you a piece of advice,—don't let him know of your errand here, or he'll take French leave of you and take the girl with him. I can't arrest him for you"—

"Courtin' 's the inalienable right of man, and, in leap year, of woman too," sputtered the deputy, with his pen in his mouth and his laugh crowding it.

"But," continued the sheriff, "as I have some business up that way, I may come over soon an' look after him, myself. Say nothin', though, about that, or you'll lose your daughter,—just one daughter."

"One darter," echoed Tubal Sims, his eyes absorbed and docile as he followed the crafty officer's speech.

"Say nothin' to nobody, and I'll see you before long." Then suddenly leaving the subject, with a briskening style he turned to the deputy. "Jeemes, take Mr. Sims before a magistrate,—Squair Purdy, I'd recommend,—on a charge of carrying weepons with the intent o' goin' armed. Let him know, though, Mr. Sims, 'twas in ignorance of the law, and a-travelin'. Remind him that the code says the statute is to be liberally construed. And remember that Jeemes can't swear that old army pistol was *concealed* on *no account*. *I* don't b'lieve Jeemes kin make out a case agin ye. Squair Purdy is mighty lenient."

"Ain't you-uns goin'?" quavered Mr. Sims, distrusting the tender mercies of the facetious Jeemes.

"No, sir," replied the sheriff, now far away in the contemplation of other matters. "Jeemes, go to the telephone and ring up the cap'n in Knoxville. I want to speak to him."

It only seemed a great babbling of a little bell in the grim twilight of the hall of the jail as the deputy piloted Tubal Cain Sims out of the door which had so obdurately closed on him. And how should his ignorance conceive that within three minutes the chief of police in Knoxville was listening to the description of poor Lucien Royce, given by the sheriff of Kildeer County, and trying for his life to reconcile its dissimilarities with the physical traits of various missing malefactors sadly wanted by the police in divers localities?

X.

IT was with a mild countenance and a chastened heart that Tubal Sims rode up to his own door the next evening, and slowly dismounted, his old brains, stiff with the limited uses of a narrow routine, dazed and racked by the brisk pace which they had been fain to conserve in the wide circuits which they had traveled in his absence. Never had the cabin on the river-bank looked so like home; never had home seemed so like heaven. For Tubal Cain Sims, in his secret soul, cared little for the bedizenments of crowns, and the superfluities of harps, and the extravagance of streets paved with gold, and the like celestial scenery of his primitive hymnology. The sight of Jane Ann Sims on the porch, her bulky arms akimbo, the flutter of Euphemia's pink dress with the dark red roses from the slope of the dell where the spring lurked, could have been no dearer to him if they had had wings,—which appurtenance, however, in his lack of spiritual imagination, would have reduced them to a turkey-like standpoint or other gallinaceous level. He hardly remembered to dread Jane Ann's questionings; and perhaps because of this beatific ease of mind, the humble works of fiction, which the puritanical might denominate lies, that had occupied his faculties during his return journey, were exploited with a verisimilitude which received the meed of credulity. He stated that the thought of Jerry Gryce, his brother-in-law, and a paralytic, dwelling in Piomingo Cove, had weighed so on his mind, in wakeful hours of the night, that he had felt obliged to rise betimes and journey thither to see that all was well with him. And a cheerful report he was able to give of that invalid,—for indeed he had stopped in Piomingo Cove on the way back,—who had charged him with some asperity, however, being a superstitious man, to have a care how he took the liberty of dreaming about him, or nourishing presentiments in which he was concerned, or viewing visions. "I kin do all my own dreamin' an' ghost-seein' too, thanky kindly," he had said satirically.

Jane Ann Sims was the less penetrating as she herself had developments of interest to detail. In a wheezy, husky whisper that had less the elements of confidential relation than a shriek might have compassed, she made plain the altered state of Euphemia's affections and the understanding which she and the juggler had reached.

It is wonderful how little mental capital a man need possess to deceive the cleverest wife. Tubal Cain Sims, seated in the open passage, tilted far back against the wall in his chair, his saddle on the floor beneath his dangling feet and his mare cropping the grass beside the step, sustained every appropriate pose of surprised interest as successfully as if Mrs.

Sims's story were new to his ears. How could she, even if infinitely more astute, have dreamed that it was the recital of these same facts which he had overheard that had sent him straight to Colbury with the instant determination to have his would-be son-in-law incarcerated on a criminal charge, before more romance could come of the juggler's stay in Etowah Cove? She had expected opposition, having divined Tubal Sims's disapproval of his guest from his perturbed and unwontedly crusty manner, and was scarcely prepared for the mildly temporizing way in which he received the disclosure.

"Humph—a—waal, we-uns will hev ter gin it cornsideration, Jane Ann, a power o' cornsideration, an'"—he suddenly remembered his piety—"some pray'r. Watch an' pray, Jane Ann."

"I'm ekal ter my prayin' 'thout yer exhortin's," she retorted, with proper spirit. "An' ef ye don't wan ter set Phemie agin ye, ye'd better do yer own prayin' powerful private." She could not forbear this gibe, albeit at the idol of them both. It was in graver and agitated mood that she revealed how the idea of an elopement had seemed to appeal to the young man's mind,—so much, indeed, that she began to fear he would welcome any parental opposition which would make it practicable. And here she found Tubal Cain at one with her own thoughts, so a-quiver with her own fears that she felt all at once bolder, as if by communicating them they had mysteriously exhaled. Not so Tubal Cain Sims. It is to be doubted whether in all his life he was ever so earnestly and markedly benign and courteous as when he again met the juggler. His whole manner was so charged with the sentiment of placation that the young man's quick discernment easily divined his state of mind and his covert terrors. It eliminated for the present any other course of action than drifting along the smooth tides of love's young dream, for no elopement was possible when there was naught from which to flee.

What wonderful days they were, as the full, strong pulses of June began to beat with the fervors of July! The long, ripe hours from early dawn to the late-lingering twilight held all the choicest flavors of the year. Never was the sunset so gorgeously triumphal; never was the dawn so dank with dew, so fresh of scent, so winged with zephyrs. The wilderness rang to the song of the thrush and of the mocking-bird, not less vocal now than with the impulse of spring. The brimming river yet ran deep in its rocky channel, and the voice of the cascade below the mill in the full-leaved joyous woods could be heard for miles on a still night. And how still were these nights of silent splendor, with the stars so whitely a-glitter in the deep blue spaces above, and a romantic mystery on the mute purple mountains below, and the great bespangled gossamer Galaxy, as if veiling some sanctity of heaven, scintillating through all the darkness!

Not till late—till so late that no one was awake to heed or behold—a yellow waning moon with a weird glamour would glide over the eastern summits, and in its precarious hour before the flush of early dawn illumine the world with some sad forecast, with slow troublous augury of change and decline and darkness.

Flowers in myriads budded at night to blow in the morning. Everywhere the strong, rich, vigorous growths unfolded to the sun. The leaves were thick in the woods, the shadows were dark and cool, and rivulets glanced in the midst of them like live leaping crystal. Anywhere down deep ravines, did one look long enough, were to be seen all the creatures of woodland poesy, evoked from the glamours of the June,—hamadryads at their bosky ease, and oreads among the craggy misty heights, and naiads dabbling at the margin of sheltered springs, and elves listening alert with pointed ears to the piping of the wind in the reeds.

These June days seemed to Royce as if he held them in perpetuity,—as if there could be no change save for the slow enhancement of all the charms of nature, bespeaking further perfections. The past was so bitter; the present was so sweet; and he thought no more of the future. He was content. He had developed a certain adaptability to the uncouth conditions of the simple life here, or love had limited his observation and had concentrated it. All the artificialities of his wonted standards had fallen from him, and he was happy in the simplest way. He wondered that he should ever have thought the girl beautiful and charming hitherto, so embellished was her loveliness now; as if she too shared the ineffable radiance and grace of the June, with the fair and faintly tinted roses known as "the maiden's-blush" that grew just outside the door. He had told her that they were like her, and when he learned the old-fashioned name he wore one always stuck in the clumsy, ill-worked buttonhole of his blue-checked cotton shirt. So pervasive was the sentiment of happiness in the house that it suffused even the consciousness of the two old people; Jane Ann accepting it willingly and with vicarious joy, and Tubal Cain yielding after many a qualm of doubt and tremor of fear, and still experiencing strong twinges of remorse. He had been led to believe, by the crafty sheriff's show of indifference to his disclosure, and repeated rejection as naught the significant points of the suspicion he had entertained, that he had been wrong from the first in his conclusion. He had begun to argue from the officer's standpoint, and he was amazed and somewhat dismayed to perceive how slight were the grounds on which any reasonable charge could be based. As this conviction grew more decided, he anticipated, with an ever increasing terror, the possible visit of which the sheriff had casually spoken. Although he was sure now that, officially considered, it could but be a flash in the pan, still it would reveal to the juggler his host's hideous suspicions and flagrant breach of hospitality, and from this Tubal Sims winced as from corporeal pain. He thought that the sheriff already considered him a preposterous fool; and albeit that judgment from so great a man—for Tubal Cain Sims's self-conceit had been much abated by his trip to Colbury—was humiliating to his pride, it would be far more poignant, multiplied by the number of inhabitants in the Cove, when published abroad and entertained by every man who dwelt in its vicinity. Moreover, the disclosure of his mission to Colbury would deliver the graceless informer, bound hand and foot as it were, into the power of Jane Ann Sims, and it might well alienate the juggler from them all and thus wreck Euphemia's happiness and prospects in life; and he had begun of late to value these. Whenever he was not mulishly resistant, he fell much under the influence of Jane Ann Sims, and her views of the preëminent qualities of the juggler's mind and manners and morals affected his estimate. She laid great stress on the fact of the young man's elaborate education, and was wont to toss her large head with a vertigo-provoking lightness as she averred, "Phemie warn't a-spellin' year in an' year out ter marry one o' these hyar Cove boys ez dunno B from bull-foot!" And Tubal Cain would sneer in sympathetic scorn, as if both he and his wife were not in precisely that sublime state of ignorance themselves. He shared her pride in a plan which the juggler had evolved to open a school in the little "church-house" when the crops should be laid by, and in the fact that this suggestion had met with the readiest acceptance for miles around, despite the prejudice touching his feats of magic.

One night, Jane Ann Sims, with the dish-cloth in her hand, was alternately wiping the supper dishes in the shed-room and cheerfully wheezing breathless snatches of a most lugubrious hymn, while Royce and Euphemia sat on the steps of the passage, where the moon, now in her first quarter, drew outlines of the vines on the floor,—with here the similitude of a nest, whence now a wakeful, watching head protruded, and now a lifted wing, and now a downy, ball-like bulk; and here, with indistinct verges, a cluster of quivering trumpet-flowers, all dusky and blurring, like the smudging black-and-white study of some impressionist artist. Tubal Cain Sims, seeking company, was aware, as he entered his domicile, that he would find no welcome here, so he betook himself, with his pipe in hand, to the leisurely scene of his help-meet's labors. There triumph awaited him, for Jane Ann Sims left the table and the dishes to the tallow dip and the candle-flies, to sink down in a chair and detail the fact that while he was gone to the blacksmith's shop to get his team shod a wonderful event had happened. Parson Tynes had been here again!

Tubal Cain Sims's lower jaw dropped. Parson Tynes figured in his mind only as the troublous advocate of a dead-and-gone love, and he thought it a breach of the peace, in effect, to seek to disinter and resuscitate this ill-starred attachment. He growled adversely, but he did not reach the point of articulate remonstrance, for Jane Ann Sims majestically waved her limp dish-cloth at him as a signal to desist, and opened her mouth very wide to emit the cause of her prideful satisfaction in a loud and wheezy whisper,—which discreet demonstration came sibilantly to the ears of the young people outside, the only other human creatures within a mile, and occasioned them much unfilial merriment.

Parson Tynes no longer dwelt on marrying and giving in marriage. Ambition had been his theme. It seemed that once, not long ago, being in Colbury when a great revival—a union meeting of various denominations—was held, he had had the opportunity to preach there through some wild rumor of his celebrity as a mountain orator; and afterward a certain visiting elderly minister had taken him aside and urged him to study and to cultivate his gifts, and above all to acquire a delivery. The visiting city minister, being a man who appreciated the Great Smoky Mountains as a large and impressive element of scenery, and having never seen them except gracing the horizon, did not realize that in all their commodiousness they had scant accommodations for learning. On his part, Tynes did not appreciate any especial superiority in the delivery of the men he had heard. His slow drawl and his mispronunciations were, of course, unperceived by him, and, speaking from a worldly point of view, he was chiefly refreshed at the meeting by the consciousness that there were many more ideas in his sermon than in that of the visiting city minister. He wondered satirically how the good man would have received the converse of this charge, had he dared to exhort him in turn to cultivate thought and acquire ideas. The meeting had done Tynes no good. It had only hurt his pride, and roused a certain animosity toward the larger world outside his life and the round of his work, and caused him to contemn as spurious the pretensions of the luckier clergy. He did not accord the advice he had received a single thought, so much more important it seemed to him what a preacher says than how he says it. But Jane Ann Sims had talked much and pridefully to her cronies in the Cove about the juggler's "readin's," and their fame had reached the parson's ears. Shortly after, he chanced to encounter Royce at the mill, and for the first time was impressed by the charm of a cultured enunciation in a naturally beautiful voice. "I'd like powerful well ter speak like *that*, now," he said to himself, with a sudden discrimination of superiority. And this afternoon he had come to say that he had heard of the projected school, and that he would like to know whether the juggler had ever been taught elocution and was qualified to impart his knowledge. Royce had read for him,—or rather, had recited from memory,—and Tynes had been surprised and delighted, and had averred that he read "better'n all the men at the union meeting shook up in a bag together, the city minister at the bottom."

"But ye would hev been s'prised, Tubal," said Mrs. Sims, her fat face clouding and her dimples turning to creases, "ter hev viewed the gamesome an' jokified way ez John Leonard conducted hisself ter the pa'son—plumb scandalous—made a puffeck laffin'-match o' the whole consarn; though arter a while the pa'son seemed some less serious, too. But he an' John Leonard air a-goin' ter meet every day, beginnin' day arter ter-morrer, in the schoolhouse, ter take lessons in readin'. An' the pa'son pays him fur it. Jes' think o' that!" Her hand with the limp dish-cloth in it extended itself impressively. "Teachin' the pa'son—the pa'son, mind ye—ter read!"

Tubal Cain Sims sat electrified by the honor. Now and again his stiff old visage relaxed with a broad smile, but this some grave thought suddenly puckered up. In the midst of his satisfaction and his appropriation of the honor that had descended upon his house, ever and anon a secret thought of his earlier distrust of the juggler intruded with a vaguely haunting fear of the promised visit from the sheriff. This he had latterly put from him, for the long silence and the passage of time warranted him in the conclusion that it had been merely a device of the officer to satisfy a meddlesome old fool, and was from the beginning devoid of intention. He hardly dared to wonder what Jane Ann Sims would have thought of his suspicion, as he remembered that from the moment of the juggler's entrance on that stormy evening she had rated the young guest as highly as now. But then, it had never been her chance to hear those strange, mysterious utterances from the turmoils of midnight dreams.

"Jane Ann," Tubal Sims said, with quavering solemnity, "I know this hyar young man be powerful peart, an' thar's nobody in the kentry ter ekal him, not even Pa'son Tynes; but what would you-uns think ef ye war ter hear him call out, like I hev done, in the night,—'way late, 'bout the darkest hour,—'But the one who lives!—fur whose life!—his life!—fur his life!—what can I do!—fur his life!—his life!—it must be!—his life!'"

As he mimicked the cabalistic phrases that had so strongly laid hold upon his imagination, the very inflections of the agonized voice were duplicated. The sentiment of mystery, of awe, with which the air was wont to vibrate was imparted anew. The despair, the remorse of the tones, sent a responsive thrill like a fang into the listener's heart. Jane Ann Sims, her face blank and white, sat staring dumbly as she hearkened. The leaves darkly rustled close to the window. Dim moonlight flecked the ground on the slope beyond with shadow and a dull suffusive sheen. The wind, rushing gustily past, bowed the flame of the guttering tallow dip, feebly flaring, in the centre of the table. As she put out her hand mechanically to shield it from extinction, the motion and the trifling care seemed to restore her mental equilibrium.

"That sounds powerful cur'ous, Tubal," she said gravely, and his heart sank in disappointment with the words and tone. He had expected Jane Ann Sims to flout the matter aside loftily, and indignantly decline to consider aught that might reflect on her much-admired guest. It was he himself who began to feel that it was of slight moment and hardly worth detailing; the sheriff had barely listened to it, without lifting an eyelash of tired and drowsy eyes. He was sorry he had told Jane Ann. What a pother women are wont to stir up over a trifle!

"Why ain't you-uns never spoke of it afore?" she demanded.

"Kase I 'lowed 'twould set you-uns agin him," said the specious Tubal tentatively.

Jane Ann sniffed contemptuously. "Waal, I ain't been 'quainted with no men so powerful puffeck in all thar ways ez I kin be sot agin a youngster, what eats a hearty supper, fur talkin' in his sleep. I'd be a powerful admirer of the 'sterner sex,' ez Pa'son Greenought calls 'em, ef I knowed no wuss of 'em 'n that."

"Wha—wha—what ye goin' ter do 'bout'n it, Jane Ann?" sputtered Tubal Cain, seeing her ponderously rising, determination on her strong features.

"I be goin' ter ax him what he means by it, that's what," said Jane Ann. And before Tubal Cain could protest, she was leaning out of the window and wheezily calling to the young people slowly strolling along the slope before the door.

"Kem in, chil'n. I want ter ax John Leonard a kestion."

She met him at the entrance of the passage, the tallow dip in her hand, glowing with a divergent aureola of white rays against the dusky brown shadows and green leaves of the vines opposite. He paused, expectant, while Euphemia, in her green dress, stood on the sill amongst the swaying vines, hardly distinguishable from them save for her fair ethereal face, looking in as if from elf-land, so subtly sweet was its reminiscent expression. But he was intent of attitude, with a question in his waiting eyes; not dallying mentally with the thoughts he had had in contemplation, but altogether receptive to a new theme.

His face changed subtly as Jane Ann Sims, watching him narrowly, repeated the words of his somnolent speech. "What air ye talkin' 'bout, John Leonard, whenst ye say them words agin an' agin an' agin, night arter night?" she asked him inquisitively.

He did not hesitate. Still, he had a strange look on his face, as if summoned many and many a mile thence. "I dream that I am dead, sometimes, and others need me back again, and I cannot go. I can do nothing. I often dream that I am dead."

It so fell out the next day that this seemed no dream. He was so surely dead that he walked the ways of this world an alien. He was not more of it than if the turf in the far cemetery, beside the marble that bore his name, grew green and lush with its first summer veritably above his breast. He had no premonition of the deterioration of the spurious animation which had of late informed the days. The dawn came early, as was its wont in these slow diurnal measures of July, and cheer came with it. The explanation he had given of his strange words was more than satisfactory, and all about him was instinct with a sort of radiant pleasure in him which diffused its glow into his own heart.

As he stood in the passage lighting his pipe, after breakfast, he noticed a salient change in the landscape. No smoke was rising from the high promontory where was situated the primitive kiln of the lime-burners.

"Ye jes' f'und that out?" said Tubal Cain, with a chuckle, as, tilted against the wall in his chair, he listlessly dangled his feet. "Thar ain't been no lime bu'nt thar fur six weeks." He chuckled anew, so cordially did he accept the sentimental cause of the juggler's lapse of observation. "I reckon that thar lime is made up inter morter an' air settin' up prideful ez plaister now, an' hev done furgot it ever war rock."

The young man placidly endured the raillery; in fact he relished it, for it was proof how genuine had been his absorption, and he was deprecatory of self-deception. That alert commercial interest never quite moribund prompted his next question.

"I don't see that lime is used in the Cove," he said, reflecting on the stick-and-clay chimneys, and the clay daubing in the chinking between the logs of the walls of the houses. "What was the purpose of that extensive burning of lime, Mr. Sims?"

"Ain't you-uns hearn?" demanded the host, with another cheerful grin expanding his corrugated leathern-textured countenance. "Pete Knowles wouldn't tell a-fust; he got the job somehows."

"Afraid of underbidding." The juggler nodded comprehension of the motive.

"So he bu'nt, an' bu'nt, an' bu'nt, an' the lime it piled up in heaps in that thar dry rock-house what 'minds me powerful o' the sepulturs o' the Bible. But it air six weeks sence they bar'led it up an' wagoned it off 'bout ten mile or mo'."

"What did they want it for, and who are 'they'?" inquired Royce, still interested.

"'They' is them hotel men over yander at New Helveshy Springs, an' they wanted the lime ter plaister the old hotel what hev hed ter be repaired an' nigh made over. They 'lowed 'twar cheaper ter git the lime bu'nt at the nearest limestun rocks 'n ter buy it bar'led an' haul it fifty mile from a railroad."

This was a proposition of a kind that might well secure the juggler's business-like consideration. But his eyes were fixed with a sudden untranslated thought. His pipe had turned unheeded in his hand, fire, tobacco, and ashes falling from it into the dewy weeds below the step, as he stood on the verge of the passage. His expressive face had altered. It was smitten with some prophetic thought, and had grown set and rigid.

"New Helvetia Springs! Summer resort, of course. I didn't know there was anything of the sort in the vicinity," he said at last. "What kind of place is it?"

"I dunno!" exclaimed Sims, dangling his feet briskly back and forth in an accession of contempt. "*I* never tuk the trouble ter ride over thar in my life, though I hev knowed the hotel ter be a-runnin', ez they call it, fur forty year an' more."

Royce stood in silence for a time, moodily leaning his shoulder against the wall of the house, one hand thrust in his leather belt, the other holding the pipe at an angle and a poise which would seem to precede an immediate return of the stem to his mouth. But he did not smoke. Presently he put the pipe into his pocket, drew his hat over his eyes, and wandered down the road; then climbing a fence or two, he was off in the woods, as safe from interruption as if in the midst of a trackless ocean. He walked far and fast with the constraint of nervous energy, but hardly realizing the instinct of flight which informed his muscles. When at last he flung himself down at the foot of great rocks that stood high above a shelving slope in woods so dense that he could not see farther than a yard or two in any direction, for the flutter of the multitudinous leaves and the shimmer of the interfulgent sunshine, he was saying to himself that he was well quit of all the associations of his old world; that he had found safety here, a measure of content, a means of livelihood, and the prospect of a certain degree of simple happiness when he should be married to a girl whom he had learned to love and who loved him,—a beautiful girl of innate refinement, who had mind enough to understand him and to acquire an education. He would do well to still resolutely that sudden plunging of the heart which had beset him upon the knowledge that his old world was so near at hand, with all those endearing glamours as for the thing that is native. What avail for him to hover around them, to court the fate of the moth? He remembered with a sort of terror the pangs of nostalgia which at first had so preyed upon him, and should he deliberately risk the renewal of these poignant throes, now possibly spent forever? Regret, danger, despair, lay in the way thither; why should he long to look in upon scenes that were now as reminiscences, so well could he predicate them on experiences elsewhere? He wondered, fretfully, however, and with a rising doubt of himself, that when he and Euphemia had climbed the mountain and looked down at the shimmer of the small towns in the furthest valley, and he had felt no stir of wistfulness, he should have interpreted his tranquillity as a willing renunciation of the life he had left,—as if the treadmill limitations and deprivations and mental stagnation of a village were the life he had left. And suddenly—although he had chosen this spot because it shut him in, because naught could be seen to deflect his errant mind, in order that he might realize and earnestly grapple with this wild and troublous lure—the illusions of a sophistry glimmered even in these scant spaces. He was definitely reconciled, he told himself, to his destiny. It was only his imagination that vaguely yearned for the status he had left. With a touch of reality the prismatic charms of this bubble of fancy would collapse,—or the glimpse of conditions native to him, the sound of familiar speech as of his mother tongue, the sight of men and women as compatriots in this long exile as of a foreign land, would prove a refreshment, a tonic, an elixir, renewing his strength to endure. He was a coward to deprive himself—for fear of discontent—of something to enjoy in the present, to remember, and to look forward to, in recurrent years.

He had not thought to notice the dwindling shadows that betokened noon and the waiting dinner which Euphemia had made ready with many a remembrance of his preferences. The sun was westering apace when, as if impelled by a force beyond his control, he found himself in the country road, forging ahead with that long swift stride, the envy of his comrades of the pedestrian club of his urban days. His heart seemed to divine the way, for he scarcely paused to debate which fork to pursue when the road diverged; he gave no heed to the laurel jungles on either hand, or, further on, to the shady vistas under the towering trees; he only perceived at last that the density of the woods had diminished. Soon peaked and turreted roofs appeared among the thinning boughs, and as he crossed an elaborately rustic foot-bridge, coquettishly picturesque, flung across a chasm where deep in the brown damp shadows a silver rill trickled, he recognized this as an outpost of artificiality. A burst of music from a band thrilled his unaccustomed ears; a vast panorama of purple and azure mountains, a vermilion sun, a flaring amber sky, great looming gray crags, and the bronze-green sunlit woods beyond were asserted in an unfolding landscape; he heard the laughter cadenced to express the tempered mirth of polite society, and the stir of talk. The verandas of the two-storied hotel were full of well-dressed people. His swiftly glancing eye marked the dowagers; their very costumes were familiar,—black grenadines or silks with a subdued inclination toward a touch of lavender decoration, and some expert softening of the ravages of time by the sparing use of white chiffon or lace, with always something choice in the selection of dainty shawls on the back of a chair near at hand (how often had he resignedly borne such a wrap over his arm in the meek train of a pretty girl's chaperon!): he knew the type,—clever, discreet, discerning. On the lawn two games of tennis were in progress, the white of the flannel suits of the men enhanced in the sun against the green grass. Along the road beyond, two or three smart little carts were coming in with the jauntiest of maidens in daintily tinted summer attire and sailor hats. An equestrian couple—the young man of a splendid physique and elegantly mounted—went by him like a flash, as he stood, dazed and staring, by the rail of the bridge. He retained barely enough presence of mind to dodge aside out of the way, and he received a volley of sand, covering him from head to foot, from the heels of the horses as they disappeared in the woods at the steady hand-gallop. On the crag at the verge of the bluff were groups of young people, strolling about or seated on the ledges of the cliff, the young men dangling their feet over the abysses beneath, such being the accepted fad; now and then, one not emerged from the hobbledehoy chrysalis would, by means of grotesque affectations of falling, elicit small complimentary shrieks, half terror, half mirth, from the extremely young ladies whom he favored with his improving society. At one side there was a meeting of fir boughs, a dank and cool dark vista, a great piling of fractured and splintered rocks, a sudden descent, and down this bosky way was so constant a going and coming that Lucien Royce divined that it led to the hidden spring.

He stared at the scene through the tears in his eyes. To him who had never had a home it was home, who had never dreamed of heaven it was bliss. He would have given all he could imagine—but, poor fellow, he had naught to give!—to be able to communicate in some mysterious way the knowledge of his quality to one of those high-nosed, keen-eyed elder women, of composed features and fine position and long social experience and much discrimination in the world's ways, and to have her commend his course, and counsel prudence, and pity his plight. He looked at the elder men, whose type he also knew,—men of weight in the business world, lawyers, bankers, brokers,—and he thought what a boon might be even the slightest impersonal conversation with one of his own sphere, his equal in breeding, in culture, in social standing. He was starved,—he had not realized it; he was dying of mental inanition; he was starved.

The next moment, two of the tennis-players, ending the diversions of the afternoon with a walk, approached the bridge: the man in his immaculate white flannels, his racket carried over his shoulder; the girl in her picturesque tennis toggery. Royce, dusty, besprinkled with sand, conscious of his coarse ill-made jeans clothes and his great cowhide boots, colored to the roots of his hair as their eyes fell upon him. In adaptation to the custom of the mountaineers, who never fail to speak to a stranger in passing, they both murmured a "Good-evening" as they went by. Royce, rousing with a galvanic start, lifted his hat, hardly realizing why they should glance at him in obvious surprise and with elevated eyebrows. For one moment he pondered fruitlessly on the significance of this trifling incident. The solution of the mystery came to him with a monition of added caution. The social training of the mountaineer does not comprise the ceremony of lifting the hat in salutation. If he would sustain the rural character he must needs have heed, since so slight a deflection was marked. He heard them laughing as they went, and he thought, with all the sensitiveness incident to a false position, that he was the cause of their mirth, the incongruity of this "million of manners" with such a subject. With an aversion to a repetition of this scene he betook himself out of the way of further excursionists, noticing that several couples were slowly strolling in the direction of the bridge. But as he moved forward from under the shadows of the fir and into the clear space of the lawn, he could scarcely sustain the observation which he felt leveled at him, Argus-eyed, from the verandas, the lawn, the tennis-court, the crags. His pride was in arms against his humble plight. His face burned with shame for his coarse garments, the dust, the very clumsiness of his rough boots, the length of his overgrown silky red-brown hair, his great awkward hat, the uncouth figure he cut in respectable society. But despite the flush on his cheek, and a thrill hot and tingling ever starting with each searing thought to his eyes, as if tears were to be shed but for the sheer shame of it, he laughed scornfully at his pride, and despised himself to be so poor, so forlorn, so outcast from his native world, yet so yearning for it. "What does it matter?" he said to himself. "They don't know me. Lucien Royce is dead,—dead forever." He walked on for a few minutes, the trained gait of an athlete, his graceful bearing, the individuality and distinction of his manner, all at their best, mechanically asserted as an unrealized protest in some sort that those lorgnettes on the verandas should not conceive too meanly of him. "I suppose I thought the ghost of a dude like Lucien Royce would be a mighty well-set-up affair, with a sort of spectral style about him and an unearthly chic. But what does it matter what they think of a nonentity of a stray mountaineer like this? Lucien Royce is dead,—dead forever!"

He had merely ventured to partially skirt the lawn, bending his steps toward the shelter of a small two-storied building at the nearest corner of it, and somewhat down the road. The lower portion of this structure, he perceived, was used as a store, containing a few dry goods, but dispensing chiefly needles and pins, especially hairpins, and such other commodities of toilet as the guests might have forgotten or exhausted or could be induced to buy. He paused in the doorway: even the sight of the limited stock ranged decorously on the shelves, the orderly counters, the smooth countenance of the salesman, seemed pleasing to him, as reminiscent of the privileges of civilization.

"Can we do anything for you, sir?" asked the clerk suavely.

Royce caught himself with a start. Then speaking with his teeth half closed to disguise his voice, and drawling like a mountaineer, he said, shaking his head, "Jes' viewin' the folks some."

He had a sense that the imitation was ill done, and glanced furtively at the face of the man behind the counter. But the clerk was devoid of speculation save as this faculty might explore his customers' pockets. Royce noted, however, a second warning, and since the sun was down and the lawn now depopulated, save for here and there a hastening figure making for the deserted verandas, he ventured out in his shabby gear upon the plank walk that stretched along the bluff where no crags intervened, but the descent was sheer to a green and woodsy slope below. The early tea was in progress; the band that for some time had been heralding its service, playing within the quadrangle, was silent now, and the shadows were abroad in the mountains; mists were rising from dank ravines on the opposite range. A star was in the flushed sky. A whippoorwill's plaintive tones came once and again from the umbrageous tangles that overshadowed the spring. Yellow lamps were flaring out into the purple dusk from the great looming unsubstantial building. He marked the springing into sudden brilliancy of a row of windows on the ground floor, that revealed a long, bare, empty apartment which he identified as the ballroom. There would be dancing later on. A cheerful clicking as of ivory against ivory caused him to pause abruptly and peer down the slope below, where a yellow radiance was aglow amongst the trees and precipitous descents. It came from the billiard-room in the pavilion, picturesquely poised here among the rocks and chasms, and looking out into a wild gorge that gave a twilight view of the darkening valley, and the purple glooms of the mountains towering along the horizon. It was the airiest type of structure. With only its peaked roof and its supporting timbers, the floor and the flights of steps, it seemed free to the breeze, so wide and long were the windows, all broadly open. Royce, looking down into its illuminated interior, glowing like a topaz in the midst of the dark foliage that pressed close about it, had a glimpse of the green cloth of the tables, the red and white balls, the dexterously poised cues, the alertly attitudinizing figures,—still loitering in white flannels, although the lights now agleam in bedroom windows told that all the world had begun to dress for the ball,—and heard the pleasant, mirthful voices.

Why did he linger here, he asked himself, as he repressed the natural mundane interest which almost spoke out his criticism as he watched the game with the eye of a connoisseur. This was not for him. He was not of this world. He had quitted it forever. And if he were mortified to fill a place in a sphere so infinitely removed from that to which he was born and entitled, would it better matters to emerge from his decent obscurity and his promised opportunities, his honest repute and his simple happiness, to the conspicuous position as the cynosure of all eyes in a criminal trial, and to the permanent seclusion of a felon's cell? For that was what he risked in these hankerings after the status and the sphere from which he was cast out forever.

He was in the darkening road and plodding homeward before this admonition to his own rebellious heart was concluded, so did the terrors of that possible ignominious fate dominate his pride, and scorch his sensibility, and lay his honest self-respect in the dust. He was tired. The drops stood on his forehead and his step lagged. Thrice the distance in the time he had walked it would not have so reduced his strength as did the mental perturbation, the inward questionings, those tumultuous plungings of his strong young heart. He was pale, and his face was lined and bore some vague impress of the nervous stress he had sustained, when at last he came up the steps of the open passage at Sims's house, and Jane Ann bent her anxious flabby countenance toward him.

"Waal, before the Lawd!" she exclaimed, holding the tallow dip in her hand so as to throw its light full upon him,—and he divined that at frequent intervals in the last two hours she had emerged thus with the candle in her hand to listen for his step,—"hyar the chile be at last! Whar in the name o' sense hev ye been, John Leonard?" she demanded, as Phemie fluttered out, pale and wistful despite her embarrassed laughter at the folly of their fright, and old Tubal Cain followed stiffly, with sundry grooves of anxiety added to the normal corrugations of his face.

"In the woods," replied the juggler; and then realizing that he spoke with a covert meaning, "I lost my way."

He slept the sleep of exhaustion that night, and the next morning he rose refreshed in body, and with the resolutions of his sober reflections confirmed.

"I am not such a snob as to care for the mere finery of existence, the mere wealth and show and fashion," he argued within himself. "It's partly the folly of my youth to care so much for those young fools over yonder,—so much like myself, or like what I used to be,—and dancing, and tennis, and wheeling, and flirting, and frivolity. A certain portion of these amenities has been the furniture of my life hitherto, and I am a trifle awkward at laying hold on it now without them. I love the evidences of good breeding, because I have been taught to respect them. I am prejudiced in favor of certain personal refinements, because I was reared to think a breach of them as iniquitous as to crash all the ten commandments at one fell swoop. I revere culture and literary or scientific achievement, because I appreciate what they require in mental capacity, and I am educated to gauge in a degree the quality of their excellence. I should like to have some conversation, occasionally, with people near my own calibre in social status and mind, and with similar motives and sentiments and way of looking at things. But I *can* live without a ballroom and a billiard-table, and, by the Lord, I'll brace up like a man and do it contentedly."

He went off cheerfully enough, after breakfast, to meet Tynes in the little schoolhouse. There he recited, in forgetfulness of his troubles, poems that he loved, and bits of ornate prose that he recalled, for he had a good memory; and he delivered sundry sound dicta touching the correct method of opening the mouth and of the pose of the body, and a dissertation on the physical structure of the vocal organs, illustrated by diagrams which he drew on the fly-leaf of the reading-book, and which mightily astonished Absalom Tynes, who learned for the first time that such things be. The leaves of the low-swinging elms rustled at the windows; the breeze came in and stirred up the dust; the flying squirrel who nested in the king-post of the roof, and who had had an early view of the juggler upon his first appearance in this house, came down and sat upon a beam and with intent eyes gazed at him. Tynes, in an unaccustomed station among the benches used by the congregation, watched and listened with unqualified commendation as Royce stood upon the platform and made the little house ring with his strong, melodious young voice. Abdicating the vantage-ground of spiritual preëminence, Tynes subordinated his own views, and when he read in his turn sundry of the secular bits of verse embalmed in the Reader—he seemed to think there were no books in the world but school-books and the Bible—he accepted corrections with the mildest docility, and preserved a slavish imitation of the spirited delivery of his preceptor. He rose into vigorous rebellion, however, when, with many a "Pshaw!" Royce rejected the continued use of the elementary Reader for the vital defect of having nothing in it fit to read, and took up, as matter worthy of elocutionary art, the Bible. Tynes, struck aghast by the change of delivery, the reverent, repressed, almost overawed tones, the deep, still gravity of the manner, listened for a time, then openly protested.

"That ain't no way ter read the Bible," he stoutly averred. "Ye hev got ter thunder it at the sinner, an' rest yer v'ice on this word an' lay it down on that, an' lift it up"—

"Ding-dong it, you mean," said the juggler, shifting quickly to his habitual tone.

"The sinner ain't ter be kep' listenin' ter sech ez that. Jes' let yer v'ice beat agin his ear till he can't keep the gospel out 'thout he be deef," Tynes contended.

"Yes, and his senses accommodate themselves to the clamor, and his consciousness sways back and forth with the minister's voice, and he doesn't hear more than one half of what is said, because the fellow yells so loud that the sound drowns out the sense. But the congregation looks pious, and folds its arms, and rocks itself back and forth with the rhythm of the sing-song, and the whole thing is just one see-saw. Do you believe that's the way St. Paul preached on Mars' hill?"

Tynes was suddenly bewildered. His manner assumed a sort of bridling offense; it seemed somewhat profane to speculate on the character of St. Paul's delivery.

"Your way ain't the way the men read at the Colbury revival, ennyhow," he urged; for the union meeting, despite his wounded pride, had become a sort of standard.

"I'll bet my old hat there wasn't anybody there who could come within a mile of my reading," glibly wagered the juggler, unabashed.

Tynes reflected doubtfully a moment. "I dunno *what*'s the matter with it," he said. "It hurts me! I couldn't git my cornsent ter read that-a-way. It sounds like ye jes' been thar yestiddy, an' it all happened fraish, an' ye war tellin' 'bout it, an' ye hedn't got over the pain an' the grief of it yit—an' mebbe ye never would."

In the pause that ensued the juggler trifled with the pages, his eyes cast down, a smile of gratified vanity lurking in the lustrous pupils.

"Well," Tynes said abruptly, "go on, John Leonard, go on."

But as the reading proceeded, the face of the slight and pallid man sitting on the bench—now and again wincing palpably from the scenes seemingly enacted before him, from the old, old words all instinct with the present, from the terrible sense of the reality of those dread happenings of the last night in Gethsemane, and the denial of Peter, and the judgment-hall—all at once lighted up with a new and vivid gleam of animation. The chapter was at an end, the lingering musical cadences of the reverent voice were dying away, and as the reader lifted his head there were tears in his eyes, and the fisher of men had seen them.

"Ye ain't so far from the kingdom, John Leonard," he said, in solemn triumph.

The juggler recoiled in a sort of ashamed self-consciousness. "Don't deceive yourself!" he exclaimed. "It is only my literary sensibility. All the four Gospels—speaking profanely—are works of high artistic merit, and they can floor me when nothing else can."

But the worldly ambition of Tynes had suddenly fled. He was baiting his hook and reeling out his line; here was the prospect of a precious capture in the cause of religion. He might not learn to read the Bible in John Leonard's illusive and soul-compelling way,—and he hardly knew if he cared to do this, so did it seem to penetrate into the very mystery of sacred things which had less poignancy under the veil of custom and indifference and a dull sense of distance in time and place,—but he would learn of him in secular things, he would remain by him, and now and again insidiously instill some sense of religious responsibility; and the soul of this sinner would indeed be a slippery fish if it could contrive to elude his vigilance at last.

He listened indulgently as the juggler declared he would have no more of the Reader, insisting that such literature would wreck his mind. But Tynes, for his own part, was not willing to trust himself to learn the arts of elocution from the sanctities of the Holy Book read with that immediate and vital certainty which tore so at his heart-strings.

"I wonder," he said, his narrow, pallid face brightening with the inspiration,—"I wonder ef thar ain't some o' them books ye speak of over yander ter the sto' what that valley-man keeps at New Helveshy Springs? They all bein' valley folks, mebbe he hev some valley books ter sell ter 'em."

"I have no doubt of it!" cried the juggler in delighted anticipation. He looked down for a moment, dubious of the wisdom of the course he had in contemplation, but with a quick joy beating at his heart. It was but natural, he argued within himself, recognizing the access of pleasure, that, young and debarred as he was from the society of his equals, he should experience a satisfaction in these fleeting glimpses of life as he had once known it, and in its attraction for him was no harbinger of regret and rue. Moreover, he judged that it would excite less attention for him to buy the book in person—he would make it appear that he was on an errand for some cottager of the summer sojourners—than if this ignorant parson should overhaul the literature of the Springs, with some wild tale of lessons from an elocutionary mountaineer. As to danger, he would hold his tongue as far as he might, and he deemed that he looked the veriest mountain rustic in the garb he so despised. "Rather a jaunty rural rooster, perhaps," he said to himself, "but as rural as a cornfield."

* * * *

XI.

ROYCE waited over one day after this agreement with Tynes, and marked with satisfaction how thoroughly his will was subject to his own control. He had seen New Helvetia once. There was naturally a certain mundane curiosity on his part to be satisfied. Doubtless, after another excursion or so thither, it would all pall upon him and he would be more content, since there was no dream of unattainable enchantments at hand upon which he dared not look.

The place was singularly cheerful of aspect in its matutinal guise. The slanting morning sunshine struck through the foliage of the great oaks and dense shrubs; but there was intervenient shadow here, too, dank, grateful to the senses, for the day already betokened the mounting mercury. Across the valley the amethystine mountains shimmered through the heated air; ever and anon darkly purple simulacra of clouds went fleeing along their vast sunlit slopes beneath the dazzling white masses in the azure sky. In a ravine, a tiny space of blue-green tint amongst the strong full-fleshed dark verdure of the forests of July bespoke a cornfield, and through a field-glass might be descried the little log cabin with its delicate tendril of smoke, the home of the mountaineer who tilled the soil. Of more distinct value in the landscape was the yellow of the harvested wheatfields in the nearer reaches of the valley, where the bare spaces revealed the stage-road here and there as it climbed the summits of red clay hills.

There was no sound of music on the air, the band being off duty for the nonce. Even that instrument of torture, the hotel piano, was silent. The wind played through the meshes of the deserted tennis-nets, and no clamor of rolling balls thundered from the tenpin-alley, the low long roof of which glimmered in the sunshine, down among the laurel on the slope toward the gorge. The whole life of the place was focused upon the veranda. Royce's reminiscent eye, gazing upon it all as a fragment of the past as well as an evidence of the present, discerned that some crisis of moment impended in the continual conjugation of the verb *s'amuser*. The usual laborious idleness of fancy-work would hardly account for the unanimity with which feminine heads were bent above needles and threads and various sheer fabrics, or for the interest with which the New Helvetia youths watched the proceedings and self-sufficiently proffered advice, despite the ebullitions of laughter, scornful and superior, with which their sage counsel was invariably received. There was now and again an exclamation of triumph as a pair of conventionalized wings were held aloft, completed, fashioned of gauze and wire and profusely spangled with silver. He caught a sudden flash of tinsel, and noted the special demonstrations of congratulation and great glee which ensued when one of the old ladies, fluttered with the anxiety of the inventor, successfully fitted a silver crown upon the golden locks of a poetic-faced young girl, a very Titania. The jocose hobbledehoy whom Royce had noted on the occasion of his previous excursion sat upon a step of the long flight leading from the veranda to the lawn, surrounded by half a dozen little maidens, and, armed with a needle and a long thread, affected to sew industriously, rewarded by their shrieking exclamations of delight in his funniness every time he grotesquely drew out the needle with a great curve of his long arm, or facetiously but futilely undertook to bite the thread.

With zealous gallantry sundry of the young men plied back and forth between the groups on the veranda to facilitate the exchange of silks and scissors, and occasionally trotted on similar errands, businesslike and brisk, down the plank walk to the store. Sometimes they asked here for the wrong thing. Sometimes they forgot utterly what they were to ask for, and a return trip was in order. Sometimes they demanded some article a stranger to invention, unheard of on sea or shore. Thus cruelly was their ignorance of fabric played upon by the ungrateful and freakish fair, and the little store rang with laughter at the discomfiture of the young Mercury so humbly bearing the messages of the deities on the veranda; for the store was crowded, too, chiefly with ladies in the freshest of morning costumes, and Royce, as he paused at the door, realized that this was no time to claim the attention of the smooth-faced clerk. That functionary was as happy as a salesman ever gets to be. There was not a yard of any material or an article in his stock that did not stand a fair chance of immediate purchase as wearing apparel or stage properties. Tableaux, and a ball afterward in the dress of one of the final pictures, were in immediate contemplation, as Royce gathered from the talk. This was evidently an undertaking requiring some nerve on the part of its projectors, in so remote a place, where no opportunities of fancy costumes were attainable save what invention might contrive out of the resources of a modern summer wardrobe and the haphazard collections of a watering-place store. Perhaps this added element of jeopardy and doubt and discovery and the triumphs of ingenuity heightened the zest of an amusement which with all necessary appliances might have been vapid indeed.

Royce could not even read the titles of the books on the shelf at this distance, above the heads of the press, and he turned away to await a more convenient season, realizing that he had attracted naught but most casual notice, and feeling at ease to perceive, from one or two specimens to-day about the place, that mountaineers from the immediate vicinity were no rarity at New Helvetia; their errands to sell fruit to the guests or vegetables or venison to the hotel being doubtless often supplemented by a trifle of loitering to mark the developments of a life so foreign to their experience. As he strolled along the plank walk, his supersensitive consciousness was somewhat assuaged as by a sense of invisibility. Every one was too much absorbed to notice him, and he in his true self supported no responsibility, since poor Lucien Royce was dead, and John Leonard was merely a stray mountaineer, looking on wide-eyed at the doings of the grand folk.

From that portion of the building which he had learned contained the ballroom he heard the clatter of hammer and nails. The stage was probably in course of erection, and, idly following the sound along a low deserted piazza toward one of the wings, he stood at length in the doorway. He gazed in listlessly at the group of carpenters working at the staging, the frame being already up. A blond young man, in white flannel trousers and a pink-and-white-striped blazer, was descanting with knowingness and much easy confidence of manner upon the way in which the curtain should draw, while the proprietor, grave, saturnine, with a leaning toward simplicity of contrivance and economy in execution, listened in non-committal silence. The wind blew soft and free through the opposite windows. Royce looked critically at the floor of the ballroom. It was a good floor, a very good floor. Finally he turned, with only a gentle melancholy in his forced renunciation of youthful amusements, with the kind of sentiment, the sense of far remove, which might animate the ghost of one untimely snatched away, now vaguely awaiting its ultimate fate. He continued to stroll along, entering presently the quadrangle, and noting here the grass and the trees and the broad walks; the romping children about the band-stand in the centre, dainty and fresh of costume and shrill of voice; the chatting groups of old colored nurses who supervised their play. One was pushing a perambulator, in which a precocious infant, totally ignoring passing adults, after the manner of his kind, fixed an eager, intent, curious gaze upon another infant in arms, who so returned this interested scrutiny that his soft neck, as he twisted it over the shoulder of his nurse, was in danger of dislocation.

"Tu'n roun' yere, chile!" she admonished him as if he were capable of understanding, while she shifted him about in her arms to cut off the vision of the object of interest. "Twis' off yer hade lak some ole owel, fus' t'ing ye know; owel tu'n his hade ef ye circle roun' him, an' tu'n an' tu'n till his ole fool hade drap off. Didn' ye know dat, honey? Set disher way. Dat's nice!"

She almost ran against the juggler as she rounded the corner. He caught the glance of her eye, informed with that contempt for the poor whites which is so marked a trait of negro character, as she walked on, swaying gently from side to side and crooning low to the baby.

He did not care to linger longer within the premises. He could not even enjoy the relapse into old sounds and sights in a guise in which he was thought so meanly of, and which so ill beseemed his birth and quality. When he issued from the quadrangle, at the lower end of the veranda, he found he was nearer the descent to the spring than to the store. He thought he would slip down that dank, bosky, deserted path, make a circuit through the woods, and thus regain the road homeward without risking further observation and the laceration of his quivering pride. False pride he thought it might be, but accoutred, alas, with sensitive fibres, with alert and elastic muscles for the writhings of torture, with delicate membranes to shrivel and scorch and sear as if it were quite genuine and a laudable possession.

The ferns with long wide-spreading fronds, and great mossy boulders amongst the dense undergrowth, pressed close on either hand, and the thick interlacing boughs of trees overarched the precipitous vista as he went down and down into its green-tinted glooms. Now and again it curved and sought a more level course, but outcropping ledges interposed, making the way rugged, and soon cliffs began to peer through the foliage, and on one side they overhung the path; on the other side a precipice lurked, glimpsed through boughs of trees whose trunks were fifty feet lower on a slope beneath. An abrupt turn,—the odor of ferns blended with moisture came delicately, elusively fragrant; a great fracture yawned amidst the rocks, and there, from a cleft stained deeply ochreous with the oxide of iron, a crystal-clear rill fell so continuously that it seemed to possess no faculty of motion in its limpid interlacings and plaitings as of silver threads; only below, where the natural stone basin—hewn out by the constant beating of the current on the solid rock—overflowed, could the momentum and power of the water be inferred from its swift escape, bounding over the precipice and rushing off in great haste for the valley. The proprietor had had the good taste to preserve the woodland character of the place intact. No sign that civilization had ever intruded here did Royce mark, as he looked about, save a book on a rock hard by. Some one had sought this sylvan solitude for a quiet hour in the fascinations of its pages.

He hesitated a moment, then advanced cautiously and laid his hand upon it. How long, how long—it seemed as if in another existence—since he had had a book like this in his hand! He caught its title eagerly, and the name of the author. They were new to him. He turned the pages with alert interest. The book had been published since the date of his exile. Once more he fluttered the leaves, and, like some famished, thirsting wretch drinking in great eager gulps, he began to absorb the contents, his eyes glowing like coals, his breath hot, his hands trembling with nervous haste, knowing that his time for this draught of elixir, this refreshment of his soul, was brief, so brief. It would never do, for a man so humbly clad as he was, to be caught reading with evident delight a scholarly book like this. When at last he threw himself down amongst the thick and fragrant mint beside the rock, his shoulders supported on an outcropping ledge, his hat fallen on the ground, he had forgotten all thought of caution, he was not conscious how the time sped by. His eyes were alight, moving swiftly from side to side of the page. His face glowed with responsive enthusiasm to the high thought of the author. His troubles had done much to chasten its expression and had chiseled its features. It had never been so serious, so intelligent, so refined, as now. He did not see how the shadows shifted, till in this umbrageous retreat a glittering lance of sunlight pierced the green gloom. He was not even aware of another presence, a sudden entrance. A young lady, climbing up from the precipitous slope below, started abruptly at sight of him, jeopardizing her already uncertain footing, then stared for an instant in blank amazement.

So precarious was the footing where she had paused, however, that there was no safe choice but to continue her ascent. He did not heed more the rustle of her garments, as she struggled to the level ground, than the rustle of the leaves, or the rattle of the little avalanche of gravel as her foot upon the verge dislodged the pebbles. Only when the shaft of sunlight struck full upon her white piqué dress, and the reflected glare was flung over the page of the book and into his eyes with that refulgent quality which a thick white fabric takes from the sun, he glanced up at the dazzling apparition with a galvanic start which jarred his every fibre. He stared at her for one moment as if he were in a dream; he had come from so far,—so very far! Then he grasped his troublous identity, and sprang to his feet in great embarrassment.

"I must apologize," he said, with his most courteous intonation, "for taking the liberty of reading your book."

"Not at all," she murmured civilly, but still looking at him in much surprise and with intent eyes.

Those eyes were blue and soft and lustrous; the lashes were long and black; the eyebrows were so fine, so perfect, so delicately arched, that they might have justified the writing of sonnets in their praise. That delicate small Roman nose one knew instinctively she derived from a father who had followed its prototype from one worldly advancement to another, and into positions of special financial trusts and high commercial consideration. It would give distinction to her face in the years to come, when her fresh and delicate lips should fade, and that fluctuating sea-shell pink hue should no longer embellish her cheek. Her complexion was very fair. Her hair, densely black, showed under the brim of the white sailor hat set straight on her small head. She was tall and slender, and wore her simple dress with an effect of finished elegance. She had an air of much refinement and unconscious dignity, and although, from her alert volant pose, he inferred that she was ready to terminate the interview, she did not move at once when he had tendered the book and she had taken it in her hand.

"I merely intended to glance at the title," he went on, still overwhelmed to be caught in this literary poaching, and hampered by the consciousness that his manner and his assumed identity had become strangely at variance. "But I grew so much interested that I—I—quite lost myself."

She had some thought in mind as she looked down at the book in her gloved hand, then at him. The blood stung his cheek as he divined it. In pity for his evident poverty and hankering for the volume, she would fain have bid him keep it. But with an exacting sense of conventionality, she said suavely, though with impersonal inexpressiveness, "It is no matter. I am glad it entertained you. Good-morning."

He bowed with distant and unpresuming politeness, and as she walked, with a fine poise and a quick elastic gait, along the shadowy green path, vanishing at the first turn, he felt the blood beating in his temples with such marked pulsation that he could have counted the strokes as he stood.

Did she deem him, then, only a common mountaineer, a graceless unlettered lout? She rated him as less than the dust beneath her feet. He could not endure that she should think of him thus. How could she be so obtuse as to fail to see that he was a gentleman for all his shabby gear! It was in him for a moment to hasten after her and reveal his name and quality, that she might not look at him as a creature of no worth, a being of a different sphere, hardly allied even to the species she represented.

He was following on her path, when the reflex sentiment struck him. "Am I mad?" he said to himself. "Have I lost all sense of caution and self-preservation?"

He stood panting and silent, the wounded look in his eyes so intense that by some subtle sympathetic influence they hurt him, as if in the tension of a strain upon them, and he passed his hand across them as he took his way back to the spring.

Did he wish the lady to recognize his station in life, and speculate touching his name? He was fortunate in that she was so young, for to those of more experience the incongruities of the interest manifested by an uncouth and ignorant mountaineer in a metaphysical book like that might indeed advertise mystery and provoke inquiry. Was he hurt because the lady, noting his flagrant poverty, had evidently wished to bestow upon him the volume which he had been reading with such delight,—so little to her, so infinite to him? And should he not appreciate her delicate sense of the appropriate, that had forbidden this generosity, considering her youth, and the fact that he was a stranger and seemingly a rustic clown? He rather wondered at the scholarly bent of her taste in literature, and her avoidance of the mirthful scenes of the veranda, that she might spend the morning in thought so fresh, so deep, so expansive. It hardly seemed apposite to her age and the tale that the thermometer told, for this was a book for study. There was something simple-hearted in his acceptance of this high intellectual ideal which all at once she represented to him. A few months ago he might have scoffed at it as a pose; he would at least have surmised the fact,—a mistake had been caused by a similarity of binding with that of a popular novel of the day with which she had hoped to while away the time in the cool recesses beside the spring, and thus the volume had been thrown discarded on the rock, while she climbed the slopes searching for the Chilhowee lily.

The fire of humiliation still scorched his eyes, and his deep depression was patent in his face and figure, when he reached the Sims house at last, and threw himself down in a chair in the passage. One elbow was on the back of the chair, and he rested his chin in his hand as he looked out gloomily at the mountains that limited his world, and wished that he had never seen them and might never see them again. The house was full of the odor of frying bacon, for there was no whiff of wind in the Cove. The rooms were close and hot, and the sun lay half across the floor, and burnt, and shimmered, and dazzled the eye. The suffocating odor of the blistering clapboards of the roof, and of the reserves of breathless heat stored in the attic, penetrated the spaces below. Jane Ann Sims sat melting by degrees in the doorway, where, if a draught were possible to the atmosphere from any of the four quarters, she might be in its direct route. Meantime she nodded oblivious, and her great head and broad face dripping with moisture wabbled helplessly on her bosom.

Euphemia, coming out suddenly with a pan of peas to shell for dinner, and seeking a respite from the heat of the fire, caught sight of Royce with a radiant look of delight to which for his life he could not respond. She was pallid and limp with the work of preparing dinner, and even in the poetic entanglements of her curling shining hair she brought that most persistent aroma of the frying-pan. The coarse florid calico, the misshapen little brogans which she adjusted on the rung of her chair as she tilted it back against the wall with the pan in her lap, her drawling voice, the lapses of her ignorant speech, her utter lack of all the graces of training and culture, impressed him anew with the urgency of a fresh discovery.

"What air it ez ails you-uns?" she demanded, with a certain anxiety in her eyes. "Ye hev acted sorter cur'ous all this week. Do you-uns feel sick ennywhars?"

"Lord, no!" exclaimed the juggler irritably; "there's nothing the matter with me."

She looked at him in amazement for a moment; he had had no words for her of late but honeyed praise. The change was sudden and bitter. There was an appealing protest in her frightened eyes, and the color rushed to her face.

He had no affinities for the rôle of fickle-minded lover, and he was hardly likely to seek to palliate the cruelty of inconstancy. He took extreme pride in being a man of his word. The sense of honor, which was all the religion he had and chiefly active commercially, was evident too in his personal affairs. Was it her fault, he argued, his poor little love, that she was so hopelessly rustic? Had he not sought her when she was averse to him, and won her heart from a man she loved, who would never have thought himself too good for her? He would not apologize, however. He would not let her think that he had been vexed into hasty speech by the mere sight of her, the sound of her voice.

"You just keep that up," he said, conserving an expression of animosity before which she visibly quaked, "and you'll have Mrs. Sims brewing her infernal herb teas for me in about three minutes and a quarter. I want you to stop talking about my being ill, short off."

As she gazed at him she burst into a little trill of treble laughter, that had nevertheless the suggestion of tears ready to be shed, in the extremity of her relief.

"I have walked twenty miles to-day, and it's a goodish tramp in the heat of the day,—over to New Helvetia and back; and I'm fagged out, that's all."

Her equilibrium was restored once more, and her eyes were radiant with the joy of loving and being loved. Yet she paused suddenly, her hand—he winced that he should notice how rough and large it was, the nails blunt and short and broad—resting motionless on the edge of the pan, as she said, "I wisht ye would gin up goin' ter that thar hotel. Ye look strange ter-day,"—her eyes searched his face as if for an interpretation of something troublous, daunting,—"so strange! so strange!"

"How?" he demanded angrily, knitting his brows.

"Ez ef—ef ye bed been 'witched somehows," she answered, "like I 'low folks mus' look ez view a witch in the woods an' git under some unyearthly spell. The woods air powerful thick over to'des New Helveshy, an' folks 'low they air fairly roamin' with witches an' sech. I ain't goin' ter gin my cornsent fur ye ter go through 'em no mo'."

She pressed a pod softly, and the peas flew out and rattled in the pan, and the tension was at an end. He felt that she was far too acute, however. He was sorry she had ever known of his visits to New Helvetia.

She should suppose them discontinued. He certainly coveted no feminine espionage.

He could not escape the thought of the place now. The face of the beautiful stranger was before his eyes every waking hour; and there were many, for the nights had lost their balm of sleep. The tones of her voice sounded in his ear. The delicate values of her refined bearing, the suggestions of culture and charm and high breeding which breathed from her presence like a perfume, had enthralled his senses as might the subtle and aerial potencies of ether. He had no more volition. He could not resist. Yet it was not, he stipulated, this stranger whom he adored. It was what she represented. He perceived at last that for him the artificialities of life were the realities. Even his own cherished gifts were matters of sedulous cultivation of certain natural aptitudes, the training of which was more remarkable than the endowment; and indeed, of what worth the latent talent without that culture which gives it use, and in fact recognized being at all? The status had an inherent integral value, the human creature was its mere incident. Nature was naught to him. The triumphs of the world are the uses man has made of nature; the forces that have lifted him from plane to plane, and sublimated the mere intelligence, which he shares with the beast, into intellectuality, which is the extremest development of mind.

As he argued thus abstractly, the longing to see her again grew resistless. Not himself to be seen, and never, never again by her! He would only look at her from afar, as one—even so humble a wretch—might gaze at some masterpiece of the artist's craft, might kneel in abasement and self-abnegation before some noble shrine. He craved to see her in her splendid young loveliness and girlish enjoyment, in gala attire, at the grand fête on which the youth of New Helvetia were expending their ingenuity of invention and expansive energy. Even prudence could not say him nay. Did fate grudge him a glimpse that he might gain at the door, or while between the dances she walked with her partner on the moonlit veranda? Who would note a flitting ghost, congener of the shadow, lurking in the deep glooms beneath the trees and looking wistfully at the world from which he had been snatched away?

It was with a lacerating sense of renunciation that he parted with each instant of the time during the momentous evening when he might have beheld her in the tableaux; for he could with certainty fix upon the place she occupied, having gathered from the talk at the store the date and order of the festivities. But he could not rid himself of the Sims family. It had been vaguely borne in upon Mrs. Sims that he was growing tired of them, and in sudden alarm lest Euphemia's happiness prove precarious, and with that disposition to assume the blame not properly chargeable to one's self which is common to some good people, who perceive no turpitude in lying when the deceit is practiced only on themselves, she made herself believe that the change was merely because she had been remiss in her attentions to her guest, and had treated him too much and too informally as one of the family. She smiled broadly upon him, with each of her many dimples in evidence, which had never won upon him, even in the days of his blandest contentment. She detained him in conversation. She requested that he would favor her with the exact rendition of the air to which he sang the words of Rock of Ages, one Sunday morning when he had heard the bells of the St. Louis church towers ringing from out the misty west; and as he dully complied, his tones breaking more than once, she accommodatingly wheezed along with him, quite secure of his commendation. For Jane Ann Sims had been a "plumb special singer" when she was young and slim, and no matter how intelligent a woman may be, she never outgrows her attractions—in her own eyes.

At last the house was still, and the juggler, having endured an agony of suspense in his determination to suppress all demonstrations of interest in New Helvetia, lest the intuition of the two women should divine the cause from even so slight indicia as might baffle reason, found himself free from question and surmise and comment. He was off in the darkness, with a furtive noiseless speed, like some wild errant thing of the night, native to the woods. He had a sense of the shadow and of the sheen of a fair young moon in the wilderness; he knew that the air was dank and cool and that the dew fell; he took note mechanically of the savage densities of the wilds when he heard the shrill blood-curdling quavering of a catamount's scream, and he laid his grasp on the handle of a sharp bowie-knife that he wore in his belt, which he had bought for a juggling trick that he had not played at the curtailed performance in the schoolhouse, and he wished that it were instead Tubal Cain's shooting-iron. But beyond this his mind was a blank. He did not think; he did not feel; his every capacity was concentrated upon his gait and the speed that he made. He did not know how short a time had elapsed when the series of points of yellow light from the ballroom windows, like a chain of glowing topaz, shone through the black darkness and the misty tremulous dimness of the moon. His teeth were set; he was fit to fall; he paused only a moment, leaning on the rail of the bridge to draw a deep breath and relax his muscles. Then he came on, swift, silent, steady, to the veranda.

Around the doors, outside the ballroom, were crowded figures, whose dusky faces and ivory teeth caught the light from within and attested the enjoyment of the servants of the place as spectators of the scene. He saw through an aperture, as one of them moved aside, a humble back bench against the wall, on which sat two or three of the mountaineers of the vicinity, calmly and stolidly looking on, without more facial expression of opinion than Indians might have manifested. He would not join this group, lest she might notice him in their company, which he repudiated, as if his similarity of aspect were not his reliance to save all that he and men of his kind held dear. The windows were too high from the ground to afford a glimpse of the interior; he stood irresolute for a moment, with the strains of the waltz music vibrating in his very heart-strings. Suddenly he marked how the ground rose toward the further end of the building. The last two windows evidently were partially blockaded by the slope so close without, and could serve only purposes of ventilation. Responsive to the thought, he climbed the steep slant, dark, dewy, and solitary, and, lying in the soft lush grass, looked down upon the illuminated ballroom.

At first he did not see her. With his heart thumping much after the fashion of the bass viol, till it seemed to beat in his ears, he gazed on the details of a scene such as he had thought never to look upon again. He recognized with a sort of community spirit and pleasure how well the frolicsome youth had utilized their slender opportunities, so far from the emporiums of civilization. Great branching ferns had adequately enough supplied the place of palms, their fronds waving lightly from the walls in every whirling breeze from the flight of the dance. Infinite lengths of vines—the Virginia creeper, the ground ivy, and the wild grape—twined about the pillars, and festooned the ceiling, the band-stand, and the chandeliers. For the first time he was made aware of the decorative values of the blackberry, when it is red, and, paradoxically, green. The unripe scarlet clusters were everywhere massed amidst the vines with an effect as brilliant as holly. All the aisles of the surrounding woods had been explored for wild flowers. Here and there were tables laden with great masses of delicate blossoms, and from time to time young couples paused in their aimless strolling back and forth,—for the music had ceased for the nonce,—and examined specimens, and disputed over varieties, and apparently disparaged one another's slender scraps of botany.

The band, high in their cage,—prosperous, pompous darkies, of lofty manners, but entertaining with an air of courteous condescension any request which might be preferred, in regard to the music, by the young guests of the hotel,—looked down upon the scene complacently. Against the walls were ranged the chaperons in their most festal black attire, enhanced by fine old lace and fragile glittering fans and a somewhat dazzling display of diamonds. The portly husbands and fathers, fitting very snugly in their dress suits, hovered about these borders with that freshened relish of scenes of youthful festivity which somehow seems increased in proportion as the possibility and privilege of participation are withdrawn. Some of the younger gentlemen also wore merely the ordinary evening dress, the difficulty of evolving a fancy costume, or a secret aversion to the characters they had represented in the tableaux, warranting this departure from the spirit of the occasion.

Everywhere, however, the younger feminine element blossomed out in poetic guise. Here and there fluttered fairies with the silver-flecked game wings that Royce had seen a-making, and Titania still wore her crown, although Bottom had thrown his pasteboard head out of the window, and was now a grave and sedate young American citizen. Red Riding-Hood and the Wolf still made the grand tour in amicable company, and Pocahontas, in a fawn-tinted cycling-skirt and leggings and a red blanket bedizened with all the borrowed beads and feathers that the Springs could afford, was esteemed characteristic indeed. Davy Crockett had a real coonskin cap which he had bought for lucre from a mountaineer, and which he intended to take home as a souvenir of the Great Smokies, although he was fain to carry it now by the tail because of the heat; but he invariably put it on and drew himself up to his tableau estimate of importance whenever one of the elderly ladies clutched at him, as he passed, to inquire if he were certainly sure that the long and ancient flintlock (borrowed) which he bore over his shoulder was unloaded. There had evidently been a tableau representing Flora's court or similar blooming theme, since so many personified flowers were wasting their sweetness on the unobservant and unaccustomed air. The wild rose was in several shades of fleecy pink, festooned with her own garlands. A wallflower—a dashing blonde—was in brown and yellow, and had half the men in the room around her.

Suddenly—Lucien Royce's heart gave a great throb and seemed to stand still, for, on the arm of her last partner, coming slowly down the room until she stood in the full glow of the nearest chandelier, all in white, in shining white satin, with a grace and dignity which embellished her youth, was she whom he had so longed to see. Her bare arms and shoulders were of a soft whiteness that made the tone of the satin by contrast glazing and hard. Her delicate head, with its black hair arranged close and high, had the pose of a lily on its stalk. Scattered amid the dense dark tresses diamonds glittered and quivered like dewdrops. Her face had that flower-like look not uncommon among the type of the very fair women with dark hair from the extreme South. Over the white satin was some filmy thin material, like the delicate tissues of a corolla; and only when he had marked these liliaceous similitudes did he observe that it was the Chilhowee lily which she had chosen to represent. Now and again that most ethereal flower showed amongst the folds of her skirt. A cluster as fragile as a dream lay on her bosom, and in her hand she carried a single blossom, poetic and perfect, trembling on its long stalk.

There rose upon the air a soft welling out of the music. The band was playing "Home, Sweet Home." She had moved out of the range of his vision. There was a murmur of voices on the veranda as the crowd emerged. The lights were abruptly quenched in darkness. And he laid his head face downward in the deep grass and wished he might never lift it again.

XII.

OWEN HAINES spent many a lonely hour, in these days, at the foot of a great tree in the woods, riving poplar shingles. Near by in the green and gold glinting of the breeze-swept undergrowth another great tree lay prone on the ground. The space around him was covered with the chips hewn from its hole,—an illuminated yellow-hued carpet in the soft wavering emerald shadows. The smooth shingles, piled close at hand, multiplied rapidly as the sharp blade glided swiftly through the poplar fibres. From time to time he glanced up expectantly, vainly looking for Absalom Tynes; for it had once been the wont of the young preacher to lie here on the clean fresh chips and talk through much of the sunlit days to his friend, who welcomed him as a desert might welcome a summer shower. He would talk on the subject nearest the hearts of both, his primitive theology,—a subject from which Owen Haines was otherwise debarred, as no other ministerial magnate would condescend to hold conversation on such a theme with the laughing-stock of the meetings, whose aspirations it was held to be a duty in the cause of religion to discourage and destroy if might be. Only Tynes understood him, hoped for him, felt with him. But Tynes was now at the schoolhouse in the Cove, listening in fascinated interest to the juggler as he recited from memory, and himself reading in eager and earnest docility, copying his master's methods.

Therefore, when the step of a man sounded along the bosky path which Haines had worn to his working-place, and he looked up with eager anticipation, he encountered only disappointment at the sight of Peter Knowles approaching through the leaves.

Knowles paused and glanced about him with withering disdain. "Tynes ain't hyar," he observed. "I dunno ez I looked ter view him, nuther."

He dropped down on the fragrant carpet of chips, and for the first time Haines noticed that he carried, after a gingerly fashion, on the end of a stick, a bundle apparently of clothes, and plentifully dusted with something white and powdery. Even in the open air and the rush of the summer wind the odor exhaled by quicklime was powerful and pungent, and the scorching particles came flying into Haines's face. As he drew back Knowles noticed the gesture, and adroitly flung the bundle and stick to leeward, saying, "Don't it 'pear plumb cur'ous ter you-uns, the idee o' a minister o' the gorspel a-settin' out ter l'arn how ter read the Bible from a onconverted sinner? I hearn this hyar juggler-man 'low ez he warn't even a mourner, though he said he hed suthin' ter mourn over. An' I'll sw'ar he hev," he added significantly, "an' he may look ter hev more."

The poplar slivers flew fast from the keen blade, and the workman's eyes were steadfastly fixed on the shingle growing in his hand.

Peter Knowles chewed hard on his quid of tobacco for a moment; then he broke out abruptly, "Owen Haines, I knows ye want ter sarve the Lord, an' thar's many a way o' doin' it besides preachin', else I'd be a-preachin' myself."

Such was the hold that his aspiration had taken upon Haines's mind that he lifted his head in sudden expectancy and with a certain radiant submissiveness on his face, as if his Master's will could come even by Peter Knowles!

"I brung ye yer chance," continued Knowles. Then, with a quick change from a sanctimonious whine to an eager, sharp tone full of excitement, "What ye reckon air in that bundle?"

Haines, surprised at this turn of the conversation, glanced around at the bundle in silence.

"An' whar do ye reckon I got it?" asked Knowles. Then, as Owen Haines's eyes expressed a wondering question, he went on, mysteriously lowering his voice, "I fund it in my rock-house,—that big cave o' mine whar I stored away the lime I burned on the side o' the mounting—this bundle war flung in thar an' kivered by quicklime!"

Haines stared in blank amazement for a moment. "I 'lowed ye hed plugged up the hole goin' inter yer cave, ter keep the lime dry, with a big boulder."

"Edzac'ly, edzac'ly!" Knowles assented, his close-set eyes so intent upon Haines as to put him out of countenance in some degree.

Haines sought to withdraw his glance from their baleful significant expression, but his eyelids faltered and quivered, and he continued to look wincingly at his interlocutor. "I 'lowed 'twar too heavy for enny one man ter move," he commented vaguely, at last.

"'Thout he war helped by the devil," Knowles stipulated.

There was a pause. The young workman's hand was still. His companion's society did not accord with his mood. The loneliness had been soft and sweet, and of peaceful intimations. His frequent disappointments were of protean guise. Where was that work for the Master that Peter Knowles had promised him?

"Owen Haines," cried Peter Knowles suddenly, "hev that thar man what calls hisself a juggler-man done ennythin' but harm sence he hev been in the Cove an' the mountings?"

Haines, the color flaring to his brow, laid quick hold on his shingle-knife and rived the wood apart; his breath came fast and his hand shook, although his work was steady. He was all unnoting that Peter Knowles was watching him with an unguarded eye of open amusement, and a silent sneer that left long tobacco-stained teeth visible below the curling upper lip. But a young fool's folly is often propitious for the plans of a wiser man, and Knowles was not ill pleased to descry the fact that the relations between the two could not admit of friendship, or tolerance, or even indifference.

"Fust," he continued, "he gin that onholy show in the church-house, what I never seen, but it hev set folks powerful catawampus an' hendered religion, fur the devil war surely in it."

Owen Haines took off his hat to toss his long fair hair back from his brow, and looked with troubled, reflective eyes down the long aisles of the gold-flecked verdure of the woods.

"Then he tricked you-uns somehows out'n yer sweetheart, what ye hed been keepin' company with so long."

Haines shook his head doubtfully. "We-uns quar'led," he said. "I dunno ef he hed nuthin' ter do with it."

"Did Phemie an' you-uns ever quar'l 'fore he kem ter Sims's?" demanded the sly Knowles.

They had never quarreled before Haines "got religion" and took to "prayin' fur the power." He had never thought the juggler chargeable with these differences, but the fallacy now occurred to him that they might have been precipitated by Royce's ridicule of him as a wily device to rid her of her lover. His face grew hot and angry. There was fire in his eyes. His lips parted and his breath came quick.

"He hev toled off Tynes too," resumed Knowles, with a melancholy intonation. "He hev got all the lures and witchments of the devil at command. I kem by the church-house awhile ago, an' I hearn him an' Tynes in thar, speakin' an' readin'. An' I sez ter myself, sez I, 'Pore Owen Haines, up yander in the woods, hev got nuther his frien', now, nor his sweetheart. Him an' Phemie keeps company no mo' in this worl'.'"

There was a sudden twitch of Haines's features, as if these piercing words had been with some material sharpness thrust in amongst sensitive tissues. It was all true, all true.

The iron was hot, and Peter Knowles struck. "That ain't the wust," he said, leaning forward and bringing his face with blazing eyes close to his companion. "This hyar juggler hev killed a man, an' flung his bones inter the quicklime in my rock-house."

Haines, with a galvanic start, turned, pale and aghast, upon his companion. He could only gasp, but Knowles went on convulsively and without question: "I s'picioned him from the fust. He stopped thar at the cave whar I war burnin' lime the night o' the show, an' holped ter put it in outer the weather bein' ez the rain would slake it. An' he axed me ef quicklime would sure burn up a dead body. An' when I told him, he turned as he went away an' looked back, smilin' an' sorter motionin' with his hand, an' looked back agin, an' looked back.'"

He reached out slowly for the stick with the bundle tied at the end, and dragged it toward him, the breath of the scalding lime perceptible as it was drawn near.

"Las' week, one evenin' late," he said in a lowered voice and with his eyes alight and glancing, "hevin' kep' a watch on this young buzzard, an' noticin' him forever travelin' the New Helveshy road what ain't no business o' his'n, I 'lowed I'd foller him. An' he kerries a bundle. He walks fast an' stops short, an' studies, an' turns back suddint, an' stops agin, an' whirls roun', an' goes on. An' his face looks like death! An' sometimes he stops short to sigh, ez ef he couldn't get his breath. But he don't go ter New Helveshy. He goes ter my cave. An' he hev got breath enough ter fling away that tormented big boulder, an' toss in these gyarmints, an' churn the lime over 'em with a stick till he hed ter hold his hand over his eyes ter keep his eyesight, an' fling back the boulder, an' run off faster 'n a fox along the road ter Sims's."

There was a long silence as the two men looked into each other's eyes.

"What air ye tellin' this ter me fur?" said Haines at last, struggling with a mad impulse of hope—of joy, was it? For if this were true,—and true it must be,—the spurious supplantation in Euphemia's affections might soon be at an end. If her love could not endure ridicule, would it condone crime? All might yet be well; justice tardily done, the law upheld; the intruder removed from the sphere where he had occasioned such woe, and the old sweet days of love's young dream to be lived anew.

"Fur the Marster's sarvice," said the wily hypocrite. "I sez ter myself, 'Owen Haines won't see the right tromped on. He won't see the ongodly flourish. He won't see the wolf a-lopin' through the fold. He won't hear in the night the blood o' Abel cryin' from the groun' agin the guilty Cain, an' not tell the sher'ff what air no furder off, jes' now, 'n 'Possum Cross-Roads.'"

"Why don't you-uns let him know yerse'f?" demanded Haines shortly.

"Waal, I be a-settin' up nights with my sick nephews: three o' them chil'n down with the measles, an' my sister an' brother-in-law bein' so slack-twisted I be 'feared they'd gin 'em the wrong med'cine ef I warn't thar ter gin d'rections." His eye brightened as he noted Haines reaching forward for the end of the stick and slowly drawing the bundle toward him.

It is admitted that a leopard cannot change his spots, and, without fear of successful contradiction, one may venture to add to the illustrations of immutability that a coward cannot change his temperament. Now the fact that Peter Knowles was a coward had been evinced by his conduct on several occasions within the observation of his compatriots. His craft, however, had served to adduce mitigating circumstances, and so consigned the matter to oblivion that it did not once occur to Haines that it was fear which had evolved the subterfuge of enlisting his well-known enthusiasm for religion and right, and his natural antagonism against the juggler, in the Master's service. On the one hand, Knowles dreaded being called to account for whatever else might be found unconsumed by the lime in the grotto, did he disclose naught of his discovery. On the other hand, the character of informer is very unpopular in the mountains, owing to the revelations of moonshining often elicited by the rewards offered for the detection of the infringement of the revenue laws. Persons of this class indeed sometimes receive a recompense in another metal, which, if not so satisfactory as current coin, is more conclusive and lasting. It was the recollection of leaden tribute of this sort, should the matter prove explicable, or the man escape, or the countryside resent the appeal to the law, which induced Peter Knowles to desire to shift upon Haines the active responsibility of giving information: his jealousy in love might be considered a motive adequate to bring upon him all the retributions of the recoil of the scheme if aimed amiss.

Knowles watched the young man narrowly and with a glittering eye as, with a trembling hand and a look averse, Haines began to untie the cord which held the package together.

"He killed the man, Owen, ez sure ez ye air livin', an' flunged his bones in the quicklime, an' now he flunged in his clothes," Knowles was saying as the bundle gave loose in the handling.

Drawing back with a sense of suffocation as a cloud of minute particles of quicklime rose from the folds of the material, Owen Haines nevertheless recognized upon the instant the garments which the juggler himself had worn when he first came to the Cove, the unaccustomed fashion of which had riveted the young mountaineer's attention for the time at the "show" at the church-house.

With a certain complex duality of emotion, he experienced a sense of dismay to note how his heart sank with the extinguishment of his hope that the man might prove a criminal and that this discovery might rid the country of him. How ill he had wished him! Not only that the fierce blast of the law might consume him, but, reaching back into the past, that he might have wrought evil enough to justify it and make the retribution sure! With a pang as of sustaining loss he gasped, "Why, these hyar gyarmints air his own wear. I hev viewed him in 'em many a time whenst he fust kem ter the Cove!"

Knowles glared at him in startled doubt, and slowly turned over one of the pointed russet shoes. "He hed 'em on the night he gin the show in the Cove," said Haines.

"I seen him that night," said Knowles conclusively. "He hed on no sech cur'ous clothes ez them, else I'd hev remarked 'em, sure!"

"Ye 'lowed 'twar night an' by the flicker o' the fire, an' ye war in a cornsider'ble o' a jigget 'bout'n yer lime."

"Naw, sir! naw, sir! he hed on no sech coat ez that, ennyhow," protested Knowles. Then, with rising anger, "Ye air a pore shoat fur sense, Owen Haines! Ef they air his gyarmints, what's the reason he hid 'em so secret an' whar the quicklime would deestroy 'em; bein' so partic'lar ter ax o' me ef 'twould burn boots an' clothes an' bone,—*bone*, too?"

"I dunno," said Haines, at a loss, and turning the black-and-red blazer vaguely in his hands.

"I do; them folks over ter New Helveshy wears sech fool gear ez these," Knowles insisted, from his superior knowledge, for in the interest of his lime-trade he had visited New Helvetia more than once,—a rare trip for a denizen of Etowah Cove.

"Thar ain't nobody missin' at New Helveshy!" Haines argued, against his lingering hope.

"How do you-uns know?" exclaimed Knowles hurriedly, and with a certain alert alarm in his face. "Somebody comin' ez never got thar! Somebody goin' ez never got away!" He had risen excitedly to his feet. What ghastly secret might be hidden beneath the residue of quicklime in that dark cavern, the responsibility possibly to be laid at his door!

Owen Haines, looking up at him with childlike eyes, was slowly studying his face,—a fierce face, with the savagery of his cowardice as predatory an element as the wantonness of his malice.

"These hyar air his clothes," Haines reiterated; "I 'members 'em well. This hyar split buttonhole at the throat"—

"That's whar he clutched the murdered one," declared Knowles tumultuously.

—"an' these water-marks on these hyar shoes,—they hed been soaked,—an' this hyar leather belt, whar two p'ints hed been teched through with a knife-blade, stiddier them round holes, ter draw the belt up tighter 'n it war made ter be wore,—I could swar ter 'em,—an' this hyar"—

Knowles looked down at him in angry doubt. "Shucks," he interrupted, "ye besotted idjit! I dunno what ailed me ter kem ter you-uns. I 'lowed ye war so beset ter do—yer—Marster's—work!" with a mocking whine. "But ye ain't. Ye seek yer own chance! The Lord tied yer tongue with a purpose, an' he wasted no brains on a critter ez he didn't 'low ter hev gabblin' round the throne. Ye see ter it ye say nuthin' bout'n this, else jestice'll take arter you-uns, too, an' ye won't be much abler ter talk ter the court o' law 'n the court o' the Lawd." He wagged his head vehemently at the young man, while kneeling to make up anew the bundle of garments, until the scorching vapor compelled him to turn aside. When he arose, he stood erect for one doubtful instant. Then, satisfied by the reflection that for the sake of his own antagonism toward the juggler the jealous and discarded lover would do naught to frustrate the vengeance that menaced Royce, he turned suddenly, and, with the bundle swaying as before on the end of the stick, started without a word along the path by which he had come, leaving Owen Haines gazing after him till he disappeared amongst the leaves.

How long Haines sat there staring at the vanishing point of that bosky perspective he could hardly have said. When he leaped to his feet, it was with a repentant sense of the waste of time and the need of haste. His long, lank, slouching figure seemed incompatible with any but the most languid rate of progression; and indeed it was not his habit to get over the ground at the pace which he now set for himself. This was hardly slackened through the several miles he traversed until he reached the schoolhouse, which he found silent and empty. After a wild-eyed and hurried survey, he set forth anew, tired, breathless, his shoulders bent, his head thrust forward, his gait unequal; for he was not of the stalwart physique common amongst the youth of the Cove. He reached the Sims cabin, panting, anxious-eyed, and hardly remembering his grievances against Phemie when he saw her in the passage. She looked at him askance over her shoulder as she rose in silent disdain to go indoors.

"I ain't kem hyar ter plague you-uns, Phemie," he called out, divining her interpretation of his motive. "I want ter speak ter that thar juggler-man,"— he could not bring himself to mention the name.

She paused a moment, and he perceived in surprise that her proud and scornful face bore no tokens of happiness. Her lips had learned a pathetic droop; her eyelids were heavy, and the long lashes lifted barely to the level of her glance. The words in a low voice, "He ain't hyar," were as if wrung from her by the necessity of the moment, so unwilling they seemed, and she entered the house as Mrs. Sims flustered out of the opposite door.

"Laws-a-massy, Owen Haines," she exclaimed, "ye better lef' be that thar juggler-man, ez ye calls him! He could throw you-uns over his shoulder. Ye'll git inter trouble, meddlin'. Phemie be plumb delighted with her ch'ice, an' a gal hev got a right ter make a ch'ice wunst in her life, ennyhows."

He sought now and again to stem the tide of her words, but only when a breathless wheeze silenced her he found opportunity to protest that he meant no harm to the juggler, and he held no grudge against Euphemia; that he was the bearer of intelligence important to the juggler, and she would do her guest a favor to disclose his whereabouts.

There were several added creases—they could hardly be called wrinkles—in Mrs. Sims's face of late, and a certain fine network of lines had been drawn about her eyes. She was anxious, troubled, irritated, all at once, and entertained her own views touching the admission of the fact of the juggler's frequent and lengthened absence from his beloved. Euphemia's fascinations for him were evidently on the wane, and although he was gentle and considerate and almost humble when he was at the house, he seemed listless and melancholy, and had grown silent and unobservant, and they had all marked the change.

"We-uns kin hardly git shet o' the boy," said Mrs. Sims easily, lying in an able-bodied fashion. "But I do b'lieve ter-day ez he hev tuk heart o' grace an' gone a-huntin'."

Owen Haines's countenance fell. Of what avail to follow at haphazard in the vastness of the mountain wilderness? There was naught for him to do but return to his work, and wait till nightfall might bring home the man he sought. Meantime, the sheriff was as near as 'Possum Cross-Roads, only twelve miles down the valley. Peter Knowles would probably give the information which he had tried to depute to the supplanted lover. Haines did not doubt now the juggler's innocence, but he appreciated the cruel ingenuity of perverse circumstances, and he had felt the venom of malice. Thus it was that he had sought to warn the man of the discovery which Peter Knowles had made, and of the very serious construction he was disposed to place upon the facts.

XIII.

WHEN this crisis supervened, Lucien Royce was at New Helvetia Springs, at the bowling-alley. His resolution that the beautiful girl, whom he had learned to adore at a distance, should never see him again in a guise so unworthy of him, of his true position in life, and of his antecedents, collapsed one day in an incident which was a satiric comment upon its importance. He met her unexpectedly in the mountain woods, within a few miles of the Cove, one of a joyous young equestrian party, and riding like the wind. The plainness of the black habit, the hat, the high close white collar, seemed to embellish her beauty, in that no adornments frivolously diverted the attention from the perfection of its detail. The flush on her cheek, the light in her eye, the lissome grace of her slender figure, all attested a breezy delight in the swift motion; her smile shone down upon him like the sudden revelation of a star in the midst of a closing cloud, when he sprang forward and handed her the whip which she had dropped at the moment of passing, before the cavalier at her side could dismount to recover it. A polite inclination of the head, a murmur of thanks, a broadside of those absolutely unrecognizing eyes, and she was gone.

She evidently had no remembrance of him. His alert intuition could have detected it in her face if she had. For her he had no existence. He thought, as he walked on into the silence and the wilderness, of his resolution and his self-denial, and he laughed bitterly at the futility of the one and the pangs of the other. He need never wince to be so lowly placed, so mean, so humble, for she never thought of him. He need not fear to go near her, to haunt, like the ghost he was, her ways in life, for she would never look at him, she would never realize that he was near; for most people are thus insensible of spectral influences.

When he sat for the first time on a bench against the wall, by the door of the bowling-alley, with two or three mountaineers whose lethargic curiosity—their venison or peaches having been sold—was excited in a degree by the spectacle of the game of tenpins, he had much ado to control the agitation that beset him, the pangs of humiliation. But after this day he came often, availing himself of the special courtesy observed by the players in providing a bench for the mountaineers, as spectators, who were indeed never intrusive or out of place, and generally of most listless and uninterested attitude toward the freaks and frivolities of New Helvetia. This attention seemed a gracious and kindly condescension, and flattered a conscious sentiment of *noblesse oblige*. There were other spectators, of better quality, on the opposite side of the long low building,—the elders among the sojourners at New Helvetia Springs,—while down the centre, between the two alleys, were the benches on which the players were ranged.

She was sometimes among these, always graceful and girlish, with a look of innocence in her eyes like some sweet child's, and wearing her youth and beauty like a crown, with that unique touch of dignity suggestive of a splendid future development, and that these days, lovely though they might be, were not destined to be her best. One might have pitied the hot envy he felt toward the youths who handed her the balls and applauded her play, and hung about near her, and chatted in the intervals,—so foolish, so hopeless, so bitter it was. Sometimes he heard her responses: little of note, the talk of a girl of his day and world, but animated with a sort of individuality, a something like herself,—or did he fancy it was like no one else? He had met his fate too late; this was the one woman in all the world for him. She could have made of him anything she would. His heart stirred with a vague impulse of reminiscent ambitions that might have been facts had she come earlier. He loved her, and he felt that never before had he loved. The slight spurious evanescent emotion, evoked from idleness or folly or caprice, in sundry remembered episodes of his old world, or evolved in the desert of his loneliness for Euphemia,—how vain, how unreal, how ephemeral, how unjustified! But she who would have been the supreme power in his life had come at last—and had come too late. How truly he reasoned he knew well, as he sat in his humble garb amongst his uncouth associates on the segregated bench, and heard the thunder of the balls and the swift steps of the lightly passing figures at the head of the alley; but surely he should not have been capable of an added pang when he discerned, with a sense almost as impersonal as if he were indeed the immaterial essence he claimed to be, her fate in the identity of a lately arrived guest. This was a man of middle height and slender, about thirty-five years of age, with a slight bald spot on the top of his well-shaped head. He had a keen narrow face, an inexpressive calm manner, and was evidently a personage of weight in the world of men, sustaining a high social and financial consideration. He did not take part in the game. He leaned against a pillar near her, and bent over her, and talked to her in the intervals of her play. He had apparently little affinity for youthful amusements, and spent much of his time with her parents. His mission here was most undisguised, and it seemed to the poor juggler that the fortunate suitor was but a personified conventionality, whom no woman could truly love, and who could truly love no woman.

When once Royce had acquired the sense of invisibility, he put no curb on his poor and humble cravings to see her, to hear the sound of her voice albeit she spoke only to others. Every day found him on the mountaineers' bench at the bowling-alley, sometimes alone, sometimes in grotesque company, the ridicule, he knew, of the young and thoughtless; and he had no care if he were ridiculed too. Sometimes she came, and he was drearily happy. Frequently she was absent, and in dull despair he sat and dreamed of her till the game was done. He grew to love the inanimate things she touched, the dress she wore; he even loved best that which she wore most often, and his heart lightened whenever he recognized it, as if the sight of it were some boon of fate, and their common preference for it a bond of sympathy. Once she came in late from a walk in the woods, wearing white, with a purple cluster of the wild verbena at her bosom. There was a blossom lying upon the floor after the people were all gone. He saw it as it slipped down, and he waited, and then, in the absolute solitude, with a furtive gesture he picked it up, and after that he always wore it, folded in a bit of paper, over his heart.

In the midst of this absorbing emotion Lucien Royce did not feel the pangs of supplantation till the fact had been repeatedly driven home. When, returning from New Helvetia, he would find Jack Ormsby sitting on the steps of the cabin porch, talking to Euphemia, he welcomed as a relief the opportunity to betake himself and his bitter brooding thoughts down to the bank of the river, where he was wont to walk to and fro under the white stars, heedless of the joyous voices floating down to him, deaf to all save the inflections of a voice in his memory. He began gradually to note with a dull surprise Euphemia's scant, overlooking glance when her eyes must needs turn toward him; her indifferent manner,—even averse, it might seem; her disaffected languor save when Jack Ormsby's shadow fell athwart the door. In some sort Royce had grown obtuse to all except the sentiment that enthralled him. Under normal circumstances he would have detected instantly the flimsy pretense with which she sought to stimulate his jealousy, to restore his allegiance, to sustain her pride. She had not dreamed that her hold upon his heart, gained only by reason of his loneliness and despair and the distastefulness of his surroundings, had slackened the instant a deep and real love took possession of him. She had not divined this hopeless, silent love—from afar, from infinite lengths of despair!—for another. She only knew that somehow he had grown oblivious of her, and was much absent from her. This touched her pride, her fatal pride! And thus she played off Jack Ormsby against him as best she might, and held her head very high.

The sense of desertion inflicted upon him only a dull pain. He said listlessly to himself, his pride untouched, that she had not really loved him, that she had been merely fascinated for a time by the novelty of the "readin's," and now she cared for them and him no more. He recalled the readiness with which she had forsworn her earlier lover, when his conscience had conflicted with her pride, and this seeming fickleness was accented anew in the later change. Royce tacitly acquiesced in it, no longer struggling as he had done at first with a sense of loyalty to her, but giving himself up to his hopeless dream, precious even in its conscious futility.

How long this quiescent state might have proved more pleasure than pain it is hard to say. There suddenly came into its melancholy serenities a wild tumult of uncertainty, a mad project, a patent possibility that set his brain on fire and his heart plunging. He argued within himself—with some doubting, denying, forbidding instinct of self-immolation, as it seemed, that had somehow attained full control of him in these days—that in one sense he was fully the equal of Miss Fordyce, as well born, as well bred, as she, as carefully trained in all the essentials that regulate polite society. She would sustain no derogation if he could contrive an entrance to her social circle, and meet her there as an equal. He had overheard in the fragmentary gossip mention of people in New Orleans, familiars of her circle, to whom he was well known. He did not doubt that his father's name and standing would be instantly recognized by her father, Judge Archibald Fordyce,—the sojourners at New Helvetia were identifiable to him now,—or indeed by any man of consequence of that gentleman's acquaintance. Under normal circumstances the formality of an introduction would be a matter of course. If she had chanced to spend a winter in St. Louis, Royce would doubtless have danced with her on a dozen different occasions; he wondered blankly if he would then have adequately valued the privilege! He felt now that he would give his life for a touch of her hand, a look of her eyes fixed upon him observingly; how the utter neutrality of her glance hurt him! He would give his soul for the bliss of one waltz. He trembled as he realized how possible, how easily and obviously practicable, this had become.

For the tableaux and fancy-dress ball had been so relished by the more juvenile element of New Helvetia that the successor of that festivity was already projected. This was to be a grotesquerie in calico costumes and masks, chiefly of facetious characters. The masks were deemed essential by the small designers of the entertainment, since the secret of the various disguises had not been carefully kept, and these vizards were ingenuously relied on to protect the incognito of certain personages garbed, with the aid of sympathetic elders, as Dolly Varden, Tilly Slowboy (with a rag-doll baby furnished with a head proof against banging on door-frames or elbows), Sir John Falstaff, three feet high, Robinson Crusoe, and similar celebrities. The whole affair was esteemed a tedious superfluity by the youths of twenty and a few years upward, already a trifle blasé, who sometimes lingered and talked and smoked in the bowling-alley after the game was finished and the ladies had gone. It was from overhearing this chat that Royce learned that although the majority of the young fellows, tired with one effort of devising costumes, had declined to go in calico and in character, still, in deference to the style of the entertainment and the importunity of the children who had projected it, they had agreed to attend in mask. Their out-of-door attire of knickerbockers and flannel shirts and blazers ought to be deemed, they thought, shabby enough to appease the "tacky" requirements of the juvenile managers, who were pleased to call their burlesque masquerade a "tacky party."

Then it was that Royce realized his opportunity. The knickerbockers and flannel shirt, the red-and-black blazer and russet shoes, in which he had entered Etowah Cove, now stowed away in the roof-room of Tubal Cain Sims's house, were not more the worse for wear than much of such attire at New Helvetia Springs after a few weeks of mountain rambles. Ten minutes in the barbershop of the hotel, at a late hour when it would be deserted by its ordinary patrons, would put him in trim for the occasion, and doubtless its functionaries who had never seen him would fancy him in this dress a newly arrived guest of the hotel or of some of the New Helvetia summer cottagers. He had even a prevision of the free and casual gesture with which he would hand an attendant a quarter of a dollar and send across the road to the store for a mask. And then—and then—he could feel already the rhythm of the waltz music beating in every pulse; he breathed even now the breeze quickening in the motion of the dance, endowed with the sweetness of the zephyrs of the seventh heaven. It was she—she alone—whom he would care to approach; the rest, they were as naught! One touch of her hand, the rapture of one waltz, and he would be ready to throw himself over the bluff; for he would have attained the uttermost happiness that earth could bestow upon him now.

And suddenly he was ready to throw himself over the bluff that he should even have dreamed this dream. For all that his pulses still beat to the throb of that mute strain, that his eyes were alight with an unrealized joy, that the half quiver, half smile of a visionary expectation lingered at his lips, the red rush of indignant humiliation covered his face and tingled to the very tips of his fingers. He was far on the road between the Cove and the Springs, and he paused in the solitude that he might analyze this thing, and see where he stood and whither he was tending. He, of all men in the world, an intruder, a partaker of pleasures designed exclusively for others! He to wear a mask where he might not dare to show his face! He to scheme to secure from her,—from *her*!—through false pretenses, under the mistake that he was another, a notice, a word, chance phrases, the touch of her confiding hand, the ecstasy of a waltz! He had no words for himself!

He was an exile and penniless. He had no identity. He could reveal himself only to be falsely suspected of a vile robbery in a position of great trust; any lapse of caution would consign him to years of unjust imprisonment in a felon's cell. He was the very sport of a cruel fate. He had naught left of all the lavish earthly endowments with which he had begun life save his own estimate of his own sense of honor. But this was still precious to him. Bereft as he was, he was still a gentleman at heart. He claimed that,—he demanded of himself his own recognition as such. Never again, he determined, as he began to walk slowly along the road once more, never again should expert sophistries tempt him. He would not argue his equality with her, his birth, his education, the social position of his people. It was enough to reflect that if she knew all she would shrink from him. He would not again seek refuge in the impossibility that his identity could be discovered as a guest at the ball. He would not plead as a set-off against the deception how innocent its intention, how transient, how venial a thing it was. And lest in his loneliness,—for since the atmosphere of his old world had once more inflated his lungs he was as isolated in the Sims household, he found its air as hard to breathe, as if he were in an exhausted receiver,—in his despair, in the hardship of his lot, in the deep misery of the first true, earnest, and utterly hopeless love of his life, some fever of wild enterprise should rise like a delirium in his brain, and confuse his sense of right and wrong, and palsy his capacity for resistance, and counsel disguise, and destroy his reverent appreciation of what was due to her, he would put it beyond his power ever to masquerade in the likeness of his own self and the status of his own true position in the world; he would render it necessary that he should always appear before her in the absolutely false and contemptible rôle of a country boor, an uncouth, unlettered clown.

At the paradox of this conclusion he burst into a grim laugh; then—for he would no longer meddle with these subtle distinctions of right and wrong, where, in the metamorphoses of deduction, the false became true, and interchangeably the true was false—he began to run, and in the strong vivacity of his pride in his physical prowess he was able to reflect that better time was seldom made by an amateur, unless for a short spurt, than the pace he kept all the way to the Sims cabin. He would not let himself think while in the roof-room he rolled the jaunty suit into a bundle. He set his teeth and breathed hard as he recognized a certain pleasure which his finger-tips derived from the very touch of the soft, fine texture of the cloth, and realized how tenuous was the quality of his resolution, how quick he must needs be to carry into effect the conclusions of his sober judgment, lest he waver anew. He was out again and a mile away before he began to debate the disposition which it would be best to make of the bundle under his arm. He recalled with a momentary regret Mrs. Sims's kitchen fire, over which doubtless Euphemia was now bending, busy with the johnny-cake for the evening meal. He dismissed the thought on the instant. The feminine ideas of economy would never suffer the destruction of so much good all-wool gear, whatever its rescue might cost in the future. Moreover, it would be inexplicable. He could get a spade and bury the bundle,—and dig it up, too, the next time this mad, unworthy temptation should assail him. He could throw it into the river,—and fish it out again.

Suddenly he remembered the lime-kiln. The greater portion of its product had been used long ago, but the residue still lay unslaked in the dry cavern, and more than once, in passing, he had noted the great boulder rolled to the aperture and securely closing it against the entrance of air and moisture. The place was in the immediate vicinity, and somehow, although he had been here often since, the predominant impression in his mind, when he reached the jutting promontory of rock and gazed down at the sea of foliage in the Cove, that surely had once known the ebb and flow of tides other than the spring bourgeonings and the autumn desiccations, was the reminiscence of that early time in Etowah Cove when he had stood here in the white glare from the lime-kiln and watched that strange anamorphosis of the lime-burner's face through the shimmering medium of the uprising heat. He seemed to see it again,—all unaware that now, in its normal proportions, that face looked down upon him from the height of the cliff above, although its fright, its surprise, its crafty intimations, its malevolence, distorted it hardly less than the strange effects of the writhing currents of heat and air in that dark night so long ago.

The young man hesitated once more. He had a certain conscientious reverence for property and order; it was with a distinct wrench of volition that he would destroy aught of even small value. But as he seated himself on the ledge, shaking out the natty black-and-red blazer, he recognized the melody that was mechanically murmuring through his lips,—again, still again, the measures of a waltz, that waltz through whose enchanted rhythms he had fancied that he and she might dreamily drift together. He sprang to his feet in a panic. With one mighty effort he flung the great boulder aside. Hastily he dropped the garments with the shoes, belt, and long blue hose, into the cavern, and with a staff stirred the depths of the lime till it rose above them. More than once he was fain to step back from the scorching air and the smarting white powder that came in puffs from the interior.

"That's enough," he muttered mockingly after a moment, as he stood with his muscles relaxed, sick with the sentiment of the renunciation of the world which the demolition of the sophisticated garb included in its significance. "I cannot undertake to dance with any fine lady in this toggery now; she'd think I had come straight from hell. And," with a swift change of countenance, "so I have!—so I have!"

Then, with his habitual carefulness where any commercial interest, however small, was concerned, he roused himself, wrenched the great boulder back into its place, noting here and there a crevice, and filling it with smaller stones and earth that no air might gain admission; and, with one final close scrutiny of the entrance, he took his way into the dense laurel and the gathering dusk, all unaware of the peering, suspicious, frightened face and angry eyes that watched him from the summit of the cliff above.

The discipline of life had certain subduing effects on Lucien Royce. He felt very much tamed when next he took a seat upon the bench placed aside in the corner of the bowling-alley, to affect to watch the game, but in truth to give his humble despair what added pain it might deem pleasure and clutch as solace, by the sight of her smiles won by happier men, the sound of her voice, the meagre realities of the day to supplement the lavish and fantastic visions of his dreams. He had reached the point where expectation fails. He looked only for the eventless routine of the alley,—the hour of amusement for the others, the lingering separation, the silence of the deserted building, and the living on the recollection of a glance of the eye, a turn of the head, a displaced tendril of hair, softly curling, until to-morrow, or the next day, or the next, should give him the precious privilege of making such observations for the sustenance of his soul through another interval of absence. Suddenly, his heart, dully beating on through these dreary days, began to throb wildly, and he gazed with quickening interest at the scene before him: the long narrow shell of a building with the frequent windows where the green leaves looked in, the brown unplastered walls, the dark rafters rising into the shadowy roof, and the crossing of the great beams into which records of phenomenal successions of ten strikes had been cut by the vaunting winners of matches, with their names and the dates of the event, the year of the Lord methodically affixed, as if these deeds were such as were to be cherished by posterity. Down the smooth and shining alley a ball was rolling. Miss Gertrude Fordyce, wearing a sheer green-and-white dress of simple lawn and a broad hat trimmed with ferns, was standing at the head of the alley, about to receive her second ball from the hands of a blond young cavalier in white flannels. Royce had seen him often since the morning when he had observed him giving his valuable advice as to the erection of the stage in the ballroom, and knew that he was Millden Seymour, just admitted to the bar, with a reputation for talent, an intelligent face, and a smooth and polished *bonhomie* of manner; he was given to witty sayings, and was a little too intent upon the one he was exploiting at this moment to notice that the pins at the further end of the alley had not been set up, the hotel functionary detailed for that duty not having arrived. Miss Fordyce hesitated, with the ball in her hand, in momentary embarrassment, the color in her cheeks and a laugh in her eyes.

Royce sprang up, and running lightly down by the side of the alley placed the pins in readiness to receive her second ball; then stood soberly aside, his hat in his hand, as if to watch the execution of the missile.

"How very polite!" said one of the chaperons over her knitting to another. "I often notice that young man. He seems to take so much interest in the game."

This trifling dévoir, however, which Royce had not hesitated to offer to a lady, savored of servility in its appropriation by a man. Nevertheless, he was far too discreet, too well aware of what was due to Miss Fordyce, to allow the attention to seem a personal tribute from him. He silently cursed his officiousness, notwithstanding, as he bent down to set the tenpins in place for the second player, who happened to be the smart young cavalier. Only with an effort Royce conserved his blithe air and a certain amiable alacrity as through a round or two of the game he continued to set up the pins; but when the flustered and hurried bell-boy whose duty he had performed came panting in, Royce could have broken the recreant's head with right good will, and would not restrain a tendency to relapse into his old gait and pose, which had no savor of meekness, as he sauntered up the side of the alley to his former seat beside the mountaineers, who had gazed stolidly at his performance.

Royce noted that one or two of the more athletic of the young men had followed his movements with attention. "Confound you!" he said to himself irritably. "I am man enough to throw you over that beam, and you are hardly so stupid as to fail to know it."

Miss Fordyce had not turned her eyes toward him,—no more, he said to himself, than if he had been the side of the wall. And notwithstanding the insignia of civilization thrust out of sight into the quicklime and the significance of their destruction, and the flagellant anguish of the discipline of hopelessness and humiliation, he felt this as a burning injustice and grief, and the next instant asked himself in disdain what could such a man gain if she should look at him in his lowly and humble estate?

Royce brooded gloomily upon these ideas during the rest of the game; and when the crowd had departed, and he had risen to take leave of the scene that he lived by, he noticed, with only the sense that his way was blocked, several of the young men lingering about the door. They had been glancing at him, and as one of them,—it was Seymour,—in a very propitiatory manner, approached him, he became suddenly aware that they had been discussing the appropriateness of offering him a gratuity for setting up the tenpins in the heat and dust while they played. Seymour was holding out their joint contributions in his hand; but his affability was petrified upon his countenance as his mild eyes caught the fiery glance which Royce flung at the group, and marked the furious flush which suffused neck and face and ears as he realized their intention. It was a moment of mutual embarrassment. They meant no offense, and he knew it. Had he been what he seemed, it would have been shabby in the last degree to accept such timely offices with no tender of remuneration. Royce's ready tact served to slacken the tension.

"Here," he said abruptly, but despite his easy manner his voice trembled, "let me show you something."

He took a silver quarter of a dollar from the handful of small change still mechanically extended, and, turning to a table which held a tray with glasses, he played the trick with the goblet and the bit of money that had interested the captain of the ill-fated steamboat on the night when Lucien Royce perished so miserably to the world. It was with a good-natured feigning of interest that the young men pressed round, at first, all willing to aid the salving of the honest pride which their offering had evidently so lacerated. But this gave way to an excitement that had rarely been paralleled at New Helvetia Springs, as feat succeeded feat. The juggler was soon eager to get away, having served his purpose of eluding their bounty, but this was more difficult than he had anticipated. He feared troublesome questions, but beyond a "Say, how in thunder did you learn all this?" there were none; and the laconic response, "From a traveling fellow," seemed to allay their curiosity.

After a little he forgot their ill-starred benevolence; his spirits expanded in this youthful society, the tone of which was native to him, and from which he had long been an outcast. He began to reflect subacutely that the idea of a fugitive from justice would not occur to men of their social position so readily as to the mountaineers, who were of a more restricted field of speculation and limited knowledge of the world. He might seem to these summer sojourners, perhaps, a man educated beyond his prospects in life and his station, and ashamed of both; such types are not altogether unknown. Or perhaps he might be rusticating in this humble fashion, being a person of small means, or a man with some malady, attracted here like others in search of health, but of a lower grade of society. "For they tell me," he said satirically to himself, "that such people have lungs and livers like the best of us!" He might be a native touched by some unhallowed ambition, and, having tried his luck in the outer world, flung back upon his despised beginnings and out of a job. He might be the schoolmaster in the Cove, of a vastly higher grade than the native product, doubtless, but these young fellows were uninterested and unobservant, and hardly likely to evolve accurate distinctions. He felt sure that the idea of crime would occur to these gay butterflies the most remotely of all the possible solutions of the anomalies of his presence and his garb. He began to give himself up unconsciously to the mild pleasure of their association; their chatter, incongruously enough, revived his energies and solaced his feelings like some suave balm. But he experienced a quick repulsion and a start of secret terror when two or three, having consulted apart for a few moments, joined the group again, and called upon him to admire their "cheek," as they phrased it, in the proposition they were about to make,—no less than that he should consent to perform some of his wonderful feats of sleight of hand at an entertainment which they proposed to give at New Helvetia. They explained to him, as if he had not grievous cause to know already, that the young ladies had devised a series of tableaux followed by a ball; that the children had scored a stunning success in a "tacky party;" that the married people had preëmpted the not very original idea of a *fête champêtre*, and to preclude any unmannerly jumping of their claim had fixed the date, wind and weather permitting, and had formally bidden the guests, all the summer birds at New Helvetia Springs. And now it devolved upon the young men to do their part toward whiling away time for the general pleasure,—a task for which, oddly enough, they were not so well equipped as one might imagine. They were going to give a dramatic entertainment upon the stage which had been erected for the tableaux in the ballroom, and which still stood, it being cheaper, the proprietor had remarked, to leave it there than to erect it anew; for no one could be sure when the young people would want it again. There would be college songs first, glees and so forth, and they made much of the prestige of a banjo-player in their ranks. Some acrobatic feats by the more athletic youths were contemplated, but much uneasiness was felt because a budding littérateur—this was again Mr. Seymour—was giving token of a total breakdown in a farce he was writing for the occasion, entitled "The New Woman," which, although beginning with aplomb and brilliancy, showed no signs of reaching a conclusion,—a flattering tribute to the permanence of the subject. Mr. Seymour might not have it completed by the date fixed. The skill of this amateur prestidigitator would serve to fill the breach if the playwright should not be ready; and even if inspiration should smile upon him and bring him in at the finish, the jugglery would enliven the long waits while the scenes were being prepared and the costumes changed.

Royce, with a sudden accession of prudence, refused plumply; a sentiment of recoil possessed him. He felt the pressure of the surprise and the uncertainty like a positive pain as he sat perched on the high window-sill, and gazed out into the blank unresponsiveness of the undergrowth of the forest, wilting in the heat of a hazy noon. The young men forbore to urge him; that delicate point of offering money, obviously so very nettling to his pride, which seemed altogether a superfluous luxury for a man in his position, hampered them. He might, however, be in the habit of giving exhibitions for pay; for aught they knew, the discussion of the honorarium was in order. But they had been schooled by the incident of the morning; even the quarter of a dollar which had lent itself to the nimble gyrations of legerdemain had found its way by some unimagined art of jugglery into the pocket of its owner, and Millden Seymour, who had a bland proclivity to smooth rough places and enjoy a refined peace of mind, was swearing by all his gods that it should stay there until more appropriately elicited.

An odd thing it was, Royce was feeling, that without a moment's hesitation he should accept the box receipts of the "show" in the Cove, on which he had subsisted for weeks, and yet in his uttermost necessity he could not have brooked appearing as a juggler before the sojourners at New Helvetia Springs for his own benefit. The one audience represented the general public, he supposed, and was far from him. The other he felt as his own status, his set; and he could as soon have handed around the hat, after one of the snug little bachelor dinners he used to be so fond of giving in St. Louis, as ask remuneration for his assistance in this amateur entertainment of the young butterflies at New Helvetia.

He burst into abrupt and sardonic laughter as he divined their line of cogitation, and realized how little they could imagine the incongruities of his responsive mental processes. In the quick change from a pondering gravity to this repellent gayety there was something of the atmosphere of a rude rebuff, and a certain dignity and distance informed the manner of the few who still lounged about with their cigars. Royce hastened to nullify this. They had shown much courtesy to one of his low degree, and although he knew—from experience, poor fellow—that it was prompted not so much by a perception of his deserts as by a realization of their own, it being the conduct and sentiment which graced them and which they owed to persons of their condition, he had no wish to be rude, even though it might seem that he owed a man in *his* position nothing.

"Oh, I'll help you," he said hastily, "though we shall have to rig up some sort of properties. But I don't need much."

The talk fell upon these immediately, and he forthwith perceived that he was in for it. And why not? he asked himself. How did it endanger him, or why should he shun it? All the Cove and the countryside for twenty miles around knew of his feats of sleight of hand; and since accident had revealed his knack to this little coterie of well-bred and well-placed young men, why should he grudge the exhibition to the few scores of ladies and children at New Helvetia, to aid the little diversion of the evening? His scruples could have no force now, for this would bring him—the social pariah!—no nearer to them than when he sat by the tenpin-alley and humbly watched his betters play. The episode of the jugglery, once past, would be an old story and bereft of interest. He would have had his little day, basking in the sun of the applause of his superiors, and would sink back to his humble obscurity at the side of the bowling-alley. Should he show any disposition to presume upon the situation, he realized that they well understood the art of repressing a forward inferior. The entertainment contemplated no subsequent social festivities. The programme, made out with many an interlineation, had been calculated to occupy all the time until eleven o'clock; and Royce, looking at it with the accustomed eye of a manager of private theatricals, felt himself no prophet to discern that midnight would find the exhausted audience still seated, enjoying that royal good measure of amusement always meted out by bounteous amateurs. Throughout the evening he would be immured with the other young men in the close little pens which served for dressing and green rooms,—for all the actors in the farce were to be men,—save for the fraction of time when his jugglery would necessitate his presence on the stage. True, Miss Fordyce, should she patronize the entertainment, might then have to look at him somewhat more discerningly than she would look at the wall, perhaps! It could surely do her no harm. She had seen worse men, he protested, with eager self-assertion. She owed him that much,—one glance, one moment's cognition of his existence. It was not much to ask. He had made a great sacrifice for her sake, and all unknown to her. He had had regard to her estimate of her dignity and held it dear. He had done her reverence from the depths of his heart, regardless that it cost him his last hope.

The powers of the air were gradually changing at New Helvetia Springs. The light of the days had grown dull and gray. Masses of white vapor gathered in the valley, rising, and rising, and filling all its depths and slopes, as if it were the channel of some great river, till only the long level line of the summit of the opposite range showed above the impalpable tides in the similitude of the further banks of a great stream. It was a suggestive resemblance to Lucien Royce, and he winced as he looked upon it. He was not sorry when it had gone, for the gathering mists soon pervaded the forests, and hid cliffs and abysses and even the familiar path, save for the step before the eye, and in this still whiteness all the world was lost; at last one could only hear—for it too shared the invisibilities—the rain falling steadily, drearily, all the day and all the long, long hours of the black night. The bowling-alley was deserted; lawn-tennis had succumbed to the weather; the horses stood in the stalls. One might never know that the hotel at New Helvetia Springs existed except that now and again, in convolutions of mist as it rolled, a gable high up might reveal itself for a moment, or a peaked turret; unless indeed one were a ghost, to find some spectral satisfaction in slipping viewless through the white enveloping nullity, and gazing in at the window of the great parlor, where a log fire was ruddily aflare and the elders perused their newspapers or worked their tidies, and the youth swung in rocking-chairs and exchanged valuable ideas, and played cards, and read a novel aloud, and hung in groups about the tortured piano. So close stood a poor ghost to the window one day, risking observation, that he might have read, over the charming outline of sloping shoulders clad faultlessly in soft gray cloth, the page of the novel which Miss Fordyce had brought there to catch the light; so close that he might have heard every syllable of the conversation which ensued when the man in whom he discovered her destiny—the cold, inexpressive-looking, personified conventionality—came and sat beside her on the sofa. But the poor ghost had more scruples than reality of existence, and, still true to the sanctions that control gentlemen in a world in which he had no more part, he turned hastily away that no syllable might reach him. And as he turned he ran almost into the arms of a man who had been tramping heavily up and down the veranda in the white obscurities, all unaware of his propinquity. It might have been better if he had!

XIV.

FOR there were strangers at New Helvetia,—two men who knew nobody and whom nobody knew. Perhaps in all the history of the hotel this instance was the first. The patronage of New Helvetia, like that of many other secluded southern watering-places, had been for generations among the same clique of people, all more or less allied by kindred or hereditary friendship, or close association in their respective homes or in business interests, and the traditions of the place were community property. So significant was the event that it could scarcely escape remark. More than one of the hereditary sojourners observed to the others that the distance of fifty miles from a railroad over the worst stage-road in America seemed, after all, no protection from the intrusion of strangers. Here were two men who knew nobody, whom nobody knew, and who seemed not even to know each other. One was a quiet, decorous, reserved person who might be easily overlooked in a crowd, so null was his aspect. The other had good, hearty, aggressive, rustic suggestions about him. He was as stiffly upright as a ramrod, and he marched about like a grenadier. He smoked and chewed strong, rank tobacco. He flourished a red-bordered cotton handkerchief. He had been carefully trimmed and shaved by his barber for the occasion, but alas, the barber's embellishments can last but from day to day, and the rougher guise of his life was betrayed in certain small habitudes, conspicuous among which were an obliviousness of many uses of a fork and an astonishing temerity in the thrusting of his knife down his throat at the dinner-table.

The two strangers appeared on the evening of the dramatic entertainment among the other guests of the hotel in the ballroom, as spectators of the "Unrivaled Attraction" profusely billed in the parlor, the office of the hotel, and the tenpin-alley. The rain dashed tempestuously against the long windows, and the sashes now and again trembled and clattered in their frames, for the mountain wind was rising. Ever and anon the white mist that pressed with pallid presence against the panes shivered convulsively, and was torn away into the wild night and the savagery of the fastnesses without, returning persistently, as if with some fatal affinity for the bright lights and the warm atmosphere that would annihilate its tenuous existence with but a single breath. The blended sound of the torrents and the shivering gusts was punctuated by the slow dripping from the eaves of the covered walks within the quadrangle close at hand, that fell with monotonous iteration and elastic rebound from the flagging below, and was of dreary intimations distinct amid the ruder turmoil of the elements. But a cheerful spirit pervaded the well-housed guests, perhaps the more grateful for the provision for pleasantly passing the long hours of a rainy evening in the country, since it did not snatch them from alternative pleasures; from languid strolls on moonlit verandas, or contemplative cigars in the perfumed summer woods under the stars, or choice conferences with kindred spirits in the little observatory that overhung the slopes. The Unrivaled Attraction had been opportunely timed to fill an absolute void, and it could not have been presented before more leniently disposed spectators than those rescued from the jaws of unutterable ennui. There sounded a continuous subdued ripple of laughter and stir of fans and murmur of talk amongst them; but, although richly garbed in compliment to the occasion, the brilliancy of their appearance was somewhat reduced by the tempered light in which it was essential that they should sit throughout the performance and between the acts, for the means at the command of the Unrivaled Attraction were not capable of compassing the usual alternations of illumination, and the full and permanent glare of splendor was reserved to suffuse the stage. The audience was itself an object of intense interest to the actors behind the scenes, and there was no interval in which the small rent made in the curtain for the purpose of observation was not utilized by one or another of the excited youths, tremulous with premonitions of a fiasco, from the time when the first groups entered the hall to the triumphant moment when it became evident that all New Helvetia was turning out to honor the occasion, and that they were to display their talents to a full house. It was only when the stir of preparation became tumultuous—one or two intimations of impatience from the long-waiting audience serving to admonish the performers—that Lucien Royce found an opportunity to peer out in his turn upon the scene in the dusky clare-obscure. Here and there the yellow globes of the shaded lamps shed abroad their tempered golden lustre, and occasionally there came to his eye a pearly gleam from a fluttering fan, or the prismatic glitter of a diamond, or the ethereal suggestion of a girl in white in the midst of such sombre intimations of red and brown and deeply purple and black in the costumes of the dark-robed elders that they might hardly be accounted as definite color in the scale of chromatic values. With such a dully rich background and the dim twilight about her, the figure and face of the girl he sought showed as if in the glamours of some inherent light, reminding him of that illuminating touch in the method of certain painters whose works he had seen in art galleries, in which the radiance seems to be in the picture, independent of the skylight, and as if equally visible in the darkest night. She wore a green dress of some silken texture, so faint of hue that the shadows of the soft folds appeared white. It was fashioned with a long, slim bodice, cut square in the neck, and a high, flaring ruff of delicate old lace, stiff with a

Medici effect, that rose framing the rounded throat and small head with its close and high-piled coils of black hair, through which was thrust a small comb of carved coral of the palest possible hue. She might have been a picture, so still and silent she sat, so definitely did the light emanate from her, so completely did the effect of the pale, lustrous tints of her attire reduce to the vague nullities of a mere background the nebulous dark and neutral shades about her. How long Royce stood and gazed with all his heart in his eyes he never knew. He saw naught else. He heard naught of the stir of the audience, or the wild wind without, or the babel upon the stage where he was. He came to himself only when he was clutched by the arm and admonished to clear the track, for at last the curtain was to be rung up.

What need to dwell on the tremulous eagerness and wild despair of that moment,—the glee club all ranged in order on the stage, and with heart-thumping expectation, the brisk and self-sufficient tinkle of the bell, the utter blank immovableness of the curtain, the subdued delight of the audience? Another tintinnabulation, agitated and querulous; a mighty tug at the wings; a shiver in the fabric, a sort of convulsion of the texture, and the curtain goes up in slow doubt,—all awry and bias, it is true, but still revealing the "musicianers," a trifle dashed and taken aback, but meeting a warm and reassuring reception which they do not dream is partly in tribute to the clownish tricks of the curtain.

Royce, suddenly all in heart, exhilarated by the mere sight of her, flung himself ardently into the preparations progressing in the close little pens on either side and at the rear of the stage. The walls of these were mere partitions reaching up only some ten feet toward the ceiling, and they were devoid of any exit save through the stage and the eye of the public. Hence it had been necessary that all essentials should be carefully looked to and provided in advance. Now and then, however, a wild alarum arose because of the apparent non-existence of some absolutely indispensable article of attire or furniture, succeeded by embarrassed silence on the part of the mourner when the thing in question was found, and a meek submission to the half-suppressed expletives of the rest of the uselessly perturbed company. It was a scene of mad turmoil. Young men already half clad in feminine attire were struggling with the remainder of their unaccustomed raiment,—the actors to take part in the farce "The New Woman." Others were in their white flannel suits,—no longer absolutely white,—hot, dusty, perspiring, the scene-shifters and the curtain contingent, all lugubriously wiping their heated brows and blaming one another. The mandolin and banjo players, in faultless evening dress, stood out of the rush and kept themselves tidy. And now arose a nice question, in the discussion of which all took part, becoming oblivious, for the time, of the audience without and the tra-la-la-ing of the glee singers, the boyish tones of argument occasionally rising above these melodious numbers. It was submitted that in case the audience should call for the author of "The New Woman,"—and it would indeed be unmannerly to omit this tribute,—the playwright ought to be in full dress to respond, considering the circumstances, the place, and the full dress of the audience. And here he was in his white flannel trousers and a pink-and-white striped blazer at this hour of the night, and his room a quarter of a mile away in a pitching mountain rain, whither certain precisians would fain have him hie to bedizen himself. He listened to this with a downcast eye and a sinking heart, and doubtless would have acted on the admonition save for the ludicrous effect of emerging before the audience as he was, and returning to meet the same audience in the blaze of full-dress glory.

"It's no use talking," he said at last, decisively. "We are caught here like rats in a trap. There is no way of getting out without being seen. I wonder I didn't think to have a door cut."

Repeatedly there rose on the air the voice of one who was a slow study repeating the glib lines of "The New Woman;" and once something very closely approximating a quarrel ensued upon the discovery that the budding author, already parsimonious with literary material, had transferred a joke from the mouth of one character to that of another; the robbed actor came in a bounding fury and with his mother's false hair, mildly parted and waving away from his fierce, keen young face and flashing eyes, to demand of the author-manager its restoration. His decorous stiffly lined skirts bounced tumultuously with his swift springs forward, and his fists beneath the lace frill of his sleeves were held in a belligerent muscular adjustment.

"It's *my* joke," he asseverated vehemently, as if he had cracked it himself. "My speech is ruined without it, world without end! I will have it back! I will! I will!" he declared as violently as if he could possess the air that would vibrate with the voice of the actor who went on first, and could put his collar on the syllables embodying the precious jest by those masterful words, "I will!"

The manager had talents for diplomacy, as well he should. He drew the irate antique-seeming dame into the corner by the lace on the sleeve and, looking into the wild boyish face, adjured him, "Let him have it, Jack, for the love of Heaven. He does it so badly, and he is such a slow study, that I'm afraid the first act will break down if I don't give it some vim; after *you* are once on, the thing will go and I shan't care a red."

And so with the dulcet salve of a little judicious flattery peace came once more.

Royce, as he took his place upon the narrow stage, felt as if he had issued from the tumultuous currents of some wild rapids into the deep and restful placidities of a dark untroubled pool. The air of composure, the silence, the courteous attention of the audience, all marked a transition so abrupt that it had a certain perturbing effect. He had never felt more ill at ease, and perhaps he had never looked more composed than when he advanced and stood bowing at the footlights. He had forgotten his assumed character of a mountaineer, his coarse garb, his intention to seek some manner that might consist with both. He was inaugurating his share of the little amateur entertainment with a grace and address and refinement of style that were astonishing his audience far more than aught of magic that his art could command, although his resources were not slight. He seemed some well-bred and talented youth of the best society, dressed for a rural rôle in private theatricals. Now and again there was a flutter of inquiry here and there in the audience, answered by the whispered conclusions of Tom or Jack, retailed by mother or sister. For the youth of New Helvetia Springs had accepted the explanation that he was out of a position, "down on his luck," and hoped to get a school in Etowah Cove. He had gone by the sobriquet of "the handsome mountaineer," and then "the queer mountaineer," and now, "He is *no* mountaineer," said the discerning Judge Fordyce to a man of his own stamp at his elbow.

What might have been the estimate of the two strangers none could say. They sat on opposite sides of the building, taking no note of each other, both steadily gazing at the alert and graceful figure and the handsome face alight with intelligence, and made no sign. One might have been more competent than the other to descry inconsistencies between the status which the dress suggested and the culture and breeding which the manner and accent and choice of language betokened, but both listened motionless as if absorbed in the prestidigitator's words.

Royce had made careful selection among his feats in view of the character of his audience, and the sustaining of such poor dignity as he might hope to possess in Miss Fordyce's estimation. There were no uncouth tricks of swallowing impossible implements of cutlery, which sooth to say would have vastly delighted the row of juvenile spectators on the front bench. Perhaps they were as well content, however, with the appearance of two live rabbits from the folds of the large white silk handkerchief of an old gentleman in the crowd, borrowed for the purpose, and the little boy who came up to receive the article for restoration to its owner went into an ecstasy of cackling delight, with the whole front row in delirious refrain, to find that he had one of the live rabbits in each of the pockets of his jacket, albeit the juggler had merely leaned over the footlights to hand him back the handkerchief. The audience applauded with hearty good will, and a general ripple of smiles played over the upturned faces.

"Ladies and gentlemen," said the juggler, picking up a small and glittering object from the table, "if I may ask your attention, you will observe that each chamber of this revolver is loaded"—

With his long, delicate, deft white hands he had turned aside the barrel, and now held the weapon up, the two parts at right angles, each cartridge distinctly visible to the audience.

But a sudden authoritative voice arose. "No pistols!" called out a sober paterfamilias, responsible for four boys in the audience.

"No pistols!" echoed Judge Fordyce.

There had been a momentary shrinking among the ladies, whose curiosity, however, was greater than their fear, and who sustained a certain doubtful and disappointed aspect. But the shadowy bullet-heads of the whole front row of small boys were turned with one accord in indignant and unfilial protest.

Royce understanding in a moment, with a quick smile shifted all the cartridges out into his hand, held up the pistol once more so that all might see the light through the empty chambers of the cylinder, then, with an exaggerated air of caution, laid all the shells in a small heap on one of the little tables and the pistol, still dislocated, on another table, the breadth of the stage between them; and with a satiric "Hey! Presto!" bowed, laughing and complaisant, to a hearty round of applause from the elders. For although his compliance with their behests had been a trifle ironical, the youths of New Helvetia were not accustomed to submit with so good a grace or so completely.

The two elderly strangers accommodated the expression of their views to the evident opinion of those of their time of life, applauding when the gentlemen about them applauded, maintaining an air of interest when they were receptive and attentive. Was it possible, one might wonder in looking at them, that differences so essential could be unremarked—that it was not patent to the most casual observer that they had some far more serious reason for their presence than the indulgent laudation of the amateur entertainment which inspired the friends and relatives of the youthful performers? The perspicacity of the casual observer, however, was hampered by the haze of the pervasive obscurity; from the stage each might seem to the transient glance merely a face among many faces, the divergences of which could be discerned only when some intention or interest informed the gaze.

Lucien Royce saw only that oasis in the gloom where the high lights of Miss Fordyce's delicately tinted costume shone in the dusk. He was keenly mindful of a flash of girlish laughter, the softly luminous glance of her eye, the glimmer of her white teeth as her pink lips curled, the young delight in her face. How should he care to note the null, impassive countenance of the one man, the grizzled stolid bourgeois aspect of the other?

The manager, keenly alive to the success of the entertainment, advanced a number of the programme since the pistol trick was discarded. Having observed the fate of this from the wings, he handed to Royce a flower-pot filled with earth for a feat which it had been his intention to reserve until after the first act of the play.

"Now, ladies and gentlemen," said the juggler, "oblige me by looking at this acorn. It is considered quite harmless. True, it will shoot, too, if you give it half a chance; but I am told," with a glance of raillery, "that its projectile effects are not deleterious in any respect to the human anatomy."

The ladies who had been afraid of the pistol laughed delightedly, and the guyed elderly gentlemen good-naturedly responded in another round of applause, so grateful were they to have no shooting on the stage, and no possible terrifying accidents to their neighbors, themselves, and their respective families.

"There is nothing but pulverized earth in this flower-pot," continued the juggler, running his hand through the fine white sand, and shaking off the particles daintily, "a little too sandy to suit my views and experience in arboriculture, but we shall see—what we shall see! I plant the acorn, thus! I throw this cloth over the flower-pot, drawing it up in a peak to give air. And now, since we shall have to wait for a few moments, I shall, with your kind indulgence, beguile the tedium, in imitation of the jongleurs of eld, with a little song."

The audience sat patient, expectant. A guitar was lying where one of the glee singers had left it. Royce turned and caught it up, then advanced down toward the footlights, and paused in the picturesque attitude of the serenader of the lyric stage. He drew from the instrument a few strong resonant chords, and then it fell a-tinkling again.

But what new life was in the strings, what melody in the air? And as his voice rose, the scene-shifters were silent in the glare of the pens; the actors thronged the wings; the audience sat spellbound.

No great display of art, to be sure! But the mountain wilds were without, and the mountain winds were abroad, and there was something strangely sombre, romantic, akin to the suggestion and the sound in the rich swelling tones of the young voice so passionately vibrant on the air. Though obviously an amateur, he sang with a careful precision that bespoke fairly good advantages amply improved, but the singing was instinct with that ardor, that love of the art, that enthusiasm, which no training can supply or create. The music and the words were unfamiliar, for they were his own. Neither was devoid of merit. Indeed, a musical authority once said that his songs would have very definite promise if it were not for a determined effort to make all the science of harmony tributary to the display of Lucien Royce's high *A*. A recurrent strain now and again came, interfluent through the drift of melody, rising with a certain ecstatic elasticity to that sustained tone, which was soft, yet strong, and as sweet as summer.

As his voice thus rang out into the silence with all its pathos and its passion, he turned his eyes on the eyes he had so learned to love, and met those orbs, full of delight and of surprise and a patent admiration, fixed upon his face. The rest of the song he sang straight at Gertrude Fordyce, and she looked at the singer, her gaze never swerving. For once his plunging heart in triumph felt he had caught and held her attention; for once, he said to himself, she did not look at him as impersonally as if he were the side of the wall.

It was over at last, and he was bowing his acknowledgments to the wildly applauding audience. The jugglery was at a discount. He had drawn off the white cloth from the flower-pot, where a strongly rooted young oak shoot two feet high appeared to have grown while he sang. But the walls of the room resounded with the turbulent clamors of an insistent encore. Only the eyes of the rustic-looking stranger were starting out of his head as he gazed at the oak shoot, and there came floating softly through his lips the involuntary comment, "By gum!"

It was necessary in common courtesy to sing at least the last stanza again, and as the juggler did so he was almost happy in singing it anew to her starry eyes, and noting the flush on her cheeks, and the surprise and pleasure in her beautiful face. The miracle of the oak shoot went unexplained, for all New Helvetia was still clapping a recall when the juggler, bowing and bowing, with the guitar in his hand, and ever retreating as he bowed, stepped off at one of the wings for instructions, and was met there by renewed acclamations from his fellow entertainers.

"You'd better bring on the play if you don't want to hold forth here till the small hours," he said, flushed, and panting, and joyous once more.

But the author-manager was of a different mind. The child of his fancy was dear to him, although it was a very grotesque infant, as indeed it was necessary that it should be. He deprecated submitting it to the criticism of an unwilling audience, still clamoring for the reappearance of another attraction. However, there would not be time enough to respond to this encore, and yet bring the farce on with the deliberation essential to its success, and the effect of all its little points.

"You seem to be the star of the evening," he said graciously. "And I should like to hear you sing again myself. But we really haven't time.

As they are so delighted with you, suppose, by way of letting them down gently, we give them another sight of you by moving up the basket trick on the programme, instead of letting it come between the second and third acts of the play,—we have had to advance the feat that was to have come between the first and second acts, anyhow,—and have no jugglery between the acts."

Royce readily agreed, but the manager still hesitated while the house thumped and clapped its recall in great impatience, and a young hobbledehoy slipped slyly upon the stage and facetiously bowed *his* acknowledgments, with his hand upon his heart, causing spasms of delight among the juvenile contingent and some laughter from the elders.

Said the hesitating manager, unconscious of this interlude, "I don't half like that basket trick."

"Why?" demanded the juggler, surprised. "It's the best thing I can do. And when we rehearsed it, I thought we had it down to a fine point."

"Yes," still hesitating, "but I'm afraid it's dangerous."

The juggler burst into laughter. "It's as dangerous as a pistol loaded with blank cartridges! See here," he cried joyously, turning with outspread arms to the group of youths fantastic in their stage toggery, "I call you all to witness—if ever Millden Seymour hurts me, I intended to let him do it. Come on!" he exclaimed in a different tone. "I'm obliged to have a confederate in this, and we have rehearsed it without a break time and again."

In a moment more they were on the stage, side by side, and the audience, seeing that no more minstrelsy was in order, became reconciled to the display of magic. A certain new element of interest was infused into the proceedings by the fact that another person was introduced, and that it was Seymour who made all the preparations, interspersing them with jocular remarks to the audience, while the juggler stood by, silent and acquiescent. He seemed to be the victim of the manager, in some sort, and the juvenile spectators, with beating hearts and open mouths and serious eyes, watched the proceedings taken against him as his arms were bound with a rope and then a bag of rough netting was slipped over him and sewed up.

"I have him fast and safe now," the manager declared. "He cannot delude us with any more of his deceits, I am sure."

The juggler was placed at full length on the floor and a white cloth was thrown over him. The manager then exhibited a large basket with a top to it, which he also thrust under the cloth. Taking advantage of the evident partisanship of the children for their entertainer, he spoke for a few minutes in serious and disapproving terms of the deceits of the eye, and made a very pretty moral arraignment of these dubious methods of taking pleasure, which was obviously received in high dudgeon. He then turned about to lead his captive, hobbled and bound, off the stage. Lifting the cloth he found no trace of the juggler; the basket with the top beside it was revealed, and on the floor was the netting,—a complete case with not a mesh awry through which he could have escaped. The manager stamped about in the empty basket and finally emerged putting on the top and cording it up. Whereupon one antagonistic youth in the audience opined that the juggler was in the basket.

"He is, is he?" said the manager, looking up sharply at the bullet-headed row. "Then what do you think of this, and this, and this?"

He had drawn the sharp bowie-knife with which Royce had furnished him, and was thrusting it up to the hilt here, there, everywhere through the interstices of the wickerwork. This convinced the audience that in some inscrutable manner the juggler had been spirited away, impossible though it might seem. The stage, in the full glare of all the lamps at New Helvetia Springs, was in view from every part of the house, and it was evident that the management of the Unrivaled Attraction was incapable of stage machinery, trap-doors, or any similar appliance. In the midst of the discussion, very general over the house, the basket began to roll about. The manager viewed it with the affectation of starting eyes and agitated terror for a moment. Then, pouncing upon it in wrath, he loosened the cords, took off the top, and pulled out the juggler, who was received with acclamations, and who retired, bowing and smiling And backing off the stage, the hero of the occasion.

Seymour behind the scenes was giving orders to ring down the curtain to prepare the stage for "The New Woman."

"Don't do it unless you mean it for keeps, Mill," remonstrated the property-man. "The devil's in the old rag, I believe. It might not go up again easily, and I'm sure, from the racket out there, they are going to have the basket trick over again."

For the front row of bullet-heads was conducting itself like a row of gallery gods, and effervescing with whistlings and shrill cries. The applause was general and tumultuous, growing louder when the over-cautious father called out "No pistols and *no knives*!"

"Oh, they can take care of themselves," said a former adherent of his proposition, for the feat was really very clever, and very cleverly exploited, and he was ready to accredit a considerable amount of sagacity to youths who could get up so amusing an entertainment. No one was alert to notice—save his mere presence as some messenger or purveyor of properties—a dazed-looking young mountaineer, dripping with the rain, who walked down the main aisle and stepped awkwardly over the footlights, upon the stage. He paused bewildered at the wings, and Lucien

Royce behind the scenes, turning, found himself face to face with Owen Haines. The sight of the wan, ethereal countenance brought back like some unhallowed spell the real life he had lived of late into the vanishing dream-life he was living now. But the actualities are constraining. "You want me?" he said, with a sudden premonition of trouble.

"I hev s'arched fur you-uns fur days," Haines replied, a strange compassion in his eyes, contemplating which Lucien Royce felt his blood go cold. "But the Simses deceived me ez ter whar ye be; they never told me till ter-night, an' then I hed ter tell 'em why I wanted you-uns."

"Why?" demanded Royce, spellbound by the look in the man's eyes, and almost overmastered by the revulsion of feeling in the last moment, the quaking of an unnamed terror at his heart.

Nevertheless, with his acute and versatile faculties he heard the clamors of the recall still thundering in the auditorium, he noted the passing of the facetiously bedight figures for the farce. He was even aware of glances of curiosity from one or two of the scene-shifters, and had the prudence to draw Haines, who heard naught and saw only the face before him, into a corner.

"Why?" reiterated Royce. "Why do you want me?"

"Bekase," said Haines, "Peter Knowles seen ye fling them queer shoes an' belt an' clothes inter the quicklime, an' drawed the idee ez ye hed slaughtered somebody bodaciously, an' kivered 'em thar too."

The juggler reddened slightly at the mention of the jaunty attire and the thought of its sacrifice, but he was out of countenance before the sentence was concluded, and gravely dismayed.

"Oh, pshaw!" he exclaimed, seeking to reassure himself. "They would have to prove that somebody is dead to make that charge stick."

Then he realized the seriousness of such an accusation, the necessity of accounting for himself before a legal investigation, and this, to escape one false criminal charge, must needs lead to a prosecution for another equally false. The alternative of flight presented itself instantly. "I can explain later, if necessary, as well as now," he thought. "I'm a thousand times obliged to you for telling me," he added aloud, but to his amazement and terror the man was wringing his hands convulsively and his face was contorted with the agony of a terrible expectation.

"Don't thank me," he said huskily. Then, with a sudden hope, "Is thar enny way out'n this place 'ceptin' yon?" he nodded his head toward the ballroom on the other side of the partition.

"No, none," gasped Royce, his nerves beginning to comprehend the situation, while it still baffled his brain.

"I'm too late, I'm too late!" exclaimed Haines in a tense, suppressed voice. "The sher'ff's thar, 'mongst the others, in that room. I viewed him thar a minit ago."

Assuming that he knew the worst, Royce's courage came back. With some wild idea of devising a scheme to meet the emergency, he sprang upon the vacant stage, on which the curtain had been rung down despite the applause, still resolutely demanding a repetition of the feat, and through the rent in the trembling fabric swiftly surveyed the house with a new and, alas, how different a motive! His eyes instantly fixed upon the rustic face, the hair parted far to the side, as the sheriff vigorously stamped his feet and clapped his hands in approbation. That oasis of refined, ideal light where Miss Fordyce sat did not escape Royce's attention even at this crisis. Had he indeed brought this sorry, ignoble fate upon himself that he might own one moment in her thoughts, one glance of her eye, that he might sing his song to her ear? He had certainly achieved this, he thought sardonically. She would doubtless remember him to the last day she should live. He wondered if they would iron him in the presence of the ladies. Could he count upon his strong young muscles to obey his will and submit without resistance when the officers should lay their hands upon him, and thus avoid a scene?

And all at once—perhaps it was the sweet look in her face that made all gentle things seem possible—it occurred to him that he despaired too easily. An arrest might not be in immediate contemplation,—the *corpus delicti* was impossible of proof. He could surely make such disposition of his own property as seemed to him fit, and the explanation that he was at odds with his friends, dead-broke, thrown out of business in the recent panic, might pass muster with the rural officer, since no crime could be discovered to involve the destruction of the clothes. Thus he might still remain unidentified with Lucien Royce, who pretended to be dead and was alive, who had had in trust a large sum of money in a belt which was found upon another man, robbed, and perhaps murdered for it. The sheriff of Kildeer County had never dreamed of the like of that, he was very sure.

The next moment his heart sank like lead, for there amongst the audience, quite distinct in the glooms, was the sharp, keen, white face of a man he had seen before,—a detective. It was but once, yet, with that idea of crime rife in his mind, he placed the man instantly. He remembered a court-room in Memphis, during the trial of a certain notable case, where he had chanced to loiter in the tedium of waiting for a boat on one of his trips through the city, and he had casually watched this man as he gave his testimony. His presence here was significant, conclusive, to be interpreted far otherwise than any mission of the sheriff of the county. Royce did not for one moment doubt that it was in the interests of the

Marble Company, the tenants of the estate *per autre vie*, although the criminal charge might emanate directly from the firm whose funds had so mysteriously disappeared from his keeping, whose trust must now seem so basely betrayed. There was no possible escape; the stanch walls of the building were unbroken even by a window, and the only exit from behind the partition was through the stage itself in full view of the watchful eyes of the officers. Any effort, any action, would merely accelerate the climax, precipitate the shame of the arrest he dreaded,—and in her presence! He felt how hard the heart of the *cestui que vie* was thumping at the prospect of the summary resuscitation. He said to himself, with his ironical habit of mind, that he had found dying a far easier matter. But there was no responsive satire in the hunted look of his hot, wild, glancing eyes, the quiver of every muscle, the cold thrills that successively trembled through the nervous fibres. He looked so unlike himself for the moment, as he turned with a violent start on feeling the touch of a hand on his arm, that Seymour paused with some deprecation and uncertainty. Then with a renewed intention the manager said persuasively, "You won't mind doing it over again, will you? You see they won't be content without it."

A certain element of surprise was blended with the manager's cogitations which he remembered afterward rather than realized at the moment. It had to do with the altered aspect of the man,—a sudden grave tumultuous excitement which his manner and glance bespoke; but the perception of this was subacute in Seymour's mind and subordinate to the awkward dilemma in which he found himself as manager of the little enterprise. There was not time, in justice to the rest of the programme, to repeat the basket trick, and had the farce been the work of another he would have rung the curtain up forthwith on its first scene. But the pride and sensitiveness of the author forbade the urging of his own work upon the attention of an audience still clamorously insistent upon the repetition of another attraction, and hardly likely, if balked of this, to be fully receptive to the real merits of the little play.

Seymour remembered afterward, but did not note at the time, the obvious effort with which the juggler controlled his agitation. "Oh, anything goes!" he assented, and in a moment more the curtain had glided up with less than its usual convulsive resistance. They were standing again together with composed aspect in the brilliance of the footlights, and Seymour, with a change of phrase and an elaboration of the idea, was dilating afresh upon the essential values of the positive in life; the possible pernicious effects of any delusion of the senses; the futility of finding pleasure in the false, simply because of the flagrancy of its falsity; the deleterious moral effects of such exhibitions upon the very young, teaching them to love the acrobatic lie instead of the lame truth,—from all of which he deduced the propriety of tying the juggler up for the rest of the evening. But the bullet-heads were not as dense as they looked. They learned well when they learned at all, and the pauses of this rodomontade were filled with callow chuckles and shrill whinnies of appreciative delight, anticipative of the wonder to come. They now viewed with eager forwarding interest the juggler's bonds, little dreaming what grim prophecy he felt in their restraint, and the smallest boy of the lot shrilly sang out, when all was done, "Give him another turn of the rope!"

Seymour, his blond face flushed by the heat and his exertions to the hue of his pink-and-white blazer, ostentatiously wrought another knot, and down the juggler went on the floor, encased in the unbroken netting; the cloth was thrown over the man and the basket, and Seymour turned anew to the audience and took up the thread of his discourse. It came as trippingly off his tongue as before, and in the dusky gray-purple haze, the seeming medium in which the audience sat, fair, smiling faces, full of expectation and attention, looked forth their approval, and now and again broke into laughter. When, having concluded by announcing that he intended to convey the discomfited juggler off the stage, he found naught under the cloth but the empty net without a mesh awry, the man having escaped, his rage was a trifle more pronounced than before. With a wild gesture he tossed the net out to the spectators to bid them observe how the villain had outwitted him, and then sprang into the basket and stamped tumultuously all around in the interior, evidently covering every square inch of its surface, while the detective's keen eyes watched with an eager intensity, as if the only thought in his mind concerned the miracle of the juggler's withdrawal. Out Seymour plunged finally, and with dogged resolution he put the lid on and began to cord up the basket as if for departure.

"Save the little you've got left," whinnied out a squirrel-toothed mouth from the front bench, almost too broadly a-grin for articulation.

"Get a move on ye,—get a move!" shouted another of the callow youngsters, reveling in the fictitious plight of the discomfited manager as if it were real.

He seemed to resent it. He looked frowningly over the footlights at the front row, as it hugged itself and squirmed on the bench and cackled in ecstasy.

"I wish I had him here!" he exclaimed gruffly. "I'd settle him—with this—and this—and this!" Each word was emphasized with the successive thrusts of the sharp blade of the bowie-knife through the wickerwork.

"That's enough! That's enough!" the remonstrant elderly gentleman in the audience admonished him, and he dropped the blade and came forward to beg indulgence for the unseemly and pitiable position in which he found himself placed. He had barely turned his back for a moment, when this juggler whom he had taken so much pains to secure, in order to protect the kind and considerate audience from further deceits of a treacherous art, mysteriously disappeared, and whither he was sure he could not imagine. He hesitated for a moment and looked a trifle embarrassed, for this was the point at which the basket should begin to roll along the floor. He gave it a covert glance, but it was motionless where he had left it. Raising his voice, he repeated the words as with indignant emphasis, thinking that the juggler had not caught the cue. He went on speaking at random, but his words came less freely; the audience sat expectant; the basket still lay motionless on the floor. Seeing that he must needs force the crisis, he turned, exclaiming with uplifted hands, "Do my eyes deceive me, or is that basket stirring, rolling on the floor?"

But no; the basket lay as still as he had left it. There was a moment of tense silence in the audience. His face grew suddenly white and chill, his eyes dilated—fixed on something dark, and slow, and sinuous, trickling down the inclined plane of the stage. He sprang forward with a shrill exclamation, and, catching up the bowie-knife, severed with one stroke the cords that bound the basket.

"Are you hurt?" he gasped in a tremulous voice to the silence beneath the lid, and as he tossed it aside he recoiled abruptly, rising to his feet with a loud and poignant cry, "Oh, my God! he is dead! he is dead!"

The sudden transition from the purely festival character of the atmosphere to the purlieus of grim tragedy told heavily on every nerve. There was one null moment blank of comprehension, and then women were screaming, and more than one fainted; the clamor of overturned benches added to the confusion, as the men, with grim set faces and startled eyes, pressed forward to the stage; the children cowered in mute affright close below the footlights, except one small creature who thought it a part of the fun, not dreaming what death might be, and was laughing aloud in high-keyed mirth down in the dusky gloom. A physician among the summer sojourners, on a flying visit for a breath of mountain air, was the first man to reach the stage, and, with the terror-stricken Seymour, drew the long lithe body out and straightened it on the floor, as the curtain was lowered to hide the ghastly *mise en scène* which it might be terror to women and children to remember. His ready hand desisted after a glance. The man had died from the first stroke of the bowie-knife, penetrating his side, and doubtless lacerating the outer tissues of the heart. The other strokes were registered,—the one on his hand, the other, a slight graze, on the neck. A tiny package had fallen on the floor as the hasty hands had torn the shirt aside from the wound: the deft professional fingers unfolded it,—a bit of faded flower, a wild purple verbena; the physician looked at it for a moment, and tossed it aside in the blood on the floor, uninterested. The pericardium was more in his line. He was realizing, too, that he could not start to-morrow, as he had intended, for his office and his rounds among his patients. The coroner's jury was an obstinate impediment, and his would be expert testimony.

Upon this inquest, held incongruously enough in the ballroom, the facts of the information which Owen Haines had brought to the juggler and the presence of the officers in the audience were elicited, and added to the excitements incident to the event. The friends of young Seymour, who was overwhelmed by the tragedy, believed and contended that since escape from prosecution for some crime was evidently impossible, the juggler had in effect committed suicide by holding up his left arm that the knife might pierce a vital part. Thus they sought to avert the sense of responsibility which a man must needs feel for so terrible a deed wrought, however inadvertently, by his own hand. But crime as a factor seemed doubtful. The sheriff, indeed, upon the representations of Sims, supplemented by the mystery of the lime-kiln which Knowles had disclosed, had induced the detective to accompany him to the mountains to seek to identify the stranger as a defaulting cashier from one of the cities for whose apprehension a goodly amount of money would be paid. But in no respect did Royce correspond to the perpetrator of any crime upon the detective's list.

"He needn't have been afraid of me," he observed dryly; "I saw in a minute he wasn't our fellow. And I was just enjoying myself mightily."

The development of the fact of the presence of the officers and the juggler's knowledge that they were in the audience affected the physician's testimony and his view of the occurrence. He accounted it an accident—the nerve of the young man, shaken by the natural anxiety at finding himself liable to immediate arrest, was not sufficient to carry him through the feat; he failed to shift position with the celerity essential to the basket trick, and the uplifting of the arm, which left the body unprotected to receive the blow, was but the first effort to compass the swift movements necessary to the feat. The unlucky young manager was exonerated from all blame in the matter, but the verdict was death by accident.

Nevertheless, throughout all the years since, the argument continues. Along the verge of those crags overlooking the valley, in the glamours of a dreamy golden haze, with the amethystine mountains on the horizon reflecting the splendors of the sunset sky, and with the rich content of the summer solstice in the perfumed air; or amongst the ferns about the fractured cliffs whence the spring wells up with a tinkling tremor and exhilarant freshness and a cool, cool splashing as of the veritable fountain of youth; or in the shadowy twilight of the long, low building where the balls go crashing down the alleys; or sometimes even in the ballroom in pauses of the dance when the music is but a plaint, half-joy, half-pain, and the wind is singing a wild and mystic refrain, and the moonlight comes in at the windows and lies in great blue-white silver rhomboids on the floor despite the dull yellow glow of the lamps,—in all these scenes which while yet in life Lucien Royce haunted, with a sense of exile and a hopeless severance, as of a man who is dead, the mystery of his fate revives anew and yet once more, and continues unexplained. Conjecture fails, conclusions are vain, the secret remains. Hey! Presto! The juggler has successfully exploited his last feat.

www.ingramcontent.com/pod-product-compliance
Lightning Source LLC
Chambersburg PA
CBHW011717240626
47153CB00009B/2898